I0678504

Zombies in New York

By Ted Stetson

*****

This is a work of fiction. Characters, names, places and incidents either are the product of the author's imagination or are used fictitiously. Any resemblance to actual persons, living or dead, events, or locales is entirely coincidental.

Copyright © 2011 Ted Stetson

All rights reserved.

Published by Three Door Publishing

Cover art by Paul Szuztka and Bob Townsend

This is dedicated to Gail.

*****

Prologue:

   With the blue and white marble Earth far below, the shuttle Invincible carefully maneuvered across the black void to the large meteor.

   When Invincible was in synchronous orbit, two doors along the back opened and an astronaut in a bulky white EVA spacesuit, looking small next to the shuttle, floated out of the cargo bay. The astronaut pressed a button on his sleeve and a silent stream of gas pushed him away from the shuttle and closer to the meteor. His breathing was the only sound in the silence of space. Like a minnow surveying a whale, Captain Lu Kim proceeded carefully to the large meteor.

   The meteor, much larger than the shuttle, resembled a large jagged rock and gleamed like a piece of coal; spiked at one end, jagged along the middle, then flat at the back. The greenish black rock was pointed down at Earth as though at a huge Petri dish.

   "So this is the infamous meteor?" Sweat dripped down Captain Kim's face despite the fans in the helmet.

   "Telemetry indicates it was slowing down," Commander Marsh said, watching from the window of the shuttle.

   "Reminds me of a burnt potato."

   "If you were moving as fast as that thing was, you'd be burned too."

   "That hasn't been verified."

   "Sort of resembles what happens when lightning hits sand," Marsh said. "Looks like a thunderbolt."

   "They get the code name from you?"

   "Hurry, get a sample. The thing gives me the creeps."

   "Try being out here with it."

   At the middle, just like the eggheads said, a piece jutted out and Kim pressed his power pack until he stopped near it. Tiny spotlights on his helmet lit up the meteor and it reminded him of a huge green-black icicle.

"Found where I can break something off."

"Roger," Commander Marsh said.

In his spacesuit Kim's heart went thumpity-thump. He breathed deeply. *The guys at NASA must be seeing the readout and wondering if I'm going to stroke.* He took another deep breath. Sweat trickled down under his arms. He gazed along the length of the meteor and suddenly shivered. This isn't right, he told himself. Something is ... very wrong.

"Doesn't really look like a rock. More like some strange composite," Kim said, talking to get time to gather himself.

"This isn't Geology 101. Just get a sample."

He surveyed the meteor again. It was a piece of jagged green-black glass the size of a giant whale. It didn't look like any meteor he'd ever seen or heard about, nor did it look like a spaceship. But it did look ... wrong; that was the only word he could think of.

"What's the delay?" Marsh said, anxiety in his voice.

"NASA sure this is safe?"

"As safe as any rock wobbling in orbit can be."

"Why did it stop here?"

"You heard the eggheads; it was just physics, the moon, the earth, gravity."

"But ...."

"Kim, if we don't get a sample the Russians or the Chinese will come with dynamite and sledgehammers. God knows what they'll do. Just do your job so we can go home."

"Aye, aye, sir." Kim located the tiny hairline crack the scientists had discovered.

On his right thigh was a tool pouch. He reached into the large pouch and took out what resembled a long screwdriver. The thick gloves made it difficult and it took longer than in training, but he finally connected the battery cable on his belt to the plug in the handle. A green readout appeared on Captain Kim's visor.

TOOL: SCREWDRIVER
USE STANDBY
POWER 0%.

He pressed computer buttons on the back of his glove. The middle readout changed to red.

USE ACTIVE

Sweat dripped down his face as he grasped the rubber grip in his right hand and worked the tip into a narrow crevice in the greenish black rock. The little crack was on an edge and when the screwdriver touched it, nothing happened. A thought flashed across Kim's mind that it was like a pull tab on a can of soda. There was no way, floating in space, for him to get leverage, so he pressed the glowing red button on the 'screwdriver' and the blade separated like a scissor jack.

He watched the readout on his visor go from 0% to 1% to 5% to 10% to 15% to 20% to 25% and stop.

POWER 25 %

Nothing ....

He tapped the escape key and the 'screwdriver' ceased its effort.

"Twenty five percent power. Nothing."

"Don't need a play by play," Marsh said nervously. "China's window will open soon. We want to get a piece and get out of here before anyone says otherwise."

Thumpity-thump. Sweat slid down under his arms.

He tapped a 5 and a 0 on the computer. The bottom line changed to: *POWER 50* %

He touched the return key and the scissor applied pressure again. It went from 25 to 30 to 40 to 50%. He felt the 'screwdriver' move in his hand, but nothing happened. He touched the escape key.

"Nothing."

"NASA says increase power," Marsh said, in a tone that suggested he was not so sure anymore.

Kim pressed 8 then the 0.

POWER 80%

He tapped the return key. Now he felt the

'screwdriver' vibrate slightly. 50 to 60 to 70 to 80%.

He looked at the green-black meteor, at the crack. It seemed unchanged.

"Nothing," he muttered and tapped the escape key.

"Maybe we should leave it alone," Marsh said.

Kim could hear voices in the background as if some of the eggheads at NASA were having second thoughts.

"Wait." Kim turned his head left and right, shining his helmet's twin lights on the meteor.

"What?"

"Something's different."

"What's different?"

"I think maybe the piece is ready to chip off."

Kim heard conversations in the background. He knew his voice was being relayed to NASA on an encrypted channel and their comments at Mission Control were being relayed back to him through Marsh's mike.

"Was that eighty percent power?" Marsh said.

"Yeah, readout says eighty."

"NASA says, shoot the works."

Kim could tell by Marsh's voice that he really didn't want him to; he wanted him to say something was not working and get the hell away from it.

"For Christ sake be careful."

Kim tapped the one then the zero then another zero.

POWER 100%

He was about to press the return key when Marsh said, "Be careful."

Kim paused. What the hell. He pressed one, three, and zero.

"Kim, what the hell are you doing?"

"A man's gotta do what a man's gotta do."

"Thought you were superstitious."

"Results," Kim said, as if that was the name of his God. "All about results."

The tool had a maximum power rating of 134.013. So what if the 'screwdriver' broke? Tools could be replaced. They wanted a sample. They might not have another chance for a sample. The damn thing seemed to be drifting away. NASA said it was being pulled toward the moon. They said it was now or never.

He touched the return key. 80 to 90 to 100%. Through the thick space glove he could feel the tool vibrate and the vibration increase -- 110. It became difficult to hold onto. 120. Sweat ran down his face. 130. Then the crack was getting bigger and suddenly he was very scared. This wasn't cracking like a rock cracks.

"What's happening?" Marsh yelled.

"I -- I don't think this thing is a rock."

"What do you mean?" Now Marsh sounded scared.

"The tool is breaking the crack, but this thing might not be a rock."

"What are you talking about?"

"Could this thing be a composite?"

"Turn it off," Marsh shouted. "Turn off. Shut down."

"Okay," Kim breathed his voice barely a whisper.

Suddenly, a hunk about the size of a silver dollar broke off. "It broke," Kim shouted. "It broke."

"We can always replace the tool."

"Not the screwdriver, the meteor broke. A piece broke off."

"Bag it and let's get out of here."

"Roger."

Kim disconnected the 'screwdriver' and tried to put the tool back into his pouch. It was then that he noticed the chrome tip had green-gray dust on it.

"Damn."

Thumpity-thump. Large drops of sweat broke out on his face, on his forehead, and he shook his head. Sweat sprinkled the inside of his face mask.

"What?" Marsh asked. "You okay?"

He breathed deeply. "Yeah." Holding the tool as carefully as he could he tried to brush the greenish dust off, but now it was on his large white glove and he could see it was definitely green-gray. His breathing sounded ragged in his ears, there was no mistaking the sound of being scared. Moving like he'd been trained to, he tossed the screwdriver up and away so that it would be caught by the Earth's gravity and burn up in the atmosphere. It tumbled, chrome tip over red handle, up and away.

Taking a breath he repositioned himself using the small thrusters. He turned around until he saw the little piece of rock floating not that far away. That's when he noticed the green-gray dust on the small joystick controlling the jetpack. Nothing he could do about that now. When he got back to the shuttle he would take care of it.

He was about to start his maneuver when he felt something against his boots. He took the small tin mirror from his belt and held it so he could see his boots. He'd drifted into the meteor. He was not far away from the broken piece of green rock and pushed off the meteor with his boots to float to the piece. He carefully grabbed it, shoved it in a pouch, sealed the pouch and maneuvered back to the shuttle.

"Everything okay?" Marsh asked.

"Isn't really dust." Kim was looking at his glove through the magnifiers in his faceplate.

"What dust are you talking about?"

"It's like tiny jellybeans. Tiny green-gray jellybeans."

"What?"

"I'll explain when I get back."

He studied a tiny 'jellybean' in the helmet's spotlight. He increased the faceplate's magnification to its maximum. "I think these 'jellybeans' are ceramic."

"What do you mean tiny jellybeans?"

"If it's ceramic, it was made by intelligent beings."

"I don't understand. Repeat. Do not understand you."

"I think we hit the jackpot." Maybe we can finally prove that there is intelligent life on other planets.

"Get inside. I want to get out of here."

As he floated into the shuttle's cargo bay, Marsh asked, "What's on your back?"

"Space shit." Kim pulled himself to the access hatch. "Look at Thunderstone."

Kim turned and looked up out of the shuttle's cargo bay. A trail of green 'dust' flowed from the hole in the meteor and was falling, streaming toward the Earth.

"Did you touch it?" Marsh asked.

Kim remembered kicking off with his feet and swallowed. "No. Only the screwdriver touched it."

Now the meteor was spiraling downward with a trail of green dust feathered behind it.

Turning back to the shuttle Kim caught a glimpse of his helmet in the cargo door's thick window. On the back of his helmet were dozens of little jellybean things.

When he reached forward to touch the door control he saw jellybean things on his glove. He pressed his glove against the wall and crushed the jellybeans. A vile looking green-gray powder came out of the tiny jellybean and coated his arm. He went to brush it off and it spread over both arms and hung like a small cloud in front of the door.

"Get inside," Marsh ordered.

"I'm coming. I'm coming." Kim walked through the green-gray cloud to the door.

*****

Chapter 1- Knife Flight

Little eight year old Kenny Stevens sat in front of the TV playing Super Mario Brothers on his old Nintendo. The jump button didn't always work; sometimes he had to press it twice to make Mario jump. A light sheen of sweat coated Kenny's face and he had to shove his brown hair out of the way to see.

Cathy, his mother, walked into the room putting on her bell earrings. Five three with blonde hair and brown eyes, she inspected herself in the mirror.

Kenny noticed the dressy pink blouse and tight black slacks and the pink eye shadow.

"Going out again?"

"What do you mean by that?"

"When are you going to spend time with me?"

"I spend lots a time with you," Cathy said, her hands on her hips. "I eat dinner with you. I sleep in the apartment with you. I have breakfast with you."

"When you're here, you're on the phone."

"You have homework anyway, young man."

"Einstein didn't have this much homework."

The TV made a funny noise when a flying turtle landed on Mario, killing him.

The two bedroom apartment was small and cramped. The beige walls badly needed repainting. The tan carpeting had been pale gold when first installed. The furniture was an assortment of leftovers that were cheap when new. Scotch taped to the walls were Kenny's crayon drawings from school. Several of the drawings were of Count Dracula and Wolfman and Frankenstein.

On the particleboard coffee table on a blue paper dish were two hot dogs, French fries, and 7-UP in a clear plastic glass.

"You haven't touched your dinner."

"I don't like eating alone and. . ."

"I'm here."

He gave her a look. "How do I know?"

"What?"

The buzzer sounded.

"Answer the door."

Enough perfume to choke on. No wonder guys don't stay around. *Whatever happened to that bubble gum perfume he got her for her birthday?*

The buzzer sounded again.

"Go get it?"

"It's not for me," he mumbled.

"Oh, one of these days. . ." She stomped to the door. Removed the security bar. Pulled back the three dead bolts. Undid the chain. "Who is it?"

A male said, "Your knight in shining armor."

Kenny shook his head as Mario jumped onto a turtle. She opened the door. "Mike. Come in."

Kenny looked down the narrow hall.

Mike Sato was a pudgy Asian guy with black hair. He wore a green shirt with wide brown stripes and baggy jeans. His shirt was open and underneath was a red t-shirt with E=mc2 printed on the front. A nerd? His mom was going out with a nerd and she was just as tall as him.

*Not the usual bad news. He won't last lon*g.

"What's that?" Cathy asked.

"Something for your son."

Her face fell. She didn't like new boyfriends bringing stuff for her son. She didn't like them using him as an angle to get to her.

Her face frowned only for an instant, but Kenny caught it.

"Hi," Mike said as he walked into the living room.

Kenny nodded, trying not to look at the present. He wanted it, but if his mom thought he shouldn't get it, he would have to give it back. "Hi."

"This is for you, Sport." Mike extended the small -wrapped box to him. He stared at it. Shiny foil paper, with Superman on it.

"Well, take it," Cathy said.

Kenny looked from her to the present. Did she really mean it?

"Kenny."

He took it.

Mike smiled at her. Not exactly a George Clooney smile. More like the rubbery face of the guy on that Jim show.

"What do you say?" Cathy said.

"Thanks."

"Are you going to open it?" Mike said.

He looked at his mother. She nodded her head yes. He smiled as he opened it and stared at the box.

"You know what it is? An action figure. A Zombie."

He nodded. He knew all about monsters. Had Dracula,

11

the Wolfman, Frankenstein, a dragon, a few Ghouls and
even a Zombie but not one as cool as this.

Cathy said, "His room is full of monsters."

"Press this button and the red eyes glow," Mike said to
Kenny. To Cathy, "Is that okay with you? I could return
it and get something else."

"No, don't bother," Cathy said. "I'll. . ."

"This is great," Kenny said and Cathy looked at him
like she wanted to say something, but it would wait until
later, when they were alone. Something like, "What did I
tell you, you don't accept gifts from my boyfriends until I
say you can." Then he'd say, "No one's trying to get to
you." At first she'd become angry like she wanted to hit
him and then she'd start crying and run into her room.

Kenny guessed she was thinking about throwing it out
when Mike left. Maybe use this as an excuse to clean out
his room. He'll just tell her they're collectibles, worth
money. That'll stop her.

Mike smiled at Cathy.

He won't last long. *Too nice.*

The buzzer sounded again.

Mike turned to the door.

"Must be the babysitter," Cathy said.

"Who'd you get?" Kenny said.

"Fran Weezer."

"Not the weasel."

"Don't call her that."

"Not her. She's mean to me."

"Aunt Fran is not. Besides she's all I could get."

"She's not really my Aunt," he said to Mike.

"If he doesn't like her we could stay here."

"It's nothing. He always pulls this."

Cathy opened the door and Aunt Fran marched in, gray
hair and round shoulders under a worn tan coat. Cathy
took her coat and Aunt Fran carried her huge pink bag of
knitting into the living room. Her long face was heavily
wrinkled. Blood red lipstick on her false teeth. Brown
eyes hiding behind ornate pink glasses.

Kenny restarted Mario. His hands were trembling.

"We'll be going," Cathy said.

"Have a good time." Aunt Fran settled into the chair like it was hers. "What time you be home?"

"Monday," Mike nudged her and Cathy giggled.

"Not too late," Cathy said.

"Don't you worry about us. Have a good time."

Kenny stared at the TV and took a breath. A cramp in his stomach. That smell. Her perfume? Smells like aftershave.

"Bye," Cathy called.

Kenny closed his mouth. He wanted to shout, say something, but after all the times of crying wolf, she no longer believed him. At the time the others seemed like wolves. Compared to Aunt Fran they were puppies.

"Bye," Mike said and closed the door.

He listened to their footsteps walking away. It wasn't too late. He could still call them back. If only he could think of something to say.

"He seemed like a nice young man," Fran said.

"Uh huh."

Her knitting needles were clicking like rat's teeth.

Kenny squeezed the control pad to stop his hands from shaking.

"GO, lock the door and put the bar in place," Aunt Fran ordered.

Kenny looked at her knitting with those long pointed needles. He watched the needles moving very fast. Last time she said she was going to poke him in the eyes. She chased him around the house and sat on him and pretended to or tried to poke him until he cried so hard he got snot on her. Then she slapped him.

"DO IT," she barked.

He jumped up and went to the door. Picked up the bar. Maybe I should run away. He looked in the living room at the back of her head. It was scary on the street at night. It was scary in here. *Where would he go?*

He locked the door and put the security bar next to it,

like he had shoved it in place. His heart was hammering like a wind up toy. He took the nebulizer from his pocket, put it in his mouth and pressed. It sprayed and he could breathe a little better.

"Come here."

He walked into the living room, his knees weak, his tummy jumping. What did she say about my feet?

"You better not drag your feet," she growled. "And you better not stomp them, if you know what's good for you."

He stood next to the chair watching her knit. He wasn't positive, but he was pretty sure there was blood on one of the knitting needles. She looked at him over her pink reading glasses. Her brown eyes reminded him of the madwoman in that horror movie: *The Madwoman of Springfield.*

"Put this in the VCR."

He took the videocassette.

"But I'm playing Mario."

"Do it."

He walked to the TV, shut off the Nintendo and switched on the VCR.

"Start it," she told him.

He pressed the button. A black and white picture came on the TV. A piano started playing. *This dumb thing again.*

"There's nothing like Bogart and Bacall."

"I thought you said she wasn't in this one."

"Mind your mouth. Get me a glass of ice and a Coke." He headed for the kitchen. "And not an opened flat one like last time, if you know what's good for you."

"Mom says we should use the opened ones first."

She stopped knitting and looked at him with those ball bearing madwoman eyes.

He walked into the kitchen. Maybe he should put something in it. Make her so sick she leaves. What's here? Nothing. Everything's in the bathroom.

He pushed a chair next to the counter.

"Stop making so much noise."

He'd rather be home alone than have her here. Someday, when he was older, he was going to tell Social Services there was nothing wrong with a kid being home alone. Kids had been home alone since the Stone Age. It was certainly better than having a dangerous crazy person in the house or putting a kid in a shelter.

He climbed up on the stool, opened the cabinet and lifted out a large glass. Last time she was angry because it was a small glass. Climbed down. Opened the refrigerator. Took out an unopened plastic bottle of Coke. He could hear his mother yelling at him for opening a new bottle when the old bottle wasn't empty. He placed it on the counter next to the glass.

"Don't forget the ice."

He pushed the stool next to the refrigerator trying to keep the noise down. Climbed on it. Opened the freezer door. Reached into the freezer.

"You drop any ice cubes and I'll put you in the freezer."

He looked into the compartment. Could see himself jammed in with the ice cream and frozen dinners, turning white and frosty. He took out an ice cube. It dropped on the counter.

"What happened?"

"It fell on the counter. Not on the floor."

"Don't put it in my drink. I've seen how your mother cleans."

He tossed it into the sink. Managed to get three ice cubes in the glass without dropping any. Took a breath. Sweat trickled down under his arms.

He carried the tall glass and the plastic bottle of soda into the living room and placed them on the table next to Aunt Fran. This close to her, he smelled the liquor on her breath under the aftershave. So that's why she wore the stinky stuff.

She took a bottle out of her bag, a bird on the label, and filled her glass half full, then added coke to it.

"Now go to bed."

"It--it--it's Friday. I--I don't have school tomorrow. Mom said I could stay up late."

She jabbed him in the stomach with the needle and he doubled over.

"Go to bed."

He held his stomach, tears in his eyes.

"God punished you. Now go."

He walked down the hall rubbing his stomach. "God didn't punish me."

"Yes, he did. You watch how you talk to me."

"You're a meanie. You're a weasel."

"WHAT!"

He heard the chair squeak and turned. She had lunged up out of the chair, her face ugly with rage. He raced down the hall, brushed the bead curtain outside his mother's bedroom so the beads would make noise and slipped into his room and belly crawled under his bed. He saw two eyes looking at him and nearly shouted. It was mom's cat, Jacko. He expected the crazy cat to scratch him, but instead it rubbed against his legs and was purring very loud. He hoped Aunt Fran didn't hear it. From down here he could see across his room, clothes on the floor, broken hockey stick, inline rollerblades and part of the light green hall wall.

Aunt Fran stomped down the hall. The floorboard by his door squeaked. The light clicked on. Light spilled into the room. Then he heard the bead curtain move and saw the light in his mother's go on. Heard her opening closet doors.

"I'm gonna get you," she said.

He held his face in his hands and shivered. *Mommy, mommy, come back.*

The bed creaked. She must be getting on her knees and looking under mom's bed. He knew what that meant. She'll look under his bed, too.

He squirmed out from under the bed and tried to run quietly. His feet were heavy. He wanted to move faster. He hit the security bar. It fell on the floor with a loud clanking sound. He took hold of the dead bolt, but his hands were sweaty and couldn't grasp hold. He tried to turn it again and again. His sweaty hands kept slipping.

Then she grabbed him by his upper arm and slammed him into the wall.

He hit his head and fell down. "Ow!" Tears gushed out. He looked up. She wasn't there. He heard her in the kitchen. He heard a drawer opening, heard her shoving things about searching for something.

He stood up and stumbled to the door.

But she was quick. She stepped out of the kitchen and grabbed him by the hair and dragged him into the living room. He saw the long carving knife in her hand and started crying.

She sat in his mother's chair in the living room and made him stand in front of her. She pulled his pants down. She placed the knife blade under his pee pee.

"Maybe I should cut this little thing off. That would teach you a lesson, wouldn't it?"

"NO! Pleease."

She smiled, the lipstick on her teeth looked like blood. Her eyes gleamed like she was enjoying this.

He couldn't hold it in any longer. Couldn't. Couldn't.

"WHAT!" she yelled and jumped to her feet, shoving him away from her, knocked him down.

He rolled away and moved quickly, pulling up his pants.

Her leg and white shoes were wet. "Look what you did."

"I didn't mean to. It was an accident. I--"

She pointed the carving knife and came at him.

He jumped up and ran, pulling over the lamp as he went past the easy chair. Heard something bang down. Glanced back. She'd tripped over the lamp and fallen.

He grabbed the dead bolt. His hands were wetter now. He rubbed them on his pants. Grabbed again. Turned. It clicked open.

She stormed down the hall.

He swung the door open and ran into the hall. He knocked on doors, pressed buzzers, no one came.

She limped out into the hall. The wet carving knife gleamed in the weak light. Her face twisted with hate.

He ran down the hall to the elevator and pressed the button. The door didn't open. It never opened when you needed it to.

She hurried down the hall after him.

He slammed through the stairwell door and raced down the metal stairs.

She came to the door and shouted, "You'd better stop, if you know what's good for you."

He paused and looked up, his heart pounding in his chest. She leaned over the banister and spit at him. He dodged back from the glob of spit.

"Leave me alone."

"God is punishing you for being such a bad boy."

"Leave me alone. Go away."

"God is punishing you."

Her heavy shoes clunked on the metal stairs.

He hurried down the steps, breathing hard and choking on his tears. He ran down the stairs, watching where he stepped. He stopped at the next floor and put the nebulizer to his mouth and squeezed. He tried to catch his breath as heard her heavy menacing steps coming closer. He rushed down the next flight, coughing, crying, and wiping his eyes with the back of his hand, and didn't stop again.

The back of his hands were wet by the time he'd raced down four floors and stopped, his breath ragged in his throat, his heart pumping so loud it was hard to hear. He couldn't hear her. He looked up. The lighting was dim. Couldn't see her.

He continued down the stairs, walking, little squirts of nebulizer, looking over his shoulder. Sweat ran down his forehead burning his eyes.

He stopped outside the ground floor door. Couldn't hear her. Was she coming? Did she give up? Breathing so hard he had to bend over for a minute, afraid he might be sick.

Maybe she died, had a heart attack. *I'll get blamed for that, too.*

He opened the ground level door.

She stood there grinning; strands of wet hair like worms hanging down her face, the knife in her hand, that madwoman look glowing in her eyes.

*****

Chapter 2- This Is It

Ryan Stone emerged from the subway kiosk just as three guys with shaved heads and jewelry in their ears were entering. They went down the stairs giving him hard looks. It seems like there were assholes giving people hard looks everywhere.

Since he had come back from the job in Portland he could taste New York in the back of his mouth and smell the hot tar, car exhaust and burnt rubber. He liked the feel of New York, the texture of it, but now he was wondering if there might be another way to live. He liked hiking Mount Hood, fly fishing the Deschutes River in Bend, lake fishing on Odell Lake; the openness of the wilderness and the quiet.

New York was so noisy. But not tonight. Tonight it was quiet, only the sound of his sneakers on the gritty sidewalk.

Too quiet.

Then he heard footsteps behind him and whirled around. Three thugs were chasing a little waif of a girl from the subway up the stairs. She was quick on the steps, but once they got on the street the longer legged thugs would catch her. He knew he should not get involved, the judge had warned him about the use of excessive force, but he wasn't about to let that little girl get hurt no matter what some Long Island judge said.

The girl had just run past him when he turned to the first thug making it to the top and gave him a shoulder that sent him flying into the other two and all of them tumbled down the hard steps. Hats and knives went flying and for a moment it looked like they might have learned a lesson. Then one of them took a gun from behind his belt and another grabbed a revolver that had fallen near him. Ryan reached for his own piece, when all of a sudden a cannon exploded next to him.

Ryan jumped back, his eardrum hurting.

The waif of a girl was holding a snub-nosed .44 magnum, which looked like a cannon in her small hand.

"Hey," Ryan said and she swung the gun toward him.

"Okay." he said, raising his hands a little. "It's not me you're mad at."

She gave him an annoyed looked and turned her cannon down the steps at the three thugs, but they were gone. Jewelry, coins, a pistol lying on the cement the only sign that they had been there.

"Damn," she said loudly and Ryan looked at her.

Now he noticed she was wearing a dark red leather jacket and red leather pants, with black spider-web boots. She raised a red cellphone to her mouth. "Got three half points, three punks got away." She stared at Ryan as she listened to her cellphone for a moment. "They took the bait, but a bystander got in the way." She nodded her head to the voice on the cellphone. "Yeah, some dumbass played hero and the dogs ran away. Right. Game on. The bait is live." She put the cellphone and large black revolver inside her red jacket.

"Is this a game?" Ryan said.

The pale white face looked at him innocently, the small right hand with the long fingers combing back her straight black hair. "Don't play, you'll get hurt."

He looked back down the subway stairs, but saw no blood and no witnesses. He was going to tell her off when he turned back, but she wasn't there. She was jogging up the block. He could probably catch her, but what for? He wasn't a cop, couldn't prove anything, and what could she be charged with? He'd probably get charged for interfering in the latest fad to hit the big city. 'Thriller' straight from the latest video game.

New York. He shook his head. Love it or leave it. You'll either make it here or little red riding hood will shoot you for trying. He continued on his way.

Cars bumper to bumper at the curb. Streetlights dotting the distance. Apartment buildings on both sides. Lights on just about every floor. But it was still too quiet. He had never seen New York this quiet. Not on a Friday night, even if it was Friday the thirteenth.

Halfway up the block a small tan dog tiptoed out of the shadows and warily approached him wagging its short tail between its rear legs. Ryan stopped and frowned down at the skinny white and brown mutt. Even in the weak streetlight he could see its ribs, places where the fur was gone. The dog made a whining begging noise. Ryan kneeled and petted the small head and felt scars and bumps the darkness hid,

"Sorry, Brownie, I don't carry scraps with me. But if you're around when I leave I'll have something for you."

The dog licked his hand.

"No collar. No family, huh? Just like me. Both strays."

In his jacket pocket he found an old piece of Slim Jim. He held it between his fingers. The mutt didn't even bother to sniff it, but greedily chomped it down.

"Hungry?" He scratched the dog behind the ear.

Up the block another dog skulked out from behind a car and made a sound. The little dog turned and ran to the other dog.

"Friend, huh?" Ryan stood up, his knees creaking. "Your friends are your family? Same as me Brownie. Same as me."

He crossed the street, loneliness tugging at his heart. A truck came slowly up the block, the engine rumbling loudly. He stopped in front of a tall apartment building and turned to look at it. The truck slowed, brakes squeaking harshly. A white Coca-Cola truck with large red letters: **THIS IS IT** !

A memory flashed across his mind. In a chopper over an Afghanistan desert. Standing in the back door staring down at a destroyed hideout, a big black hole in the sand. The pilot yelled, "THIS IS IT!" and banked, but he was late. An artillery shell screamed past and exploded in the bunker. Must have hit ammo or gasoline. A huge ball of fire mushroomed. The helicopter pitched. His harness tore free.

He was blown out the door and twisted in the air, an angel without wings. Tried to grab at the helicopter, but it was engulfed in flames. He rolled over and saw the black hole coming at him full of jagged pieces of metal.

He woke in the hospital with cuts and lacerations and a broken left leg. He was lucky to be alive.

Got out quietly, no hurrahs. Lost his job. No disability now that his leg was mended. He was slimmer, a little gray in his brown hair and sadness in his brown eyes. Went from job to job. Night watchman while in school. Taxi driver. Bookstore clerk. Salesman. Construction work after he left school. House painting, mostly on Long Island. Now a security guard. Some P.I. work on the side, mostly checking resumes. Falling through life grabbing at failure.

The truck engine roared and he continued toward the apartment building. Too many memories outside waiting to come out of the dark.

He crossed the lobby to the elevator. Cigar smoke hung heavy in the air. Someone left a copy of Newsweek on the plastic ashtray. He picked it up and pressed the red up button. The magazine was opened to an article about the meteor in space.

The door opened and he stepped inside. He pressed button 17 and the elevator rose and he leaned back against the railing inspecting the small metal room. The floor had gray tile and there was tan fabric on the walls. Looking down at the floor, he blinked and for an instant he saw beneath him that black hole in the Kuwait desert.

Grabbing the railing he glanced at the ceiling. Was the elevator suspended by an old cable? *An old rusty cable*? He gazed at the floor. How solid was the floor? Was it rusting? Over a dark black hole? He turned to the magazine.

On the cover page was a blown up picture of the **Thunderstone** meteor. Supposedly touched up by an artist; made prettier so people saw a green-black jagged potato and not an ugly hunk of rock.

The picture, supposedly taken by the Hubble Space Telescope and computer enhanced, looked a lot like a frozen lightning bolt. For size comparison they showed a blue whale next to it. The whale was a lot smaller.

WHAT IS IT? The magazine asked on the cover in blood red letters.

WHERE IS IT FROM? In yellow letters.

The magazine opened to the start of the article.

On the top half of the page was a guessed at trajectory, jig-sawed together from radio telescopes. It showed the Thunderstone coming from the Andromeda constellation, a constellation seen in the Northern Hemisphere.

Under that were the first paragraphs of text.

***

For days the world has been in turmoil. Scientists state they do not know what it is, but world leaders re-iterate that the thing poses no threat to us. "If it had been a threat it would have done something by now," Secretary of Defense Martin Gross said.

"We are not on Defcon Three," General Lawrence Tucker said.

"You can take my word for it," Joint Chief of Staff General Kyle Greene said, "Everything is under control."

What is this **THUNDERSTONE?**

Scientists have had a hard time agreeing on exactly what happened. Some postulate that something happened

-- an explosion or an unknown gravitational force -- that sent the meteor in our direction (i.e. Milky Way's direction) millions of years ago. Once it neared our solar system, it was caught by the sun's gravity and came into orbit with the earth.

(Below was a picture of the meteor with Jupiter behind it.)

"Our radio telescopes and the Hubble Space telescope have not shed any light on it," Doctor Kevin Yates said at NASA. "We have concluded from the computation of its orbit that it is hollow. Therefore if it falls to earth, it will burn up and not cause any severe damage."

Doctor Morris Breitkopf, an eminent scientist, testified that whenever we want we can blast the thing out of orbit. He speculated that the meteor, nicknamed THUNDERSTONE, could be a treasure chest of information about the solar system.

***

"Thunderstone," Ryan said.

When the elevator stopped he hurried off, rolled up the magazine, need this for the ride down, and shoved it in his coat pocket.

Tan carpet in the hall, off-white walls, bright white ceiling. Lighted sconces shaped like shells added a nice effect to the overhead lights. One of the neighbors had sprayed the hall with Pinesol again.

He pressed the buzzer to apartment 8. The door was opened by a shapely woman with skin like brown silk. The former Patricia Hernandez, now Mrs. Ronald Parker was short with long brown hair, chocolate eyes and a smile that could melt a steel heart. Stylish jeans and a loose white silk blouse enhanced her figure.

He walked in and breathed deeply. He loved this apartment, the view of Jersey across the river, the roomy ambiance, the cleanliness and warmth. Beige couch that you really sank into. Friendly pictures on the walls of country scenes. Furniture finished in light oak.

He breathed the aroma of steak grilling in the kitchen

and Chanel No. 5's reaction with Pat's skin smelled of silk sheets and warm kisses.

"I missed you," she said.

"Talk is cheap."

She came into his arms and he hugged her, and she wrapped her arms around him.

"Much time before your husband comes home?"

"Have to be a quickie."

"I heard that," said a male voice in the kitchen. Ron Parker stepped into the foyer holding a carving knife.

"He's been after me again."

Ryan reached under his coat. "Want me to?"

"No. His insurance isn't high enough."

"How do you like your steak?" Ron was a slender, light-skinned African-American with a handsome face.

"Burnt on the outside, rare on the inside."

"Texas style?"

"Just don't fry it."

Pat took Ryan's brown leather jacket glancing at the gun in the shoulder holster. He saw the look in her brown eyes, guns scared her, had ever since she'd lived in the projects.

"When are you going to get a new jacket?"

"I like that one."

"They're having a sale at. . . ."

Ryan was already shaking his head.

"Well, I tried," she said.

"What's up?" he asked as she hung up his jacket, his shoulder holster and his gun.

She shook her head. "He won't tell me."

Ryan noticed the new framed poster on the wall:

Donald Trump's
Great New York Balloon Fair

Pictures of colorful balloons floating over Central Park. The Donald had planned a balloon race across the country to Central Park until he was informed how hard it would be to take off and land in New York. Now he had balloons on display in Central Park and was getting millions of dollars in free publicity.

Ryan walked into the oak cabinet and stainless appliance kitchen and Ron handed him a bottle of Coors. He leaned back and took a sip, tasting the cold beer on the back of his tongue and wanting the feeling to go on and on and on.

"Nothing better than that first cold beer."

"Nothing?" Pat dropped the magazine on the counter, the picture of the meteor on the cover.

Ryan took another sip gazing at the red tinted glasses hanging upside down like in a restaurant. It reminded him of those alien monster eggs in that movie. Goose bumps crawled up his arms.

Pat was staring at him. They made eye contact and she made a face. He noticed the way her hip leaned against the counter. Why can't I meet a nice girl like her? Why do I always meet girls who are interested in my wallet? How old are you? What do you do? How much do you make?

The buzzer sounded and Pat walked to the foyer. The deadbolt thunked and the door opened.

"Hey, beautiful," Hector Mendoza said, leaning on the doorjamb, "what's going on?"

"Mary Anna couldn't come?"

"Alex is still sick." Hector stepped inside.

Through the doorway Ryan saw he wore loose black slacks and a white shirt open at the collar.

"I'll call her later," Pat said.

"What's so important? Have to drop everything and rush over?"

"He won't tell me."

"You looking good. Let's get it on."

"You guys. . . ." Ron frowned at Ryan.

"Shouldn't have married such a pretty woman."

"She wasn't this pretty when I married her."

"I heard that," Pat said from the foyer.

"What's up?" Ryan said.

Ron shook his head as he turned the steaks over.

"You should have been a cook."

"When I retire I plan to open a--"

"I know. I know."

Hector sauntered into the kitchen. "What's the rush?"

"Later." With the large fork Ron added a fourth rib eye. It sizzled and smoke went up the hooded vent over the stove.

"Hey," Hector said to Ryan, "what you doing here? After all those emails I thought you moved to the northwest."

"I really liked it there."

"I know. I know."

"Thought maybe we'd travel there and look around."

"Not me," Ron said. "I was born in the city. The city's in my blood." He motioned at Hector.

"Not me. I was born here, I'm gonna die here."

"Be careful before you eat those words."

"Will you guys stop," Pat said.

Ryan shook his head; we're just getting warmed up.

"What's so important you rushed back from Florida?" Hector said "Got tired of the beaches and golf courses, you had this urge to burn some beef?"

Ron said, "Why couldn't you get here first? And Ryan, who likes his rare, can arrive last."

"Hey man," Hector said. "Start cooking mine when you turn on the stove. Steak can never be overdone. A little ketchup and it's okay."

"For this I buy good meat?" Ron stabbed a steak and slapped it over, black furrows from the grill on the meat.

"What's got him so keyed up?" Ryan looked at Pat, but she shrugged.

"Gimme a clue."

"The brass wanted to run it tonight; I was going to anchor it." Ron turned over a steak.

"How come you ain't?" Hector said.

"Showboat demanded the story. He's flying back from England."

"Wasn't he supposed to interview the Queen?"

"Canceled. Tomorrow night he'll anchor a special news report. We'll promo it all day."

"That big?" Ryan said.

"You should have seen the Vice Presidents at the network bouncing out of their offices like pinballs."

"Anything to do with the shuttle we lost contact with?"

Ron turned to Hector. "We didn't lose contact."

"But NASA said. . . ."

Ron made a face. "They have a private line. A camera inside the shuttle recorded something. They called the President. NASA went on red alert and kicked all the reporters out, and they flew the only copy to the White House -- or at least they think it's the only copy."

"You dog," Hector said.

"I'll be an anchor after this."

"What is it?" Ryan said.

"Don't know. Didn't have time to watch it. Made a copy and split. Security was so tight I had to sneak out of NASA. Drove like a madman to Jacksonville and flew straight here. While the V.P.'s were ricocheting around patting each other on the back, I had someone make me a copy."

"Let's take a look," Hector said.

"After dinner."

Ryan leaned against the counter. Nearby was the *Newsweek* he'd brought upstairs. The cover had a blowup of the jagged meteor in space. Above it in large red letters:

THUNDERSTONE

Ryan said, "Does it have to do with that meteor?"

Pat turned to him and shivered.

The apartment was very silent. The meat sizzled on the grill and in the distance a police siren screamed. Then another. And another.

*****

Chapter 3- The Monster

Kenny was paralyzed with fear. His mouth worked,
but no words came out. He could hardly breathe, his heart
was pounding so hard. He wanted to use the nebulizer, but
if she saw it she'd take it away from him.

Aunt Fran moved angry fast. She grabbed his arm and
yanked him into the hall. Her claw hand squeezed his arm,
nearly lifting him off his feet.

"No. No," Kenny said.

"Gotcha now, smarty pants. Sass me, will ya?"

"No. No. Lemme alone. Lemme alone."

"Shaddup," she yelled her face grotesque with rage.

She pulled him into the elevator. Stabbed the number 8
button with the knife. The plastic cracked and the door
closed. The elevator lurched upward, his stomach sank.

"Smarty pants. Talk back to me? I'll teach you. Put
you in the dishwasher. That'll wash the sass outta you."

"No. No. Please no."

"Shaddup!"

Kenny cried. Tears coursed down his face. He sniffled
and wiped his nose on his sleeve.

"Pig." She twisted his arm.

He cried, snot dripped down over his mouth, his eyes
blinded with tears. She gripped his arm so hard it hurt.

"Thought you could get away, Mister smarty pants.
Fooled you. Ha. Took the elevator." She cackled.
"Teach you to be mean to me. The dishwasher for you."

"I'll die," he sobbed.

"So? The Catkins' baby drowned. Kept crying.
Taught him a lesson. Police questioned me. Think Mrs.
Catkins did it. Ha!"

The elevator stopped with a clunk and the metal door
opened. She clumped off the elevator, dragging him with
her.

He scanned the hall. Hoped someone would be there. Anyone. Even drunk Mrs. Brown who complained about every noise he made. But the hall was empty.

She pulled him down the dimly lit hall, hiding the knife behind her back. "Walk or I'll cut you."

Kenny stumbled alongside. He cried, looked left and right hoping for a door to open and someone to come into the hall. His apartment door, number five, coming closer and closer. Fear crawled up his stomach. "No," he whimpered.

"You live on the eighth floor in apartment number five." She glowered at him. "You know what eight and five are? Thirteen. Your lucky number."

Her grip loosened, but was still tight. He stared at her feet plodding along. She had funny white shoes and walked oddly. Maybe I can stick my foot out and trip her. The guys do it to me at school, but I'll never get away with it. Not now. Suddenly, he remembered she had Bun-onions, whatever that was. She was always complaining about her sore feet.

They were almost at the door. Once inside she'd hurt him terribly. It had to be now. His heart was beating so hard, like that little bird he'd found in the park. Beating like it would bust out of his ribs. He wanted to use his nebulizer, needed to.

When she stopped at the door to grab the doorknob, he lifted his right foot high and stomped down on her left toes. She yelled and swung the knife, but he'd already jerked his arm free. The wet blade sliced the air where his face had been.

He jumped back staring at the knife. It had come so close. She glowered at him. Then her face contorted and she reached down for her foot and fell over.

He couldn't believe it. So easy! He could've done it before. Hit her on the toes with his baseball bat and she'd never come back.

She raised her head, her mouth a snarl of pain and hate, face red as hell, and looked at him. Those dark madwoman eyes glowing with rage like that movie. She started to crawl toward him.

He backed up, told himself he should be moving. He'd wasted time watching her. Time he should have used running, but his feet seemed frozen. He had to force himself, will himself to get going. He put the nebulizer in his mouth and squeezed once.

He raced for the elevator. Hit the button hard. The door opened. He leaped inside and hit the '1' button and glanced back, expecting her to be right behind him. She was still on the floor, trying to use the wall to stand up.

"I'll get you," she said, struggling to get up.

He pressed the button again. The door didn't close. Come on. Come on.

"I'm gonna get you," she warned as she limped toward him, her face was so twisted with anger she looked like a monster. Her injured foot thumped the floor as she walked. Thump! Thump! Closer and closer.

He slapped the button again and again.

"Don't you close that door."

He smashed the button with his fist. The door started to shut, but she was very close. His heart pounded against his chest as he backed into the rear wall.

"Come on. Come on."

She reached for the door. If she got her hand between the doors it would open.

He reached in his pocket for some marbles. Threw a few at her. She flinched, her hand protecting her face. He'd missed her, but the door closed.

Oh God.

He leaned against the wall. Sweat dripped from his face. "Oh Mommy."

The elevator started down haltingly. He heard the metal door on the fire stairs slam open. He knew what that meant. She's coming down the stairs. How fast is she? Can she beat the elevator?

Above the door the floors slowly went by. It seemed to pause at every floor as if making up its mind.

"Faster. Faster. Come on. Come on."

The numbers inched down. Four. Three. Was that noise her pounding down the stairs? He put his ear against the wall. Heard the machinery cranking.

Could she beat the elevator? He hadn't when he took the stairs. But she's big and takes bigger steps, even when she's limping. She's so mean she might jump all the way down.

It approached the ground floor. Number one. His heart beat faster. He moved back and licked his dry lips.

Should he wait or try to dodge past her? Don't want to be on an elevator with her again. Might not make it to my floor.

The elevator stopped and he froze, his legs shaking.

When the door opened, he dived outside, rolled into her. She was standing over him.

"Noooo." He covered his head with his hands. When nothing happened he looked up.

It was drunk Mrs. Brown, her blonde wig crooked on her head. She gave him a startled look.

"Dumb kid." She stepped onto the elevator and pressed a button.

"Mrs. Brown," he gasped. "Someone's chasing me."

"I don't sees no one." She drunkenly looked around the elevator.

"She's trying to kill me."

"Prolly have it comin'."

"But she's after me."

She made a face as she pushed the button again with her thumb. She looked past him, impatient for the door to close.

"I need your help."

Drunken Mrs. Brown stared down at him. "What have you ever done for me?"

The door closed.

He stared at the closed door. He couldn't believe it. How many times had his mother told him, "Be nice to Mrs. Brown, she'll be nice to you." And, "Take in her mail for her." How many times had he done something for her and now when he needed her she smiled at him like she was hoping he'd get it.

A noise from the stairwell. His head spun, looked at the door. He walked to it. His hand trembling, he pushed. Aunt Fran had fallen down. She was lying on the stairs, a crease of blood across her forehead. She was breathing hard, like Mrs. Brown's fat old bulldog.

She looked at him. "Help me," she pleaded.

Before he could stop himself, he stepped into the stairwell. Then he saw the hate burning in her eyes and backed up.

"You little bastard." She climbed to her feet, holding onto the banister, and hobbled down the metal stairs cursing. "Cheap white trash like your whore mother."

He turned and feeling a little light-headed, ran down the hall, but he knew it was too late. The monster was going to get him. The monster was going to grab him and cut him with the knife. His heart felt like it'd freeze up. His lungs wouldn't breathe, he put the nebulizer in his mouth and squeezed and it was a little better.

He went out the front door and down the steps. The street was dimly lit. Cars parked at the curb. Very quiet outside, the street deserted. No one around to help.

Up the street empty garbage cans lay on the sidewalk next to the building. The super hadn't taken them in again. He raced to the trash cans. He crawled into one and it began to roll. No good.

He sat on the gritty sidewalk and strained to pull the bent tin garbage can over him just as the apartment's street door banged open. He should've run away. He could've outrun her on the street. By now he would've been a half a block away. Why didn't he think of that?

"Where are you?" she shouted.

He shivered inside the garbage can. Go away. Go away. God, please don't let the monster get me.

The inside of the can smelled yucky, like rotten bananas, old cabbage, furry potatoes and used kitty litter.

He touched the side of the tin can, it was slimy and cool. He gagged.

"I'll find you." Her voice sounded funny, but it sounded much closer. "You ain't gone far. I'll get you."

Mommy, help me. Mommy, mommy where are you?

A small bullet hole in the can let light in. He peeked out. Had to lean real close. Tried to do it without touching the slimy can.

She was walking up the street looking in the cars. "Hiding behind a car, are you?" The knife blade glinted in the streetlight. "You better come out, if you know what's good for you."

He started to cough and put his hand over his mouth almost choking himself. But he didn't cough. Fresh tears came to his eyes. *Mommy*.

He wiped his eye with his hand and put his eye to the hole. At first he thought he couldn't see, and then he realized her back was nearly against the garbage can.

"Don't make me wait," she warned.

He trembled and leaned away from the peephole. She's gonna lean against it, bump it, something. Once it moves, she'll know I'm inside. Then she'll get me.

He waited and waited. He couldn't hear very good in the can. It was cold. He shivered. He looked through the peephole expecting her to be looking in. But she wasn't near the trash can. She was next to the cars under the streetlight. And the strangest thing, she wasn't looking at the cars or under them. She was looking up at the sky.

Chapter 4 - Dust

Ron and Pat sat on the cushy tan sofa, Ryan and Hector perched on the edge of twin easy chairs viewing the DVD. The 52-inch Sony showed the shuttle's interior in crisp detail, like watching from within the curved glass of a fish bowl.

Commander John Marsh was standing at the side of the shuttle's cockpit. His short blond hair gleamed in the overhead light as he stared out the window. He floated to his seat at the console in the lower center. His blue eyes looked up at the camera. "The meteor is heading toward earth."

At the top center of the curved view Captain David Kim entered, stocky with close cut black hair, a strong chin and dark brown eyes, wearing a white jumpsuit with a diamond NASA patch on the shoulder. He floated through the cabin to his seat in the lower left corner. "What a mess."

"Get rid of those 'jellybeans'?" Marsh said.

"Doctor Martin is finishing up. They had something on them, stuck to everything they came in contact with."

"Got samples?"

"Enough to make everyone happy. What's going on?"

"NASA's thinking of shooting it down.".

"Why bother? It's unstable; it'll break up."

"You don't think it'll make it to Earth?"

"We're two hundred and fifty miles up. It'll burn up. The pressure and temperature will destroy it."

"What about those jellybeans?"

"Fragile, easily crushed. Strange, though."

"What's strange?"

"When I accidentally crushed a few, they had a powdery green-gray dust inside."

"Just dust."

"Yeah. Whatever it was must've turned to dust a million years ago, when it was traveling through space. Smelled like rotten eggs."

"So that isn't you?"

"Very funny."

"Wasn't the sunset a little gray tonight?" Pat said.

"Shssh," Ron said.

"You sure that was dust?" Marsh said.

"Take my word for it. I know vile shit when I see it. Whatever it was it turned to dust a million years ago. Only thing left is the awful smell. Martin's examining it. Our microbiologist will say it's safe, trust me."

"She said it's safe?"

"She's in hog heaven."

Marsh glanced down at the controls, and then went back to looking through the window at the meteor. "NASA, you getting this?"

"Roger," said a voice over the radio, "we copy."

"If you guys back at the Cape want," Kim said, "we can track it and watch it breaking apart. Take some nice home video."

Over the radio: "We are keeping an eye on it."

"Make sure everyone knows it's not us."

Over the radio: "Why did it start falling?"

Marsh gave Kim a look.

"Not sure," Kim said.

Over the radio: "Were the jellybeans like tiny ceramic containers?"

"Stop worrying," Kim said. "No one's invented ceramic that strong."

"Don't they have ceramic cars in Japan," Marsh said. "Who knows what advances aliens might have made."

"Stop sweating the small stuff. It's junk. Space garbage. Some alien race was probably throwing garbage into their sun to destroy it. Something happened; it drifted a few million years in space. Whatever it was, it rotted away a long time ago, decomposed and turned to dust."

"Would aliens throw garbage into their sun?" Pat said.

"Might," Hector said. "Something too dangerous to put in a landfill or burn on their own planet."

"Maybe it wasn't garbage," Ryan said. "Maybe it was a missile that was launched in a war and it went off course and no one's left alive to claim it."

"Mr. Armed-to-the-teeth would put a cheerful spin on it," Ron said.

"Hey, all I'm saying ...."

"Shssh," Pat said. "I can't hear."

Turning toward the rear of the shuttle Commander Marsh said, "What's that?"

"What?"

"Thought I heard something." Commander Marsh twisted to look at the rear door, his short blond hair shiny gold in the shuttle's interior light.

"It's nothing. You got space willies."

Marsh reached up and flipped a switch. "Doctor Martin?" He waited. "Lydia, everything okay?" When no reply came he turned to Kim. "Check it out."

"Do this. Do that." Kim floated out of his seat. "Some day I'll be in charge and tell others to do this do that, but by then it'll be robots and that won't be any fun." By handholds he pulled himself to the rear entry. "I can hear something now. Sounds like bees."

"Bees?"

"Valve on my EVA suit must've jammed again."

"Make sure Dr. Martin's okay."

"She probably just threw up again."

Kim reached for the door handle.

"Don't open that door," Pat said.

Ryan glanced at her, saw her hands clasped together as if she was praying, trembling.

Kim twisted the handle and the door swung open. An orange light inside the rear room was flashing off and on, making it difficult to see. "Martin," Kim said as he pulled himself into the room and out of camera range.

Marsh floated up close to the window on the right. The camera swung with him. He looked out the window. Beyond his face they could see the meteor dropping to earth. "It's wobbling," he muttered. "Won't be long before it breaks apart."

Suddenly Kim started screaming, "Aeeeeeh!"

Marsh spun around. The back of his blond head blocked the camera. Someone at mission control switched to another camera; now Marsh was to the right and the back of the shuttle with the darkened rear door open on the left.

Kim floated into the cockpit on his back, his head toward the camera. He slowly turned over and they could see his face, what was left of it. His nose and left eye and part of his mouth had been eaten away as though he'd been dead for some time. A fluid red ribbon of blood trailed behind.

Marsh started forward and stopped, and then he started backing up.

Into the open cabin door came Dr. Martin. The once pretty redheaded microbiologist looked like she'd been dead for a week. Her skin was gray with a slimy greenish sheen; her black lips were parted back from long teeth. Her bulging eyes were frozen open. Clumps of her red hair had fallen out of her white skull. Her white jumpsuit was spattered with blood.

"Dr. Martin," Marsh shouted, "what's the matter?"

Groaning lowly like a primeval beast, Lydia Martin turned toward Marsh, her wide open eyes settled on him. She jerked forward slowly, stiffly, as if she did not have the coordination necessary to move smoothly in space.

"Stay where you are," Marsh warned.

His voice only agitated her and she reached her hands out to him. Behind her a greenish-gray dust drifted into the cabin. More and more dust was pouring into the cabin. Over the floor, walls and ceiling a fog of dust advanced into the large cabin.

Marsh whirled back to the console. His scared eyes darted right and left. He pulled himself close to the console; hit a switch on the panel. "NASA! Do you see this?" He glanced over his shoulder. "NASA!" His voice close to panic. "NASA? COME IN!" He listened, breathing hard. "NASA! HELP!"

The radio was switched off.

The sound of radio silence filled the apartment.

"Strange," Ryan said. "The dust is moving, but not like it's in an air current. It's almost like it's after him."

Marsh pushed off -- the camera following him. He yanked a large red fire extinguisher from the wall. He shoved Dr. Martin with the end of the cylinder and she floated back, away from him. Then he sprayed CO2 foam at the wall of dust coming toward him and the front part of the wall he hit stopped moving, but the dust behind that wall separated into flanks and floated to the sides and away from the foam blast as if trying to go around the foam. When the foam hit the flank the dust stopped moving and separated, parting up and down, trying to move around the foam. When those flanks of dust touched the foam, again they separated, this time flowing down and into the consoles. The walls of dust behind the foam had split into many fingers as if to reach around the foam.

Marsh was holding his own, spraying, up, down, left and right.

"What's going on?" Pat said.

"Is it intelligent?" Ryan said.

"Watch out," Hector shouted. "Behind you."

A finger of dust floated down to the floor and under the console and around the foam and now was coming up at Commander Marsh from behind. Suddenly sparks flew from the console and the picture blinked and then half the picture was filled with static. Marsh glanced at the camera, his eyes more excited, his mouth moving as it he was shouting, but not a sound was heard.

Commander Marsh was turning when the dust landed on the left side of his face. It spread quickly, radiating out, turning his pink skin gray-green. He put his hand up to his face to brush it off, to make it stop, and his hand turned gray-green. First the fingertips, then the fingers, then his hand. It went up his hand to his wrist turning his skin gray-green, his veins turning dark black-green. Marsh's face contorted as if he was in terrible pain, he opened his mouth to scream, but no sound came out. Then slowly softly sounds came back on as Marsh's scream became a whimper. Spittle and drool spilled out of his mouth, then it was greenish drool, becoming thicker and thicker as he struggled.

Slowly at first, then more violently he started vibrating from fingers to hands to arms, till his body vibrated like a string on a guitar. When he stopped vibrating his whole body was gray, his eyes bulged whitely and his lips had turned black and pulled back from his teeth. The blonde hair on the left side of his head had mostly fallen out revealing a network of green-black veins beneath the pale gray skin. Now he looked like he'd been dead for days.

By the time the thing that had been Dr. Lydia Martin got to Marsh, he was like her. He hissed at her and she hissed back, then they turned toward Kim's body, floated to it and started eating it. Kim's head turned to them.

"He's not dead," Ron whispered.

"Shit!" Ryan said.

"Oh, dear God," Pat breathed.

"Zombies," Hector whispered.

The camera swung to Kim. His arms outstretched, he floated in the cabin. The two things were feeding on him. Parts of his skull showed. His face a grimace of pain, every now and then he quivered. Through a hole in his neck an artery throbbed.

"My God, his heart was still beating."

"Turn it off!" Pat shouted. "Turn it off!"

Ron pressed the remote button and the TV switched off. "There's more."

"I don't want to see it." Pat put her arms around herself and shivered violently.

*****

Chapter 5 - Road Into Hell

The aged black Mustang with the Georgia license plates rumbled northward on the New Jersey Turnpike. Cars, SUV's and trucks roared past in a splash of bright headlights. Horns blared as cars came up behind it then jumped into another lane and raced by.

Howard Farrell concentrated on driving. He'd had enough problems in the last few hours without asking for more. He watched every car that came up behind him. His hands gripping the steering wheel, he squinted as every vehicle flew past, and then blinked to see again.

Thomas Nathan Tolliver in the seat behind him pressed his knees against the back of his seat again. Howie could feel it in the small of his back. Howie hated that and Tommy knew it, but Howie kept his mouth shut. He didn't want to upset Diane with another argument.

"How many cylinders is this rust bucket running on?" Tommy asked.

"Five," Howie said. "Two more than you."

Howie glanced in the mirror. He couldn't see Tommy. Sometimes, in the splash of lights, he could see Tommy, especially when he combed his blonde hair.

"Why didn't we take your folks' four door Mustang?"

"Mustangs don't come in four doors."

Tommy folded his arms across his chest.

"Notice how quiet it is with the new muffler?"

"If we'd taken my Mini-Cooper," Tommy said for the umpteenth time, "we'd've been there already."

"With eight speeding tickets, T.N.T."

"Don't call me T.N.T." Tommy slapped the back seat and dust rose into the air. "Look at this wreck, two hundred thousand miles and never had a tune up."

"It's cute," Diane McDavid said, brushing her short black hair. She was thin with a nose that was a bit too long. Her narrow face had a strong chin and wide forehead. Blue eyes the same shade as her jeans.

"It probably has the original tires on it. Now my souped up Mini .... "

"Give it a break." Diane put the brush in her purse.

"We had tickets for Radio City tonight."

"Can it." Howie shook his head. Tommy sure had changed since high school. "We had a flat. It happens."

"To you, things happen. Things don't happen to me."

"Isn't that what you told Jenny?"

The knee pushed the back of the seat again. Howie gritted his teeth, mumbled, "T.N.T."

"Leave her out of it," Tommy said.

"Yes, please, let's not talk about her anymore." Diane watched the gray cloud dip down; lights from below lighting it up, it almost looked like claws coming down.

"Look at how dark these windows are," Tommy said. "We'll get a ticket from the first cop who sees it. Against the law for windows to be tinted this dark."

"It should be against the law for your mouth not to have a muffler on it."

"Will you two stop arguing?" Diane turned to Tommy in the back seat.

"We could've gone in my car with no problems. Spent the weekend in New York and had a great time."

"We're still spending the weekend in New York," Howie said. God, he wanted Diane to have a good time. It wasn't just that he liked her so much. Since last Christmas it was like a pin had pricked her wonderful sense of humor. He hoped the trip would give her a lift. "And we can still have a great time."

"But we could've ridden in comfort." Tommy's knee pressed on the seat. Howie breathed deeply.

"Who knows, maybe because we're going in my car it will save our lives."

"Yeah, right."

"Like we didn't go too fast and die in a traffic accident or something."

He looked in the rearview mirror. Tommy stopped combing his blond hair. He saw the look on Tommy's face. Tommy's hand came into view with three fingers held up: read between the lines.

"Where'd the traffic go?" Diane looked at both lanes of the highway.

"Da-da-da-dum," Howie said in his terrible rendering of the Twilight Zone theme. Then in a Rod Serling voice added, "They were on their way to New York when they entered the Twilight Zone."

"A few minutes ago cars were zooming past."

"Slow as this crate goes everyone zooms past."

"Now there aren't any other cars."

"Don't see any taillights in front," Howie said.

"No cars going the other way."

"Did we take the wrong exit?" Tommy said.

Then in his terrible Rod Serling impression Howie added, "T.N.T. you're now on a road in hell. Watch out. Up ahead is the Twilight Zone exit."

"Give it a break," Tommy said, "before I--"

Diane twisted around in the seat. In the mirror Tommy's smile faded. His eyes became uncertain. Howie enjoyed it. The mouth-of-the-south was silenced.

"Not another word. Not another putdown. Not another impression. Nothing. Understand?"

"I was just--"

She grabbed the door handle. "Stop the car."

It surprised Howie, but if that's what she wanted. He lifted his foot off the gas and the car slowed.

"Okay, but where's the other traffic?"

"Must be a break in the traffic." Howie looked in the mirror. Tommy was pouting again. For an office manager, he sure does pout a lot. Wonder if that goes along with the job description; must pout when annoyed.

"I didn't say anything."

Howie smiled. God, I love it when he whines. He leaned back which usually caused Tommy to push on the back with his knees, but not this time. Now there was no pressure. Nothing. Silence in Mouthville, Arizona.

After the flat, when the car wouldn't start, Tommy had fooled with the wires until he stopped him. Now they had only yellow parking lights and tail lights. Even the dome light was out.

Tommy said, "Reminds me of that book--"

Diane whirled glaring at him. "Don't even think it."

Tommy sighed.

Howie had to bite his lip so he wouldn't smile.

"Do you know what bridge to take?"

"I thought we'd take a tunnel."

"I'll check." Tommy picked the map off the seat and flipped open the top of his Zippo lighter, the one he'd won at the county fair which he never let them forget about. The smell of lighter fluid filled the car. He thumbed the striker wheel and a blue flame leaped up. "Should be a sign up a ...."

"There it is." Howie pointed. Across the shimmering Hudson River was New York City. Huge towers of stone. Buildings rising up like tall castles. Millions of lights.

"It looks like a birthday cake," Diane said.

"Whose?"

"The Zombie Birthday cake," Tommy whispered, in an awful Boris Karloff impression. "Hop aboard for a thrilling ride."

"I heard that." Diane turned to Tommy. He made a face and she laughed. Tommy laughed too.

"Here's our exit," Howie said. A sign overhead, white letters on green:

LINCOLN TUNNEL

"Can we check into the hotel and go somewhere to eat?" she asked. "Emma's on her senior trip and I promised to call."

Howie said. "If that's what you want, Princess."

"Let's skip the show."

"We missed it by now, anyway," Tommy grumbled.

"Let's walk around and see the sights."

"It's going to be quite a night."

"It sure is."

Howie took the exit and the black Mustang drove into the dark night.

*****

Chapter 6 - Now What?

"You sure that's real?" Hector said. "Maybe it's, you know, a gimmick, like that new movie I heard about."

"What? You think it's an ad for a movie?" Pat said.

"It's real?" Ron said.

"What happened to the shuttle?" Ryan asked.

"NASA must want the President to give the order to destroy it."

"Can they?"

"Probably."

"Was that yesterday?" Hector said. "What happened to that Chinese spacecraft that launched last night? It should have gotten to the shuttle by now."

"Don't know. I left NASA this morning."

"Was did you say about the sunset?" Ryan said.

"Please stop." Pat sat in a corner of the couch shivering, she reminded Ryan of a little girl frightened by campfire stories. "Ron, I need a drink."

Ron stood up, took a breath to stop trembling. He paused as if he was unsteady on his feet. "Shouldn't wait till tomorrow."

"Show it right now," Ryan said.

Ryan and Ron exchanged a glance, sharing the same chilling thought: It's falling to earth now. Tomorrow might be too late.

"Ron?" Pat said. "You okay?"

He motioned at the bar. "How about the rest of you?"

Hector said, "I'll have whatever you're having."

"Why didn't NASA stop it?" Ryan said. "Surely there's a system for stopping it. Like putting out a fire or venting the atmosphere."

"Too busy crapping in their pants," Hector said.

"Assuming they can stop it," Ron said. "That they had a procedure in place and have trained and practiced using it."

"Mother of God, help us," Pat said and motioned to Ron she needed that drink now.

"I don't like it," Ryan said. "They should show this immediately. What the hell are they waiting for?"

"Hey, man," Hector said, "everyone would panic."

"Maybe they should," Ryan said. "Hey world, hey movers and shakers, we're going into space, but we going to act like fools so watch out, here we come."

Ron carried in a tray with bourbon and waters on it. Ryan grabbed his glass. It was warm. He didn't care. It tasted great. If only his hand didn't shake. Spilled some on his chin but got most in his mouth; it went to work fast, burning as it went down. His hand slowed its trembling.

"Now what?" Pat said after a drink.

"I lost my appetite," Hector said.

"The steaks!" Ron rushed to the kitchen and turned the stove off. Stabbed the steaks with a fork and put them on a platter.

Ryan smelled the burnt steaks. The odor upset his stomach. He walked to the window. On a clear night he could see lights across the river in Jersey. Tonight had been clear, but Jersey seemed dark like a fog covered it.

"Maybe we should watch a little more," Ron said.

"I can't," Pat said almost jumping to her feet. She was visibly shaken. "You go ahead. I need to take some aspirin. I don't feel good." She hurried out of the room, one hand on her stomach.

"What you think?" Hector grinned. "There a disclaimer?"

"Disclaimer, hell." Ron shook his head not amused.

"Might be useful," Ryan said. "To see more of it."

"That's what my father said about my joining the Marines," Hector said. "It could be useful. It was. I beat his ass when I came home on leave."

Ron pressed the remote control.

The picture filled with Kim's body floating inside the shuttle cabin. A bone white hand drifted by the camera.

The monsters that Martin and Marsh had become were feeding on parts of Kim's body. Even though they had devoured most of Kim and were partly bloated, they didn't seemed to be satiated.

"Hey," Hector said. "They ate him, but they're still hungry. Maybe they're my relatives."

When the last of Kim was gone the two monsters looked around, then at each other. They started attacking each other. Marsh ripped off Martin's arm and started eating it. Martin attacked Marsh's head and ripped off the right side of his face and started eating it. With one arm ripped off she didn't bleed much, a rope of thick blackish blood spiraled from her body and then it stopped as she continued to feed on part of Marsh.

"Oh man," Hector said. "That is gross."

Suddenly foam squirted down from a nozzle in the ceiling and the monsters were repelled.

"NASA woke up," Ron said.

When the foam stopped the lights inside the cabin were turned on brighter so the monsters could be seen. The monsters turned to the spotlights. Marsh to the one over the cockpit, Martin to a light in the back.

"They're attracted to lights," Ron said.

The spotlights went off and the camera switched to infrared. The infrared lights in the ceiling and in the console made the monsters look even more ghoulish. A recessed light in the ceiling came on and the monsters, with their mouths hanging open, looked up at it.

Out the side windows they could see the space craft rolling over. Then the recessed light went off.

"NASA is flying it." Ryan pointed at the TV screen.

The craft rolled and bright sunlight came in the darkened window. The sunlight shined on the monster that had been Marsh and he turned to the light and put up his hands as if to protect himself and then he stopped moving and floated in the zero gravity as if he was dead. The monster that had been Martin crawled into the shade and hid from the sunlight.

"NASA do that?" Hector said. "They're experimenting with them?"

As if in answer the window darkened and red lights inside the cockpit came on.

For a few minutes Marsh's corpse did not move. Then he started moving in a stiffer manner. He turned toward what was left of Kim and resumed feeding. NASA lightened the windows and the cabin was flooded with bright sunlight. Monster Marsh pulled Kim's body down into the shade under the control panel.

Now the camera swung to the rear of the cockpit and found the Martin monster hiding in the back. When the front windows darkened and the lights in the back brightened the monster came forward. It moved slowly, strangely, half floating, half jerking its way along, ropes of bloody drool hanging from its black mouth. Its bulging white eyes stared at things as if the synapses in her brain were made of molasses. It watched the Marsh monster eating Kim then it went over and ripped the white jumpsuit away from Kim's loins and starting eating.

The tape went blank.

"I thought there was more," Ron said.

"You see it?" Ryan said.

"No. Heard them talk at NASA about the length," he glanced at his watch, "A few minutes at least."

"Must've been edited. Too gross for the President."

"Too gross for me," Hector said. "And I've seen gross shit."

Suddenly the screen cleared. The shuttle windows were darkened and Mission Control turned on an overhead spotlight and increased its intensity. The Marsh monster and the Martin monster crawled way under the control panel out of the light, pulling Kim's body, now in parts, with them.

The screen went dark as Mission Control went back to infrared lighting. The monsters came out from under the console gnawing on bones. Now Mission Control kept the camera on the Martin monster as it was eating. Then

NASA undarkened the windows and turned on the spotlights. The monsters turned away from the light and dragged what was left of Kim into the darkness.

"What is this, Science 101?" Ryan said. "Let's see what we can make the monsters do?"

"Before I managed the bookstore. I worked as a guard for this research company. They were working on the prototype of a creature to send to some planet to eliminate a hostile life form. They wanted to be able to take over a planet and make it suitable for humans without nuking it."

"That was only microbes. Not creatures."

"That powder in the jellybeans," Hector said. "Been in space for a few million years, who knows what happened. Maybe it started out being something beneficial, but, you know, after a million years something happened."

"You're saying this is a foothold situation?"

"I'm only saying what if, you know."

"This thing was drifting in space for a few million years; Earth was different a million years ago."

"Maybe it wasn't even supposed to come to Earth," Hector said, "They're guessing it was drifting for that long. They don't know. They have no idea."

Now the led lights in the consoles blinked and the leds of the various computer systems in the ceiling and walls blinked as if NASA was checking the systems.

The monsters moved out from where they were hiding and looked at the flashing lights.

"Colonel Marsh," a demanding voice over the loudspeaker said.

The Marsh monster did not react to the voice.

"Dr. Martin," the voice on the loudspeaker said. "Doctor."

The Martin creature turned toward the loud speaker in the panel.

"They want to see if it can understand," Ron said.

"Want to see if they can control them," Hector said.

"Not the same voice we heard earlier," Ryan said.

"What are you saying?" Ron said.

"Maybe a military man took control of the mission and shut everything down. The blank spot in the tape. Now it's the military seeing what the situation is."

"Dr. Martin," the authoritarian voice said.

The zombie moved toward the speaker in the center of the console. It didn't move its eyes, but turned its whole head to see in that direction.

"Dr. Martin, can you hear me?" the voice said. "Nod your head if you can hear me."

Suddenly the zombie started beating on the console where the speaker was.

"That didn't prove anything," Ron said.

"Yeah it did," Ryan said.

"It's attracted to sound," Hector said.

"Proved they can't control shit."

"Tell me something I don't know."

The screen blipped and went blank. Ron pressed rewind and stopped with the zombie facing the camera. The zombie's white eyes looked straight at them. The gray-green face had gashes on the forehead and cheeks. The black lips were split. Ropes of pale greenish drool hung from the jagged mouth. Some of its hair had fallen out. The left ear was partly torn off and hanging down.

"It's no longer intelligent," Hector said.

"More intelligent than some network brass for not showing this," Ron said. "What a bunch of idiots."

"Show this they got a riot on their hands," Hector said. "Probably better they didn't show it."

Ryan didn't feel so good. The creature appeared to be studying the camera. He could see it coming out of the TV and crawling out of the TV screen. He shivered.

"They're eating humans. Does that mean the dust genetically engineers them to eat people?"

"I read this article in Popular Science," Hector said.

"Anyone ever tell you, you read too much?"

"All the time. But in this article they said a virus could be created to destroy the frontal lobe which makes rational decisions for planning, morality and stops impulsive actions, but this virus leaves motor skills such as walking, ripping flesh apart intact. In the 1950s they discovered a prion epidemic in New Guinea where members of a certain tribe would tremble and burst into uncontrollable laughter. Doctors traced this back to the tribe's cannibalistic funeral practices of brain-eating.

"And in the 1990s what is called mad cow disease would cause misshapen prions to make sponge like holes in people's brains. So it would not be a giant step for some advanced alien race to create a virus to spread a prion disease."

"Prion?" Ron said.

"This doctor Prusiner coined it, combining the words protein and infection. Prion diseases affect the structure of the brain."

"You saying some evil earth genius did this?"

"No, I'm saying the other things were a wake up call, but as usual world leaders have been more concerned about power than our safety."

Ryan walked over and refilled his drink. He sipped it. The liquor tasted like water; not a good sign. He checked the bottle to make sure it was liquor. Wild Turkey. He was so shook up the liquor had no taste.

"What is the President going to do, shoot the shuttle down?" Ryan said.

"They can't let the shuttle bring that stuff to earth.".

"Must be what they're up to at NASA," Ron said. "Closing the base off to get another shuttle up there right away or launching a nuke to destroy it."

Ryan leaned against the radiator under the window. All those tiny jellybeans floating in space. How much dust in each jellybean? Would the jellybeans be destroyed, burn up if they fell to earth? If the shuttle fell to earth? When was that video taken? How long would it take the tiny jellybeans to float down? He looked out the window. High above New Jersey a feather green cloud dipped downward as the cloud fingers turned into claws.

Ryan noticed Hector staring at the sky. In the moonlit

night the cloud was floating lower and lower.

"When did the shuttle have its accident?" Ryan turned to Ron. Ron was staring at the TV screen.

"Ron."

Ron blinked and looked at Ryan. "Was at Cape Kennedy this morning. Think this was shot yesterday. Don't know where the shuttle was."

"If this was taken about twenty-four hours ago," Ryan said, "why'd it take so long to get it to the White House?"

"Don't know when the White House got it. They kicked us out yesterday afternoon. But they missed me. One of the engineers I'm friendly with --"

"Kelly?" Hector winked.

"-- was showing me the new computer system and they missed me. She made me a copy of the tape, but I couldn't just walk out of there with it; they were searching everyone so thoroughly. Had to sneak out. Then I went to town and rented a car. Drove to the Jacksonville airport, had to wait for a flight back."

"The President has known about this for twenty-four hours?"

"Maybe that's why he lit out for Camp David this morning," Hector said.

"You still got that telescope?"

"In the closet."

Ron hurried down the hall.

Hector said to Ryan, "You don't think?"

Ryan motioned to Pat standing in the doorway, her brown eyes wide like she was screaming inside. A shriek waiting to come out. She pointed to the window. Her arm, hand, finger shook wildly.

The claw cloud was coming down. Parts of it seemed to have touched New Jersey. The tip of another claw was coming close to Manhattan.

"Oh dear God."

*****

Chapter 7 – Hide

"Dial phone," Alexei Antonov said.

Mikhail 'Mika' Solinsky stood across the glass coffee table watching the way the boss handled Betty Garza. One thing he had to admit, Alexei knew how to handle women. He watched her shivering in the green silk dress; saw the goose bumps on her pale skin. She was so small and frail he almost felt sorry for her. Almost.

Alexei's gray eyes stared at her like she was furniture he owned. He had a way of frowning that was intimidating. He was average height with short black-gray hair and a face that could have been that of a car salesman when he smiled, or an attorney with those gray eyes. His teeth were yellowed from years of smoking. The long nose gave his face a ruthless appearance as if his thuggish past was hiding under the surface. With his gray pinstriped suit and gray shirt and dark gray tie he looked like a respectable businessman.

"Dial," he growled, leaning close like he was going to bite her. Like he enjoyed scaring her, which he did. She started to speak and he jabbed her in the ribs with his finger. She winced. "DIAL!"

Betty, thin with white blonde hair, was shaking so bad she had to touch the numbers twice to get it right. Her green eyes darted about; the green eye shadow could have been put on with a spray can. The green silk dress was slit up her skinny white thigh.

"It-it's ringing." She sounded relieved as she held the red phone shaped like a woman's lips for Alexei to hear. Her hand shook. Mika nearly smiled, the phone looked like it was trying to plant a kiss on the boss.

On the second ring an operator said, "Hello. This is the White House, may I help you?"

"I want to speak to Leon Johnson."

"He's unavailable," was the nasal reply. "May I take a

message?"

"Tell him it's Betty Garza. It's important. He'll take my call."

"Hold on, please." Muzak played over the phone.

Betty's green eyes darted nervously to Alexei.

Alexei ignored her and glanced at Luka, Luchezar 'the Bear' Krokovsky, his cold gray eyes saying look at the crap I have to put up with, and Luka's right eyebrow went up agreeing, he always said Alexei was too nice to skirt scum.

Alexei's eyes swung to Mika, and Mika got that feeling that Alexei knew a lot more than he let on. The way those shark eyes went over his slender body, stared at his wide mouth. He tried not to look away and breathed evenly. Alexei was more dangerous than Luka. You could prod Luka for a long time without getting a rise out of him. But not Alexei, one wrong move and he'd never let you forget it. Never.

"Hello?" said an anxious male voice on the phone.

"Leon, it's me." She held the phone sideways for Alexei to hear. The gray eyes looked at her like he was angry with her.

"I--I can't talk now," Johnson said.

"Got some candy for you." Betty gazed at the baggy of white powder, cocaine, on the coffee table.

"Not now." There was a pause on the phone, he whispered, "Hide!"

"What?"

"Have to go."

"When can I see you?"

The laugh was short and strange.

"When? That's a good one," he said.

"What?" Betty said, "What does that mean?"

"Hide," he whispered again and hung up.

Betty's frightened green eyes looked to Alexei begging him to understand. What could she do? His eyes scowled as though they could shoot holes in her. She was shaking like she was going to wet the couch.

"H--he sounded funny. You heard him. Something's going on."

"Not my problem. What about investigation?"

"I couldn't. You heard him. Something's the matter."

"He paid to keep me informed. He try to cheat me."

"No. Not him. I do what you tell me, but I can't do him long distance."

"Damn!"

Betty jumped.

Alexei marched to the window. In the distance the Statue of Liberty glowed against the night sky. Next to him on a table was a statuette of a balloon with a basket and around it beads of glycerin ran down the nylon strings to the basket.

"A--A--Alexei." Betty stood up uncertainly. She glanced at Luka and Mika. "Why don't we ... go into m--my room ... and talk?"

Alexei eyed the doorway to the bedroom. "Sure. What else I got to do?"

He walked across the pale green carpet like a man used to getting what he wanted.

Betty paused, looked at the small baggy on the table. Her hand clenched and unclenched. She saw Alexei was ahead of her and left the baggy and hurried after him. She entered the bedroom behind Alexei and closed the door, once more glancing at the baggy. Behind the closed door she started saying, "Master . . ."

Mika turned to Luka, what did that mean?

Luka Krokovsky smiled his teeth like kernels of corn. Scars crossed the rubbery face. A nose like a potato hit with a hammer and brown steel marbles for eyes. Six feet four, two hundred and sixty pounds, short black bristling hair, five o'clock shadow an hour after he finished shaving. Big Luka laughed as he lumbered to the table and picked up the baggy. "Hate to waste good shit," he whispered. He slipped the baggy in his coat pocket and using his fingernails dropped another baggy on the table. "Rat poison."

Mika stared at the little clear baggy of white powder, then at Luka not sure what to say.

"Boss think Feds onto her. Why Johnson not talk on phone."

Luka stepped to the window, his large elbow bumping the balloon statue. "Hey, don't Miss Liberty look great? Look at all spotlights on her. Lit up like beauty queen.

Mika strolled past the table. In a deft move he picked up the poison baggy and put another in its place. Luka's eyes looking at the dark mirror window didn't blink, but a crinkle appeared next to his eyes.

Mika stood next to Luka at the window. He was nervous. Tried to breathe normally. "Yeah, something." Lady Liberty was across the dark water and in the window, reflected in the dark glass, was the white baggy on the table. He breathed easier seeing the baggy there, knowing he had made the switch. Tomorrow the Feds would raid Betty's place and find Alexei's prints on the baggy.

"Remember when we took this?" Luka gestured at the statue on the table.

"Yeah," Mika said. "Everyone at funeral. We went dressed in moving company clothes."

"Took everything."

"Was lotta junk, I could not fence."

"Like to have seen look on her face. Remember when she was disrespectful to Alexei? Miss High and Mighty. Two weeks later her husband's buried. Come home to empty apartment. Her face must have looked like shit." He laughed a hard cold sound.

Minutes later Alexei came out of the bedroom and headed straight for the front door. He barged into the hall to the elevator. Luka shoved Mika and they rushed to beat Alexei down the hall. Mika caught up at the elevator, but Luka was a few steps behind him.

In the doorway, Betty posed with a hand on her hip and said, "When am I gonna see you again?"

Alexei grumbled as he left, "What am I, boyfriend?"

Franciszek 'Frankie' Fedorova waited by the elevator.

Slender with a face like a hungry wolf his brown eyes slid away from Betty as he adjusted his brown jacket, and straightened the brown tie on the brown shirt.

"Anybody tip you?" Alexei laughed.

"Prolly got brown underwear," Luka said.

Mika sensed something was wrong. He could feel it. They were kidding Frankie, not him. He looked at Frankie, the brown eyes turned away from him.

They stepped inside and Frankie jabbed the button and the door closed. The elevator rumbled downward. A drop of sweat inched down the side of Mika's face.

Alexei looked up at Luka. "Switch vork?"

"Yeah." Luka winked. "Just like you figure."

Mika saw Luka wink and his mind reeled. Did Alexei know he switched the baggy with one that had his fingerprints on it? Took two months to get it. Coated the bag lightly with oil. Left the bag around for Alexei to pick up. Now the frame was ready. But why the wink? What was going on?

Alexei turned to him. "Mika, you still wearing gloves? You think we gonna make hit?" He smiled at him.

"Thought we going to do something."

"We did."

Mika took off the black gloves, his hands were sweaty, and he rubbed them on his dark green shirt.

Luka said, "Why you no let me. . ."

"Nyet," Alexei said. "Cold better."

Mika stiffened. Cold what? Revenge?

Luka shook his head. "You boss."

A phone rang.

Mika took a cell-phone out of his pocket. Unfolded it, put it to his ear. "Yeah." He listened, then said to Alexei, "The blacks are upset, they no like to wait."

"Tell 'em we held up in traffic," Frankie said.

"Who the HELL are they?" Alexei said. "Tell them screw them self. We get there when we there."

Mika spoke into the phone. "You wait."

Alexei pointed at Mika. "That your trouble, Mika. No

got balls to be tough. Always nice. You gotta slap them around, keep them in place. Slap them with words, not just hand. The bigger they act, the harder you slap 'em. And if they screw you, get revenge. Remember, to always get revenge."

Luka laughed. Frankie stared at the floor like he knew something and was afraid if he looked up he'd spill it. Mika breathed, his heart thumping in the back of his throat. Sweat dripped down his sides. He stared at the numbers over the door. They knew. Maybe Alexei was sizing him up right now. One nod to Luka and . . .

"Look at him." Alexei said to Luka. "Mika, you may be smart, but you rattle easy as punk. Who think it be so easy to get under skin. That why you always be soldier, never leader."

"Here's our floor," Frankie said.

"It stops in Hell." Luka laughed.

*****

Chapter 8 - Double Cross

Alexei's black Mercedes limo slowed as it came to a little park alongside the Hudson. The street was dark and usually deserted, but tonight cars crowded the curb, including three Cadillacs with enough extra chrome to cover a spaceship.

"The brotherhood," Luka said, as Frankie parked beside a fire hydrant.

Big Luka stepped from the front seat of the limo and looked around. The postage stamp park had some trees, walks and a few benches. Across the river was the Statue of Liberty, lit with many spotlights. The park was unusually dark as if some streetlights were out. And no people strolled about.

A butane cigarette lighter flared next to the wrought

iron fence along the river walk as someone lit a cigar, the red tip glowing with each puff. Luka motioned at three men with cigars standing at the railing. Once Luka's eyes adjusted to the darkness he saw other men standing in shadows further along the river walk. It was okay; the boss had men hidden around the outskirts of the park.

Luka said over his shoulder, "They here."

Frankie climbed out from behind the wheel. Mika stepped out of the back and held the door for Alexei.

Alexei got out with a topcoat around his shoulders like a cape. He marched into the park, a Russian general in command of an army. Luka and the others followed, their hands not far from their guns. As they crossed the park the odor of the Hudson River was replaced by the aroma of Cuban cigars.

They walked through an open area and then down a path to the river walk, a cement walkway following the river, lampposts every few yards.

Alexei stopped at the edge of the walk and looked at three black men: Mohammed Jones, Big George, and T-Bone Tabari. Then turning right and left he saw the men waiting in the shadows.

"WHAT!" he said.

Big George his shaved head gleaming in the streetlight turned from leaning against the lamppost, his diamond ear studs gleamed and looked at Alexei and his men. Behind Big George, across the river, spotlights shined on Lady Liberty.

Big George was so much bigger than Alexei that Alexei moved to a park bench facing the river and sat down. Big George sat on the other end of the bench and puffed on the cigar.

"Why call emergency meeting? What emergency?"

Big George puffed on his cigar. "We've been getting along lately, sharing information and not fighting. Thought we might be able to work something out."

"What this about emergency?"

"Got a cousin that works at the Cape." Big George

looked at Alexei, then Luka. "You know, Cape Kennedy, the spaceport."

"So? What spaceport got to do with us?"

"My cousin called me told me something happened." Big George motioned with his cigar at the sky. "He said something coming our way."

"Your cousin watches too much TV."

"Dude's been in the army, fought in a war, he knows some shit."

Alexei shook his head. "What you saying?"

"My cousin said to get all the guns and food I could get my hands on and find a safe place to hole up in."

"Your cousin sound like he got one too many joker. What he mean?"

"He didn't explain, but since we're allies, cooperating and all, I thought maybe I would share this and we'd still be allies."

"How you mean?"

"If anything does happen we should split up the Big Apple not fight each other."

Alexei studied him.

"You know like a contingency plan so if something serious happens we don't wind up shooting each other."

"Why we shoot each other?"

"I know you got stockpiles of weapons and I thought maybe we could share them before anyone gets hurt."

Alexei looked at Lady Liberty. Out of the corner of his eye he saw Mika wanted to speak to him; probably about the government guy telling Betty to hide.

"For this, you call me from business?"

"Tryin' to save your ass, work something out here."

"You got cousin who used bad shit and had bad trip and you call ME?"

"He's not a user. He worked for me in the army. Set up supply lines for me when he was overseas, got wounded, came home a hero. Now he's lying low, working part time, 'til they're done investigating him."

"I think you want excuse raid my warehouse. You say

it because some fool say something. Then later you say, oops, you make mistake, so sorry."

"Hey, I'm being serious here, we're both serious men. I'm showing you respect."

"This how you show respect, you say come alone and you bring army?"

"That ain't my army and that ain't your army behind them." Big George punctured his words with the cigar. "That's just our palace guard." He smiled a mouth of white and gold teeth.

Alexei glanced over his shoulder at the park and at all the brothers standing in the dark shadows.

"We both know you got men outside the park." Big George inclined his head as if he was the king of Manhattan and Alexei was in his territory.

"Your men bigger I need more," Alexei said and Big George's round face smiled as if that was the point.

"Mika, what you think?" Alexei asked.

Mika gazed at the dark hostile eyes. "Not trust him. Supposed to bring only one man and show up with army. Call it palace guard, whatever, still army."

"I cover my ass." Big George smiled. "This part of the Big Apple is crawling with your men. I'm the king of my territory and I come to your side of the island to work out a truce before shit hits the fan."

"Then we both agree," Alexei said. "This my turf."

Big George's face took on a hostile expression.

Alexei had a lifetime of studying people. His old man had made him steal things when he was young and could get away with it, then took everything away, including the credit and beat him. When his father was in jail his mother blamed his father and him for their predicament and made him sleep in the hall while she entertained.

Then there were teachers who wanted him to read about a kid floating on a raft when he needed to know how to eat for a week with no money. Or about Stalin when he needed to learn how to stop his mother's boyfriends from beating him. Or how to write legibly when he needed to know how not to get beaten for swiping money. He got kicked out for beating some kid.

Then he got caught breaking in. One of those winter nights when it was too cold to sleep on the hall floor and he wanted someplace warm with a blanket. Reform school was bad. Beatings. Rough kids. Taught him how to survive. When he was released, his father was home and kicked him out, mostly at his mother's urging, afraid he might talk. He moved in with an older woman. Katrina taught him a lot of things. Mostly not to be a sucker. A contact from juvie got him a job being a lookout. From then on it was easy. Some hard guy jobs. A stretch in jail got him a big time connection. When he came out, he was on his way.

There was one speed bump. He caught a guy with his woman. Boris Machronov was rich, a computer whiz. Alexei took a baseball bat to him. Last he heard, Boris was still in the hospital making things with Popsicle sticks and, once her face healed, Katrina went home to hide. Then everyone start calling him Tough Alexei. He got respect from people who years earlier wouldn't give him the time of day.

"You want truce or you want weapons?"

Big George waved the cigar. "We're important men. We should come to an agreement before our soldiers," he glanced at Mika, "a lot of our palace guard, get hurt."

"How much you pay for weapons?"

Big George's heavy eyes stared at Alexei as the muscles under his cheeks moved and the corners of his mouth drooped downward. His expression said he was annoyed at the Russian for taking his time and not treating him with the respect he deserved.

"Enough bullshit," Big George said. "I can just take it; I'm trying to be a nice guy about it."

Alexei looked at the gold teeth. "Where my baseball bat when I need it?"

"What?"

"You have a few soldiers, that's all." Alexei saw Big

George didn't understand and figured it was from his soft American upbringing.

"I'm trying to negotiate here," Big George said. "You want them towel heads to take over?"

"What take over? What you talk about? No one take over anything."

"You and me we ain't like them. Those Arabs will ruin this country. . We're in a position to stop them."

"If there is this emergency you talk about."

"Oh there is, I got more'n one contact." Big George studied Alexei. "You can contact your Washington man and verify what I'm telling you."

Alexei stared at Lady Liberty across the river. *How he know about my Washington man?*

"Boss," Mika said.

"Not now," Alexei said.

"What? What's going on?" Big George said. "You know something?"

"All he know is not to keep mouth shut," Alexei said.

Big George looked at the slender man. "What is it?"

Mika shook his head. "It nothing."

"Ain't got time for this," Big George said. "I come to you in good faith and you know something and you're holding back."

Alexei turned to Big George. "What I know I paid for and I not give away because you scared."

Big George flung the cigar up, across the walk, and over the railing. The cigar went up, the red end glowing brightly, and then tumbled like a rocket out of control, down out of sight into the dark river.

Big George's men stirred as if to come forward.

"If I want, you is dead meat." Big George leaned forward and pointed his thick finger at him. "All your men outside the park, they dead too if I say so."

"Then you should not speak," Alexei said.

"You better show respect," Big George said.

Alexei studied him.

"You dis me in front of my men, you history." Big

George raised his fist. "When my hand drops, you old news." He glared at Luka, the big man looked like he was about to yawn.

"One liddle thing," Alexei said.

"I was gonna share Manhattan with you, now I just kick you and your Arab friends off it."

Alexei was about to say something, but held the remark back. He breathed, stared at Big George. Their eyes locked for several moments. His voice as cold as hell, Alexei said, "Five to bump him off now."

"What!" The corners of Big George's mouth twitched. "You is one dead mother."

"Dime you do it now. I sick of looking at ugly face."

"Why you. . . ."

T-Bone yanked a nine-millimeter Glock 17 from behind his back and aimed at Alexei, and then he turned and pointed it at Big George, twisted it sideways and fired. The shot rocked Big George back on his seat.

Big George's hands went to the bullet hole in his chest; blood flowed out between his thick fingers as Mohammed Jones pulled a nickel plated .357 from a shoulder holster and also shot Big George. The .357 sounded like a cannon as it echoed across the river and down the cement canyons and Big George tumbled off the bench onto the cement walkway and lay still, his face on the ground, as if he was staring at something on the sidewalk, a red puddle spreading around his body.

The other brothers up the walk and in the park pulled guns and were about to start shooting, but Mohammed Jones and T-Bone turned about and raised their hands and shouted for everyone to be cool. Jones held up the nickel plated .357 for everyone to see, gun smoke still curling from the end of the barrel. T-Bone, the other captain, raised a dark and boxy Glock 17 in the streetlight. Jones and T-Bone exchanged a look and glanced down at Big George sprawled on the cement walk, the puddle of blood around him. The smell of gunpowder overpowered the odor of cigars and the river.

"We share the leadership?" Jones said.

"Sure," T-Bone said.

"Why not," Alexei told them. They'll share leadership for one night. Tomorrow one or both be dead.

"The cut?" Jones said.

"Same plus more. We talk."

Both men exchanged looks and agreed.

"You hear what he talk about?"

"Nah," T-Bone said. "The brother been acting funny. Think it was some bad drugs he took."

"We talk later."

Light-skinned T-Bone smiled, his dark eyes sized up Jones. Mohammed Jones had a cold look in his eyes.

Alexei stood up and the others followed.

T-Bone motioned at some men and they hurried over and lifted George's body to the railing and heaved him into the river. There was a splash and the men looked down at the water. The walk, the railing had blood on it.

T-Bone swaggered away. Jones left, trying not to look like he was hurrying after him. Their men, their soldiers, sauntered away like it was no big deal.

Alexei walked to the railing and looked at the river. It was so dark he could not see the body. He turned to Mika, his face like stone, his gray eyes hard as nails.

"I'm sorry boss, I thought what we heard at Betty's was important."

"Important to us, not to him, not to these ... men."

Luka held two baggies of white powder in his thick paws.

Mika paled, his mouth flopped open, his Adam's apple bounced. His eyes skittered about looking for a place to run to.

"We change baggy you left with one with your prints."

Mika tried to speak, but when his mouth moved it was so dry, he couldn't speak.

"Go get her body, come back here and dump her with black gangster."

Mika stared at the baggy and realized it was last week

65

after he spoke to the D.A. that he'd touched it.

"What the matter? You not like you not so smart?"

Mika shook his head.

Alexei slapped him hard across the face; Mika stumbled back a few paces and almost went down.

"When you come back, make sure park is clean. No want blood here." He motioned at Lady Liberty across the dark water. "Give place bad name."

Mika's head throbbed, his left ear rang.

Alexei noted Mika's mouth quivered and the way he shook. He grinned at the fear.

"Try anything again, you rat bait."

"Uh huh," Mika whispered. Alexei was going to let him live. He was going to be alive. He was so happy he wanted to fall on his knees and thank him.

Alexei turned to Luka. "Good job."

Luka straightened his arms and from out of the sleeves of his black leather coat two hammerless pistols dropped into his hands.

"Frankie," Alexei said, "Go nearby apartment, get bucket, wash blood away, no one know what happened."

"Thought Mika vas cleaning the ground," Frankie said.

"He go to Betty's and wipe prints off everything."

Alexei patted Frankie on the face and then walked to the limo, followed by Luka.

*****

Chapter 9 - Something Wicked

American Airlines flight 706 from Orlando was crowded. The passengers, mostly senior citizens, were going to the northeast during the summer. A few businessmen were hurrying home for the weekend.

The engines roared as the plane circled in traffic above La Guardia. The flight attendants handed out extra drinks, pushing carts up and down the aisles.

"I don't like it." At eighty years old, tall and thin, Paul Dachtera had a full head of gray hair and good flash teeth. He wore tan cotton slacks with an elastic waistband and a light blue long sleeve shirt with a pair of drugstore cheaters in each pocket.

Helen, his white haired wife of fifty years, looked past him out the window. With her glasses perched on her nose she was flipping through a magazine. "You're not seeing meteors, are you?"

"No, Dammit."

"Then what's the problem?"

"We should be on the ground already. What's all this hurrying and boarding early and flying so fast if we just have to wait up here all night? Could've driven up here 'fore we land."

"It's not all night. It's just till they have room for us to land."

"Everything okay?" P.J., the pert flight attendant, asked. She was lanky and very thin with short red hair.

"He's just grumpy," Helen said.

"No, I'm not," he said, sounding very grumpy.

"More meteors?"

"Ain't right the way they went across the sky, it was like they were hollow?"

"Maybe they were," Helen said, and then to the flight attendant, "Can't meteors be hollow?"

P.J. smiled sympathetically, but didn't comment.

Paul scowled, unhappy about being patronized.

"He hasn't had his dinner and he's grouchy."

His thin face reddened. "That's not it."

Helen said, "We're visiting our grandchildren."

"We move to Florida, live close to Rat World, so they can visit. Have a house with a pool. You know how much it costs to maintain? And do they visit us? Hell no. We have to visit them."

P.J. frowned. She wanted to remind him about his language, but feared if she did, it'd set him off.

"Would you like something to eat?" P. J. said.

"No," Helen said. "It will ruin his dinner."

"Stop talking about me like I'm a child. I'm right here. I'm not senile. I can hear fine. And I can answer for myself, thank you."

He stared at Helen. A time back a remark like that would've brought tears to her eyes, but now he couldn't tell if she heard him. Probably needs new batteries.

The stewardess was still standing over them. He was about to ask what she was waiting for, when it came to him, she was waiting for him to speak. "What you got?"

"We still have some chicken parts."

"That stuff. It's like rubber. Worse than a frozen dinner. Last time I had one of those dinners, my stomach blew up till it was hard like a drum. Couldn't go for a week. Doctor had to give me special medicine."

"Paul!"

"It's true."

"I don't think we'll have--"

"Got any drumsticks?"

P. J. smiled as she tried to remember if they still had the hot sauce on board. "I'll see what we can put together."

She walked down the aisle.

Bob watched her long legs until he felt something at the window. His head whipped around. Not a foot from his face was a large black spider. He shouted, "AW!!!!"

"Oh!!!" Helen jumped, her hand over her heart.

"Dickie!" a woman shouted in the seat behind them.

The woman yanked the little pole out of her son's hand. On the end of a string was a small plastic spider with six red led eyes.

"I'm sorry," the woman said.

Paul held his chest and breathed. "I could've died of fright. What the hell type of manners you teaching that rug rat?"

"You okay?" Helen asked.

"Lost another ten years."

"Dickie!!" That was followed by a slapping sound. Dickie wailed. "Shut up," she said. "You frightened that old man. He could've got a heart attack."

Paul smiled. It wasn't that bad.

The woman continued, "We would've been sued. Your father'll never let you go to Disney World again."

"I frightened him? He was the one had everyone looking out the window for meteors."

"Dickie, he's just old," she said in a low voice. "When someone is old they sometimes get touched in the head. You know like Uncle George."

"I'm tired of listening to him," Dickie said.

Helen gave Paul a please bear with it a little longer, he's-just-a-kid look.

"For two cents," Paul said.

"I know. I know."

"You should apologize to him," his mother said.

"To him? He took so long in the bathroom I nearly peed my pants."

"Shssh, he might hear you."

Paul leaned back and ran his tongue over his teeth. I hope you have to go again before we land. I'll mark all the others out of order and. . . .

"Here you are, sir." The stewardess bent over. Her perfume smelled like bubblegum. Paul started to feel sick just smelling the stinky stuff.

P.J. handed Paul a plate of small breaded chicken legs. Paul looked at the reheated microwave food. Each leg was made of pulverized chicken, shaped in the form of a small leg and breaded and fast fried and frozen and packaged to be reheated when opened. Looking at it he had the sinking suspicion it'd been frozen during the Eisenhower presidency.

He started to reach for a leg then pulled his hand back. How old is it? That's what I need, a bellyache at my daughter's house. I'd never hear the end of that. Remember when Gramps visited and his belly blew up like a balloon? Ha. Ha. Ha.

"Sir?" P.J. was doing her best to smile. Her feet were killing her; if she didn't need this job she'd tell him to assume the position and feed it to him South Park style.

"Give it to the kid behind us." He deserves a bellyache.

For a moment P.J. frowned, then the plastic smile returned and she showed the plate of chicken legs to the woman behind them.

"Would your son like this?"

"Did he spit on it?"

"Dickie!"

"What's a matter with it?"

"Nothing." P.J.'s voice was starting to show the strain of putting up with fussy passengers.

"You tried to give it to the O. F. and he didn't want it. Why give it to me?"

"Dickie."

"If he doesn't want it, I'll take it back," Paul said.

"You want it or not?" P.J asked.

"We'll take it," his mother said.

P.J. started to walk away. A passenger said, "Do you have any more? I haven't eaten since breakfast. I'd certainly like something." P.J. shook her head as she walked down the aisle. "I'll see what I can do."

Another passenger called out, "Hey, can I have something to eat? We've circled so long, I missed my connection."

"I missed dinner. I'd like something, too."

"I'll see what I can do." P. J. gave Paul an icy smile as she headed to the galley.

Paul leaned back. How long before we land?

"Why are you smiling?" Helen asked.

He waved her question aside. Twenty minutes? Two hours?

Tonight in the news. Several passengers on an American Airlines flight from Florida came down with food poisoning. Worst among them was a boy by the name of Dickie. His stomach was so swollen.

Helen said, "Don't you put up a fuss if Jack wants to

take us out on his boat."

"Humph. Last year, it was his super-sized TV, before that it was his fantastic cell-phone, then computer this, computer that. Now he's got a boat. Damn fool can't swim, and he acts like he's a sailing expert."

"You be nice."

"Okay. Okay."

He watched the lights of New York go by, the skyline lit up like a birthday cake. Sure is beautiful from up here. He leaned close to the window looked at the skyline and then looking up to see if he could see another meteor. What he saw took his breath away. It wasn't exactly a meteor; it was as if it was raining dust. Gray-green dust. Then the plane flew through a dust string and he saw it wasn't dust. It was ... he wasn't sure. Then he saw a piece of dust had hit the wing and was trapped in the tiny groove where the aileron joined the wing. He stared at it and his mouth fell open. It looked like a very tiny jellybean. A gray-green jellybean. Then the jellybean seemed to melt and from out of the jellybean oozed dust. Gray-green dust. More dust seemed to come out of the jelly bean than was possible. Could it have grown when it touched the air? No, that was impossible. But, still, it was strange. Goose bumps grew on his arms. He rubbed his forearms, but they wouldn't go away. He sat upright, suddenly breathing hard, suddenly frightened.

"What is it?" Helen said.

Paul leaned close to the window and looked out at the wing. The dust was gone. The turbulence blew the last of the dust away. He turned to see where it had fallen and saw some part of Queens or was it Long Island below him?

"What is it?" Helen repeated.

He shook his head, it didn't make any sense. It was probably nothing. It--

"Mom!" Dickie said, "I don't feel so good. I gotta go."

"You can't, the stay seated light is on."

"I gotta go. Gotta go."

"Well ... hurry."

Dickie climbed out of the seat, bumping the back of Paul's seat, his stomach rumbling loudly like thunder. He raced down the aisle.

Paul chuckled softly.

"How did you know that?" Helen whispered.

"Didn't," he whispered. "It was an educated guess; guesses get better when you get older.

"That wasn't nice."

He nodded and remembered something. "Remind me to stop at a drug store."

"Did you forget you pills again?"

"I got them," he snapped.

"Then why should we stop?"

"Knowing him I'll probably need a few more."

"Don't you dare say anything."

"I won't. I told you."

"Just nod your head and say how nice it is."

"Don't tell me what to do."

"Be nice."

"Just don't."

She sighed and he turned back to the window.

*****

Chapter 10 - The Palace

Howie parked the black Mustang in the parking garage. The attendant had offered, somewhat reluctantly, to park the old Mustang, but he'd insisted on doing it himself, not over fear of the attendant stealing anything, but he'd heard how these parking valets treated cars and was afraid the guy might do something that broke the car and he'd have to pay a fortune to get it repaired in New York just to drive home. So he said no, much to Tommy's annoyance.

He turned off the engine and patted the dash. Thank

God, we made it. He breathed with relief. He'd wanted to take Tommy's car, afraid of what would happen if they took his, but Diane said she didn't want to be in the front where Tommy would touch her leg every minute with a lame joke and riding in the back made her sick. Now he hoped his car would be able to take them back home to Atlanta Sunday night.

He stepped out of the car. Parked nearby were Mercedes, Cadillacs, Lincolns and Lexuses. His car looked as out of place as a poor relative. Even in the dimly lit garage the other cars' chrome gleamed and paint shined more than his old car did on its best day.

You look about as out of place here as I do.

Nearby was a gray metal door with a bright red neon sign above it.

HOTEL ENTRANCE

A gossamer spider web wafted in a cool draft over the sign. Howie shivered. "Spiders."

He reached forward and opened the door and entered a long plush hall. Tan carpet, golden beige wallpaper above the polished oak wainscoting. Every few feet was another painting. Everything was tasteful and expensive.

He wanted to leave. He was used to a room in a seedy motel near a machine that had soda cans booming down the chute. This luxury made him feel out of place and nervous. Tommy might be able to 'BS' his way into ritzy places, but even here the Mouth of the South was out of his league.

He hurried inside following the signs to the lobby.

Tommy and Diane were waiting for him. In jeans and rumpled shirts they looked like hicks as they stood there gawking at everything. People walked past dressed up, not really snubbing their noses, but with an attitude that said, what are you wrinkled, sweaty people doing here. Don't you know you don't belong?

Howie could feel everyone's eyes on him as he walked up to them. Look, the Hillbillies are staying here.

"What took you so long?"

"Wanted to make sure it was close to the door."

A blonde woman about Diane's size strutted past in a sequined dark blue gown that glittered with every step she took and she took every step as if everyone always watched. He wished he could buy Diane a gown like that. The older woman noticed him staring and with a smug grin glanced away as if he'd been interested in her. It bothered him her expression said that. What's her problem? She had nothing he wanted. Except maybe her money, her clothes, and her jewelry, but not to rob, just to give to Diane so she could wear it.

"How'd you get a room here?" Diane said to Tommy. She'd seen Howie staring at the blonde and watched her sashay away as if she was special.

"Contest at the bank," Tommy said. "My section showed the greatest improvement."

"How'd you win?" Howie said.

"Fired everyone who wasn't over a hundred percent."

"How could you do that?"

"Hired people that were really hungry." He chuckled, an unpleasant sound. "The rest of the staff filled in."

"Did they work more and get paid overtime?"

"Overtime wasn't allowed. They took the work home or did it on their lunch hour." Tommy grinned as his eyes swept around the expensive hotel like he belonged there, like he was a young king coming into his own. Shrugged his thickening shoulders. Tommy was the same height as Howie, but fifty pounds heavier and his blonde hair fell across his forehead like his expensive hairdresser designed it.

"You didn't fire that nice Mr. Haldeman with the four kids?" Diane said.

"He was constantly taking vacation or sick leave cause of the kids. I warned him. Hell, he should've thought of that before he had four kids."

"Four kids." Howie glanced at Diane. He'd like to have four kids with her.

"You bastard." Diane marched a few feet ahead and stared at a large poster on the wall.

DONALD TRUMP'S
GREAT BALLOON FAIR
CENTRAL PARK, NEW YORK CITY

"I had to." Tommy hurried up next to her. "If I didn't, someone else would have, or they would have fired me. It was either him or me. That's the way it is in the corporate world. I told him before his wife had the fourth kid he was taking too much leave. He wouldn't listen."

"You weren't his boss then," Howie said. "Who are you to tell some guy to stop having kids?"

"Hey, I was just trying to wise him up."

"No wonder foreigners are taking over the country. They come here and have a dozen kids and are willing to work themselves to death and we fire our own citizens if they have more'n two because it'll cost too much insurance premium."

Diane glared at Tommy. "You didn't work hard. You partied weekends while your staff busted their asses."

"It wasn't like that. It wasn't."

"Big man. Your staff jumped when you said jump just like your ex-wife's lawyer made you jump."

Tommy turned from Diane to glare at Howie. "I got us this, didn't I?"

"Maybe we should stay somewhere else?" Diane said to Howie, even as her tone said she longed to stay here.

Howie wanted to say yes, but thought of how much money was in his wallet, how little room was left on his charge cards and how much a room in a decent hotel in New York cost. God, he so wanted to say yes.

"No. No. Don't be like that. Stay here. I wasn't Scrooge. My boss, the company, wanted to get rid of certain people. I can't hire or fire anyone. He told me what to do. I just talk a lot. I objected to some of his choices, but I had to do as he said or I'd've been fired."

"Why didn't you say something?" Diane said.

"I--I--I couldn't." Tommy hung his head. "I like to, you know, sound important, but I just take orders like everyone else."

Howie studied Tommy a moment. What an act. Tomorrow Tommy would be laughing to him at how he put this over on her. And if Howie said anything to her she'd think he was just out to get Tommy. "Might as well register."

The lobby was like a castle. Ivory ceilings with crystal tear drop chandeliers. Pale white walls with rosewood partitions, crystal sconces, wooden banisters with gold filigree, green marble columns, expensive carpeting. Porters, bellmen, staff in neat red jackets waiting to serve them.

Like hicks from the country they walked across the lobby gawking at everything. Looked up at the stairs, at the richly furnished elevator bank, at the marble floors, the art work on the walls, at the guests walking past. Listened to jazz being played on a piano somewhere. Breathed in the clean new smell.

They went up to the front desk. A short old bellman waited with their baggage -- they'd unloaded it at the front door -- he had dark circles under his eyes. A very thin woman behind the marble desk in a red jacket greeted them with a professional smile. A nametag:

RANA
Will be glad to serve you

"May I help you?" RANA was Indian with dark skin and intelligent dark brown eyes, long black hair rolled up in a bun on the back of her head.

"Thomas N. Tolliver. I have a room reserved."

"T.N.T.," Howie whispered under his breath. "Tell him what he wants or he'll explode."

"Shush," Diane said playfully.

"Oh, Mr. Tolliver." The smile left her face and her eyes looked away as if saddened. "So sorry, your reservation has been canceled."

"What!"

"There's a message." She delicately handed him a note on hotel stationery as if she was so sorry for giving him bad news, but it was a part of the job and must be done at all costs, so she did it with regret.

Tommy opened the note. His eyes moved down the page slowly. He read it again.

"What's the matter?" Diane asked.

"I've been fired. The whole section was fired this morning. My boss has been transferred. He canceled the reservation."

"Oh Tommy." Diane touched his arm.

Howie saw the compassion on Diane's face, the way she touched Tommy's arm and he wondered if this was for real. Was this a trick to get Diane?

"The bastard. He wasn't paying for the room, the bank was. They wouldn't have known."

"But why fire you?"

Tommy shook his head, his eyes glazed. "Who knows? I won't know till I go back and clean out my desk. Probably the department was downsized."

"Should I have the bellman call you a cab?" RANA had heard it all before, from people who really were hurt and from people trying to hustle a free room. 'A million stories in the Naked City.'

Tommy turned to RANA. His mouth worked like he was chewing sand, like he wanted to speak, but didn't know quite what to say.

RANA watched his expression closely; was it real or was it a scam?

To Howie, Tommy looked like he'd been punched in the groin and somehow still managed to stand. He could envision a long weekend of Tommy crying on Diane's shoulder. Maybe she'd sleep with him. Then in a few weeks T.N.T. will have another job and be smiling and laughing as if it never happened.

"Sir?"

"I want a room."

"It'll cost a bundle," Howie whispered, hoping Tommy wasn't going to ask him to chip in. He would if he had to, but he didn't have a dime.

"I'll pay for it." He took out his wallet and pulled out his gold American Express card.

Howie recalled how over-extended Tommy was. Plastic maxed out. Ex-wife eating him alive. He reached for his own wallet and stopped, he couldn't chip in.

Tommy grinned seeing the expression on Howie's face. "I'll pay for it."

"But--"

"You don't have to." Their eyed locked. Howie could feel Tommy saying, I always go first class.

RANA glanced at the bellman, their eyes saying they had seen this before and it had been touching the first hundred times, but now it wasn't. The bellman, dark-skinned like he'd just emigrated from the Middle East.

"No. That's not it." Howie lowered his voice. "Let's go some place that won't cost so much."

Tommy gazed at the expansive foyer, the nicely-dressed guests hurrying by and a look came over his face as if he'd come this far and 'they' weren't going to throw him back on the train to Hicksville.

"Never been to New York before. Let's do it in style."

He handed the desk clerk his credit card.

"Very good, sir." RANA ran the card through a machine. "One room or two?" Her eyebrows rose as her dark eyes went from him to Diane to Howie.

"We're married." Tommy chuckled and hugged Diane. She submitted good-naturedly. "He's her crazy brother. One room."

"If you say so." RANA punched the keyboard behind the desk. She gave Marco a look and he grimaced, who were these kids fooling? Still, seeing how they were, the two guys caring for the one girl, brought back memories of her own youth and she gave the young man the special discount government employee rate.

Tommy grinned at Diane.

Howie was surprised; even though Diane pulled away she made a face like she was impressed. She wouldn't ride in Tommy's car, but maybe was willing to act like they're married. Women. Go figure. He turned away.

"One bed or two?" RANA asked.

"What about the room that was canceled?"

"The suite's occupied, but I have very nice room."

"How much?" Howie asked, he couldn't help himself, he always asked how much, from burgers to fries.

Tommy's hazel eyes told him to shut up.

RANA quietly mentioned the price.

Tommy's mouth fell open. Even he was surprised.

Howie held his breath. Jesus, for one room. He thought of all the things he could buy for that much money; a computer, new jeans, a tune-up, take a date to a monster truck rally every weekend for a month.

"We'll take one room with two beds," Diane said as if she had to take control before they screwed it up.

RANA smiled, perhaps her dark eyes showing some concern. Another story in the big city. Marco nodded liked she was doing the right thing giving these kids the special rate for a nice room.

She handed the bellman a key card and Tommy his gold card. "Eighth floor. I'm sure you'll like your room."

Howie stepped up to the desk. "I thought hotels didn't have an eighth floor."

"It's the thirteenth floor." RANA smiled as if everyone knew that. "Enjoy your stay."

"I could've told you that," Tommy said when they walked away from reception as though Howie had embarrassed him.

"How can you afford this?"

Tommy chuckled.

"What?"

"I ain't paying, the company is. My boss canceled the reservation, but the stupid ass forgot to cancel my company credit card." Tommy grinned at how clever he was.

"Won't they make you pay?"

"By the time they get the charges a month, six weeks from now, I'll have another job. I'll say there was a mix-up or my boss, Larry Dalton must've screwed up, again."

They followed Marco, the short bellman with a long nose and dyed dark brown hair as he pushed the bags on a small cart.

"You see them meteors?" Marco asked. "Little red glowing things?"

"Looked like dust," Howie said.

"Hard dust going to fall," Tommy sung like it was the lyrics of a song and laughed. "They were pretty neat."

"I thought you said they were space debris?" Diane said and Tommy blushed.

Howie paused by a poster on a stand.

DONALD TRUMP'S
GREAT BALLOON FAIR
CENTRAL PARK, NEW YORK CITY

The poster had pictures of colorful balloons: a Bart Simpson balloon, a red, white and blue balloon, a Pepsi can, a baseball balloon, a red Coca-Cola can balloon.

"What's going on?" Diane asked. "There were balloon decorations on the front of the hotel."

"Balloons!" Marco said, as if it was another gimmick to keep the masses poor and to make the rich richer. "Balloons were supposed to fly to New York from different cities and land in Central Park. Only in the City the winds are too dangerous, so they fly to nearby counties with farms and were hauled into the park. Inna morning you see them across the street. Really sumthing." Marco stepped forward as an elevator door slid open and a gray-haired man dressed in a tux and a fat woman in a purple sequin dress stepped out and walked across the lobby.

Howie wrinkled his nose. "I can smell her perfume downwind in a hurricane."

They entered the lift and the door closed behind them.

Marco pressed the button and it slowly rose.

"Mister Trump thinks it's good for business if there was balloon race from Chicago to New York," Marco said, like he was waiting tables at his day job.

"The Donald wanted it from L.A.," Howie said, "but the F.A.A. was against it."

"Was that why the race was canceled?"

Marco told them, "The balloons are going to be in Central Park over the weekend so people can see them. I see them this morning, really sumthing."

"And too dangerous to land in Central Park."

"Hell, this is New York," Tommy said. "Breathing the air is dangerous."

"They have police and security people guarding them," Marco said.

"How many balloons?"

"Don't know. Hotel has a balloon. Asked me if I would go for a ride. I tell them I go up as far I want in an elevator."

"What if there's a wind?"

Marco's watery brown eyes smiled. "Be on the six o'clock news." He coughed and put his hand over his mouth and Howie made a note not to shake that hand.

"Might be fun to go see," Howie said.

"Looking is for free," Marco said as if everyone employed in the hotel had them figured out.

Howie glanced at the elevator, ornamental wood and burnished glass and golden hand rail. "This is furnished better than my apartment."

Tommy and Diane now studied the walls, carpet and ceiling. Diane agreed and Tommy laughed that big laugh of his like he was so cool and you aren't.

The lights blinked and dimmed and came back up to near normal brightness.

"Welcome to the city." Marco coughed.

The door opened and they followed Marco down the carpeted hall.

"We've been friends for years," Tommy said and

Howie nodded waiting for what he had to say. "You were brought up in a nice middle class home, while I was raised closer to the tracks, if you catch my meaning. We both went to the same college, so how come I'm making over twice as much as you."

Howie sighed, he could tell Tommy the truth, but that'd upset him. He'd told Diane he didn't want to be a salesman like his father and spend five days a week on the road and never see his wife and kids. Or take a job where he had to screw his fellow employees to get ahead, like Tommy did. And jobs didn't fall into his lap like they did Tommy. "Luck," he said.

"Come on," Tommy smiled. "You can tell us."

Howie gazed at him debating whether he should wipe that smile off his face with the truth. "You're lucky, I'm not."

"Come on, don't get upset." Tommy was smiling ear to ear like he'd just put Howie down and Howie didn't have a comeback.

"I'm not upset T.N.T.," Howie admitted. "You're just very lucky I'm not."

Tommy looked at him and wanted to say it wasn't luck, he worked twenty hours a day. It wasn't luck that he kissed his boss's ass. It wasn't luck that he worked so hard he didn't have time for finding new girls and was stuck seeing Diane and the old gang. Then he noticed Howie staring at the walls and saw Howie was upset he had brought it up and he smiled.

"Boys," Diane linked each of her arms in theirs, "we're here to have fun, let's not fight."

Tommy was already smiling. "Okay, by me."

Howie shrugged. "Sure."

Marco stopped in front of Deluxe Room # 805. He swiped the key card in the slot and opened the door. The walls were pale beige, the carpet was beige. On the right was the marble bathroom, Diane remarked, she'd never seen such a gorgeous bathroom, multiple head shower, whirlpool tub, towels twice as plush as what she bought in

Wal-Mart. They walked further into the room itself, it was furnished with taste and elegance. A large flat screen TV, a polished oak writing table, old fashioned paintings on the wall in gilt frames, cushioned chairs in a pale green fabric, two double beds with a plush bedspread and ornamental gilt headboards.

Tommy picked up a laminated plastic sheet off the dresser that had detailed instructions for operating the computer gizmos; one side for the bedroom, the other side the bathroom.

But the most astonishing thing was the view. The thick posh drapes had been pulled back and in full view was Central Park. It was beautiful at night with lights and spotlights, and the large colorful helium balloons, lit by spotlights at rest just above the trees.

Howie, Diane, and Tommy stood at the window staring at the sights, until they heard a cough behind them. They turned. Marco stood there. He had wheeled the bags into the room and stood waiting.

"His tip," Diane whispered.

Tommy took out his thick wallet and opened it. Inside were a dozen of credit cards and no cash.

Howie took out his wallet and opened it. All he had were fives. Gas on the Turnpike cost a lot more than he had figured. When the machine had rejected his credit card he had paid with cash. He needed the cash for New York, he'd planned to borrow Tommy's credit card for the trip home, something he knew he'd be ribbed over for a long time.

"Charge it to the room," Howie said.

"Gotta give him something." Tommy took two fives from Howie's wallet and handed them to the bellman.

Marco nodded like he expected more, but it would do, and turned.

Howie looked down at his almost empty wallet.

Tommy chuckled and Diane tried not to notice the stricken expression on Howie's face. She was determined to have a good time no matter what these clowns did.

"I have the shower first," Tommy said.

"Don't take all night," Diane said and Tommy grabbed his bag and rushed into the shower. When Tommy closed the door she turned to Howie. He had put his wallet away and was looking out the window.

"I'll lend you some money if you need it."

He didn't nod or shake his head; he just stared out the window. "Not how I planned."

"It'll be okay."

He sucked in his lower lip and chewed on it.

She wanted to go over and give him a hug or maybe even a kiss, but she struggled against doing that. He was a grown man, not a kid.

"Let's unpack."

He went to the dolly got his duffle bag and looked at the door to the room and wanted to keep on walking, get in his car and drive away, leave her and Tommy to this dumb dance they were doing; later he wished he had.

*****

Chapter 11 - Closer

Mika stepped off the elevator at the seventeenth floor and walked to Betty's apartment. He'd put on a black leather car coat over his suit jacket in case it was a little messy; he didn't want to ruin a good suit. He shoved his black leather gloves on tighter and looked up and down the hall. He didn't like it. The place was too quiet, but if Alexei said do it, he had better. If he went to the Feds now, they'd find his prints on the baggy. He was fortunate Alexei didn't want revenge for that little trick of his. What was he thinking trying something so stupid?

He stopped at the door. What would she look like? Twisted ugly by pain? Maybe she had done something to herself the pain was so bad. He shook his head.

He reached for the doorknob and stopped. He didn't have a key. He felt along the top of the doorjamb and couldn't find it. He would have to kick it open. He stepped back and took a breath. He wasn't very good at this. Luka could do it like they did on TV, but Luka wasn't here. He was about to kick it open when he paused, reached forward and tried the brass doorknob. It turned and the door opened.

He paused with the door open a crack and steeled himself for what he would find on the other side. He took a breath, held it and gently pushed the door open. The door swung inward easily and silently. He stepped inside steeling himself and pushed the door closed. It swung shut until the lock clicked.

By now sweat was dripping down his face. He trembled slightly. He breathed out and in, through his mouth, so he wouldn't smell anything and walked straight into the living room, the deep pile green carpet soft under his feet.

At first he was surprised seeing Betty lying on the pale green couch in a green negligee. She didn't look so bad, sort of had a strange expression on her face. She sort of looked nicer dead than alive.

He was about to step forward when she moved and he nearly jumped.

She sat up and looked at him, not really surprised. Too high to be surprised.

"Mika? Didn't hear you knock." On the coffee table was a spoon and syringe, a piece of rubber tubing on the floor. Her eyes were glazed, a lazy smile on her face.

"That baggy," he said.

"I lost it," she said, as though she didn't care.

"What?"

She shrugged so drugged she didn't understand.

He saw part of a small baggy behind her foot, under the couch. He got down on his knees and reached under the couch and grabbed the baggy and was about to sigh with relief when he saw that it wasn't the right baggy. The one he'd left had a blue zip lock, this one was red.

"Where baggy?" he demanded.

"There." She pointed at the baggy and laughed.

"Where other baggy?"

She smiled, feeling no pain, and spread her thin legs, her pale white right leg coming out of the slit in the green negligee. "You want?"

He hated talking to dope heads; they were such pain in ass. He knew guys who would do her. He considered it, then getting her to snort some of the poison. Might even be fun. But Alexei would be even more pissed when he found out. And somehow Alexei would find out.

"Just want baggy." He looked around, wondering if he should shoot her or break her neck.

"You old druggie." She laughed and smiled at him as if now she saw him for what he was.

He sat in the padded green silk chair across from her. Sitting so close he could smell her expensive perfume. Out the window was the Statue of Liberty and in the distance behind it a gray-green cloud was coming down.

"Take off your pants and stay awhile." She giggled.

"Give me baggy."

"Traded it for some H."

"Traded! With who?"

She blinked. Looked at him and grinned, a stupid druggy grin. "Guess. You'll never guess who."

"Just tell me, you dumb slut."

She picked up her glass from the coffee table and stood up as if she was going to the wet bar, took a few steps, wobbled and sat in his lap, put her arms around his neck. "Who you calling dumb?"

He pulled her arms down. "Where is it?" He gently pushed her off him, back to the couch.

"You're no fun."

"Alexei want it back. I need it, now."

"He gave it to me."

He stared at her for a moment. He couldn't tell her the truth. And he didn't want to tell her something that would piss her off. He needed her to cooperate with him. This was turning out to be a nightmare and he needed to keep things under control so he could live through the night and maybe escape tomorrow.

"Alexei said it not good enough for you. He want me take it back so he can give you better."

"He does?"

"After what you did for him," he motioned at the closed bedroom door, "he does. Where is it?"

"Why doesn't he just give me good stuff?"

"He want old stuff back first. He no get that back, you no get better stuff."

"Why?"

"Cheap stuff, it meant for Long Island, not for you. I get mixed up which baggy go where, he tell me to get it back or else."

She frowned. "Ut-oh."

"What you mean ut-oh? That doesn't sound good."

"I gave it to my friend."

He stared at her not sure he'd heard her correctly. "You got friend? You gave it away? Who?"

She motioned at the closed bedroom door.

Mika jumped to his feet and yanked his pistol out the pocket of his black vinyl shoulder holster. He held the nine-millimeter Glock down at his side like he'd seen the cops do on TV. He hurried to the closed door and stood alongside it ready to shoot as his heart pounded in his chest and he breathed as if he'd been running.

She scrambled after him.

"Don't hurt him," she begged.

"Him? Your friend a him?"

Her face crumpled, she'd been such a fool, but it wasn't her fault. She didn't like being alone. She needed to be with someone when she got high.

He wanted to hit her with the gun. His hand was shaking with anger. This was turning out to be terrible night. He put his ear against the door and listened. The other side of the door was quiet.

He turned to her. She was staring at him. He whispered, "What his name?"

She shrugged like it was no big thing. "T-Bone."

His brown eyes shot to her, his mouth flopped open. "Big George's man?"

"He killed Big George. Now he's as big as Alexei."

He stared at her. How can she be so dumb? He rapped on the closed door with his knuckles and stood back, ready to shoot. He motioned to her.

"T-Bone," she called and Mika aimed at the door.

No answer.

She looked at him.

Sweat dripped down under his arms.

"We just do drugs together," she said.

"How long he in there?"

She raised her shoulders in a gesture of doubt. "Don't know. A while."

His shook his head, licked his lips, his mouth dry. He slowly opened the door and stepped into the bedroom. He pointed the gun ready to shoot anything that moved. Nothing moved. T-Bone lay on the bed, his face twisted in pain. His shoes and shirt off; his skinny chest was covered with tattoos: chains, the initials MLK, designs, knives, and the head of a black panther, his brown skin turning gray in death.

Betty followed him into the room and cried out, "Oh, Jesus," and stumbled into her dresser.

For a moment they both stared at T-Bone, then Mika slapped her hard and shoved her into the bathroom and told her get cleaned up. Mika threw the green silk sheet over T-Bone. He saw T-Bone's body outlined by the green silk sheet and almost expected T-Bone to sit up. He saw T-Bone's gun on the night table and shoved his own pistol in his should holster and put T-Bone's Glock, which had back spatter blood on the barrel from shooting Big George, in his coat pocket.

When Betty came out of the bathroom he told her to hurry get dressed.

"Why?"

"You help dump body. Body cannot be found here."

"Why me? I didn't kill him."

"If he found here, it start war."

"But I didn't do anything. T-Bone and me, we just got high together. We don't do anything else."

Mika didn't believe her. Alexei certainly wouldn't. The Feds wouldn't.

"His friends will think you kill him for Alexei. They will kill you, and then they come after Alexei."

She looked around the room for her cell. "I'll call and tell Alexei I was getting information from T-Bone."

"You think Alexei believe that?"

She blinked several times and stared at him; tears welled up in her green eyes and ran down her face.

"T-Bone's friends, they come after you."

"Alexei will protect me."

"This after you tell Alexei what T-Bone doing in bedroom, with no clothes on?"

She glanced at T-Bone understanding dawning on her pale face. "You won't tell Alexei would you?"

"What you think?"

"T-Bone said he'd protect me."

He looked at T-Bone's body.

"He can't protect you now."

"He was always so nice to me."

"He use you to get to Alexei. Maybe that why Alexei think Feds after him. You tell T-Bone things. He tell someone else."

"I didn't tell him anything."

"Is because you know nothing. But what you think, this no make Alexei angry?"

"I'll tell him I killed T-Bone for him."

"How? How you kill him?"

She stared at T-Bone then her eyes looked at the baggy on the night table.

"Were those drugs bad?"

"That why I rush over here." He picked up the baggy

and stuffed it in his coat pocket. "Get dressed."

Her wet eyes blinked several times and her mouthed opened. "Oh." She shook her head like she couldn't get her mind around it and he got fed up with her not doing what he said and shoved her into the dresser.

He said, "You dress now." While he wrapped the body in the green sheet she stopped dressing and turned to him as if she was finally figuring things out.

"Is Alexei going to kill me?" She stood there wearing only a green silk blouse over thin pale legs.

He was scared and thinking fast like he did when he played chess with Alexei.

"You hide until I can explain things. I tell him T-Bone try to rape you and you fight him and kill him."

She looked at him as if he was her only friend in the world. "What's going to happen to me?"

"You help me dump body, then stay at friend's place. You got friend?"

"I got a sister in Jersey."

"Stay there till it over."

"Is Alexei coming here?"

"He no come here. I tell him you gone."

"He going to have me killed?"

"You stay out of sight until all forgotten and he not kill you."

She swallowed. Now she was starting to shiver.

"How long?" She tucked the green blouse into the tight jeans.

"Until I call and tell you to come."

"Thanks, Mika. Anything you want," she said it to him so he would understand, "anything."

"Want to get this over before Alexei take it out on me."

"Why'd he do that?"

"Who introduced Alexei to you? Hurry now."

While she finished dressing he pulled down a drape cord and used it to tie T-Bone in the green bedspread.

She threw some things into a small carryon suitcase, zipped it up, opened the front door and rushed to the elevator and held the door open.

Mika carried T-Bone over his shoulder, and watched her standing there nervous and shivering. Her mascara had run down her cheeks.

"I tell Alexei you do favor for him. With T-Bone gone it easier for Alexei to keep control."

"You think he'll buy it?"

"I tell they will think whores work for him and they will not know who to trust."

He stepped into the elevator and she pressed the button for the Lobby. He carried T-Bone on his shoulder, surprised at how light he was. The thug had dressed like he was a big man with padded shoulders, but he was lighter than some women he'd had to carry away.

"You're a real friend." She reached over and gave his arm a squeeze.

"You make it up to me when this over."

"I will, Mika. I really will."

She studied him as he looked up at the floor numbers. "Is it true T-Bone killed Big George?"

"Alexei told T-Bone and Jones to do it and like they Alexei's soldiers, they shoot Big George."

"Lying slime bag. T-Bone said it was all his idea."

"He like dog Alexei tell to bite someone."

She nodded, seeing it in her mind. "So he wasn't equal to Alexei?"

"No one equal to Alexei."

The elevator door opened. "Open front door."

She ran across the lobby to the front door and held it as Mika carried T-Bone's body to his dark green Ford Explorer parked at the curb. He pressed the key fob opening the doors. She got in the front while he dumped T-Bone's body behind the second row of seats. He slammed the hatch, got behind the wheel and turned the key. The engine roared to life.

"What now?"

"Dump him in river."

"You need me for that? Why can't you drop me at the

bus station?"

"Need lookout. You volunteered."

"Alexei going to be there?" She felt she should jump from the moving car and run for her life. "If he's there so help me God, I'll say it was a threesome."

Mika looked hard at her. "I save your life and now you double-cross me?"

"I didn't mean anything by it; I'm just not going to be set-up."

"You not set-up. I not shoot you when I find T-Bone there, remember that."

"Mika, I'm sorry. It's just that a girl has to be careful." She reached over and gave his arm a squeeze. "Thanks, Mika." She studied his face. He seemed scared and she smiled thinking her threat got to him. He might have guns and fists, but she had a mouth that could do more damage.

Suddenly, a noise in the back. Mika stomped the brakes. Betty was almost thrown to the floor.

Mika looked in the mirror. T-Bone sat up behind the rear seat, the silk sheet had come off his head and he looked around, confused. Betty started screaming like she thought he'd come back to life. Mika tried to yank his Glock out of his coat pocket, but it snagged on the leather pocket's broad ridge and he had to yank harder, tore his side pocket before it would come out and extended his hand toward the back and shot T-Bone twice. T-Bone was slammed back into the cargo area. Blood spattered the rear window, dripped down the glass, two holes in the tinted glass. Mika leaned over the seat and fired once more into T-Bone's body to make sure he was dead.

His ears were ringing from firing in a confined space. Betty was crying. He could not hear what she said

"SHUT UP," he shouted.

She jerked bolt upright and looked at him as though seeing for the first time that he was a murderer, not just some errand boy. Then she twisted around, grabbed the door handle to jump out and run. She froze when she felt the gun against her back.

"How far you get?" he shouted.

"Lemme go."

He couldn't hear her, but he guessed what she'd said. He cocked the hammer and shouted, "You try to leave now I shoot you dead."

She shied away from him as his heart pounded in his chest. She was still gasping, breathing hard when she put on her seatbelt.

"You didn't have to threaten me," she said.

He didn't hear her. "First dump body."

Mika placed the gun between his legs and grabbed the steering wheel with both hands. He glanced at her. Why couldn't he kill her now? Why did Alexei want to him to take her to the river walk and kill her? Maybe he knew about T-Bone and wanted to send a message. Maybe she was also involved with some other gangbanger. He didn't know, but he'd disobeyed too much already. It would be safer to do exactly as he was told.

Down the side streets as he drove to the river, he saw fog rolling in over Jersey and shook his head. Fog on top of everything else, what a f-ing night.

*****

Chapter 12 - Happening in the Park

In light traffic Mika drove to the park and stopped in a no parking zone. The normal foot traffic had disappeared. He'd never seen the place so empty, so quiet. The gunfight must have chased the people away. Or must be something going on. Maybe on TV. He gazed at the nearby apartment buildings and saw no one watching him. He turned to Betty to ask her if there was something on TV and saw that she had shrunk within herself. Either she had come down off the drugs or she had realized that what she'd done was not going to go unpunished. If not today, then in the future; only a fool would believe that Alexei wouldn't punish you for betraying him. But Alexei wouldn't do anything to him, he needed Mika and they were friends, friends were allowed a little leeway and they were men at war with this decadent society, men trying to make something of themselves. He shoved the gun, still warm, in his jacket pocket and climbed out of the dark green Ford Explorer and walked around to the back, eyes darting up and down the street making sure the coast was clear.

His hearing had returned and his footsteps sounded strange in the quiet night. Now that his hearing had returned everything seemed too quiet. It made him nervous. Should be people walking about, maybe noise from an apartment. Something.

Alexei wanted him to dump T-Bone in the same place to make it look like they'd had a fight. Alexei said the cops will find T-Bone's bullet in Big George and think Mohammed Jones killed T-Bone. They would not suspect Alexei was involved.

He opened the back of the Explorer. "Jesus." The cargo area was filled with blood. The blood had sloshed around and it smelled like hell. He would have to burn it. Shit. Replacing the SUV would be a pain. He turned to the side to breathe and not puke.

He was going to carry him over his shoulder like he'd done at her apartment, but he saw all that blood from the bullet holes and his stomach rolled and he thought, Jesus H. Christ. He grabbed T-Bone's hand. The corpse was still warm, but starting to cool. The skin was turning grayish. He let go and rubbed his hand on his pants. He glanced down the street. Too damn quiet.

He grabbed an ankle; the flesh was soft, wet. Took his hand away. It was covered with blood. The coppery smell and the metallic taste on the back of his tongue was sickening. He swallowed the bile in his throat. He wiped his hands on a dry section of sheet, then touched T-Bone's leg and shivered. Grabbed and pulled the legs to the edge of the compartment.

Bile was coming up and he swallowed again and again. Took a drink from a pint in his glove box. Betty stared at him; she had cleaned off her eye makeup, now her eyes looked dull and stupid. "What's going on?"

He offered her the bottle and she shook her head. He stepped to the back and took another drink, saw he'd left bloody fingerprints on the bottle and tossed it in the rear. Now he turned his head away, took a deep breath and grasped a wrist and pulled the body to the edge.

He gasped for air, breathing hard, his heart hammering, sweat running down his face. Again he swallowed the bile coming up his throat, then glanced down the empty street. Across the park, across the dark water Lady Liberty glowed. A gray-green cloud surrounded the torch. Pollution, he mumbled and turned back to the car.

On the way over he'd wondered how Alexei knew about the baggy. Had he mentioned it to Frankie? He wasn't sure. Maybe when they got high. Could Frankie have remembered? That was over a month ago. The jerk must have said something. Alexei was smart enough to put it together. Not everything or he'd be dead. Must a thought I got a soft spot for Betty and didn't want to see her die. He looked at Betty smoking a joint, her hand shaking real bad.

"Give me a hand," he shouted, his voice echoed up the dark street. "A hand ... a hand." She didn't move. "Betty, get your ass over here." She looked at him as if to say who the hell was he? "NOW!!!" He motioned her to hurry up.

She slid out of the seat and came to the back of the Explorer with an attitude. "Oeuw, it stinks." She put her hand over her nose.

"Grab his hands."

She shook her head and started backing up like she might turn and run away.

He took out his gun and pointed it at her face.

She stared at the gun, and then her frightened green

eyes went to him; what is this about? In that split second she figured out that her life was in Mika's hands.

"Okay, already." She motioned him to lower the gun.

He shoved the gun back in his coat pocket and saw that his hands were shaking and his fingers were bloody.

Mika grabbed the brown gabardines over T-Bones' ankles and felt the material squish into the soft flesh underneath. Betty hadn't moved and he gave her a hostile look to do it or else and she tried to wrap the bed sheet around T-Bone, but on seeing it was all bloody, she pulled her hands back, then grasped T-Bones' wrist and cried out and let go and stood shivering.

"Damn you," Mika said. "Just do it."

She looked at him; her eyes said she hated him.

"Hurry the hell up."

She grabbed the wrist and pulled and Mika pulled and lifted the ankles and T-Bone's lifeless body slid out of the SUV. At the last moment, Betty had squeezed the wrist and the flesh squished under her hands and she'd cried out, let go and jumped back hopped around, shaking her hands and gagging, every sound loud in the quiet night.

T-Bones' bald head hit the asphalt like a coconut. Blood spattered everywhere.

"Damn you, Betty!"

"I can't," she cried. "I can't. I can't Mika, I just can't." She sobbed, her thin shoulders shaking. She shook her hands then wiped them on her jeans, then touched her face, smearing blood on her cheek.

"Grab the bedspread and sheet."

Mika grabbed the ankles and pulled the body to the curb, up and over the curb and down the cement path.

"Come on," Mika shouted at her and she hurried over shaky legged and nervous a skinny dog ready to bolt.

"Why don't you just put him over your shoulder again?" she said and he wanted to shoot her. Just take out his gun and put one in her face, but Alexei had told him to wait until he got to the seawall so it didn't leave a mess and it looked like something T-Bone or Mohammed Jones had done. As he pulled the body he could see it was leaving a trail of blood, but he didn't care. He just wanted to get it over with.

Across the dark water, Lady Liberty stood tall and proud, the gray-green cloud now flowing down over her, obscuring the torch. The breeze from the river eased and he smelled the blood. Shit! What a stink.

As he pulled the body to the river walk he thought about taking his Explorer to a car wash and filling it with water. A few gallons of bleach then shoot a hole in the trunk so it could drain and no one would ever know. T-Bone was heavier now that he was dead weight and he had to pull hard to drag him. He listened to the sound the body made scrapping across the sidewalk. It was so quiet outside he could hear everything, even his heart pounding in his chest. The quiet before the storm, a voice in his head said.

T-Bone's belt caught on a stake at the edge of the grass and Mika lost his grip and let go. He stood there breathing hard and glanced over his shoulder. The fog had descended to the ground and filtered the many spotlights around the base of Lady Liberty. The grayish-green fog hugged the ground and moved over the water toward the shore. He wanted to be away from here before the fog rolled in. He didn't like fog. When anyone asked him what he was afraid of, he always said nothing. He couldn't tell them he was afraid of fog. Whoever heard of someone being afraid of fog? When he was a kid he'd seen his brother standing frozen in the icy fog in Siberia. A memory that never left him. Didn't need fog on top of everything else.

He held the ankles and dragged T-Bones' body down the walk. Where is everyone? The body's back rasped over the cement walk, then he lost his grip on the right ankle again and let go. He leaned against a tree, breathing hard. The smell wasn't so bad with the breeze from the river. He fought the urge to stop and have a smoke. Sweat dripped down his face and he wiped sweat out of his eyes before he remembered his bloody hands and looked down at his hands. He shook his head, didn't want to see what he looked like. God, he needed a drink.

"Hurry up," Betty said and he saw her standing there. She had dumped the sheet and bedspread over the wall, and he wanted to hit her. She had lit another joint and was smoking, T-Bones' blood on her hands on the joint and now on her mouth. She was disgusting.

He looked at his car parked at the curb. On the sidewalk was a trail of blood, visible even in the dim light. He'd get some water, maybe a fire extinguisher and wash it down. Then he thought maybe not. Somehow he'd make the cops think that Mohammed Jones did it. He took a deep breath, reached down and grabbed the ankles again.

He dragged the body to the wrought iron fence. The body seemed to have gained weight. He tugged, stopping every few feet to breathe and wipe his slippery red hands on his pants. He'd burn his pants later. He grunted from the strain. This was taking way too long. Hope no cops come along. He stopped at the fence and leaned against it, breathing hard when spotlights came on. Mika whirled around looking for a place to run, but was blinded by the circle of light and too beat to run. He reached for the gun in his coat pocket.

"Don't!" a loud voice shouted.

He froze. It sounded like a cop. Shielding his eyes he made out shapes, men standing behind the glare of lights, guns drawn. Saw uniforms. Police.

A big man with square shoulders stepped forward.

"Lieutenant? That you?"

"Got you this time, Mika," Roy Boggs said.

"Hey, not this." He motioned at the corpse. "Find him in trunk." He started to reach for his gun.

"Don't try it."

He put his hands up.

"You make mistake."

"Drop your gun on the ground." Mika took T-Bone's gun out of his coat pocket and dropped in the walk. "Kick it away from you." Mika kicked it across the walk. "And the other one." Mika took his own gun out of his shoulder holster and dropped it on the walk and with his foot nudged it toward the cop.

"Come on, gimme break."

"Sergeant." A policewoman stepped forward holding a video camera. "Yes, Sir."

"Got it?"

"Every word."

"Pack up, Sherl."

"Yes Sir." She walked away, the spotlights went off.

Lieutenant Boggs reached into his coat pocket and tossed something to him. He caught it, turned it over.

"Recognize this?"

Mika looked at the .357. "Nyet."

"Sure?"

Mika held it up. "Definitely not mine. I use automatic." He motioned at his gun on the walk and handed the .357 back to the Lieutenant.

Boggs put it in his pocket. "Got your prints on it now. One of the guns used to kill Big George."

"Hey." Mika stepped forward and was slugged by a left cross. He staggered into the fence. While he was shaking the stars out, something metal snapped against his wrist. He struggled to his feet and pulled, his right wrist was handcuffed to the wrought iron railing. "Hey!"

He yanked on it, not believing they'd done that. What the hell was going on? What were they doing here? He was Alexei's man, they knew that. Oh no. Alexei had set him up. His throat squeezed tight with fear, but then he realized even Alexei must know if he rolled on him he'd get in witness protection and Alexei would do hard time. He almost started to smile, but when he looked up; Boggs was putting on one of the sheer rubber gloves they wear at a crime scene. He picked up Mika's Glock and pointed it at Betty; she was standing twenty feet away against the railing, shivering like it below zero. "Don't," she cried. The Lieutenant fired and she went down. The Lieutenant slid Mika's gun across the ground between Mika and Betty.

Now Boggs and the other cops were walking away. Where were they going? What the hell was going on?

"Hey, what's going on?"

They acted like they didn't hear him. But he'd shouted real loud. They had to hear him. He tried again, "HEY!" They continued walking away like he didn't exist. *This is crazy. What the hell is going on?*

Alexei's black limo pulled to the curb. The dark back window slid down. Mika shook his head.

"You made point," he shouted.

A rifle barrel stuck out the window. A red laser dot skipped along the ground till it found him and danced across his chest. "HEY!" he yelled, ducking, left and right not letting the red dot settle on him. Oh God. Oh God.. Any second the gun would shoot and the slug would hit him. He kept moving, dodging away from the red dot. Then he saw the red dot had stopped on the walk about ten feet from him.

He looked at the limo's rear window. The barrel was still there. *Maybe he wants me to beg.* He saw Alexei's face in the window. He was leaning out the window.

"Hey. Come on. You know me. I your friend."

Alexei didn't answer. He wasn't even looking at him. He was staring behind him. Mika glanced over his shoulder. The Statue of Liberty was dark like the lights had gone out. And across the river was New Jersey. Wait. Where were the Jersey lights? What happened to Jersey? A power outage? Then he saw it. Hard to see against the black night. That dark wall of ... fog? Swirling clouds crossing the river. Something was strange with the way it moved. No, not strange, wrong. Very wrong. The wall of fog was a gray-green color.

Lady Liberty was completely hidden, the fog blocking her from view. The fog cloud glowed. It was over ten feet high. Were those screams coming across the river? Gunshots echoing from Jersey? The fog was still coming.

Coming closer. It wasn't like a wall; parts of it reached out toward wherever people were moving. Toward the cops running, toward Betty wounded trying to stand.

"HEY," Betty cried. She had been shot in the chest and her blouse was covered with blood. She struggled to her feet.

That's when he saw Alexei's limo drive way. "NO!" he screamed, but the black lim did not stop.

Mika's fear broke and he turned to run. He took one step and was yanked back down by the handcuff. He cried out. It hurt like hell, he'd dislocated his shoulder. He got to his knees and held his shoulder. The handcuff was covered with blood; blood running down onto the ground. His shoulder hurt like a live wire inside was sending electrical jolts through him. He leaned against the fence.

He turned to shout at the cops, but some were running, others froze like statues. The fog moved after the runners. One cop fell to the ground and was clutching at his chest. Another cop came back and helped him to his feet. The fog went in their mouths, eyes, and ears.

Across the river he couldn't even see Liberty Island. Where was Lady Liberty? His heart pounded.

He tugged on the handcuff. The steel cut into his wrist. Blood ran down his arm, spread on his hand, and soaked his shirt sleeve. His legs were shaking so bad he could not stand. Like a runner out of breath, he breathed in gasps

Now he couldn't see up or down the river. The fog had rolled to the shore and like octopus arms reaching out, tendrils of fog came ashore. Strange sounds came from the fog, people screaming, others seemed to stop as if frozen in place.

He yanked on the handcuff. It wouldn't budge. Put his foot on the fence and pulled as hard as he could. Blood greased the handcuff. His hand was starting to come through, the skin ripping off as it came. His hand was on fire. He glanced up, fog tendrils came on shore and through the metal fence and swirled over the park.

Betty was staggering away, down the walk. Holding

her bloody chest, Betty stumbled into the park.

He yanked on the handcuff the pain almost made him pass out. When he looked up Betty was running back.

"Hey," he shouted. "Give me hand."

She looked at him and stopped, too frightened and confused to move. A tendril of fog floated over the park and followed her.

"My car!" He pointed at the dark green SUV at the curb. "Bolt cutter in back. You get."

She looked at him, then smiled and went to his car.

"What about me?" he shouted.

Suddenly she stopped on the sidewalk near his SUV. She turned left and right. Maybe she was coming back for him. She leaned against the SUV sobbing.

He didn't understand until he saw the people coming out of the fog toward her. They moved stiff limbed and silent, their white eyes bulging. They shuffled under the lights and he saw their gray faces, black lips, open sores and wounds, dark blood oozing out.

Then the gray-green fog rolled over T-Bone, went in his open mouth, went in the bullet holes, and the dead gangster moved jerkily, sat up and climbed to his feet.

"Zombies." The wind from the river, as damp and cold as any breath from hell, licked the back of his neck.

Betty swung around to him and had started toward him when they, the zombies in the fog, grabbed her and began eating her where she stood screaming and struggling. They chewed on her arms, ripped flesh off her face. She screamed until the scream became a gurgle and was buried under a mountain of zombies.

Now the zombies turned toward Mika. T-Bone turned to him and they staggered toward him, dozens of zombies, zombies who had been cops, Big George's men, civilians, all coming his way. He tried to break free of the handcuff. He yanked and yanked, but it wouldn't break. They were almost upon him. That's when he started screaming.

*****

Chapter 13 - And Closer

Through the telescope Hector watched the gray-green cloud cross the river. Numb, he stepped aside. His face pale, he was trembling.

Pat took a look and gasped and jerked her head away. Ron hugged her as tears ran down her face. Ryan peered into the aperture. His stomach curled into a knot.

"Coming fast," Ryan said.

Hector turned to him. "Mary Anna and the kids!" How could he have forgotten? *Was he that scared?*

He rushed to the phone. Dialed. Missed the numbers and hung up. Dialed again. The line buzzed busy.

"It's busy."

"Let me hear." Ryan grabbed the phone. "A land line."

"Could only afford one cell phone," Hector said. "Graduate school cost too much."

"The circuit's busy. Lot of people calling. The lines are jammed."

"You sure?"

"Once installed phones."

"What haven't you done?" Hector hurried back to the telescope and looked again.

Ryan gazed out the window and shook his head.

"Gotta get them."

"It's too far," Ron said.

"Stay here," Pat said, shivering against Ron.

"No." Hector headed for the door. "Stay here, I'll call you, try to come back here."

Pat rushed to the drapes. "Are you sure it isn't fog? It looks like fog."

"You saw my cell phone with my cousin in Jersey," Hector said. "You saw the picture he was streaming."

"Too small to be insects. Maybe microbes. Maybe a thousand microbes all together look like a no-see-um, a midge."

"I'm coming with you," Ryan said.

"You'll slow me down." Hector yanked the door open. "Call Mary Anna for me. Tell her I'll be right there."

"But the lines--" Pat said.

Ryan ran to him. "You'll need help."

"Just don't slow me down."

"Wait." Ron ran to the closet and pulled out a green Army pack. "The General gave this to me."

"What is it?" Ryan slipped on his shoulder holster and his brown leather jacket.

"Survival stuff. Walkie-talkies." He took out two walkie-talkies, put one back in the pack and tossed the other on the couch. "The phone lines might not work. Call me, I'll be listening."

Ryan slung it over his shoulder and ran out the door after Hector.

Up the hall old Mrs. Moon opened her door wearing a ratty pink bathrobe, her thin white hair covered by a scarf. "Something the matter?" In her small arthritic hand was a huge blue-black 1911 Colt .45, probably owned by her grandfather in World War One.

"Better lock your door and go back inside," Ryan said.

"You want you should take this?"

"You keep it."

"I have others."

"Give it to Ron, Mister Anti-gun," Ryan told her. "He can use it. I'll be okay." He heard the lie in his voice.

She stepped up the hall and handed it to Ron. He glanced over his shoulder at Pat; she was at the window and wasn't paying attention. "I better not," he whispered and handed it back. "But thank you."

Mrs. Moon's expression said he was being stupid. She went into her apartment, closed her door and shoved the bolts in place. Ron nodded to Ryan and Ryan raced down the hall after Hector.

"Come on," Hector called from in front of the elevator, he'd pressed the button. He looked over the door at the numbers; the elevator was taking its time.

Ryan ran to him, leaned against the wall and panted.

"Ron's neighbor offered me a gun."

"You should've taken it."

"Got mine." Ryan patted his holster and saw the look on Hector's face, he wanted a gun too. He should have taken the gun for Hector.

"Come on, come on." Hector stared at the numbers over the door. "What if Pat can't get through? Mary Anna could be sitting on the stoop on a night like this. Jesus, Mother Mary, I hope not."

The indicator moved slowly down to their floor. "Come on, will you? Hurry up for God sake."

Doors along the hall opened. People put their heads out. Some tenants stepped out.

"What's going on?" a middle-aged man asked.

A woman in a flowery silk bathrobe said, "I was talking to my sister in Jersey and the line went dead and now I can't get the operator."

A lady with rollers in her hair poked her head out. "It's a storm. You see the storm cloud across the river?"

"That ain't no storm," an old man said. "It's the end of the world. God's punishing us for our sins."

The woman stared at him like he was a loco.

The elevator bell rang and the door slid open. Hector and Ryan jumped inside.

The old man scurried down the hall. "Wait for me."

"Where you going?" Hector asked.

"With you."

Hector pressed the down button. The door closed in the old man's face.

"Safer he stay here."

Ryan's expression soured, he was going to be sick.

Hector said, "Come on," to the elevator going down. Dear God, what can I do? "Gotta get Mary Anna and the kids, pack and leave the city."

Ryan opened the backpack and looked inside.

"You think it's safe upstate?"

Ryan looked at him wondering the same thing.

When the door opened, Hector ran across the lobby and into the street. People were rushing outside, throwing suitcases in cars and trying to maneuver out of parking spaces. Bumpers crashed. Horns beeped. People shouted, cursed. The street was jammed.

A woman was saying, "Was on a webcam with my brother in Newark when the fog turned him into a monster."

"He's a zombie," a redhead with a heavy nasal accent said. "Same thing happened to my cousin at the Shore."

"They were broadcasting the game," her husband said, "when the fog rolled in and everyone it touched turned into a monster."

"Not everyone," the redhead said. "Most, but not everyone."

The man jumped into the car. "Come on, get moving."

Hector and Ryan ran up the block. Hector took the lead, weaving around cars and people lugging their belongings outside. A white haired man jumped in front of them, held up his hands.

"I'm Allen Spellman, you must've heard of me, I'm a congressman. My back went out. I'll give you a hundred dollars to load my car." He pointed at bags on the sidewalk next to a gray Lexus; expensive luggage with separate black leather cases for his Ipad and laptop.

"Out of my way." Hector started to shove him aside.

Spellman tugged an automatic pistol from his trench coat pcoket and pointed it at him. "Do it or I'll shoot."

Ryan was a few steps behind Hector and shouted, "Stop!" and the guy pointed the gun at him.

Hector picked up a duffle bag, swung it and knocked the gun out of Spellman's hand, it skittered under the Lexus. Then he hit him in the mouth and Spellman went down and covered up in a ball on the ground.

Hector felt sorry about the bastard on the ground but didn't have time to find out if he was alright. He raced on, Ryan running next to him.

"Man, you see that?"

"Aren't you glad I came along?" Ryan was puffing hard like he wasn't going to make it.

Hope Ryan can keep up. Hate to leave him.

"Trying to save my kids and that fool wants me to load his laptop. You should've shot him."

"Waste of a bullet."

"Should've taken his gun," Hector looked at the man on the ground, but didn't see the little automatic.

They sprinted to a subway kiosk across the street. Ryan paused on the top step and looked up at the sky. He made a gasping sound.

Hector stopped a few steps down and turned.

Why's he stopped? What's he looking at?

The gray-green cloud was coming closer, long tendrils like tornado funnels dangling down to the ground. In the distance the murky green fog rolled down the street. People ran from the fog. When the fog swallowed the people they stopped running. Some just seemed to stand there; others fell down, and then were lost in the darkness.

Hector raced down the steps and jumped a turnstile.

"Hey!" a transit cop yelled.

"Up there," Ryan yelled and the cop turned in the direction of the stairs.

They ran down the platform toward an express about to pull out. They leaped on board, the doors closed and the subway train lurched down the track.

Hector grabbed the pole and held on, bending over panting, sweat running down his face, his shirt coming out of his trousers. He tried to project his thoughts. Mary Anna, take the kids and hide. It was no good. A thousand fears got in the way. The astronauts in the shuttle .... Why hadn't there been an announcement?

A splitting headache battered his forehead. He closed his eyes and winced. This is not the time for a migraine. Suddenly, he was trembly sick. He opened his mouth and saliva oozed out. Knees weak, he wanted to sit on the floor, but he clasped the pole tightly and remained standing.

Ryan was sitting on a bench breathing hard, head between his knees. Big drops of sweat rolled down his face and dripped to the floor. Must not get sick. Ryan looked up at Hector. Hector nodded. Yeah, I'm sick too.

Ryan motioned at the subway map on the wall at the other end of the car and stood up and shakily made his way down the car to it.

Hector looked at the other passengers as the subway car rocked. Every time the lights flicked an ice pick stabbed his migraine. Some passengers were looking at him. A large woman in a bulky dark gray coat with a knitted green scarf around her neck clutched a large black purse like it was a life raft. His head pounded so hard it was a minute before he caught on she wanted him to look behind him.

"Lookie what we got here," said a taunting voice.

Half dozen gangbangers swaggered toward him like a pack wild dogs. Hector rubbed his forehead. Must be the night for assholes.

"Not now. I'm not in the mood."

"What'd you do, spic, just rob a liquor store?" said a pale youth with an "X" tattooed on his cheek, chains dangled from his hairy wrists. "On the lam?"

"Crawl back in your hole."

The gangbanger pulled a chrome metal thing out of his pocket, flipped his wrist and out snickered a knife. He pointed the knife at Hector.

"Okay spic, hand over the green." The guy motioned with his other hand that he was in a hurry.

"Leave me alone." Hector pointed at the ceiling, still gasping for air, his heart pounded, the migraine making everything a problem. "Fog, something bad coming'."

The gangbanger made a face. "Oh sure." His buddies snickered, crowded close to enjoy this guy trying to talk his way out.

"Fog coming ... across the river from Jersey ... here any minute." He looked at the gray ceiling as the subway car rocked down the tracks. Probably here already. On the streets. People attacking people. He shuddered.

"It's Jersey swamp monsters." One of them said.

"Damn dope head. Didn't give us any."

Hector noticed several passengers were scared. They believed him. The woman with the purse was clutching it to her, pretending she wasn't looking at him. He saw Ryan staring at the map like he was trying to memorize it. He didn't know what was happening right behind him.

"Up there." Hector pointed up.

"Shaddup and give me your money."

That was it. He'd had enough. Had to save his family and this asshole was in the way. The headache was going away. He took a breath, feeling the anger coming, a volcano of rage rising up inside him.

The leader jabbed the knife at him and he exploded, batted the thick arm aside and punched the guy's chin. The head snapped back, his teeth bit into his tongue. He yelled and dropped the knife, blood dripping from his mouth.

Hector punched the leader's belly, knocking him into the skinhead behind him.

Ryan rushed to help, but a punk on the right swung a chukka catching him in the side of the head. He saw stars as he went down and lay there struggling to clear his aching head.

A thug slashed at Hector, but Hector was so keyed up, the guy seemed to be moving in slow motion. He caught the wrist with his left hand and twisted hard and the guy cried out and the knife fell to the floor.

As the thug fell back Hector whirled around in time to catch the one swinging the chukka. He blocked the chukka with his forearm, man that hurt, and kicked him in the groin. The punk bent over and Hector punched the side of his head. The punk stumbled backward, holding his ear, screaming obscenities.

A short squirrelly-faced hood stepped forward and pointed a small nickel-plated pistol at him. Again, Hector watched as if it was slow motion. The punk raised the gun, squinting, turning his face away afraid of the blast. In his mind Hector was screaming, NOOO! moving as fast as he could to get out of the line of fire.

The bullet hammered his chest, knocking him back. He grabbed at the air trying not to fall, seeing the ceiling tilt in front of him and felt himself falling back, back, back. He hit the floor hard and seemed to be lying there for an eternity. He wouldn't be able to rescue Mary Anna and the kids because of some gangbangers, damn punks on a subway. He tried to sit up but his body would not respond. He felt like a swimmer being sucked under water, an impossibly heavy weight in the middle of his chest. The punk stepped close to him and he wanted to reach up and hurt him, hurt him bad for stopping him from saving his dear sweet Mary Anna and the kids.

The punk pointed the gun at Hector's face. "Any last requests, asshole?"

Hector couldn't believe it. He was dying and this punk was talking like some damn movie. Tried to grab him, but his arm flopped at his side.

The punk turned his eyes away again and squinted.

Ryan came slowly out of the numb starry world. He saw Hector lying wounded on the floor. He hadn't heard the shot and now saw the punk aiming to shoot Hector again. Quickly, he reached under his leather jacket and yanked out a Smith and Wesson blue-black.357 and pointed the short big gun and squeezed the heavy trigger and fired. The gun boomed in the subway car. The squirrel-faced punk was knocked back into the tall one behind him, but he didn't go down. Ryan didn't know if he only nicked him or what. He was still blinking, trying to clear the cob webs, when he saw the punk move. Maybe he was raising his gun to fire back or maybe his buddy was shoving him away. No time to take chances. He fired again. The tall punk winced and let squirrel-face fall. The tall punk staggered back, blood flowing from his arm. He sat heavily on the edge of a bench; stared scary eyed at the wound in his arm, the punk who had held the gun sat on floor looking at the bleeding bullet hole in his chest.

Ryan pointed the gun at them, not knowing if the others had guns, afraid they all did and would all draw on him. And he wanted to shoot again. God did he. Wanted to pay them all back for hurting Hector. His mouth dry, he felt like he might be sick.

The train jarred to a stop and everyone hurried out of the car and along the platform. One of the punks helped the wounded one sitting on the bench out the door, then left him and ran away. People boarding the train were knocked aside. Those who saw Hector stepped back off. Other passengers started hurrying off the subway. The punks stomped up the stairs.

Ryan ran to the door. He was shaking, out of breath. He leaned against the door holding on. "Stop!" he yelled, but his heart wasn't in it.

The leader, surrounded by a sea of fleeing passengers, raised his middle finger.

Ryan fired at the ceiling and hunks of tile showered down on the punks. The gunshot echoed in the tunnel and someone cried out. Ryan was on the verge of chasing them when he looked back at Hector lying in a puddle of blood. The punks were escaping up the stairs.. He really wanted to get them now, but the puddle of blood under Hector was spreading.

He put the gun away and kneeled next to him.

"Mary Anna. The kids," Hector gasped. "Save them."

"I will. You know I will."

"The fog," Hector said painfully. "Kept the fog away from ...." He coughed up blood.

"Don't talk. Save your strength. I'll get a doctor."

Hector shook his head. "Too late," he whispered. "Save Mary Anna, the kids."

Ryan glanced at the station. The train was pulling away. The columns went by. He looked back down. Hector stared at the ceiling, not seeing it, his lifeless head rocking with the motion of the train.

Out the window, the leader ran down the stairs and sprinted along the platform; he was pointing up and shouting. He tripped and tumbled along the platform as the train entered the tunnel.

The express plunged into the tunnel and Ryan couldn't see the station. The train raced through the tunnel beneath the city. Ryan's knees were soaked with blood. The dead punk had two chest wounds. He would not live to steal another day. He picked up the punk's gun, a .32 automatic, wiped the blood off on the punk's jeans and put it in his coat pocket.

He closed Hector's eyes. Should say a prayer. His mind was blank, then he stumbled through the Lord's Prayer, "Our Father, Who art in Heaven. . ."

"He's gone," the fat lady said. She leaned forward on her seat, clutching a big automatic in her fat little hands. "There's nothing you can do for him now."

"Why didn't you help?" Ryan said. "Just pull the gun out and wave it around."

"So they shoot me," she said. "Or press charges. I gets in trouble and you and your friend disappear and don't know nothing."

Ryan looked down at Hector too angry to speak.

"Save his family," she said. "That's what he wanted."

He nodded, no longer hating her, well maybe a little, but he had too much to do and hate got in the way.

The train shot past another station. Deserted. The lights blinked. Nothing unusual, lights blink on the subway all the time. Suddenly the lights went out and the train rolled to a stop. It was quiet in the train. The fat lady took a large flashlight out of her purse. Shined the light up and down the car.

"Don't worry." She shined the light in Ryan's eyes. "Just the subway system."

Then from up above, through the tunnels and kiosks, and down the subway gratings were the screams of people, yells, gunshots and cars crashing.

The other passengers, some watching this drama unfold in front of them, other oblivious that anything had happened, sat upright and looked around. They all started talking at once. "What the hell's going on?" "He was right." "It sounds like war." "What's this about a fog?" The fat lady rushed toward the front of the subway car. "Follow me."

Ryan watched her knocking people out of her way as she plowed toward the door to the next car. People jumped up, dropping their things on the floor, scurrying after her. They rushed out the door at the back the car and the coach became pitch black.

Emergency lights dimly lit up the car and the tunnel.

He noticed the army pack on the floor, reached in and pulled out a small flashlight, twisted the handle and shined the dim light around. He was alone in the car except for two dead men. The yells, stomping sounds of the other passengers hurrying to the back of the train was fading away.

He put his hand on Hector's chest and finished his prayer. By the time he finished, the noise of the passengers had stopped. Silence. His heart hammered. Sweat ran down his face. Suddenly, he was cold. He looked up. What had happened on the surface? Then the flashlight beam dimmed to pale yellow, dimmed to a pale glow, dimmed to a red filament in a small bulb then went out. He twisted the handle, it broke and the light didn't come back on.

*****

Chapter 14 - I've Got You

Little Kenny sat with his face in his hands, his eyes closed tight. He couldn't hear in the garbage can. It was cold and he shivered. When he lowered his hands and peered out the bullet hole Aunt Fran was still looking up at the sky, now she was backing up. The carving knife trembled in her hand as she backed toward him.

Oh no, he thought, stop. But she didn't.

The garbage can banged his head when it was knocked off. She stood over him with the long sharp knife in her hand, but when she looked down at him it was like she'd forgotten who he was. Her eyes were confused. Wormy strings of wet hair framed her face.

Then she heard something behind her and whirled around with the knife raised like a weapon. Fear vibrated through her and her whole body trembled. He saw wetness spread on the sidewalk by her feet and he back-crawled deeper into the garbage can. She stared at a wall of murky gray-green fog rolling down the street. On the other side of the wall was the sound of screams and car crashes and gunshots.

Fran forgot about Kenny and backed away. She turned and ran a few steps to a streetlight, panting and staggering like she might fall over.

Kenny lay in the garbage can. He was so afraid, shaking so much, it hurt. He watched the foul smelling -- like rotten eggs -- gray-green fog flow down the street. The stench was so bad it made him gag.

Aunt Fran stood against the light pole as if she was about to start screaming, then the fog rolled over her and she stood with the fog rolling past and looked around. When nothing happened she turned to the garbage can and grinned.

Without thinking, Kenny put the nebulizer in his mouth and squeezed. He felt the medication in his throat, breathed and watched her come in his direction.

Then she looked up the foggy street. Her mouth flopped open. Her false teeth fell to the ground. She shook her head, her mouth moving, no sound coming out. She seemed to be saying no, no, over and over. She pointed the knife, her hand trembled.

"St--sta--stay b--ba--back," she said.

One by one they emerged from the fog and moaning they shuffled to her. A thin old man in a green army type coat shambled to her, his cheeks had been ripped open and gray flesh and black blood vessels hung down his face.

She stabbed his chest and he paused to gaze down at his wound dripping black blood, then he reached for her. Aunt Fran pulled the knife out of his chest and slashed his head and the old man fell down. But others were coming at her, reaching for her. She slashed right and left, cut off fingers, pieces of face flew off. Some of the walking dead went down, others didn't.

Terrified Kenny whispered, "Zombies." He put his nebulizer in his mouth and stopped; the sound might attract them.

There were so many of them they were eating Aunt Fran while she fought. She cried out. They tore at her and tried to chew her as she swung the knife and stabbed and slashed. So many of them came for her, they knocked the garbage can and it rolled away.

Little Kenny put his hands over his head against the slimy smelly garbage can so it wouldn't touch his head as it rolled like a terrible ride at the fair. Kenny never liked those rides. When it was done rolling he couldn't see Aunt Fran in the swarm of monsters.

Now the Zombies seemed aimless and wandered about. Kenny smelled the worst rotten eggs. Up the street someone was shooting. Some of the monsters headed toward the sound. Streetlights went out on the block one after another. The zombies were wandering in and out of the darkness up and down the street.

As quietly as he could, Kenny crawled to the back of the garbage can. Shaking, he listened to them shuffling about. Every now and then he would peek and see then going into the apartment buildings. The sight sent shivering goose bumps up his back. Tears streamed down his face. He put the nebulizer to his mouth and gave a little squeeze. It was empty.

"Mommy," he breathed. "Where are you? Mommy, help me. Mooommmmy."

*****

Chapter 15 - The Big Apple, Part 1

Miss Susan Goodwin clutched her clipboard tightly. She stood tall and straight in the lobby of the New York City Downtown Holiday Inn. Her short frosted brown hair was sprayed in place with enough shellac to seal a ship. She wore a blue Atlanta Braves windbreaker, over the left breast was a button:

I GAVE MYSELF TO CHRIST.
DID YOU?

"Stay in groups of two," she ordered loudly above the voices of everyone. "If you have a disagreement, stay together 'til you get back here. That is a must. This is New York City, the Big Apple; they eat little munchkins like you for snacks. It is extremely, do you hear me, extremely perilous out there. Everyone understand?"

"Yes, Miss Goodwin," several high school students said and Miss Goodwin touched the small gold cross around her neck.

"Frank and David. You understand?"

"Yes ma'am," both boys said.

"You're all eighteen an' you've been told how to handle yourselves, but New York is a big city that can gobble you up if you're not careful. Everyone back by eleven o'clock. No excuses. No delays. Come to my room and check in. Tomorrow night is the dance; I don't want anyone to miss it. And I don't, you hear me, I don't want to visit anyone in the hospital or God forbid, in the jail. Do ... you ... understand?"

"Yes, Ms. Goodwin."

As the students left, she wrote a number next to their names. 1- Beau Dooley and Sally Bailey. 2- Bonnie Silverman and James Cooney. 3- Tori Hutchinson and Laura Fielder. 4- Rebecca Kelly and Kevin Colvin. 5- David Pidgin and Frank Sullivan. And so on.

She watched them go. Oh, to be so innocent. And so naive. She sighed, to be young again. She walked down the carpeted hall to the restaurant. The sign said: Wait to be seated. But a young woman quickly led her to a small table in the middle of the large dining room.

The responsibility weighed heavily on her shoulders. Mr. Paine was supposed to be here, but he changed his mind when he realized she wasn't a teacher he could put one of his moves on. She sat at a table all alone, gazing around to see if any man, George Clooney perhaps, was looking at her. The crowd was thin and no one showed interest in a forty-six year old spinster.

She took a compact out of her purse and looked at her hair in the mirror. Maybe she should dye it. Men seemed to like blondes. No. Why should she lie, put on airs, this was who she was. Who was she kidding? Who'd want a skinny woman with a pinched face even if she had blonde hair? Look at Mrs. Shea, the librarian, had going blonde her helped her? No, of course it hadn't.

She dropped her large purse on the chair next to her in such a way it would appear she was expecting company. Kicked her shoes off, wiggled her toes. She was startled when a thin tan man appeared at the table. Started to think, Spain I'd love to, then saw the waiter's nametag: Ricardo and her brown eyes frowned. "I'll have a Martini."

"Yes ma'am," Ricardo said.

She glanced around making sure no kids were spying on her and touched the crucifix on the gold chain around her. She looked back at Ricardo and for an instant she saw him with white eyes and a gray face with black holes in it. She blinked and he was back to himself. She hoped that wasn't one of her visions, she didn't need that now along with everything else.

"Make that a double."

He wrote on the order sheet.

"Does a double cost a lot more?"

He smiled sympathetically. "For you, on house."

She felt her spirits lift at the kindness, breathed easier. He handed her the menu and she scanned down the page. Several of the prices were so high she had to look at them twice. No, it was no mistake. She wanted to order the cheapest thing on the menu, but he had been so nice to her. She shouldn't let him down and be a tightwad and only get an appetizer. Something to show she had culture, taste.

"I'll have a small dinner salad and for my main course Welsh rabbit." *Was it very expensive to import rabbits all the way from Wales?*

"Senora means Welsh Rarebit?"

"Of course," she said, not sure what that meant.

"Very good choice." He wrote on his order pad. "Blue cheese dressing? Or ranch, thousand island, raspberry vinaigrette, or red wine vinaigrette?" He talked with a slight accent, she thought, to make it adorable.

"What country do you come from? Or aren't you supposed to say?"

He smiled sympathetically at her. "Brooklyn."

She nodded as if she was not surprised.

"What do you recommend?" She looked into his eyes.

"Italian."

She paused. "I'll have the house dressing."

She handed him the menu.

"Something to drink with your meal?"

"Water." She saw him frown. "Maybe some wine."

"Would you like to see a wine list?"

She guessed what the prices on that would be.

"The house red wine will be fine," she said and hoped you drank red wine with rabbit, after all it was a meat and you drank red with meat, didn't you?

He smiled kindheartedly as if he understood the choices one must make.

She watched Ricardo walk away. Watched the way he moved in his tight black pants and wondered if that was affected. Did that mean he didn't like women? She was unsure; the big city was so different from where she grew up in Ohio, from where she taught in Fayetteville.

She took the compact from her purse and looked at her face. Maybe she should have put on a little makeup. Some eye shadow would help. No, he probably wasn't interested. And he's not from Spain. Brooklyn by way of Puerto Rico if that. And he's not rich and if he's single he's a ... no, she didn't know what he was and what difference did it make if she did.

She looked at the other diners. They seemed to know what they were doing. Why was she always so unsure, and felt like she'd been left in the dark about things?

Ricardo put a glass of red wine on the table. She picked it up and smelled the wine. Smelled okay, but she hadn't smelled much wine in her life. You didn't smell wine in Blakeslee; you put 7-up in it. Maybe it smelled cheap and she didn't know she'd been gypped. How much does it cost? Too late now. She supposed they wouldn't put it back in the bottle. She took a sip. It was sort of familiar like that stuff she bought in Publix.

"Is okay?" Ricardo said.

"Fine." She smiled. "Just fine."

He smiled and walked away She took a bigger drink. The wine was room temperature, smooth down her throat, fire in her belly. She coughed and fanned herself. She felt her face turning red and looked about to see if anyone noticed. Then she remembered she had ordered a Martini and he hadn't brought it. She wanted to say something, but didn't want to seem like one of those people who always complain about something. She hoped it wasn't on her bill as she sipped the red wine.

She was halfway through the glass when Ricardo brought her salad. She smiled at him. God that wine went right to her head. Maybe he put something in it, the little devil. She laughed.

"Madam likes the wine?"

"Oh yes."

"Would madam like another glass?"

She grinned, but the first thing that came to mind was the price. How much did the stuff cost?

As if reading her thoughts, Ricardo said, "On house, since I forgot Martini."

"Oh, I forgot too." She smiled like they shared a secret. Her face lit up, glowing with blushing highlights. On the house she could afford.

He went to a nearby station and returned with a carafe of red wine. He started to lift the bottle to refill her glass.

"Oh! The children. I can't."

He raised an eyebrow like Mr. Spock. He must think she was talking about her own kids.

"You see, I'm a teacher. I have to be awake until all the kids come back from their night on the town. I'm chaperoning them."

He bowed as if she was doing the right thing and walked to one of his other tables. He must think she was trying to ... pick him up. How foolish. She giggled, touched the cross. Her voice sounded very loud in the quiet restaurant and she put the linen napkin over her mouth.

When she finished the salad he brought the Welsh rabbit. At first she was confused and it must have shone on her face for he said, "Welsh rabbit, like you ordered."

She stared at the melted Cheddar cheese on toasted wheat bread with fried tomatoes on that and a Branston pickle. She'd forgotten. Welsh rarebit had no rabbit.

"Would madam like something else?" Ricardo asked.

"No, this is fine," she said. She was a firm believer in you ask for what you get and you get what you pay for. "Thank you."

Ricardo nodded and walked to one of his other tables.

She tasted the Welsh rabbit. It was okay. The dark wheat bread gave it a very nice flavor. The hot cheese made her thirsty and there wasn't enough water. She had another glass of wine, drank it slowly, rolling it around in her mouth.

She asked Ricardo if they had a little sampler bottle. "Just for you," he handed her a small complimentary bottle, which she took to her room. Sitting in a hot bath she drank most of it. Just a glassful left.

A long towel wrapped around her and feet on another chair, she stared out the dark window, the lights of the city in front of her. Oh George, oh Brad, oh Mel where are you when I need you? If only I'd known life would be like this. Sitting alone in a fancy hotel in New York City, no one back home to call, no one to be with. With tears running down her face she gazed at the lights and hoped the kids were alright.

She'd voted against their coming and still was picked to chaperone. The big mouthed proponents should have come so they could worry. But they'd said she was the lead teacher, it was up to her, but if anything happened she'll get blamed. Be a terrible shame if any of them got hurt.

Her purse was on the table with the plastic bottle of Valium. If things get too bad she could take them. She could always do that. God would understand. That's why he's God. He always understands. She was going to take them before they left, but she could wait. Maybe tomorrow. Wouldn't that be something? Everyone would be wondering about it. "Why did Ms. Goodwin take those pills in New York?" "The least she could have done is see the kids home." "Not leave them stranded in New York." What a bunch of fool kids, but the Bahamas were out since that girl died. So was Mexico with all the drug violence. So New York it was. Hurrah for parents who are idiots.

She looked at her reflection in the window. The tired face. The thin lips. Who'd want to make love to that? She'd had a chance to do something with her life. She was at the top of her class at St. Thomas. If only things hadn't turned out the way they did. Never would have expected to wind up like this. Not her, of all people. With a little luck she could've been someone important.

Men, where are you? A forty-six year old virgin is waiting for you. Hell, she'd take Ralph Kramden all three hundred pounds of him.

She had a few hours before the kids started straggling

in. She sipped her drink. The TV was on -- background noise. She saw gray-green fog rolling across the city. Is that what fog was like in the city. The drink was getting to her. Her eyes were so heavy. She lowered her head and started snoring. The TV switched to a printed message:

SPECIAL NEWS BULLETIN

A pretty woman came on the screen. "This is Diane Sawyer with a special news bulletin. The President has ordered all branches of the service, the Army, Navy, Air Force and Marines to active duty. He has called out the National--"

The TV blipped and the screen went blank.

***

Hand in hand Beau Dooley and Sally Bailey walked past Macy's window. Some people stood looking at the display; most people glanced at it as they strolled by.

"Sure is nice." Sally was so excited being here in New York chills kept crawling up her back.

"I'm hungry," Beau said.

She smiled at him; how nice his short brown hair looked. "You're always hungry."

"For more'n just food." He leaned toward her.

She pushed him away. "Not until we're married."

He patted her rear and she pushed his hand away. "Guess we'd better feed you."

They walked up the streets. Past the stone lions in front of the Library. Beau sat on one and she took his picture. She sat next to it and he took her picture. They talked a black guy walking by into taking a picture of them sitting on each side of the stone head. They walked from the Empire State Building to Penn Station. Then they headed north. They found a Tad's Steak House and stood outside looking at the menu taped to the door of the restaurant.

"We can go someplace else."

She shook her head. "We're saving for the wedding. This is fine."

They went inside, grabbed trays, ordered medium and well-done. Carried the trays to the back. When they finished, they walked up Fifth Avenue.

"What's that?" Sally pointed to the west.

"A storm cloud."

"Let's get inside before the rain hits."

"There." They ran for a subway kiosk. As they were going down the steps they glanced back at the sky.

"That's not rain," Beau said.

"Wh--what is it?"

"It's fog."

They exchanged looks and watched fingers of fog reach out and envelope people. From out of the fog came horribly disfigured people who lunged at other people, grabbed them and tried to ... eat them?

Sally and Beau whirled around and raced down the steps as things stumbled down the tunnel steps after them.

***

The street was dark and quiet. The doors opened and people filed out into the night. The night filled with the sounds of people talking and walking, cars driving away. Taxis stopped and passengers climbed in. Most people strolled down the street enjoying the night.

Blonde Bonnie Silverman and redheaded Jim Cooney walked east. Bonnie and Jimmy wore Wrangler jeans. He wore an Atlanta Falcons windbreaker, she an Atlanta Braves windbreaker.

"Let's get something to eat." Jimmy was small, pear shaped with blue eyes.

"Wasn't David Letterman funny?" Long blonde haired Bonnie had brown eyes and a plump figure.

"Paul Schaefer has a great band."

"Never seen a TV show before. It was something."

"Wonder how much of it was rehearsed?"

"You don't realize there are so many people that you don't see."

"Bet you they all went to school to learn their jobs."

"He seemed pretty nice," Bonnie said.

"Wonder how much he makes," Jimmy said.

"Wasn't that top ten list great? But I thought number one was wrong. The monster I'd least like to have a date with is Dracula."

"No, it was least likely. Not who you'd want to have a date with. Besides if Dracula looked like Tom Cruise the women would be lining up to let him suck their blood."

"I guess. I'm hungry. Watching him sampling that food made me hungry."

"Where do you want to eat?"

"There's a cafeteria by Times Square."

"Can we can walk there?"

"You bet," Jimmy said. "You see that suit Letterman was wearing? Must have cost a thousand bucks. I had a suit like that, I'd look good too."

They stopped at the traffic light on the corner and she faced him. "You look good to me."

He took her in his arms and they kissed. People walked past. The kiss was wet and noisy. They started really getting into it when someone shouted. They barely heard it. Other voices rose in shouts as he grabbed her butt and squeezed. He thought they were talking about them and smiled. She smiled too. Then people ran past them and someone bumped into them.

"Hey!" Jimmy shouted.

Everyone was running away. A woman who ran past pointed behind them. They looked back behind them.

At the end of the street was a gray-green fog; at the front edge of the fog were people? Strange looking people. Ugly injured people? They walked weirdly like they had problems moving. They saw these monsters attacking people, grabbing them and biting them first, for almost a second, they thought it might be a joke, one of those TV shows that try to scare you, and then a monster tore off chunks of flesh with his teeth. Another monster started eating the arm of someone who tried to push him away. Other monsters ate people's faces. Most of the people fought back. Some of them, after being bitten, changed into ... monsters. The monsters chased after the people running away from them.

Bonnie and Jimmy started running, not knowing where they were or where they were going. They smelled ammonia and rotten eggs behind them. Heard people shouting and crying out. A police car with its lights flashing raced toward the monsters. The car screeched to a stop and the cops got out of the car and started shooting. Then the fog rolled over them and the shooting stopped.

Bonnie and Jimmy ran for their lives. In the next block she tripped and fell down hard. He ran back to her.

"Leave me."

"Get up."

"Can't, I broke my ankle."

"Try."

"It hurts."

"Try, dammit."

A woman ran past, her red hair messy, her eye makeup smudged, and her face a mask of terror. "They're coming. The zombies are coming. The zombies are coming."

He pulled her to her feet and had her hold onto a streetlight pole for a moment. He turned to face the attack and flexed his shoulders and squeezed his fists. The fog and monsters came forward. Jimmy hit and kicked and knocked a few down.

"Bonnie, you okay?"

When she didn't answer he turned. She was just standing there with her head lowered.

"Bonnie?"

Her head came up and it was Bonnie, but she had changed. Her brown eyes bulged, her skin was gray-green, and her black lips pulled back from her teeth.

"Bonnie?" he said and her bulging eyes looked at him and her hands reached to him. Her fingernails were black now. She grabbed him and tried to bite his face. He shoved her away and the other zombies swarmed over him, pulling him down to the ground.

*****

Chapter 16 - Big Apple Part 2

They carefully emerged from the subway kiosk and surveyed the neighborhood, two meerkats looking for predators. The streets were dark and empty. In the distance they saw lights and heard music.

"So this is Greenwich Village." Tori Hutchinson had awe in her voice.

"Want to be a writer?" Laura Fielder pushed the glasses up on her ebony nose. "This is where you start."

They were dressed in loose-fitting jeans and grungy army jackets. No makeup. Hair needed brushing. Trying so hard to look like they fit in, they stood out, like strangers in a strange place.

"Ain't anything like I imagined," Tori said, the awe starting to fade.

The buildings were dark and the streets quiet. Streetlights like spotlights shined down the street into the distance. At the corner was a small club. In the window a dim neon sign: NO GIRLS ALLOWED.

"On a nice night like this, why aren't more people outside?" Tori said. "Why ain't there artists walking around. Someone playing music on a stoop or in an apartment. It's always like that in the movies. It's like everyone's inside. Why?"

"Let's take a walk."

They crossed the street and headed for the lights. They had gone only a short distance when two heavily made-up, statuesque ladies, in sequined evening gowns, one red the other blue, and high heels, with red and blonde hair piled high on their heads, sashayed down the sidewalk.

"Will you look at them?" Laura said.

"Holy cow. Must be going to a party."

"Maybe we can go."

126

"Like this?"

"Gawd, those heels must be five inches high."

"I'd get a nose bleed from the altitude."

They giggled. Then stifled the laughter as the tall ladies came near them.

They walked down one street after another. Soon they were lost. They found a little park and sat on a bench. There were other people in the park. A homeless guy was playing a guitar. People paused to listen. A few people dropped money in a nearby coffee cup. They thought he played good, but were nervous about taking out money.

A scruffy looking guy wandered over and stood at the end of the bench they were sitting on. He smiled at them. Tori looked at his straggly beard and his torn clothes and nudged Laura. Laura shrugged as if to say leave me alone.

"Nice," the guy said when the guitar player took a break.

Tori furtively glanced at him and felt he had moved closer. Again she nudged Laura. Again Laura shrugged her off, leave me alone, I'm enjoying this.

Tori started to shiver, afraid what would happen next.

"Hey," the guy said like they were friends, "you got some money for coffee?"

Now Tori looked at him and the guy smiled. It wasn't an unfriendly smile, but there was something not right about it, goose bumps raced up her back. She shook her head and nudged Laura real hard.

"What?" Laura turned to Tori, angry that she was being poked.

"Money for coffee?" the guy said.

Laura's mouth opened and she froze like a rabbit in a spotlight.

"No," Tori said and grabbed Laura's arm and stood up, forcing Laura to stand up with her. Laura looked at her and Tori's eyes told her to shut up and come along. Tori pulled her along the walk and out of the park. When they were out of the park, Laura shook her arm off.

"What's the matter?"

"There was something about that guy."

"He just wanted coffee money."

"God, you're sooo naïve."

"And you imagine things," Laura protested.

"At least we're safe."

"Stop it, will you?" Laura was tired of her friend's over protectiveness. She looked behind them.

"Don't look," Tori said.

"Oh my God."

Tori didn't have to look, she felt it up her spine, like in that horror movie.

"He's coming."

They turned at the first corner they came to. They street was dark. They went a ways up the dark street, before they realized how alone they were.

"We should have gone back to the park," Laura said.

"Can we go back?" Tori rushed ahead not wanting to look back.

"I—I don't know."

Tori glanced behind them. The stranger was walking fast trying to catch up to them. He seemed bigger now that they were away from the park. He took long aggressive strides.

"Hurry," Tori said.

They rushed up the dark empty street. At the first corner, Tori made a left turn. Laura turned with her. Now that they were off the dark street, they started to run. They'd taken a few steps when they realized they were in an alley. A dark alley filled with garbage cars and locked back doors.

They stopped dead and looked about. There was no way out, except the way they had come. They spun around toward the entrance. He wasn't in the entrance. No one was.

"Can we get out?" Laura said, shivering like she was naked in a snowstorm.

Tori was too scared to answer. She pulled Laura behind boxes filled with garbage. They squatted on the ground next to something that smelled so bad Tori had to put her hand over her mouth to stop gagging.

Laura had to peek to see if he was there. She saw a tall shadowy figure at the end of the alley; he had something that gleamed in the night like a knife in his right hand. She ducked back behind the carton bumping Tori. Tori almost fell over and put out her hand to stop herself. She put her hand in the gooey stuff and almost cried out. She shivered as tears ran down her face.

The stranger threw a bottle into the alley. It shattered against the wall opposite them.

"Come out, come out, wherever you are," he called in a gruff voice.

Laura turned to Tori, not knowing what to do, afraid of what was going to happen to her.

"We don't have any money," Laura called out and was poked so hard by Tori she almost cried out.

"I don't want money," the stranger said as he stepped into the alley.

"Come on," Tori growled and yanked Tori further back into the alley.

They ran a few yards and slipped and banged into garbage cans, making enough racket to raise the dead.

The stranger laughed; as if this was great fun being the hunter.

Tori had fallen and picked up a garbage can lid and handed it to Laura.

"What's this for?"

Tori picked up another lid. She showed Laura how to hold it in front of her like they were playing 'World of Warcraft'. She faced the stranger.

The alley was dark as night. The end of the alley was grayer. Some light shined down from a window high above. They could see the stranger at the opening to the alley, but they could barely see each other.

"What's that you got?" he said.

"Swords," Tori said.

"Shields," Laura said.

The stranger stared into the darkness. He didn't believe they had swords, but he couldn't see.

"You ain't got swords," he said.

Tori took a breath and spoke, trying to keep the tremble out of her voice, "Come taste my steel."

Laura looked at her like she was crazy. What the hell was she doing?

The guy backed up a few steps. "Weirdoes." Then he turned and ran.

"Come on," Tori said and ran to the alley entrance with the garbage can lid as a shield in front of her.

"Watch out," Laura said, thinking it was a trap.

As they got close to the alley entrance people were running past. They went into the street and looked around. People, the guy with the guitar from the park, were racing past.

They whirled around. The world seemed to stand still. In one terrible moment all their dreams and plans were lost and insignificant. They backed up. Up the block came swirling dark clouds, a strange storm was heading toward them.

"Fog?" Laura said.

"Ain't like any fog I've ever seen."

The fog swirled and twisted like it was filled with nasty little bugs. At the front emerged terrible looking people savagely attacking other people.

"Zombies!"

"Come on," Tori said.

They ran up the street to the corner.

"Where's the subway entrance?"

"Wrong corner. This way!"

Ran to the next street, their green army jackets flapping and turned down the next and ran till they were out of breath. They stopped and panted. Now they jogged a few steps, walked a few. Jogged and walked.

"I'm sick."

"Shut up and keep going."

"How'd we wind up in a park?" Laura said.

"Where the heck are we?"

"Don't cry now."

"What's that smell?"

"R--r--rotten eggs."

They jogged up a dark street, panting so hard it hurt, heard steps and muttered sounds coming behind them. They turned the next corner and ran until they were in a dead end street. They turned back to the entrance. Too late, the gray-green fog roiled down the alley.

***

Becky Kelly and Kevin Colvin walked out through the double doors with the rest of the patrons. The large marquee over the row of doors shined:

RADIO CITY MUSIC HALL

"I've never seen the Rockettes before," Becky said.

"Me neither." The handsome dark-haired quarterback took the small hand of the blonde Homecoming Queen and they strolled up the street. Kevin swung her hand like they were kids.

Becky looked stylish in an emerald green suit and a green blouse that set off her green eyes and matched her green bag and shoes. He walked with a hand in the pocket of his gray slacks, his blue sport coat open, his white shirt open at his thick neck and black Nikes that looked like shoes.

Kevin ran a hand through his hair. "Want to eat?"

"Not yet. Let's take in the sights."

"Where you want to go?"

"Let's walk to Times Square and then walk to Rockefeller Center. Then let's go to Central Park." She looked up at the tall buildings as they walked.

"Ain't going to walk through Central Park at night."

"Course not, silly." She squeezed his hand. He could be so sweet at times, worrying about her safety. "We'll take a horse and buggy ride."

"They got that?"

"Yes. I checked it out."

"Cost a lot?"

"My treat. We'll be going to college next year and I want us to remember this trip."

"Okay with me, Honeycakes."

"Not in public." She looked around; no one was interested in them or their conversation.

They strolled to Times Square marveling at the millions of lights on the signs above them. She looked at the stores. He gawked at the intersection of the world crowded with people, more people than he could count.

There was a farm boy from Kansas, a married couple from Newark, tourists from Japan, a family from Italy, two sailors from England, an immigrant from Russia, a Marine and his girlfriend from Long Island, teenage girls from Brooklyn and people from everywhere, but mostly he looked at the girls walking around in short skirts, a few smiling at him.

As they waited at a corner for the light to change he noticed someone in a nearby coffee shop.

"Hey." He pointed. "Davy."

"What's he doing there?" Becky said.

"Probably trying to get laid."

"Oh Kevin, not all boys are like that."

He scowled. "Pizza face is."

"Who's that girl?"

"She ain't doing social work." He stared at her legs.

"Maybe I should go in and tell her I'm his girlfriend."

He grabbed her arm. "Let the Pimple King alone. He needs all the help he can get."

They walked up Seventh Avenue, crossed 49th Street and turned east. The streets were crowded and adequately lit but it was thrilling and somehow dangerous to be alone walking in the Big Apple. For awhile they gazed at the water fountain in front of Rockefeller Center. Watched the spotlight lighting up the water and people strolling by. As they were leaving, sirens blared and car horns sounded way off the west.

"What's going on?"

He scanned the street. At first he didn't believe what he

saw, and then he took her hand and started running.

"What's the matter?"

"Just run."

"What?" She looked behind them. "Fog?"

"In the fog."

"Oh my God."

"Run."

"I can't run in these shoes."

He anxiously looked back up the street while she yanked off her shoes. He bounced on his feet, eyes checking left and right at the people shouting, screaming, and running away.

She tore a slit up the side of skirt and they took off. She let go of his hand and raced alongside him.

He thought he'd have to slow down so that she could keep up, and then remembered she was on the girls' track team.

At the next street she tripped and went down. Her emerald green purse skidded across the road. He stopped and looked back at the fog. His nerves on edge, his muscles quivered as his eyes went down to her.

"Help me," she said. "I twisted my ankle."

He started to go to her and stopped. He remembered in practice when the guys filled the football with rocks. He couldn't run fast carrying and they caught him. Can't outrun the monsters carrying her. If she'd trained like he told her she wouldn't keep twisting her ankle.

He rushed back to her, his brown eyes darting up the street. Oh God! It's coming fast.

She reached her hand to him. "Help me." He started to grab her hand, and then paused as his eyes swung to the onrushing storm. He felt himself shivering inside.

"Kevin," she yelled sounding just like his sister.

He reached down and helped her to her feet. She put her arm around his shoulder and he hurried on, her limping, him walking fast and jogging. He glanced over his shoulder. The fog was gaining on them.

"We can't make it like this," she said.

He let go, thinking she was volunteering to take one for the team.

"We need a car," she said.

He was surprised, why hadn't he thought of that. He jogged along looking in car windows for keys. He jogged up a side street looking in windows then went back to running.

Becky was doing the same, but she was taking longer to do it.

"Hurry up," he told her as he waited on the corner to help her to the next street.

"Shut up and give me a hand," she told him.

He didn't like the sound of that at all. Reminded him of his last girlfriend. She reminded him of Mrs. Daye, the assistant principal, who hated jocks. Still, he started up the side street looking for a car he could use, when Becky tripped again.

He ran over to her.

"Now I've injured my other ankle."

He looked at her holding onto the side of a car struggling to get to her feet and remembered how she was always getting injured. Fell out of his car and cut her knee. Tripped walking down the stairs and if he hadn't been there to catch her, she probably would've busted something. She banged her head on a locker at school. His mother said with her it was always something. Everything flashed through his mind as he watched her struggling, holding onto the car, to get to her feet.

The fog was only a block away now.

He turned and was running before he knew it.

"Kevin!" she called. He raced away. Only her scream caught him. Nagged him. Took hold of his heart and started eating. He ran like he was playing against the meanest defense in football. His knees came up and he pumped his legs. He leaped over a car at the corner of 52nd Street, the driver looking up at this blur going over.

At 53rd, a wino walked in his way with his hand out. "Hey buddy. Can you spare. . ."

Kevin stiff armed him so hard the wino fell to the ground and rolled to the curb and was unconscious when the zombies came to him.

Kevin ran through people shrieking on the sidewalk. Ran through people racing every which way, knocking a few of them down. At 55th he was winded and looked back; the fog was still gaining and he got his first good look at the monsters. Before, he wasn't too sure what they looked like. He saw the fog coming steadily and the monsters, now he knew they were zombies, at the front of it, attacking people, eating them. He saw when the fog touched some people they changed into monsters, but not everyone. The monsters ate those who didn't change; they chewed their face off, bit their arms, yanked out their intestines, and ripped off their flesh with their teeth. Once injured the person slowed and the other monsters swarmed all over him.

Up ahead trees were lit were by spotlights, large hot air balloons glowing above the trees. Must be the park was ahead and as he crossed the street more zombies were coming from the west. He was running north. If he had run east he might've out distanced them. But he was too winded now. His heart beat fast and painfully hard. He panted, gulping air.

He raced into Central Park. They were closing fast. Ran down a path. The monsters cut off his route up the trail. He noticed water on the right and sprinted for it. They were almost on him when he dove into the water.

He swam underwater to the bridge, touching bottles and slimy things. He didn't know how long he could hold his breath. He was surprised he made it so far, had stayed under so long.

When his lungs were about to burst he came up slowly, just his head and breathed. He was under the bridge in a few feet of water, slimly muck up to his ankles and the water didn't feel clean.

He was trying to figure what to do when a zombie slid down the bank and sloshed into the water after him. The monster had red hair and wore a green blouse.

"Becky?" he said, his breath like frost.

The zombie looked at him and smiled and it was that smile that sent arctic chills up his spine. Her face was gray-green, her lips were black, and her teeth seemed to have grown longer and looked to be broken with projecting sharp points as if she had chipped them gnawing bones.

He voided himself as he stepped back.

"Becky," he cried.

The zombie groaned something low and guttural, perhaps a moan, but he didn't hear it as he backed up into a swarm of zombies that had lurched down the bank behind him and was torn apart before Becky could get a good bite.

*****

Chapter 17 - The Big Apple, Part 3

David Pidgin and Frank Sullivan meandered across Times Square. The busy intersection glittered with millions of lights on billboards and signs. The streets were filled with cars, horns honking, the sidewalks crowded, people walking, gazing at the sights.

"The neon forest," Frank said and David knew he had read it somewhere. He was always reading stuff and saying things like he'd thought of it and half the time he didn't know what it meant. David shook his head at the five foot six apple shape. Frank should have listened to his advice and lost weight, maybe he wouldn't be as thin as him, but anything was an improvement.

"Can't believe it. One beer and you're zonked." David ran a hand through his blonde hair

"Hey, I didn't have anything to eat."

"Look at the lights." "Look at the pussy." Frank waved his fingers at some black girls in short tight skirts talking to the cars going by.

David frowned. "They're whores." He believed that any girl in a tight skirt or wearing a lot of makeup was a prostitute.

"Since when were you so finicky?"

"Thought we were going to score."

"That's scoring." Frank smiled at a thin white girl who swaggered past with her nose in the air. "My brother was in some Mexican border towns. He said the whores were just like this before they cleaned them up."

"Paying for it? Ain't never paid for it."

"And you ain't ever had any, zit man."

"Ha, fart mouth," David snorted. "Lot you know."

A tall black girl in a silver wig strutted by with a short Puerto Rican girl wearing a curly red wig. Both wore bright halter tops and miniskirts. Frank turned around staring at them with his mouth hanging open.

"Look at the ass on that one."

"This is going out on the town? Thought we were going to a ball game or a movie."

"We're in the Big Apple and you want to see a movie? Get a life."

A guy was standing in a doorway barking for customers, "Hey, youse, come dance with pretty girls."

"You said we'd see a skin flick. We can look at whores back home any time."

"But these are New York whores."

"What does that mean? Does being laid a million times make them better?"

"We came here to get fucked."

"There's getting fucked and gittin' fucked."

"What do you think; we were going to meet nice girls on our first night in New York? God, you're so immature."

"And paying a slut that's been laid at least a hundred times today is mature?"

"You're a douche bag. A terminal case of zits."

"Takes one to know one, fart mouth," David replied,

wishing he had a better retort.

They stopped on the corner of Broadway and 43rd Street. Traffic raced past. People were six deep on the corners waiting to cross the street. A small black girl stepped back from the curb and looked at the two youths. Frank smiled and she smiled back. He winked and she motioned him over with her long red fingernail.

"A sperm box waits." Frank walked over to her.

David shook his head. I mowed lawns and was a bag boy to save for this?

Frank grinned over his shoulder at him as he strolled over to the girl.

Big man. David sighed. Mean-looking black dudes lounged nearby. Girls sashayed over to cars and bent over to the window and talked.

Frank hurried back. "Need ten more bucks."

"Where's your money?"

"In the hotel room. Come on. She won't wait long."

"As long as you got money, she'll wait."

"Davie old boy."

He held his wallet close to his chest, opened it and took out a twenty.

Frank grabbed it quickly.

"That's a twenty."

"Owe you twenty."

"I'll never see you again. They'll find your body in an alley somewhere and Ms. Goodwin will blame me."

Frank walked away next to the short girl with the balloon butt. He waved. "Ta. Ta."

"Asshole."

Frank tried to put his arm around her, but she shook it off.

"I'll wait for you here," he said.

Frank waved as if he didn't hear him.

David looked around. Now that he was alone everyone seemed to be looking at him, sizing him up, especially those big mean black guys by the white caddie. The lights of a small coffee shop beckoned.

He was walking toward it when a tall black girl with yellow blonde hair, asked, "You want to have some fun?" He wanted to say yes, but knew he should say no.

"Just down here," she said. "Let me show you."

He walked behind her. After a few steps he was going to say no, but she was too far ahead.

"Hey," he called. "Hey you. I changed my mind."

She walked faster and he kept following.

"Hey you," he called louder. "I changed my mind."

She hurried ahead.

He had to run to catch her.

"Hey you," he said and she turned about to face him.

"Who you calling hey you?" she demanded.

"I just wanted you to know I can't. I gotta get back."

"What you talkin' about?"

"Y'know, back there, you said if I wanted to have fun." He used his thumb to motion to the back.

"I never said no such thing, what type of girl you take me for?"

Before he could answer, appologize, something hit him on the back of the head and he went down.

***

He woke up in a dark alley, naked except for his white socks and underpants and black t-shirt. His head hurt like that time he fell out of the tree. They stole his pants, but left his Wal-Mart sneakers. He staggered to his feet and slipped the black sneakers on his feet. He stumbled to the sidewalk. The street was quiet. He looked toward Times Square. Can't go back there.

At the entrance to the alley a wino was lying on the sidewalk. The wino looked at him.

"Do you remember who did this to me?" David said.

"Life," the wino said and laughed. He laughed so hard he started coughing.

David hoped the guy coughed himself to death.

Suddenly the wino looked like he was going to die, and David feared he was going to be blamed. Then the guy puked. Brown chunky vomit hurled across the alley and on David's socks. David jumped back. He carefully reached down and took off his socks.

When he looked up the guy had passed out. He was lying on his back, his open mouth filled with puke.

He's going to die. And they're going to blame me.

David realized he had to roll the guy on his back. He went to grab the wino, but didn't want to touch him, so he yanked the ratty tan raincoat and turned him over. As he pulled the dirty raincoat came off. He stumbled back, the smelly raincoat in his hands. He looked at the wino. The guy was now snoring.

He held his nose with one hand as he put on the dirty raincoat. Then he headed to the corner, once he knew the street number he'd be able to figure out how to get back to the hotel. I'll tell them I was mugged. No one will laugh at that. Won't mention the girl. Especially not to Frank. Can't tell the Mouth anything. He'll tell everyone.

He was partway up the street when he heard police sirens. His heart jumped. He knew the police were after him for stealing the raincoat. He spun toward Times Square. Beyond it, in the distance, was the fog.

He'd seen enough movies to know something was very wrong. It didn't look like regular fog. Cars drove into it and crashed. Behind it was screams. Gunshots briefly lit up the dark fog like flashes of lightning. He could see things in the fog, but could not make out what they were. Then people were running toward him.

Hundreds of people running and strange looking people, injured people, coming out of the fog, shuffling, chasing them. The people chasing attacked the people standing around looking at the fog like they were wild animals. More people were running and screaming. Cars raced up the street, one a big white caddie convertible packed with guys and girls, so many they were lying across the trunk holding on.

He spotted the girl on the trunk.

"Hey you!" he shouted.

She didn't hear him. They were yelling and screaming.

There was a grayish person in the car trying to bite them. The caddie swung a wild turn at the corner and Lois fell off the trunk. There was a loud crack when her head hit the road. Then she rolled into the curb and lay still.

More cars raced by. The fog was coming closer. He started running. Momentarily he stopped by the girl lying in the gutter the blonde wig partially off her head almost covering her face. He pulled it back, looked at her face. She looked dead, her face gray, her lips black. He heard screams and looked back up the street. The monsters, the zombies, were coming.

He turned to run and felt cold slimy fingers on his left leg. He tried to jerk his leg away. She had hold of his leg and she was trying to bite him. He yanked his leg away and his left sneaker came off.

She reached for him and he turned and ran. It was hard running with only one sneaker on. It wasn't like running in the country. Bits of glass cut his left foot; pieces of broken cement gashed him. His sock was soon shredded.

He looked back over his shoulder. The monster fog was coming closer. He ran, his heart pounding in his chest. He jogged one block over and saw the white caddie had crashed into another car. Several people were lying in the road, others were limping away. Jane was lying on the ground reaching up to him. "My leg's broke." He shook his head and backed away.

"Please," she begged. "They made me do it."

He stepped up to her and helped her onto his back and jogged. She was too heavy to run with. He was barely able to stay on his feet. He smelled rotten eggs and when he glanced back the fog was almost up to him. He tried to go faster. Sweat poured down his face. He turned down a side street and tripped and fell down. He smacked his head trying to clear out the cobwebs.

Jane limped behind a car. Limped like her leg wasn't broke. He staggered to his feet.

"Help me," she mumbled and reached out to him.

He started to go to her to help when he stopped. Her

face was now gray; black lips pulled back from her long teeth. Her fingernails were like black claws. She went to speak and snarled at him. He backed up. She lunged for him. He dodged from her, turned and ran away. He turned and looked back over his shoulder and saw the fog was thinning out. Maybe he could out run it?

***

Miss Goodwin woke suddenly. She was ice cold. Had a strange dream. Something about fog and monsters. God, how she hated those horror movies the kids watched. Wasn't fond of science fiction either.

She rubbed her eyes and looked out of the window. The glass was dark. She squinted. Strange, the whole city was dark. Here and there were rapid flashes of bluish light. It wasn't lightning. Could it be gunshots? She stepped back knocking over the chair. That's when she noticed the TV was off. Then the room lights flickered and went off.

"My God." A shiver rippled through her and she grabbed the small crucifix around her neck.

She backed into the bed. She remembered the room had one of those card keys with the electronic lock and trembled with fear at the thought of being locked in. She ran to the door, bumped into her bed, and yanked on the doorknob and was surprised when the door opened.

The hall was lit by yellow emergency lights. One at each end and one by the elevator. She started to step out of her room and stopped. There were strange sounds coming from the elevator like there was a wild animal trapped inside. And there were sounds of struggles coming from some of the rooms. And the smell of rotten eggs in the hall, was there a gas leak?

Then the stairwell door next to the elevator opened and someone stepped into the hall.

"Hello," she called and he turned toward her.

She could barely see him, the lighting was so bad. She made a mental note to complain to the management. He started coming to her and she saw the white jacket and the tight black pants. A waiter? She couldn't see his face, but he seemed about the right size.

"Ricardo, is that you?"

A strange gurgled reply like he couldn't speak.

"Do you know what hap ....?"

His white shirt was torn. Now she saw his face in the dim lighting. His face was gray, his flesh hung out of open wounds, his eyes bulged, and his black lips were pulled back from his snarling mouth. He moved stiffly, but came at her with outstretched arms.

"HELP!" she cried and some of the doors along the hall opened and she saw that it was other people horribly transformed like the waiter. They too were all coming for her. A door up the hall opened and nosy Leslie Dubois stepped into the hall.

"Go back into your room," she shouted and Leslie stared at her as if to say who are you to shout at me?

Then the monsters had Leslie and starting biting her and ripping at her. Ms. Goodwin took a step to help Leslie, but the monsters had her down and now others were turning to her. She jumped back into her room and closed the door. She remembered the card didn't work and threw the deadbolt just as the monsters slammed into the door. The monsters started beating on the door and she backed up. She was shaking her head no and backing up.

"Go away," she cried, and they beat harder. The sound was deafening like she was inside a drum and she put her hands over her ears and backed up until the window stopped her. The door was starting to give way. She could see more light around the top and knew they would break in and come to get her.

She stood with her back against the window and sobbed. She knew she was doomed. Then she saw something hanging out of her purse. She grabbed her wooden rosary beads and kneeled on the carpeted floor and prayed. The sound seemed to lessen. Perhaps they were going away, but she didn't stop praying.

*****

Chapter 18 - One, Two, Three - You're Out

Mike and Cathy sat in the bleachers behind first base. Yankee Stadium was crowded on this warm night. From the second level they could see they whole field; it was like they were sitting right over the field. Up and down the aisles vendors called: "Get your cold beer. Ice cold beer. Ice cold beers here." "Hot dogs! Corn dogs! Polish sausage!" "Coke! Seven-up!" "Popcorn! Peanuts! Cotton Candy!" The smells of hot dogs and mustard and beer and popcorn drifted over Cathy but she fought the urge to ask for something. She wasn't about to give him the satisfaction.

She had told him she would go out with him, but she meant a dinner at a nice restaurant or a movie or a show. God, there were so many shows in New York you could just about get in for free, but she never gave any indication she wanted to go to a sporting event. A baseball game? They could've brought Kenny along; she could've saved herself paying the babysitter. This was about as romantic as fishing on the docks. And that fool behind her had a mouth like a foghorn.

"Another beer?" Mike raised his hand.

She shook her head, she was wearing part of her last beer. When Jeter got a hit, she was bumped and the beer spilled.

The Yankees were trailing the Red Socks 7 to 6 in the top of the eighth. The Yanks were up. Pedroia was on first and Ellsbury was on second. David Ortiz came up. People in the stands were shouting, "Get a hit." "Get a hit." "Throw the bum out." "Hey batter, don't just stand there." "Easy out. Easy out."

Cathy sat arms folded, legs crossed, mouth bent into a tight scowl. If this was what he thought was showing her a good time, he had a lot to learn and in about five minutes she was going to tell him a thing or two.

"Come on, Ortiz," Mike shouted. "One hit, you tie the game."

"I thought we were going out to eat." She was barely hiding the anger.

Mike held up his fourth hot dog and grinned, mustard dripping down the side of his chin. "We are."

She pouted. His laughing was not making it any better. She sat back and refolded her arms. If only she'd remembered to take some money with her. But he'd seemed like a nice guy, someone easy to handle.

"When this is over we'll go someplace nice."

"You're just saying that."

"I promise. Cross my heart." He crossed his heart on his shirt, making a yellow mustard mark, and grinned at her, bits of hot dog on his teeth.

"Where?"

"You pick."

"Really?"

"Hey, if that's what it takes to make you happy." He took a bite out of his frank. Yellow mustard dripped down his chin.

She smiled, thinking of the clubs they would go to. The places she would put in an appearance. Oh yes, we just came from the ball game, box seats. Thought we'd stop by and say hi. Got a party we have to go to.

Mike gazed at her. "I thought you liked baseball."

"I do." She liked Nintendo baseball or baseball on TV; she really didn't understand being at a game.

"Swing!" he yelled at the batter. "It was a strike, you jerk. Give the bat to your seeing eye dog."

Cathy shrunk in her seat. He was yelling so loud she expected the people in front of them to turn around and make an ugly scene. But no one did, though occasionally someone gave her looks.

He nudged her. "You see that? My kid sister can play baseball better'n that bum."

"When are they going to kick a field goal?"

Mike choked on his hot dog. "You're kidding, right?"

She blushed slightly. "Of course."

C.C. Sabathia, the pitcher wound up and the stands became quiet as the white ball streaked toward home plate. The batter swung and hit the ball, the sound echoing across the stadium. The ball flew down the first base line; a foul.

"Straighten it out," Mike yelled.

"Who's the center?"

He paused with the hot dog halfway to his mouth. "The guy on the pitcher's mound." He pointed.

"A LAY UP!" she yelled.

People in nearby seats looked at her.

She felt her cheeks redden and glanced at him. "Wrong sport?"

"You were close."

The batter hit a ground ball down past first base. The ball bounced into the outfield. The right fielder picked it up and threw it to home plate as Ortiz rounded first. Ellsbury stopped halfway down the third base line and dashed back to third. Pedroia went back to second.

The fans were cheering and shouting. The screen on the scoreboard lit up: A HIT.

"Bases loaded."

"Is that good?"

"Could be. If Youkilis gets a hit."

Kevin Youkilis approached the batter's box. The Red Sox manager walked out to the pitcher's mound. The stadium of Yankee fans jeered.

"Talk to him all you want," Mike said, "it's too late."

Suddenly, someone in the upper outfield bleachers stood up and shouted and pointed outside the stadium. One by one other people stood up to look and they too started shouting. People on the upper decks stood up, but no one on the lower stands could see what they were excited about. A few people in the upper decks raced up the stairs and down the concourse behind the seats.

From where they sat Cathy and Mike could see the

outfield wall and the outfield stands and something grayish beyond that.

"What's going on?" Cathy said.

"Maybe a fight on the street."

More people started shouting and pointing. Then they saw it coming over the outfield wall, a strange gray-green fog, moving slowly. It seemed thicker than a normal fog and smelled terrible, like rotten eggs. And it didn't exactly move like a wall, tendrils of fog moved toward people in the stands. Some fans in the outfield stands turned and looked at it. The fog seemed to be alive with something, and then tubes of fog came forward and covered people in the stands.

"It's so thick they should call the game," the guy with the foghorn voice behind Cathy said.

The fans quieted as the fog descended into the stadium. Then things started happening. People inside the fog started shouting and screaming. They could barely make out things happening right behind the fog wall. They saw some people freeze, become motionless; other people fell down, but not much else. The stadium, the inside of Yankee stadium became very quiet.

Then as the gray-green fog rolled down toward the field a woman ran down an aisle in the right field stands and jumped onto the field. Security raced out across the outfield to her. As they came close to her she pointed behind her, she was easy to see outlined as she was in the spotlights on the green grass. Yankee stadium was so still -- as if holding its collective breath -- so lit up, everyone could see her point.

Out of the fog they came; dressed like people, but they looked like monsters. They walked oddly and their clothes were ripped and their skin was gray, their eyes bulged, and they attacked everyone.

"They looked like they're dead," foghorn said.

A male security guard ran to them and tried to get them off the outfield and they attacked him. While one grabbed his head and tried to eat it, another ripped an arm off and started eating his other arm. A woman in the upper decks screamed and that scream was echoed by a thousand others and now more of these monsters were in the stands attacking people. The security guards let go of the woman who had run onto the field and ran to help the guard who was being ripped apart. The first few security guards on the field were attacked. They held their own, beating the monsters back. More and more zombies came at them until they were overwhelmed and went down under the tidal wave. Other security guards turned and ran.

The people in the stadium who had been watching the game starting running away. The fans in the upper bleachers raced down the stairs for the exit. Pedroia on second base ran for the dugout. Ellsbury sprinted away from third base. Ortiz raced for the tunnel. More and more fans raced for the exits. It became a stampede and that turned into a wild mob. People were pushed down, shoved aside as the mob raced for the exits.

Cathy and Mike stood together in a little knot of people that were hemmed in and couldn't move.

"What's that?" She gestured at the fog.

"I don't know."

The fog moved slowly across the stadium. Coming closer and closer. Just behind the thinning wall of fog came the monsters, the zombies.

People were screaming. One woman a row over fainted. The stadium vibrated with the thunder of thousands of people panicking, stampeding for the exit. Someone fell off the upper deck, turning over and over, crashing to the hard seats below.

Some zombies lunged ahead of the wall of the fog and the people fought them. Many people stopped the zombies, and threw them out of the stands, bashed their heads in, guns fired here and there. Even though many people stood up to the zombies, there were many more zombies, and wherever the fog rolled more people became zombies and the people were swarmed over or changed into zombies or were beaten back.

The scoreboard lights and spotlights exploded and the field was in darkness as the zombies fought and the people ran. The stands vibrated as if they would shake apart from people running, jumping, jostling for the exits, but all the exits were jammed. The aisles were jammed. People were screaming. Children were crying.

Cathy felt faint. Her stomach clenched in a tight knot. Her jaw hung open. Her heart pounded and she couldn't catch her breath. She plopped onto the seat, and then slipped to the sticky floor.

Mike picked Cathy up and hurried over the seats. He was almost to the exit when he tripped and went down. She crashed into a seat and crawled back to him. He was unconscious. They were between rows. She huddled against him, looking left and right and listening to the people around them screaming, and feeling the stadium shaking. Heard someone crying -- strangely familiar -- and realized it was her.

*****

Chapter 19 - Monster Fog

Alexei put the sniper rifle down and waved with his hand like Star Trek's Captain Jean-Luc Picard. "Go."

Luka didn't move. "What they do to Mika?" It was so quiet in the car it was like they were watching a movie.

"Eat him. What you think they do?"

"What is happening?" Luka asked.

"I look like rocket scientist?"

"Are we at war?" Luka said.

"Who hell knows? Just drive car, go. The fog is coming we got to stay out of fog." Alexei's accent became worse as he became scared.

Luka turned the key and kept it turned, the starter made a sickening noise. Alexei shouted, "LUKA!" Luka released the key and the engine roared to life.

"Drive slow. Keep lights off, no use horn and keep off brake."

"How I stop?"

"Use emergency brake." Alexei pressed the button to raise the window.

Luka spoke, his voice a scared whisper, "Okay."

The black limo edged away from the curb.

"Wh--where we go?" Frankie was shivering so bad, his foot was bouncing on the floor.

"Shad-up." Alexei pointed to the corner. "Turn left."

Luka turned the steering wheel, his big hands suddenly so wet he had trouble gripping it, and the car eased slowly ahead.

"Drive little faster; we got stay ahead of fog. Stay ahead of it."

"We need find place to hide," Frankie said.

"I got place," Alexei said.

"Where?"

"Stop with questions. Need time to think."

They went a few blocks. The fog rolling down the side street next to them. Most of the people coming out of the fog were zombies. Not everyone turned into a monster, the monsters ate the people who were not monsters. People were fighting the zombies and holding their own, but there were too many monsters.

"Fog touch people and people change into monsters and eat other people," Alexei said as he watched. "Some people that fog touch not change, but if get bitten they turn into monsters."

"Zombies." Frankie shivered. "They call them ... zombies." Sweat crawled down Frankie's face. He looked at Luka in the rear view mirror, the big man's eyes were as big as headlights and nothing ever scared him. Frankie's stomach roiled into the back of his throat.

"What are they doing?" Frankie pointed to some monsters wandering around as if confused.

"Not know. You want find out?"

"Nyet. Nyet. Nyet." Frankie's head shook like his neck was a spring.

Then they turned a corner and the fog was in front of them. Luka stopped and looked over the front seat at the rear window as he prepared to backup, but the fog was coming from behind also.

"What we do?" Luka said his voice almost showing panic. ""Fog in front and behind."

Frankie saw the fog coming from in front and turned around on the seat and saw it coming from behind. Looked to the front. Looked to the rear. "Are we gonna turn into zombies?"

"You not remember?" Alexei spoke in a hoarse whisper. "Put on air filtration system."

"Oh, right." Luka turned to the dashboard and stared at the rows of toggle switches. He flipped up a half dozen.

"What system?" Frankie asked his voice getting higher and higher.

"Got car from ex-Senator who take it on what they call fact finding trips overseas. He got system so he and his girlfriends would not be -- how you say -- interrupted, and be on six o'clock news."

Frankie turned and watched the fog roll over them. Tiny little green things in the fog touched the tinted glass and spiraled on the glass like tiny worms and stopped as the fog moved on.

"That's what they do to your brain," Alexei said. "They spiral into the brain and eat it and infest the blood, so that if they scratch someone they get infected."

Frankie sat there shivering, almost crying.

"But not everyone," Luka said.

"My guess some people got immune system or built up better antibodies. Who knows?"

As the fog moved past so did the mindless herd, denizens of the dead-fog.

"How long we stuck in car?" Frankie said sounding close to panic.

Alexei pulled a cloth tab and a compartment under the

seat opened. He pulled out gas masks. "Till you talk too much."

"Could they be looking for some – some – some leader?" Luka breathed, wiping the sweat from his eyes with the back of his hand. "For some monster to tell them what to do, where to go."

"Nyet, fool. They mindless freaks." Alexei turned and stared at Luka in the front seat as if he couldn't believe he said something so stupid.

Luka nervously stomped on the gas pedal and the limo accelerated, shot out of the fog.

"Slow down, big fella," Alexei said cause Luka liked that term and wanted him to listen to him.

The limo went slowly, staying a half a block ahead of the fog. Cars had crashed in the street, on the sidewalk. Monsters were everywhere. People fought monsters everywhere, battled then valiantly and mostly lost. There were too many zombies.

"Like this world," Alexei said. "God put too many monsters in it for man to survive in a fair fight, so man must either surrender or be part monster."

Frankie gazed at the boss as if he was cracking up.

"I not for surrendering."

Frankie nodded his head, not about to disagree.

"Give me your three-fifty-seven," Alexei said to Luka, preferring it to his nine-millimeter Beretta M9. Luka handed him a nickel-plated Colt .45 semi-automatic that weighed 2.5 pounds, and felt as heavy as a small barbell. Alexei rolled down his windows and aimed at a nearby monster. He shot it in the chest. The monster went down, green-black blood oozed from the wound. For a moment it didn't move, and then it struggled to get up.

"That should've killed it," Frankie said. "It-it-it re-animated."

Alexei fired and hit it again; this time in the gut. Again the zombie went down, the new wound oozed more of the blackish blood, and after a moment it struggled to stand up.

As the black limo was moving along slowly a monster turned and came at the car and Alexei shot it in the head. The heavy slug from the Colt snapped the monster's head back and nearly lifted it off its feet. The monster flew backward and lay with its arms spread and didn't move.

"Only head shot kill it," Frankie said.

"Da." Alexei saw another zombie nearby and shot it in the leg. Blood and gore splattered out of the exited hole and the monster spun as it went down. Alexei aimed and shot it in the back. After a moment the monster lay still, green-black blood ran from the wounds like thick syrup. Then the monster started moving. Unable to move its legs it pulled itself after the limo, by its arms.

"Gross," Frankie said.

Alexei aimed and fired and took off part of the monster's face. The monster still kept coming. Alexei fired and missed. "Only seven rounds."

Luka reached in the glove box and handed a magazine over the seat back to Alexei.

"Get out of here," Alexei said and Luka steered the limo down another street, bumping into a few zombies and rolling over them, their bones cracking against the underside of the car.

"T--t--they're e--e--everywhere," Frankie said.

They rolled past the theater district.

"How we gonna get out?" Frankie said.

Alexei laughed. "If car only fly."

They stopped at Times Square.

"Whores not get off street in time." Luka's voice didn't sound so scared.

"They need money for drugs. Not matter now."

"Crossroads of world," Luka said.

"Crossroads of hell," Frankie said, his long nosed face shiny with sweat, his dark eyes scared, his thick black hair wet with sweat like he'd run a race.

Alexei felt Frankie trembling on the seat. He reached in the compartment behind the front seat, took out a bottle of Cold River Vodka and handed it to him.

"Take drink."

Frankie took the cap off and put it to his mouth: He tilted his head back. Liquor splashed down his chin.

Alexei yanked the bottle away. "Not get drunk."

Frankie wiped his mouth with the back of his hand. He hadn't tasted it. He licked his lips. He was so scared it tasted like water.

Alexei handed the bottle to Luka.

"Thanks." He raised the bottle to his mouth. The liquor splashed in his mouth and over his chin.

Whores, tourists and cops laid on the ground. And monsters were eating them. The zombies were everywhere. They moved around slowly. A teenager, about five six, brown eyes, black hair, wearing a green shirt and green jeans was shuffling slowly along, gray-black blood dripped from his torn clothes.

"Look at that one," Frankie said.

"He not one of them."

"What you mean?"

"Watch?"

As the limo rolled past the short fat teenager suddenly veered toward them. He was across Times Square. He tried to wave as a monster might wave.

"You not leave him," Frankie said.

Alexei gave him a look, then relented and motioned to Luka. Luka slowed the car to a stop.

Once the limo stopped the fat kid started hurrying to it. The zombies noticed the movement and chased after the teen. The fat kid grabbed a gun off a dead cop and started shooting at monsters that neared him. But he wasn't a very good shot and one bullet hit the car.

"You try to get us killed?" Alexei said.

Frankie shook his head like he was sitting on a block of ice.

The teenager's shooting attracted more attention. Half a block from the limo the gun ran out of bullets, but now the monsters were all around him. The teenager tripped and went down and the hungry monsters swarmed on him.

"Seen enough." Alexei sat back, deep in thought. Frankie was pale.

A man crawled out from under a big white caddie. He got up and started to run toward the limo.

"Is that Mohammed Jones?" Luka said.

"He dead."

Frankie faced Alexei. "You not gonna. . ."

"Why bother."

With the zombies distracted by feeding on the teenager it seemed as if Jones would have a chance. A monster got in his way and he punched it knocking it down. Another got in his way and he clubbed it with a Tech 9 pistol.

"Must be out bullets," Alexei said.

Using the gun as a club Jones fought his way across the street. He was a good street fighter, but there too many of them.

"You want help him?" Alexei asked Frankie.

"Nyet." Frankie couldn't tear his eyes off the fight; he was fascinated by the spectacle.

Jones hit a monster with a gun and the monster bit his hand and he let go of the gun

"Ut oh," Frankie said. "Now he's infected."

Jones took a switchblade from his pocket and started stabbing the monsters, stabbing let and right like a wild man. He slashed up and down and to the side and was covered in the green-black blood to his elbow.

"Should have sword," Alexei said, "With sword maybe he have chance." Luka grunted agreement.

Soon Jones had a swarm of monsters around him. The monsters dragged him down and he was lost to sight. A moment later the monsters were ripping parts of him off and eating them.

"Oh God." Frankie reached into the liquor rack and fumbled another bottle out of it. He ripped the cap off and drank from the bottle. "What a way to die."

"What you mean dead?" Alexei said.

Frankie's jaw fell open. "Wh-wh-what?"

Jones minus an arm and part of his face stood up and

oozing green-black blood, sluggishly walked to the limo.

Alexei motioned to Luka. "Go."

Frankie started to say, "Maybe we should do. . ."

Just then a monsters came up to the window, it tried to reach in the open crack and grab Frankie.

"Ahhhh!" Frankie cried and Alexei slugged him.

He pushed the button and the window slid up. The tips of the fingers were cut off and wiggled on the floor.

"Keep quiet. You crack now and you out door."

Frankie, his feet on the seat, stared at the wiggling fingers on the floor. "W--why they not attack car?"

"Must be black color and tinted windows, can't see us. Or maybe it not smell human. Smell like oil and gas."

Frankie shivered. "When window was open. . . ."

"It saw us or smell."

"Or heard us," Luka said.

"They like wild animals," Frankie said, "fast movement, lights, attract their attention."

Alexei said, "Like only sub-section of brain working."

Luka did not know what had happened, but he knew the boss was the only man smart enough to figure a way out. If any man could get out of this, it was Tough Alexei.

"Drive slow. Head to Brooklyn. Be safe there."

The black limo quietly drove away.

*****

Chapter 20 - Follow the Rules

Kenny watched the zombies chomping on the babysitter. It was gross and he had to turn away before he got sick. They heard him retching; it was what his mom would call surreal sort of like as if '*South Park*' met *'Night of the Living Dead'*. Then the monsters left. They shuffled down the street. One bumped into a different garbage can, but left it alone and moved on.

Kenny peeked out of the garbage can certain a zombie was waiting to grab him, but there were no more monsters nearby. He crawled out of the garbage can and it rolled a few feet, making a loud tinny noise. Far up the street a zombie turned in his direction.

Kenny sat perfectly still on the sidewalk looking around. No other zombies were coming. It was quiet. Up the block a zombie slowly limped away, dragging an injured woman, with him. Kenny didn't know what was left of the babysitter, he guessed she was dead, pulled apart and eaten, but Fran Weezer, was now a zombie and turned its head toward the sound and saw him. Its one eye, the right eye, watched Kenny get to his feet and head to the apartment. One arm was ripped off, hunks of its flesh had been chewed and bitten off and half of its face gone, but now it felt hunger like it'd never felt before and struggled to get up. Its one eye watched the boy go into the apartment building and it struggled even harder. ""Food," it cried, sounding like "'Ooood!"

Kenny hurried inside the building. Yellow emergency lights glowed dimly. He pressed the elevator button. It didn't light up. The elevator wasn't working. The building was very still, more quiet than early in the morning.

He opened the stairway door slowly. The stairwell was dark. Pitch black dark. He couldn't see anything. He stepped inside and waited for his eyes to get used to the dark like his mother said, but they didn't. It felt cold and damp. An emergency light faintly glowed on every floor. Holding the banister, he climbed the stairs, his small steps echoing in the empty stairwell. The place smelled bad, like there was another gas leak.

On the third landing something scurried away from him in the dark. He yelled and nearly tumbled back down the stairs. When he could hear over the noise of his thumping heart he heard, Meow. Mendelson's cat, Sharona, got out again. That black cat with the white face was always getting into things.

Kenny hiked up the stairs. Finally he reached his floor.

Cautiously he opened the metal fire door and peeked into the hall. It was quiet. The emergency light was dim. The cat sneaked though the crack, touching his legs, almost making him jump.

"Sharona."

He ran down the hall. At his door, number 8, he stopped to listen. He couldn't hear anything. All he could hear was his heart hammering and his ragged breathing. He opened the door and went inside. The small emergency lights that one of mom's dates, the guy who was afraid of the dark, gave her glowed pale yellow from two light sockets; one in the kitchen and the other in the living room. He liked the guy, but he wasn't much fun.

He hurried to the phone, dialed 911 and listened. No dial tone. The phone was deader than the babysitter. He stared at the see-through plastic phone. He wanted to call his mom. She was probably at that dumb club she once took him to. She was always going there. But if the phone was dead, how could he call her?

Please God, let her be okay. Maybe that guy, Mike, will take care of her. He seemed better than her other dates, but maybe he isn't. Knowing mom's luck in dates, he could be another jerk. Why does she always go out with losers? Mike might not be able to help her; she might have to help him. He shook his head. Just like mom to find a guy she had to help. She was always taking in the strays who stayed a month till they took her emergency money and left and she never heard from them again.

He'd have to help her, but he couldn't call the police. He'd have to do it himself. He sort of remembered the way to the club. They had to walk home one night because someone took her purse. It's not that far, she was always saying that and saying she was counting on him to be the man of the house. Now he could show her. She'd be proud of him.

He looked out the window and saw a few zombies shuffling about. He remembered the look on Fran's face when she saw the zombies. She was so interested in hurting him; she forgot Rule Number One- watch out for monsters. He'd made his own rules up after watching '*Man vs. Wild'* on TV. Bear had his rules, Kenny had his own rules.

He started for the door, stopped and looked at himself in the mirror. Can't go like this. He had to follow Rule Number Two- be prepared. He'd have to change.

"Meow."

Now what?

He walked into the kitchen. Jacko was sitting in front of the refrigerator licking her lips. Mendelson's cat, Sharona, was rubbing itself against Jacko and purring like it was a she. Some days Sharona acted like a she cat. The Mendelson's named it Arona, after a place they went on their honeymoon, but when the kids saw the cat with other cats they nicknamed it Sharona, much to the Mendelsons' annoyance. He took a carton of milk out, placed a soup bowl on the floor and filled it, left the milk on the counter and marched down the hall.

Can't go like this. What should he wear? Rule Number Three- you can't be over prepared.

He went into his bedroom and looked around. Against the dresser was a Yankee baseball bat and his red hockey stick. In his open closet was his Black Hawk peewee football uniform: shoulder pads, black knee pads, black helmet and hockey skates.

"Yeah," he said and started taking off his clothes.

When he was dressed he went into the living room and looked at himself in the mirror. He saw the blade on the hockey stick was broken. That wouldn't do. He went into the kitchen and found a roll of black duct tape in the utility drawer. Then started opening drawers trying to find the biggest sharpest knife he could. He found a long carving knife. He put the knife, the hockey stick and the duct tape on the kitchen/dining room table. He taped the handle of the knife against the hockey stick blade. He wrapped more and more gray duct tape around it until it was a fist with a knife blade sticking out. Then he wrapped the rest of the duct tape around the top of the hockey stick forming it into a hard ball about as big as a soft ball, a duct tape bludgeon.

He shoved an extra carving knife in his backpack and stopped on the way to the door to look at himself in the mirror.

"More over, Mr. Death," he said and started for the door. Then he stopped and went back to the mirror and lowered the helmet over his eyes. Now he lowered his voice as he said, "Luke, I'm not who you think I am."

With grim determination on his face, he headed to the apartment door.

*****

Chapter 21 - Unwanted Ghost

Howie, Tommy and Diane walked down the hall to the elevator. They were dressed for a night on the town; Tommy wore his expensive dark green blazer, gray slacks, gray silk shirt, pink Donald Trump tie. Howie wore a J.C. Penney blue blazer, button down blue shirt and pressed jeans. Diane wore a homemade black cocktail dress that didn't hide her pretty legs. Crystal pendant earrings swung as she walked, sending out rainbows of colors.

"Where to first?" Howie asked as he pressed the elevator button.

"What?" Diane said. "I still can't hear from T.N.T.'s boombox being so loud. I may be permanently injured."

Tommy laughed. "Hey, just wanted to liven things up. Can't blame a guy for wanting to have a little fun."

"Happens all the time," Howie said in his Boris Karloff voice. "Guys get in trouble for having fun, for thinking 'bout having fun."

"What'd you say?" Diane cupped her hand over her ear.

"Okay," Tommy said, then mumbled. "It's no longer

funny."

"I'm surprised someone didn't call the manager. You had it so loud."

"They've all gone out already."

"We're so late." Diane looked at her wrist watch.

"Surprised if we don't get a water bill."

"Hey, when I take a shower, I take a shower."

"Man takes shower," Howie sounded like Rod Serling, "uses all the water from Niagara Falls. News at Eleven."

"Good one." Diane smiled at him.

Howie stopped. "Thought I heard a siren."

"In New York?" Tommy laughed. "Big surprise."

"Where we going to go?"

"I'm hungry," Tommy said. "Let's eat."

"We can eat later. Let's drive around and see the city at night. Maybe we can go by Emily's hotel and say hi."

Howie heard the anticipation in her voice. He didn't want to go near the car until they left. It might not start. But if she wanted to ride around, he'd chance it. He took his key ring out of his pocket and twirled it.

Diane admired the textured wallpaper. "This is nice."

"Sure is quiet." Howie now imitating Sean Connery. "Be on your guard, Moneypenny."

"Stiletto," Diane corrected, and Howie bowed an apology

"Of course it's quiet, this is an expensive hotel." Tommy looked around. "What do you think? We're at Motel Six?"

The elevator door opened and they stepped inside. Howie remembered the shortcut to the parking garage and pressed the button. The door closed and he thought he heard something scratching on the roof of the elevator and looked at the ceiling. Couldn't see anything. There it was again.

"We're in one of the best hotels in the world, what do you expect?" Tommy knocked on the wall. "Walls aren't paper thin."

Howie shrugged. The hotel really was quiet. A

scratching sound on the roof again.

"You hear that?"

"What?" Diane said.

Howie pointed to the ceiling. "Sounds like something's on the roof of the elevator."

Tommy made a face. "Sure there is. Sure there is."

"There it is again."

"Maybe I should drive." He reached for the car keys.

Howie turned his hand over so he couldn't touch them.

"Hey, I heard something too," Diane said.

Tommy listened to a clicking sound. "Cicadas?"

"In New York City?" Diane said.

"It's a bug." Tommy chuckled. "Making mountains out of nothing, again. The world is full of bugs."

"We're inside an elevator, and we can hear it."

Tommy shook his head. "Here we are in the Big Apple and you two are talking about bugs. I tell you, you two are driving me bugs."

The elevator stopped on the second floor.

"This isn't the lobby," Tommy said.

"Shortcut to the car."

"I want to see the balloon exhibit," Tommy said.

"It won't go away," Diane said. "You can see the balloons tomorrow."

"He'll just drool over the blonde handing out brochures," Howie said in.

Tommy scowled at him, he was paying for the room and being put down, what kind of a friend was that?

"Her balloons will be there tomorrow," Diane said.

Howie and Tommy exchanged looks and laughed.

"No," Diane said. "I didn't. Not again."

"That was good," Howie said.

Diane frowned as they went down the hall to the parking garage. "Why do I always do that?"

"Where is everyone?" Howie asked.

"Already out having a good time," Tommy said, "because they didn't drive here at forty miles per hour."

"If we had a sail, T.N.T., with your mouth we'd've

been here yesterday."

"And if you didn't stop to look for bugs in the elevator," Tommy added.

"You're the only bug I see," Howie said.

"Hey, you two," Diane said, "cut it out."

Tommy nudged Diane. "How about we take a ride in a horse drawn carriage through Central Park? Howie can follow in his car. If he can keep up."

"Did you really want to look at the blonde?"

"On the brochures her balloons are handing out."

She laughed and punched him.

Howie opened the fire door to the parking garage; it was as dark as a Georgia country road on a moonless night. "What happened to the lights? Some fancy hotel you booked us in."

"Must be a fuse."

"Here." Diane took her keys from her purse. They were on a key ring with an Atlanta Falcons souvenir. She pressed the button and a small light shined barely enough light to see where they were going.

"Let's get a bellman with a flashlight," Tommy said.

"You going to tip him?" Howie said.

"I tip on my credit card when I check out."

Howie glanced at T.N.T. Tommy's expression said if you dish it out you'd better be able to take it.

"I parked the car close to the door." Howie pointed to the third car in the row. "Here it is."

"Black mustang with black chrome," Tommy said, "did you buy this wreck off a backwoods movie or from white lightning smugglers?"

"Planning to make a fast getaway?" Diane kidded.

"That ain't such a bad idea," Tommy said. "I could say my card was stolen."

"Knew you'd think of a way to screw someone on the trip."

"As long as you don't have to pay." Tommy started to smile and saw Diane giving him laser eyes and wondered what he'd done. He started to climb in the back and saw the tinted windows. "With the windows so dark, I won't be able to see anything."

Diane thought of him in the back seat where he was -- sort of -- far away but that mouth of his would be right in her ear and that could ruin everything. In the front seat he couldn't run or hide. She sighed. "Okay. Sit in the front. I'll sit on your lap."

A smile leaped across Tommy's face. "All right." He winked at Howie.

"Hey, what's that?" Howie pointed in the exit. "Thought I saw something."

A man in ragged clothing shuffled down the street. His face looked gray in the light.

Tommy chuckled. "First you hear things on the roof of the elevator and now you think some bum is a monster. I know you don't want me saying anything, but Howard, I think you took a turn into the Stephen King Zone." To his surprise Diane didn't show any agreement and Howie ignored him. Tommy settled into the bucket seat and Diane sat on his lap and swung her pretty legs in.

Howie gazed over the roof of his Mustang at the exit. It did look like a bum, but in a way, it didn't. He climbed in and closed the door. He said a silent prayer before he twisted the key, but the starter turned quickly and the engine rumbled to life on the first try. As a matter of fact it didn't sound so bad.

"Hey," Howie said, then like Karloff, "it's alive, it's alive."

"All that hard driving tuned it up," Tommy said like he knew about such things and wasn't making it up.

As Howie backed out of the parking place he thought he saw something in the rear view mirror. He whirled around to look out his open window, but he saw nothing. He drove slowly down the ramp.

As he drove away a zombie limped after the car in the darkness.

Howie tried his headlights. "My headlights still aren't working."

"Don't sweat the small stuff," Diane said.

"With this wreck you sweat everything."

"Maybe I should break your headlights and see how you take it," Howie said to Tommy.

"I just pushed some loose wires out of the way and you go blaming everything' on me."

"You're calling what you did an accident?"

"Can it," Diane said.

Howie drove slowly. Without overhead lights in the garage or headlights, he had to be careful. Didn't want to crash into a parked car and have his insurance go up again.

"Hey," Tommy nearly shouted, "I forgot to call down about the TV not working."

"You can call tomorrow," Diane said. "It must be something with the cable."

"But I wanted to see what Saturday morning TV is like in New York."

"Afraid you'll miss Bugs Bunny?"

"I heard they have some really weird stuff on TV."

"Is it like the porn stuff on late night?" Howie asked.

"I don't know. I just wanted to take a peek."

"He came to New York to take a peek," Howie said in his Rod Serling impression, "and disappeared into the --"

Together Howie and Diane said, "Twilight Zone," and laughed.

Tommy sighed; he was tired of Howie's impressions and tired of Diane ganging up on him.

Howie stopped at the exit. No one was in the booth to check tickets. The barrier was broken.

"What are you waiting for?" Tommy said.

"There's no one to take the parking pass."

"We're guests; we don't have to pay. Let's go."

Howie rolled down the driveway to the street. They saw cars parked here and there and even in the street, but no moving traffic.

"It's so dark," Diane commented.

"The moon hasn't risen yet," Howie said.

"When does it rise?"

"Later after all the vampires have fed," Tommy said in an accented vampire voice.

"Why are the cars stopped in the street?"

"It's New York," Tommy said.

"Where's the traffic?" Howie said.

"Who cares, let's go to Central Park," Diane said.

Howie swerved around cars parked in the street, past delivery vans frozen in time and followed a sign to Central Park Drive. Entered Central Park. Greenery on the right and left.

"Your headlights still aren't working," Diane said.

Howie hit the dash with his fist, the headlights came on. He grinned. "For milady."

Tommy shook his head; this bucket of bolts should be put out of its misery.

"This is spooky," Howie said. "Where are the people, the joggers, the bicycle riders, anybody."

"First the elevator, then the parking garage, now Central Park." Tommy shook his head. "Are you trying to turn this into a horror movie and ruin the weekend?"

Howie glanced at Tommy, but didn't say anything.

"This is nice." Diane said and they looked at her.

Howie drove slowly down the winding street, past a lake to the right. On both sides spotlights lit up colorful hot air balloons. A baseball balloon to the left and a red and yellow rainbow balloon way to the right soared over the tops of the trees. They didn't see any security guards or police; the lighted balloons were unguarded, moving gently in the breeze. A blue propane flame blazed at the bottom of one balloon filling it with hot air.

"How can they do that?" Diane said. "Don't they need someone to monitor it?"

"Read about it in 'Popular Science'," Howie said. "Done by computers. A sensor in the balloon signals a computer on the instrument panel. The pilot presets it to how much pressure or lift he wants and the burner automatically goes on. That's how they can get away with leaving them unattended at night, instead of deflating them at night and starting in the morning."

"It's romantic," she said, "the lights and everything."

"Maybe we can go for a little ride."

"Who's paying for it?" Howie said.

"I'll pay for me and Diane." Tommy grinned at Howie.

Walks on the left and right, guard rail on the left, streetlights on the right partly hidden by trees. They drove on a bridge over a road.

"65th Street something," Tommy turned his head as they went by and tried to read the sign.

"There's someone," said Diane. Through the trees, way over across a field they saw more balloons and someone running and a bunch of people chasing him.

"That isn't football," Tommy said.

"Looks more like tag," Howie said.

The guy fell down and everyone jumped on him.

"Rugby," Tommy said.

Clothes flew up in the air.

"Are they taking his clothes off?" Howie said.

"Football is rough in New York," Diane commented.

"No piling on," Tommy yelled out the window.

Someone turned to the car and then the others turned and started coming toward them, but they were way across the field and the black Mustang went around the bend.

"What's their problem?" Howie said.

"Bad losers." Tommy winked at Howie like he was one too.

"Did you see the way they moved? Like something was wrong with them."

"Don't start," Diane said. "Just don't."

Tommy grinned at Howie.

They went around a long curve to the right. A traffic light wasn't working at the crosswalk, so Howie paused briefly then continued around a bend to the left, toward two more colorful balloons. Another traffic light not working, two roads combined into one with a sign: East Drive. The road, now East Drive, continued curving.

"Almost look like tall stone monoliths," Howie said,

"like we're in some prehistoric world."

Tommy gave Diane a look and shook his head, as if to say Howie was losing it.

Trees lined the narrow road. Above and behind the trees stood all buildings, every now and then the burner from a balloon lit up and dispersed the thin fog. There was a cement sidewalk on the left behind the guard rail. No joggers tonight. Up ahead was another pedestrian crossing, with the traffic light blinking red.

Howie stopped at the crossing. They heard something or someone in the bushes.

"What's that?" Diane asked.

"Just go," Tommy said.

Howie stepped on the gas and went right at the 'Y'. Around the bend, East Dr. merged into 72nd Street Transverse. A balloon resembling a Dr. Pepper can floated on the right, to the left a colorful rainbow balloon. At the next traffic light a limo was stopped on the sidewalk, apparently it had run into a cement park bench. The driver's door was open, no one was around.

Howie slowed as he and Tommy craned to look.

"Just go." Diane said her voice a little shrill. She rubbed her arms. In the dim light Howie could see her arms were covered with goose bumps.

Howie drove to the next traffic light, again a light not working, and turned right onto 5th Avenue.

"You got air conditioning?" Tommy said.

"Got to go eighty-five and roll down the windows."

"Maybe we should roll up the windows."

"You want some heat?"

"Duh." Tommy gestured at the frightened expression on Diane's face.

They rolled up the windows and he turned on the fan to get some fresh air circulating. When Howie switched on the fan, unknown to them, all the exterior lights went off, and probably saved their lives. The black car rolled almost silently down the dark streets like an unwanted ghost.

*****

Chapter 22 - City of the Dead

The noise of the car's engine echoed up and down the cement canyons sounding like there were other cars on other streets, making it impossible to tell where the car was and where it was going. It echoed back at them sounding like several cars moving on other distant streets.

The lights inside the car, the dash lights, gauges, instrument lights, all went out. Even the brake light didn't go on when Howie stepped on the brake.

Tommy shook his head. "Does anything in this car work?"

"Your point being?"

"Ever have the coolant checked?" Tommy said.

"At the prices they want?"

Upset at being in such a loser car, Tommy looked out the window. "How come the side windows are tinted so dark?"

"Way I got the car."

"Can't see anything." Tommy leaned close to the windshield trying to look up at the tall dark buildings. "Lights out everywhere."

"Don't make a big thing out of it," Diane said. "Probably has to do with a transformer or relay station going out."

"Do you know anything about what you just said?" Tommy said.

"No and neither do you. That's what they say on TV."

"Where to, Milady?" Howie said.

"I always wanted to see Times Square at night."

"We're headed there." Howie looked up and down the street for traffic, but it was empty. That was weird. No working streetlights in the distance. No one walking. Only the silently blinking (red) traffic lights. "Where's all the traffic?"

"They heard you were driving your demolition derby reject and high-tailed it." Tommy laughed, it echoed spookily in the quiet.

"T.N.T., you ought to get a job as a comedian. Then you can be fired from two jobs at the same time."

"Guys." Diane sighed, at times she felt like she was babysitting.

Howie drove very slowly down Fifth Avenue. The dark boulevard was empty of moving traffic. Cars stopped in the street. No streetlights. No one walking. A riderless police horse waited at the curb.

Tommy and Diane stared at Central Park on their right. In the distance they could see people wandering around. They didn't seem to be together and they weren't really on any path.

"Sure is dark," she said.

"No wonder there are so many muggings."

"Think that's dark?" Howie said. "Look at the streets."

On the left were office buildings, corporate headquarters, hotels, apartments. Tall dark towers that seemed abandoned. All the lights in the buildings were out; here and there a flashlight beam slashed the darkness. Someone in a tall tower, behind a glass window, was yelling at them, but they couldn't hear and couldn't really tell; maybe it was nothing. Between the tall cement cliffs were ribbons of dark asphalt that ran straight into the distance.

"No lights in any of the windows," Howie observed.

"That's weird," Tommy said.

"Maybe just a power outage." Diane rubbed the goose bumps off her arms.

The buildings rose like dark cliffs in the silent night. They drove past Pulitzer Fountain on the right and the Plaza without realizing it; they were so engrossed by the strange dark night.

"Everyone went somewhere for the weekend," she said.

No cars moved. Many were parked in the street. A

few cars smashed into each other. Some had jumped the curb and gone across the sidewalks and hit a building and stopped.

"Is this demolition derby weekend?" Howie said.

"No tow trucks," Tommy said incredulously. "No ambulances. No one anywhere. Something's wrong."

"What's happened?" Howie said. "Look at all the accidents. The police should be all over the place.

"It must've happened when you were in the shower."

"It's probably nothing," Tommy said.

"T.N.T., if you hadn't played that boombox so loud we might have heard something."

"Maybe it's a drill or something we don't know about," Diane said. "Maybe they're making a movie."

"Where are the actors?" Howie whispered.

"Stop it. You're scaring me."

"There." Tommy pointed. Down the street they could see a few people wandering about, some people were in the street, others on the sidewalk. They saw a few people watching from the dark interior of buildings. Some people in the buildings waved at them, at their car, as went by. "They're making a movie. There must have been signs to stay off certain streets."

"You see," Diane said relieved, "some director is going to come out and tell us to get off the set."

"We'll tell him we were auditioning," Tommy said. "The hicks from out of town."

Howie stepped on the brake and slowed the car. "What's that?" He pointed at something on the sidewalk by a subway kiosk.

"Move closer," Tommy rolled down his window, "but don't stop."

"Oh, what's that smell?" Diane held her nose.

"Rotten eggs," Tommy said. "A gas leak. It's just a gas leak."

"The stinkiest gas leak in the world." Howie clamped his nose with his fingers to stop gagging. He breathed with his mouth like he had a cold.

A man lying on his back was being dragged by something across the sidewalk. They couldn't get a good look at it in the dark. The man's head, trunk, then legs, went down the subway entrance.

"Wh-what was that?" Diane said.

"Dunno," Howie said. "Special effects?"

"I know." Tommy grinned. "It's that new practical joke program I heard about. You know, they play these scary practical jokes?"

Diane and Howie exchanged looks of disbelief.

"Let's go back to the hotel," Diane said.

"I think it'd be better if we found out what's going on." Howie drove past Rockefeller Center. An emerald green purse lay in the road.

"Stop," Tommy shouted.

Howie kept his foot on the gas pedal.

"I could have returned that for a reward."

Howie glanced at him like he didn't believe him.

"Nice try," Diane said.

"I would of, really."

"The sidewalks are empty." Howie's mouth was very dry.

"It's night," Tommy said. "An emergency curfew."

"Is that why the lights are off?" Howie asked.

"That smell. A massive gas leak?" Diane speculated. "The Governor or Mayor ordered everyone off the streets. We missed it because T.N.T. was listening to very loud music in the shower. The hotel has a backup generator. It was quiet because everyone else at the hotel was in a ballroom or meeting room waiting for instructions."

"That doesn't explain the wrecked cars."

"Lights went out and people got scared causing accidents. Chain reaction. Police rushed everyone off the streets."

"In New York?" Howie twisted around and looked down the side streets. "And that thing at the subway entrance?"

"We really didn't see anything," Diane said. "Guy was

probably getting mugged."

"Diane McDavid," Tommy said, "you are the--"

"Shut up," Diane said sharply. "That's all it is. It's not anything serious."

Howie heard the panic in her voice. He circled Rockefeller Center. It towered above them, dark and eerie like an abandoned castle.

"Isn't it usually lit up?" Tommy said.

"Like a birthday cake," Howie said.

"What's that?" Diane pointed high up.

Howie slowed to a crawl. High up something glowed in the moonlight. "Looks like thin silvery threads."

"Look," Tommy stuck his head out the window, "on the side of that building. Looks like a giant spider."

Now that Howie knew what to look for he could see them moving in the breeze, thin white strands hung down from the tall building. Others waved in the breeze high above the ground, catching the silvery moonlight with their radiance. Others twisted in the night breeze.

Diane shivered so much Howie felt her against his arm. He looked at Tommy. His mouth was slack and his eyes were open wide like they might fall out. Howie nudged Tommy and gestured to cool it with Diane.

"Maybe they're making a new Spiderman movie," Tommy said.

Howie looked up at the building. The wind changed and the giant spider web slipped down a few dozen floors on the outside of the building and then floated to the street.

"It's a giant balloon webbing," Howie said, relieved.

"It must have broken loose."

"Maybe that's what this is about," Diane said. "One of those balloons in Central Park broke loose and landed on a power station and shorted everything out."

Howie didn't think so, but he kept his mouth shut as he turned the steering wheel. It was like driving in a graveyard. The only sound was the noise of their car engine echoing down the cement canyons. At 50th Street he turned onto Seventh, heading south again.

"Shouldn't there be someone around, HAZMAT, or something?" Fear edged into Howie's voice.

Tommy said, "Must be a hell of a big gas leak."

"Are you sure?" Diane asked.

"New York probably has more gas pipes than the rest of the world combined. This a huge gas leak. The mayor or governor ordered the electricity turned off so it wouldn't spark an explosion. And all the cars were told to stop and left where they are. Whole areas of the city must have been evacuated."

"Should we be driving?" Howie asked.

Tommy waved for Howie to continue.

"That's all this is ... a gas leak?" Diane said.

"What else could it be? It isn't anything weird or scary." Tommy prided himself at being so smart he could figure out anything.

Diane gave him a hug. She turned to Howie. "Don't say a thing; it's just a gas leak." She playfully shoved him. "No big deal."

Howie drove slowly down Broadway.

"Look!" Howie pointed.

In the dim moonlight they could see something on the ground, like turned over garbage cans. Black shapes moved in the shadows.

"Oh shit," Tommy said.

Tommy reached under the seat and pulled out Howie's five cell Radio Shack flashlight. He put it out the window and turned it on. Its powerful beam sliced across the dark courtyard.

That wasn't garbage. It was hundreds of bodies. They could see bodies being dragged along the ground. Some were devoured as they watched. The things in the shadows were people or had been people and they were devouring people. They were hideous looking with open sores, gray skin, bulging eyes, black lips, black fingernails and had lost clumps of hair. Many were wounded or injured, and dripped green-black blood.

Monsters everywhere they looked. Thousands of them.

Whitish eyes glowed in the light. Some stopped what they were doing and walked, shuffled, toward the light. Other monstrosities shuffled out of buildings and plodded toward them. Some crawled. None of them spoke; they wore ripped, torn, bloodied clothing, some were seriously hurt.

"The light," Diane said. "It's attracting them."

"Huh?" Tommy glanced at her. Howie saw he'd been numbed by the terrible horror out there.

Diane knocked the flashlight out of Tommy's hand. It fell to the street and rolled away from the car.

"Go!" Diane shouted at Howie.

He gazed at her. She pointed and he stepped on the gas and the Mustang raced down Seventh Avenue.

Looking behind them, he saw most of the monsters going to the light, others slowly coming after the car.

"They're attracted to light," Diane said. "And maybe noise. Slow down."

Howie stepped on the brake pedal and pulled an empty Coca-Cola bottle from under the seat. He drove to the curb and tossed the bottle on the sidewalk. It bounced and then rolled across the sidewalk in the moonlight. They watched two people, monsters that were shuffling about start toward it and stop when they saw what it was.

"And sound," Howie breathed, fear quivering his voice. "Maybe movement."

"Turn off what lights are on. Keep your foot off the brake so the brake light stays off."

"All the lights are off," he informed her. "The brake lights don't work."

"Oh."

"You sure?" Tommy twisted the light switch. The headlights that hadn't worked suddenly blazed. Seventh Avenue was lit, bodies everywhere. Monsters turned to them. Whitish eyes gleamed at them. More zombies turned in the direction of the headlights.

"The lights!" she said.

Howie grabbed the switch and twisted it until all the lights went off. He put his hand on his chest. His heart beat as if it wanted to burst. He was panting. He glanced at Diane. She had her hands on her chest too. Her mouth hung open and eyes were popped open, the whites so big.

"You see them?" he said.

Diane nodded. They turned to Tommy. He was pale and shaking.

"Drive," she said.

Howie pulled away, keeping the car moving.

"Tommy?" he said. Tommy didn't answer. "Tommy."

His jaw hung limp. His breathing was shallow.

"Shit," Howie said. "Just what we need."

She slapped Tommy. His head recoiled back. He blinked and stared at her.

"D--d--did y--y--you s--s--see them?"

"Yeah," Howie said. "We saw."

"Are you okay?" Diane asked.

"The dead are alive," Tommy whispered. "They're zombies."

"I wonder if it's a new biological weapon," Howie said. "Who attacked? The Chinese, the Iranians or the North Koreans? Terrorists?"

"Does it matter?" Diane said.

"Guess not," Howie said.

"Dead ... are ... eating ... people?"

"But if it's a war, are our soldiers dead?" Diane said.

"Don't think so. But that's just a guess."

"Let's get out of here," Tommy said. "Fuck my clothes. Fuck the hotel. Let's hit the highway and drive."

"Okay." Howie gazed at Diane. "Which way?"

"Where's that map?" Tommy said.

"Glove compartment."

Tommy opened it. Half the contents fell out. Diane squirmed her way onto the console between the seats and Tommy sorted through the junk till he found a map. "I can't see."

Diane reached into her purse and pulled out her key ring. She turned on a key light aiming it at the map.

"Keep the light low," Howie told her.

Tommy bent down under the dash and opened the map. Diane leaned close so she could see.

"Turn it off," Howie said, the little light lit up the inside of the car alarmingly bright.

"We can't see," Diane said.

Howie saw zombies turn to the car as it passed. "It's making us visible. Roll up the windows."

He looked around. Now that he knew what he was seeing, he saw the sides of the road were littered with bodies. It wasn't a garbage strike. Cars had come to a stop on the sidewalk or against other cars or on top of bodies. Among the bodies moved groups of zombies, every now and then their whitish eyes catching the moonlight and gleaming.

"We're near Times Square," Howie said, trying to stop his hands from shaking on the steering wheel.

"Keep going," Tommy said. "At Thirty-Ninth Street turn right. We'll take the Lincoln Tunnel."

"A tunnel?" Diane said. "You think that's smart?"

"What other way is there?"

"What about a bridge"

"I don't know what bridges are nearby. We'll try this first."

Howie drove slowly forward.

Times Square was a mess, cars, bodies everywhere. They could barely squeeze around the cars. Then Howie saw the bones in the moonlight. Skeletons lying in the road -- some had been picked clean -- lining the side streets, scattered across Times Square.

Zombies were feasting on the bodies. Squatting next to corpses like cannibals at a banquet they ripped the bodies apart as they fed. Some looked up at the passing vehicle. Others turned away as if afraid.

"Oh my God," Howie said.

He slowed to a crawl.

"I can't go around."

Tommy twisted in his seat. "We can't go back. The ones we passed are coming after us."

Howie stared at the highway of skeletons in front of them. His mouth dry. His heart thumped fast and hard. Sweat trickled down his face.

A carpet of bones covered the street, gleaming dully in the pale moonlight. It was like a street in hell, a graveyard where all the bones suddenly rose to the surface. Round skulls, smashed skulls, ribs like fallen tree branches and thick bones like tree roots crisscrossed the street. Here and there a piece of clothing flapped in the breeze. A piece of paper rustled along like a dry leaf. Jewelry glittered on the ground. A body hung from a light pole too high up for the zombies to reach. Like rats zombies came from the dark broken windows of stores, from out of the abandoned cars, from the insides of the buildings, more and more zombies came toward them.

"Go," she said. "You have to."

He stepped heavily on the gas pedal; his hands shook on the steering wheel. His teeth rattled together he was so scared. He slowed as he came to the first bodies.

Tommy shoved his hand down on Howie's knee. The Mustang surged ahead. It rolled over a few bodies, the bones banging, thumping against the undercarriage of the car, most bones crushing like sticks in a forest, crunching under the heavy tires. Some broken white bones flew out from under the tires and clattered against other bones.

Diane cried, tears dripping down her pale face.

"Can't go around them," Howie said.

"Go. Go," Tommy said sounding so very sacred.

Suddenly a zombie crawled on the hood. Diane nearly screamed. She held the scream back by jamming her hands over her mouth. The zombie clawed at the windshield trying to get to them. Howie stepped on the brake and the zombie fell off the hood. Now he stepped on the gas and they heard the front bumper whack into the zombie, then the car rolled over it, the bones breaking like sticks of wood. They inched across Times Square. The stench of rotting bodies made their eyes water. Tommy turned his head to the side and twisted around and threw up in the backseat.

Just as the path started to clear, a group of zombies came at the front of the car. Howie stepped on the brake and the zombies continued to shuffle toward the car.

"You have to step on the gas," Tommy said, his voice had the urgency of someone close to cracking.

Howie slowly eased ahead.

"Faster," Diane said. "I can't take going slow."

Tommy shoved Howie's leg again and the Mustang surged ahead a few feet. It ran over the three zombies and stalled. The monsters under the front of the car struggled to get out.

"They're not dead?!" Diane said.

"You did it too hard," Howie said.

"Fuck your car."

"Fuck you."

"Stop it, you two!" Diane yelled.

Howie turned the key and the engine turned over slowly like it did not have enough juice to start.

"We should have taken my car," Tommy said.

"Well, we didn't, did we?" Howie said and stopped trying to start it, wanting to wait a minute and let it rest. "If we'd taken your car we'd be dead."

"Let me try," Tommy said.

"Don't touch it," Howie warned.

"Stop fighting," Diane cried.

Tommy wrapped his arms around her and held her tightly.

Howie pushed down on the gas and turned the key. The engine turned over once, and then coughed to life like a mean drunk. He shifted into drive and stepped on the gas. The zombies crunched, thumped, bumped under the car.

Diane shivered violently and Tommy struggled to hold her. "It's okay. It's okay," he whispered to her and gave Howie an angry look.

"Go around, go faster."

"Shit," Diane said. "Shit."

The street seemed to go on forever. Now it was hard to imagine what Times Square looked like when it wasn't full of dead people. Howie felt like he was driving after a nuclear holocaust. It took only a few minutes, but it seemed like hours. At one pointed he turned and saw a carpet of bodies down a side street. That almost did it for him. He forced his hands to hold onto the steering wheel and made himself concentrate on his driving. Concentrate before he lost his mind.

"Not everyone turned into a zombie," Tommy said. "Those who did ate those who didn't."

"Why didn't they?" Diane said sounding like a frightened little girl.

"We didn't," Tommy said.

"Why?"

"We were inside," Howie said. "The window wasn't open. Remember the air conditioning wasn't on. Tommy's boombox was so loud we couldn't hear what was happening."

At Thirty-Ninth Street he turned right. There was no traffic. The streetlights were out. Cars had driven onto the sidewalk and stopped. A few cars were stopped in the street. Some traffic lights blinked, others were out. He saw a green sign, white lettering: LINCOLN TUNNEL.

The entrance to the Lincoln Tunnel was almost a parking lot. Cars were stopped at the sides. No lights flashing. No people around. A police car had crashed into a light pole. There was a thin open path between the stopped vehicles.

"Pull to the side," Diane said.

"Stop telling me what to do," Howie yelled.

He drove to the side and shifted into park.

"We wait," Diane said.

"For what?" Howie said.

"Just wait," Diane said.

"Maybe we should get out and walk through," Tommy said.

Howie turned to him. He can't be that stupid? Or was

he that scared?

"No," Diane told them.

In a few minutes a black Caddie limo roared past. The headlights were white cones in the dark night. Zombies clung to the limo. They were on the hood, the roof, the trunk. A man stood in the sunroof clubbing them with a shotgun. Some had broken a side window and were hanging out of the car.

The Caddie entered the tunnel, the bright lights shined far into the tunnel. Now they could see the monsters inside the tunnel. A wall of monsters was shuffling, coming out of the tunnel when the Caddie hit them. They could hear the bones breaking, see the monsters tossed aside.

The Caddie went into the tunnel, the tunnel roadway turned and it was lost from sight. The zombies walked after it. They heard the car roaring down the tunnel. Saw it lights reflected on the walls.

"Maybe we can follow it," Tommy said.

Diane turned to him.

"Okay, we'll wait."

Howie watched the lights receding away slower and slower. "It's slowing down."

"Why?" Diane asked.

"Thousands of monsters," Howie said.

Then they heard a crash. Metal breaking, tearing, bending. A car horn blasted for a moment echoing up out of the dark tunnel.

"It hit something," Tommy said.

"Probably another car," Howie said.

Smaller white lights shined deep down the tunnel.

"It's backing up," Howie said.

There was the sound of a car crash, then after a minute the lights went out. Now they saw blue flashes and heard guns firing. Then the blue flashes stopped and the guns were silent.

"All those zombies," Howie said.

"Now what?" Tommy said.

"Any bridges we can try?" Diane asked.

Tommy bent over almost under the dash and turned on the little flashlight.

"Is the George Washington Bridge north of here?"

"Yeah," Tommy said. "Not that far--"

"LOOK!" Howie shouted.

Out of the dark tunnel came dozens of zombies. They looked in car windows. Then their whitish eyes swung in the direction of the Mustang and they headed toward it.

Howie threw the transmission into reverse and stomped on the gas. The Mustang shot backward until he swung a wild U-turn. The zombies hurried after them. He shifted into forward and the black Mustang raced away with the zombies chasing it.

*****

Chapter 23 - Beat It

Paul Dachtera, struggling to keep up, hiked up from the dock with his son-in-law. He breathed the fresh breeze off the bay. Smelled the saltiness, could almost taste it on his tongue it was so salty, and behind that aroma was the sweet smelling freshly cut lawn he walked on. The stars twinkled down on him.

Jack McKenna strolled across the damp grass. His round face going soft. His hair thinning. Blue eyes like the Atlantic Ocean.

"Nice boat," Paul said reluctantly.

"Glad you like 'Victory'," Jack said. He had a perpetual smile on his face that irritated Paul, and curly red hair that he didn't care for either, even if it was thinning. Gina had said she hated men with curly red hair and then she goes and marries one.

"It's a Hunter twenty-eight, sleeps six, sixteen horsepower diesel, modernized galley, everything computerized, GPS, transponder, satellite dish, depth finder, AM/FM radio. Improved the Groco head, the hull, deck and rigging. Everything's been updated and redone. Practically sails itself." Jack smiled at the boat like he'd built it from scratch himself. "Now that everything's been modernized and replaced I'll moor her at one of the nearby marinas."

"Didn't know you liked sailing," Paul said trying to keep the anger out of his voice.

"Always wanted to," Jack said. "Wait till we go out tomorrow. You'll love it."

"A boat like that must cost a pretty penny." No wonder you can't afford to visit us. Who's going to pay for the children's college? Especially on Long Island where nothing is cheap.

"Actually, I got it at a bargain, traded Gina's old Mercedes to my boss for it. Got a customer that specializes in redoing boats, got that done at a bargain too. Whenever I want to sell her, I'll probably get back more than I paid."

"Still must be expensive."

"I'm the head salesman in my division now. I can't be the head salesman and look like a poor schmuck. The bosses at the company have sail boats. Of course this is nothing compared to theirs, but this will help them see I've got the right mind for management."

"Can't get much use out of a boat up here," Paul said, "what with the short summers and the hard winters."

"We'll use her in the spring and fall."

"Down in Florida, I can see owning a boat. Sailing year round. Why folks even live on it. But up here. . ."

"We're thinking of sailing her down the coast."

Paul stopped walking. "Sailing to Florida?" With the grandkids on it?

"Yeah."

Stupid ass. Paul turned away and continued walking up the sloping lawn.

"But I don't have enough time off," Jack said.

Thank God for the little things.

"And Gina doesn't think the kids are old enough."

"They could fly down with Gina and wait for you."

"We make them wear life jackets all the time."

"Even while they sleep?" Paul asked ready to disbelieve his answer.

"We've only slept anchored to the dock."

Paul faced his bigger, square shouldered, son-in-law. God, make me twenty years younger for five minutes so I can beat some sense into this fool. No, just give me two minutes. I could do it in two minutes.

"Daddy, Daddy." Gina came running out the back door. "There was a news alert on TV about a meteor falling. The whole country is put on alert. The National Guard's been called up."

Helen hurried after her, a tissue to her wet eyes. "Then the TV went off the air.

"Off the air?" Paul faced to Helen. "The meteors I saw."

"Yes," Helen said grudgingly. "You were right again."

"What about the Emergency Broadcasting System?" Jack said.

"Can't find it," Gina said, her voice shook a little, fear starting to show on her face.

"They said the meteor might've caused a disease or a virus that has turned some people into monsters. The people who turned into monsters, zombies are attacking and killing and eating the people who didn't turn into monsters."

"Zombies?" Bob said as if this was not happening.

"Is this a joke?" Jack said.

Gina stared at him, like she wanted to kill him. "This is no joke."

Abruptly the house lights blinked and went off.

"It's all right," Jack said. "We have candles. We'll wait inside until they make an announcement."

Suddenly, their neighbor Steve Hayes pushed his way through the hedge. He was six foot eight, had played basketball at Seton Hall, and shaved his black head. His green t-shirt with Jets across the front in large white letters was torn. His skin was gray and his eyes white and his lips black. He shuffled stiff legged like his joints were not working properly.

"Hey, Steve," Jack said. "What's up?"

Gina cried out and Steve veered toward her with his bloody hands stretched out toward her.

"That's what people turn into," Helen said, her eyes wide with fear. "They showed a picture on TV."

Paul hurried in front of his daughter. Jack gave Paul a look like he was overreacting; this was just part of the joke, that's all.

"Stay back," Paul warned, and Steve reached out and grabbed him. Paul tried to shove him back, but Steve had grabbed him and wouldn't let go.

"Steve, stop fooling around," Jack said, his face confused, half expecting Steve to let go and start laughing like he had done last Halloween.

Steve started hissing and trying to bite Paul. Paul struggled to keep him away from biting him.

"JACK," Gina said, her voice rising, starting to sound frantic. "Do something."

"Like?"

"Stop him."

"He looks just like they showed on TV," Helen said, Jack looked at his mother-in-law and saw the terror on her face.

"Steve, stop it," Jack said, fearing how this 'sick joke' would haunt his relationship with his in-laws for years to come. He stepped forward and grabbed his friend and neighbor Steve and tried to pull him off his father-in-law, but Steve wouldn't let go. He finally yanked him away and then Steve turned and came at him, trying to grab him and bite him.

"Steve, stop it." Jack shoved him back, but Steve hissed and came at him again and Jack shoved him back again. Steve came at him again and Jack said, "Steve, stop fooling around," and pushed him way back. And still Steve came at him. Finally Jack punched him in the face. Steve backed up a step and raised his hands and came at him again.

"Jack, he's a zombie," Helen said.

Jack glanced at her, trying to be nice and humor her.

"Stop it," Jack yelled, but Steve wasn't listening to him.

Just then a shovel flashed into view. The shovel hit Steve's right arm and sliced his hand off. Jack looked at Steve's hand on the ground and it flashed through his mind lawsuits, charges being brought and his reputation ruined. "Oh my God, Steve, I'm sorry."

However, Steve barely looked one at his black-blooded stump before going back after Paul holding the shovel. But he didn't go after Paul wild and crazy and angry like a person might; he still reached for him like he was on drugs.

Paul kept on pushing what had been Steve back with the blade of the shovel, but zombie Steve kept on hissing and trying to reach Paul's face.

"Look at his severed hand," Helen said and Steve looked. "It's dripping black blood like they said on TV."

Jack stepped up to stop Steve and Steve reached for him. Taken by surprise Jack tripped and went down and Steve lunged on top of him and tried to bite him. Jack was barely holding his own when Gina came into view and hit Steve with a rake. The force of her blow knocked the zombie off Jack and Jack hurried to his feet.

Jack looked at the rake sticking in Steve's back and said, "That's going to be one hell of a lawsuit."

Steve struggled to get on his feet.

"Hey, old buddy," Jack said to Steve. "We can talk this out, can't we?"

Again Steve tried to bite Jack until Paul stepped in and smacked Steve in the head with the shovel. Steve went down and Paul hit his head with the shovel again and again like he was whacking a rat.

"You still don't seem to get it," Paul said as he whacked

the zombie with each word. "This thing is no longer your neighbor." He hit him again.

Jack pulled Paul away afraid he would have a heart attack. Jezz, the shit couldn't get much worse. Steve would sue him over a practical joke gone bad and his father-in-law would die of a heart attack and somehow everyone would blame him.

"Since when did your neighbor bleed black blood?" Helen said. Jack looked at the zombie on the ground, at the puddle of thick blackish blood around him.

Paul smashed the zombie in the head with the shovel one more time and the zombie lay still.

Jack looked down at Steve. "What about my tools he borrowed?"

Gina shook her head.

Paul pointed at the boat. "How long it take you to get that thing going?"

"It's ready now."

"Supplies?"

"Stocked with rations for two days."

"Get the kids."

"Dad," Jack said, "it can't be that bad and I really don't think we should. . ."

"He's right," Gina said. "Tomorrow could be a lot worse. Or tomorrow we could be out on the ocean, where nothing can get to us."

Jack looked at his father-in-law, then down at his dead neighbor - if he left now the police might not blame him for Steve's death – and then at his boat. "Sure, why not?"

Paul regarded his son-in-law. He doesn't really understand, just wants to show off his goddamn boat.

Helen said, "They read a list of cities under attack."

"How close?" Paul said.

Helen wrung her hands together as if trying to squeeze out the fear. "Don't remember all of them. New York, Chicago, Dallas, Atlanta, Los Angeles."

"New York?"

"They showed this poison cloud sweeping over the

city." Helen turned to Paul. "You were right."

"Let's go." Paul hurried to the kitchen door. "Extra clothes for everyone in a pillow case."

Helen pulled Gina by the hand. Gina looked scared, everything was moving too fast like an out of control the merry-go-round and she wanted off.

Paul turned to Jack. "You have containers of water?"

"Water's gotten so crummy. I get purified water."

Does he have to brag about everything? "Where?"

Jack hurried into the kitchen, and opened the louvered pantry doors. He proudly motioned to the water cooler and an extra five gallon jug on the floor.

"Bought the cooler at Sam's Wholesale Club," Jack told him. "Filled the jugs myself at the supermarket."

God, what a long-winded fool, no wonder he's a good salesman.

"Take 'em both," Paul said.

Jack lifted the plastic water container off the cooler. Paul grabbed a blue plastic Rubber Maid laundry basket and dropped it on the floor by the kitchen cabinets and started tossing in canned goods. He glanced at Jack. "What are you staring at? Get that boat ready to go. They'll be here any minute."

"Who?"

"The zombies, God Dammit. More infected people like your good buddy Steve."

Jack glanced across the lawn at Steve lying on the grass. Fear finally gripped Jack's blue eyes. Paul thought he'd have to hit him to get him moving, but just then Jack took hold of the neck of a jug in each hand and lugged them out the door.

Paul heard the kids waking upstairs and asking questions as he continued dropping supplies in the basket. There were mumbled replies and dresser doors opening.

Gina came down the stairs with towheaded Richie and Joey. Each boy had a sleeping bag under his arm. Richie held a Mutant Ninja Turtle and Joey a Batman.

"Boy oh boy, Gramps," Richie said. "We're going

camping on the water."

Paul smoothed his grandson's hair. What will happen? Can they live in tomorrow's world?

Gina herded the boys out the door.

Paul filled up the laundry basket to overflowing and pulled it close to the door.

Helen rushed by with little Maria sound asleep in her arms. Gina raced through the kitchen and up the stairs.

"Hurry," Paul said.

Paul found a mesh sack hanging on a nail in the pantry and starting tossing supplies in it. Powered milk. Ivory dishwashing liquid. Pancake mix. Glad garbage bags.

Helen came back and grabbed extra Duracell flashlight batteries off the shelf and dumped them in the laundry basket. She groaned as she lifted it.

"That's too heavy for you," Paul said. "You'll hurt yourself. Don't need you hurt."

"Stop telling me what to do. You just hurry yourself."

He watched her stagger out the back door. The screen door slammed shut.

He felt a little shock of stabbing pain in his chest and paused. He stood still and breathed deeply. He gave a little cough. Nothing pained him. He breathed deep.

Gina struggled down the stairs with several stuffed pillow cases and his and Helen's smaller suitcases. "You'll need clothes too."

Paul grunted as he followed her out the door struggling under the weight of the filled sack. The dock seemed half a mile away now that he was lugging stuff. The draw string on the sack cut into his hands. He felt his heart beating dangerously hard.

Jack clambered out of the boat to help him. He grabbed the plastic clothes basket and easily carried it to the boat.

Paul was panting. His heart thumped painfully in his chest and he felt a constriction down his left arm. Not now. God, not now. He reached into his pants pockets for his pills. Opened the little plastic bottle-- only a few left.

He'd forgotten to bring the refill, left it on the dresser in Orlando. No time now as he put a pill under his tongue.

He turned away. The pain had subsided and he breathed easier. The sky clear, the moon was rising in the east. He heard Helen asking the boys where to put things to keep them occupied.

"I've got emergency stuff," Jack said.

Paul mumbled, "Hurry," as he sat down in a white plastic chair on the dock. He looked around the backyard, didn't see the neighbor. "Where's Mr. Hayes?"

Jack hooked his thumb at the canal. Paul glimpsed a body floating away in the dark waves and wanted to say, stop wasting time.

"Fishing poles, hooks, guns?" Paul said. "You got any of that on the boat?"

"Oh shit." Jack raced to the house.

"Where's he going?" Gina asked.

"Forget his ass if it wasn't attached."

"Dad," Gina said, "Why do we have to bring guns? You know how I feel about guns. We aren't going to fight the Russians or anything."

Paul looked at his daughter, sometimes she was so thick. It was from Helen's side of the family.

"We're not the Swiss Family Robinson." Gina's face caught between a smile and a cry. "The government will have this thing cleared up by tomorrow. You know they will. You do, don't you?"

"When did you start depending on the government to do everything for you? You need to do things for yourself, you can't wait for the government to baby-sit you."

"Dad, come on, get real."

"We don't know what's going to happen tomorrow," Paul told her as gently as he could. "We might have to shoot birds to eat them."

Her look said she still didn't believe him like he was secretly planning to rob a Seven-Eleven or something.

"I'll get the front lines." Gina made her way to the front of the boat.

Jack stumbled out of the garage with a duffel bag on his back, a large bucket cooler in his left hand and two five gallon pails in his right. One of the white plastic buckets had fishing poles and fishing gear. When Jack dumped them on the deck, Paul saw a cast-net in the other.

"Bait, rifles, fishing gear," Jack said.

"You got weapons?"

Jack stared at him like he was the last person he expected to hear that from. He glanced at the front of the boat; Gina's back was to them. He lowered his voice so Gina would not hear, "A four-ten shotgun and a twenty-two rifle. I was going to use them for target practice on the ocean."

"Where?"

Jack opened the old green duffel bag so Paul could see the stocks on the shotgun and rifle.

Paul pulled out the twenty-two. He'd never fired a gun. Knew next to nothing about them. "How many bullets?"

Jack said. "A box for each."

"How many in a box?"

"I don't know. Is it really important?"

"Guess not, no place we can get more tonight."

They were both looking at the rifle when Ricky Garcia, the neighbor on the other side came through the hedge. Ricky was short and thick. He normally had little to do with Jack, but tonight he looked so scared he didn't know what he was doing.

"Ricky," Jack said.

"Stop where you are," Paul said.

Ricky looked at them, but he was too scared. He kept coming.

"Stop," Paul said and aimed the rifle.

"Dad, don't," Jack said. The only time he'd ever called him dad.

Paul aimed and Jack pulled the rifle barrel down. The twenty-two Ruger fired, a small popping sound, and Ricky went down.

They rushed over to him.

"Is he a zombie?" Jack asked, looking at Ricky lying on his back on his nice green lawn.

"Why'd you pull the rifle?" Paul said. "Don't you keep the safety on?"

"I've never used it," Jack said. "I don't know how to use the safety."

"Is he dead?" Paul said. "Up close he doesn't look like a zombie."

"Give me that." Jack grabbed the rifle away from Paul. "You shouldn't have shot him."

"He was a zombie."

"No, he wasn't."

While they were arguing Ricky sat up. Ricky may not have been a zombie before, but he sure was one now. He reached for them.

Paul noticed him and jumped back.

Ricky lips were turning black. Blackish blood oozed from the wound in his side. His eyes had turned white.

Jack looked and jerked back and fired the .22 caliber rifle at point blank range. The bullet hit Ricky in the head and he fell back onto the lawn.

"You killed him," Paul said.

"I didn't mean to," Jack said. "You made me."

Paul looked at his son-in-law and shook his head.

"Guys," Gina called.

Paul rushed to the dock. "Jack just killed your neighbor. You keep on killing neighbors like this and you won't have any left"

Jack hurried to the dock. "I didn't mean to."

"Who?" Gina said.

"Ricky Garcia."

Gina shook head. "That little greaseball kept coming on to me."

"He did?" Jack said. "Why didn't you say anything?"

"I tried to tell you."

"That's no reason to kill him," Paul said.

"Who shot him?" Gina said.

"I did," Paul admitted, "but he wasn't dead and he wasn't a zombie then."

"But he became a zombie," Jack said. "That's when I shot him."

"Good," Gina said.

"You shot him by accident," Paul said. "You didn't mean to kill a zombie. I don't even think you knew for sure he was a zombie when you shot him."

"Dead is dead," Jack said like all of a sudden he was a Wild West gunfighter.

"Guys," Gina said and pointed.

Across the lawn Ricky had gotten to his feet and was shuffling toward them.

"Some shot," Paul said.

"I'm casting off the bow line," Gina called.

Jack jumped on board and helped Paul climb on.

Jack untied the stern lines and pressed a small button on the console. A motor puttered to life and the sailboat slowly motored away from the dock and into the channel. Ricky came down to the dock and stared at them.

"Lights?" Paul motioned at the lights.

"Running lights," Jack explained.

"Turn them off."

"Against the law. We're not suppose to."

"You don't know what we're dealing with," Paul said as calmly as he could, holding his anger back before he said something stupid. It was just like his thickheaded daughter to marry someone just as thick. It wasn't the stubbornness he minded. If only Jack was smarter, but for all his possessions, he just wasn't that bright. Dammit, he was just like Gina.

From out of a neighbor's house people stumbled out onto their back yard.

"Just going sailing," Jack called and Paul lunged at him and tried to put his hand over Jack's mouth.

"Stop it. We've known them for years."

Just then one of the neighbors fell into the water. The others shuffled down onto the neighbor's dock. In the solar dock light they could see the stiff legged way they walked, their white eyes open very wide, their hands stretched out in front of them. One of them stumbled and fell into a small rowboat tied to the dock.

"That was Dickey," Jack's voice trailed off.

"Lights," Paul reminded him.

Jack flipped a switch and the lights went off.

It was dark on the water. Small waves lapped against the side of the boat as the sailboat motored down the channel in the moonlight. From the narrow channel Jack steered the boat past the buoys, Gina stood on the bow shining a flashlight on them. Soon they were in the open bay, and the houses and the shore dropped behind them. As they moved into Great South Bay they could see more of the sky to the west and north.

"No glow from the land," Jack said. "No lights from the houses, from Robert Moses Causeway."

"Huh," Paul grunted.

Gina gave her father a look. Was he alright?

They moved into the bay and the wind picked up. Now they could smell the death and destruction behind them.

Gina held her nose. "Rotten eggs and ammonia."

"What's that awful smell?" Richie asked from below deck.

"The dump," Helen said. "We're going past a garage dump."

"No garage dumps here, Grandma."

"Well, that sure smells like a dump to me," Helen said, "so we must be going past one."

Jack turned off the motor and gave Paul the wheel. Jack and Gina hoisted the jib and the foresail and the mainsail. Paul felt the boat come alive. He'd never felt anything like that before. It was strange and exhilarating. He could see himself sailing off to foreign lands. Captain Paul and ... Jack came back and grabbed the wheel. Paul didn't want to let go. He wanted to hold it, feel the boat move to his touch.

"Now where?" Jack said.

Paul said, "Sail to open water."

"How far out?"

"So they can't smell us."

"You think it's that bad?"

He pointed back at Long Island. It was almost as dark as when the first settlers landed hundreds of year ago. They could see flashes of light and echoes booming across the water -- "Gunfire," Jack said -- and then it was still and dark.

*****

Chapter 24 - Fort Fear

Ron and Pat had barricaded the windows. They had wedged the queen sized mattress over the bedroom window, where the fire escape was, and then the box springs over the window in his office. They upended the dining room table in front of the living room window and wedged the sofa to hold it in place. He turned off the window air conditioner units and duct taped towels over them to prevent the green-gray fog, the dust, whatever it was from getting inside the apartment. They pushed and carried the brown leather La-z-boy recliner in front of the front door. The door was steel and the hinges reinforced so they didn't think it would be a problem.

"What about the wall," Pat said and Ron looked at her. "I mean if they can't get in the door, won't they try the wall next to it?"

"No, why would they?" He said it in such a way as if he knew what he was talking about.

Pat got out incense candles she had bought at a *Partylike* party and he wished she hadn't made him get rid of the M9 Beretta he had wanted to keep in the apartment for protection. The thought bothered him and he changed into his jeans. He felt kind of stupid defending his apartment in dress pants. He took the hand-size portable shortwave radio from the backpack and put it on the coffee table and tried to find a station.

Pat pressed the TV remote and the cable box displayed the number for each channel but the TV screen remained black. "No channels."

Ron grunted.

"What happened to the Emergency Broadcasting S--"

"Maybe the cloud landed on the cables company's dish."

"Why should that interfere with reception?" she asked.

"Don't know." When he looked up her eyes were filled with panic. "Maybe whatever it was in that fog got into the electric circuits."

"Or the people who are supposed to monitor it?"

"Yes, maybe."

"The water supply might run out or get contaminated," she said.

He agreed and shook his head.

She started filling everything she could with tap water. Pots, pans, washed out old bottles from the recycle bin.

Suddenly a voice blared over the radio.

***

This is the Emergency Broadcasting System. We have interrupted regular programming to bring you this special bulletin. A meteor carrying dangerous biological material fell to earth. Tiny parts of the meteor have broken off and released a gray-green dust. At this time the powder is believed to be a virus that has infected a large percent of the population. According to the CDC, those infected have lost all higher brain functions and have become carnivorous flesh-eaters. One bite or scratch from one of these 'zombies' infects the victim and turns him into a zombie. Hordes of zombies

are attacking major population areas. ... "
Iil--Interference--
The U. N. Security Council issued the
following statement: The epidemic is
worldwide. An emergency meeting of the
Security Council has been called to
formulate a plan of operation.

*** *

"As soon as they stop hiding," Ron said.

*** *

Stay tuned for further instructions.
In the meantime we will broadcast the news.
All communication has been lost with Japan,
Australia and India. There are reports from
China that their army had been compromised
and the Chinese leaders have gone into
hiding. England, France, Spain, Germany and
Russia have declared national emergencies.
"We have received reports that Rome is
burning. The streets of Greece are filled with
zombies. No one is left alive in Cairo,
Baghdad, Tehran, Tripoli or Tel Aviv.
The Russian army fought the zombies
until they ran out of ammunition. Moscow
has been evacuated. Toronto, Montreal and
Rio de Janeiro are burning. Fires
are raging out of control in Lisbon,
Havana, Mexico City and across Africa.
Johannesburg is under martial law.
The President's motorcade was attacked
.. on its way to Camp David.
The President hasn't been heard from since.
No word on the Vice President."

*** *

"Probably hiding under his bed," Ron said.
"I don't blame him," Pat said.

*** *

"All National Guard units have been

called up. The Army reports heavy
casualties. The Air Force has been
grounded. The Navy has tried to position
its ships at sea away from the virus fog.
We urge you to listen carefully to the
following instructions.
 The announcer paused, his voice trembling.
Stay indoors. The greenish powder from the
meteor that looks like dust are really microbes
that swarm together resembling fog.
Once the fog touches someone, the microbes
invade the blood system, go to the brain and
destroy the host and take over.
Most people become infected immediately.
At the present there is no antidote.
We will notify you when the fog has dispersed.
If you are attacked, the only way to
kill an infected person is with a blow to the
head. Blows to the body do not stop them.
Infected blood changes to green-black and
coagulates and immediately seals all superficial
*wounds. Only critical injuries stop them an*d--

***

A blast of static and the radio went dead.

"What happened?" Pat asked.

Ron shook his head.

The apartment's lights blinked and went out. A nightlight/emergency light in a plug next to the kitchen counter cast muted light across the apartment.

Ron rushed to the window. He pushed the mattress aside and looked out. "The city's dark."

"Dark?" Pat said as if that was the most terrifying thing in the world; the empire city, the metropolis of the world without lights. "The whole city?"

They had seen brown outs. With Con-Ed living in New York was sometimes an adventure, but this was something else.

Pat hurried to the window and stood beside Ron.

Across the street was another apartment building and next to it another and another and they were all dark. All the buildings in all directions, all the streetlights, and all the city lights were out as far as they could see. It was darker than the darkest jungle and because it was unexpected it seemed darker and blacker. Here and there a flashlight beam lit up a window, shined into the night. Some people put a candle in their window. It seemed poetic that in the Big Apple a small candle here or there signified life and hope.

"I should get a candle," Pat said.

"No," Ron said and grabbed her arm.

"Why?"

He pointed at a flashlight beam shining on the street. "It lets them know there's food where that candle is."

"What?" she said, thinking he was mistaken.

"Look," he told her.

She craned her head and looked down at the street. The nightlife in New York now consisted of zombies wandering up and down the streets. But when a flashlight shined, they turned and like a slow moving pack of wild animals migrated to the lights. Even from their apartment on the 17th floor they could hear windows and glass doors breaking, shots being fired, screams echoing up and down the street.

Ron quickly pulled the mattress back in place.

"Are they in the building?" Pat said.

"They may not have had to break in," Ron said.

"Oh," Pat said, then thought about it and said, "OH."

He led her back to the kitchen counter. She fumbled him the box of matches. He took a wooden match out and struck it on the side of the box. The small flamed wavered in his shaking hand. He lit the candles on the counter. She took a lit candle and the matches and lit two candles on the TV.

"How romantic," he said. "Don't light too many, we don't know how long we'll need them.

She smiled nervously at him and blew out a match and

then they heard something scratching on the door. He swung his flashlight around. The scratching went over the whole door, rattled the doorknob and continued up the doorjamb. The scraping moved around and around the door.

"They're looking for a way in," he whispered.

"They're here already?" she said.

"The fog infected them, maybe one of our neighbors. Who knows how many are infected."

"C--can they get in?"

"God, I--I hope not," he said, his voice wavering.

*****

Chapter 25 - Flying Pigs

Luka guided the black limo through the dark streets. It didn't look like New York. Never was the city this still, this dead. It was even deader than some of the war ravaged cities they'd been in. It sort of reminded him of Chernobyl without the radiation poison. Dead bodies littered many of the streets. Once he ran over a monster on a purpose. At one street people waved at him from an apartment complex and he kept going, sometimes having to drive on the sidewalk. Once he had to put the Lincoln's heavy bumper against a wrecked black Mustang and push the old Ford out of the way.

After hours of navigating the horrors, they viewed the Eighth Wonder of the world, the Brooklyn Bridge. Two brick and cement towers, almost two miles across, once called a work of art. He didn't have to be a genius to know they were never going to cross it.

The ribbon of asphalt was blocked with wrecked vehicles. Monsters were everywhere. Uninfected men and women and children had climbed up the suspension cables to the towers. There was no more room for anyone else on the towers. Other people crowded up on the cable close to the towers. Many people sat on the curved suspension cables: one on each side, two in the middle. Some people had climbed down onto the girders under the deck and were hiding in the dark down there.

The zombies tried to get to those up on the towers and suspension cables. Theyclimbed up the thick suspension cables at the bridge ends or in the middle of the bridge and tried to walk or crawl up to the people. The people on the bridge kicked or knocked them down. The zombies fell into the water or smacked down on the bridge. Other zombies waited on the bridge for people or zombies to fall. They shuffled about as they looked upward and moaned as if from hunger. Some zombies tried to shinny up the suspender cables, almost all of them were unsuccessful.

The people on the superstructure would knock a zombie down; it would fall to the pavement or to the river and another zombie would try to climb up to get them. Hundreds of people were on the towers and cables. The bridge roadway and walkway were packed wall to wall with zombies. Once in a while someone slipped off the suspension cables, probably passed out from exhaustion, and fell to the roadway and the zombies would tear the person to shreds. Every so often someone trying to kick or bat a zombie off the suspension cable was grabbed by the zombie and both fell to the roadway. Each fall, each death excited the zombies and more would climb the suspension cables and try to climb up to the tower.

"Only matter of time, before they get them."

"Too many monsters," Alexei grumbled, "but maybe they make it. What odds you give?"

"None." Luka shook his head.

Frankie trembled and laughed strangely. He whispered, "We should put them out of misery."

"Screw that," Alexei said. "Not have enough bullets and it attract monsters to us."

"Why we put them out of misery?" Luka said as he looked in the mirror at Frankie. "They dumb, they pay for it. Stupid gun laws. Only police have guns. Where police now? I should not have gotten fine."

"Luka, not now," Alexei said. "Try Manhattan Bridge."

"Stupid." Luka pulled away slowly.

"You drive good with lights out," Alexei said. "Cop try give you ticket for driving with lights off, I handle him."

"With the tinted windows I not see behind or sides, but front okay. And zombies not see us. Give me ticket now, cop. Where are you?"

"Lower side windows," Alexei said.

"Don't!" Frankie said his voice a little too high and Alexei looked at him like he was seeing what he always suspected and waved to Luka to do as he said. The side windows in the rear rolled down. There was no longer any greenish-gray dust in the air, but the air didn't smell fresh. There was a stench that made Frankie sick.

"Smell like dump," Frankie said.

"Nyet, smell like death, like war zone." Alexei looked at Luka. "Remember?"

Luka looked in the rearview mirror and nodded. Boss was something. Making jokes and planning how to escape when most men would be crumbling, cowering on the ground. Of course Luka remembered, but he saw Frankie shaking he was so scared.

Luka headed up a side street, ignoring one way signs, zombies and bodies in the road.

"Look, Boss." Luka pointed then put his fingers on the center console ready to make the windows on the right side of the car go up.

On the building was a billboard advertising the Great New York Balloon Fair. Across the building were painted pictures of colorful balloons.

"Look at balloon that look like flying pig."

In the middle of the painting of a balloon on the side of the building a man was waving from a small window. He threw a rope made of sheets out the window -- oddly the pink sheets resembled the balloon as if the balloon was coming unraveled -- the man crawled out the window and started lowering himself. He appeared to be crawling down the side of the balloon. The makeshift rope didn't go all the way to the ground. When the man got below the balloon basket he stood out like a human spider on the side of the building. His movement attracted zombies to the barren ground below him. They stood there shuffling side to side, doing a slow dance.

"What?" Luka said. "Are we supposed to go over and risk our lives and kill zombies for him?"

"Where percentage in that?" Alexei said. "We fire one gun and attract ten monsters for every one we kill."

"Buried alive, trying save one fool," Luka said.

"Maybe we should do something," Frankie said.

"Okay, you do something," Alexei said.

Frankie reached over and grabbed the door handle and froze. His right hand on the door handle trembled. He looked back at Alexei wanting him to stop him. He realized that his talking with the window open had attracted a zombie and he pushed the button to roll up the window. At first the button wouldn't work and he started jabbing it many times to get the window to close. Then he saw Luka smiling at him. Luka had stopped the window from closing by pressing a button on the front console. Luka pressed a button to close the window.

When the tinted window closed, the zombie turned away.

"We doing something," Luka said looking at the guy waving at them, and attracting more and more zombies to the lot below him. "We stay alive to fight another day."

Suddenly the guy slipped and fell; he crashed down on several zombies. He struggled to get up and made it to his feet and started across the barren lot when the zombies buried him. Zombies that had not been attracted to the man now joined the feeding frenzy and others came out of the shadows. For a few seconds the man's screams echoed in the quiet night.

From both ends of the street and out of small alleys the

zombies came. Some walked, most shuffled, a few came slightly faster, as if they had very recently become infected; in a short time a few became many, then many became a mob.

"Go," Alexei said. "Before we next on menu."

Luka drove through congested streets. He pulled over to where they could see the Manhattan Bridge. No traffic moved on the bridge. No cars. Thousands of zombies shuffling down the street.

The car was very quiet. Alexei opened the sunroof, any sound including the sound of the roof opening loud in the quiet night. He stood up and looked around. He put night vision binoculars to use and saw zombies in the shadows everywhere. Frankie stood up next to him, he could feel Frankie shaking he was so scared.

"What are we going to do?" Frankie said his voice quivering with fear.

"Williamsburg Bridge," Alexei said his voice faraway as if he was considering a chess move and did not want to be bothered with small talk.

"Prolly the same," Luka said.

"Try it," Alexei said tiredly. "Turn on the police radio. Try all bands. Maybe there way out."

"Been on automatic scan since Brooklyn Bridge." Luka pointed at the earplug in his left ear. "It'd stop on any channel that had something."

"Nothing?" Alexei said.

Luka shook his head.

"The radio?" Frankie asked.

Luka pulled the earplug out of his left ear. "Something on public channel. Said was national emergency. President dead. Can't find Vice President."

"Jesus Christ!" Frankie said.

"Like this everywhere: Europe, Asia, South American, Africa, Russia," Luka said.

"What about army?" Alexei asked.

"Haven't heard anything. No one here; that tell us something."

Frankie plopped down in the seat. "They not coming. No one come."

"No one in charge." Alexei sat down and closed the sunroof.

Frankie looked at Alexei. The boss was staring straight ahead, his jaw set, his dark eyes staring straight ahead at nothing. "What you think, boss?"

"Country in chaos. Politicians hiding. Country need someone to take charge." Alexei stared ahead, a thought forming in the distance darkness. "When we come out of this, when zombies eat themselves out of food, whoever in charge be hero, have anything he wants. Feds no press charges. People respect someone who takes charge. "

"What about politicians?" Frankie said.

"Who cares? They put us here. Where are they? People ask what you do when things went bad, and when they say, they hiding, they not here, they not helping, people not respect them."

"Those fanatical groups?"

"Not worry about fools who kill their own."

"Now you talking," Luka said. "Get them 'fore they get us." He pulled over to where they could see the Williamsburg Bridge. "Same."

They watched someone trying to run across. He was carrying a flashlight. He ran around zombies and slugged them when he couldn't run past them.

"Come on," Alexei cheered. He stood in the open sunroof to watch. "Come on, run you fool."

The guy made it partway across, but his progress had attracted many zombies and his forward passage was blocked by a horde of zombies.

They saw flashes and heard the echo of gunfire as he tried to shoot his way across. Shooting zombies cleared a path, but attracted many more. He made it a little further and then there were too many of them and he was swarmed over.

Alexei sat down heavily.

"Too many vehicles in way for car," Luka said.

"We could go together," Frankie said. "Cover each other's back."

"What then?" Alexei said. "When we get across. What about monsters on other side?"

Frankie shook his head, his eyes wide open.

"Get going," Alexei said.

"Look!" Luka pointed.

A zombie turned the corner and shuffled toward them. Then another and another. Soon there were a dozen of them coming toward them.

"There are too many of them," Frankie said his voice high like he was about to scream.

Alexei slapped him across the face. Frankie was stunned. A red welt on his face.

Alexei said, "Go to warehouse in Soho. Maybe something we can do."

Luka stepped on the gas and ran down some zombies as he turned the corner. A few banged on the fenders. One bounced on the hood and rolled off.

"With President dead and Vice President hiding," Frankie said, "who running country?"

"Me," Alexei announced. "Everyone's disorganized. Get men behind us and we take over. Like Stalin did."

"There were zombies back then?" Frankie said.

Alexei looked him. Frankie's stupidity never failed to amaze him. "You go school?"

"Moscow and here," Frankie said. "Not a whole lot."

"For moment, you have me worried." Alexei motioned Luka to drive as he sat back and stared out the window.

*****

Chapter 26 - Action Hero

The apartment opened and Kenny stepped outside wearing roller-blades, soccer knee pads, football shoulder pads, a football helmet, and holding a hockey stick. On his belt was an 'L' shaped Boy Scout led flashlight which he switched on. The new batteries lit up the dark hall.

He took a few steps, the roller-blades very loud in the quiet hall. All of a sudden a door up the hall opened and drunken Mrs. Brown staggered outside. Her old bulldog Brownie raced out the door glad to be out of the apartment. The heavy dog lumbered to the elevator, its nails clicking on the tie floor.

Mrs. Brown didn't look like Mrs. Brown any more. She looked like one of those zombies. Her whitish eyes turned to Kenny and her hands reached out and she shuffled toward him.

"Mrs. Brown, stay back," Kenny warned.

She kept on coming. Her black lips pulled back from her teeth and she hissed at him.

Kenny skated up the hall. When he came close and she reached for him, he swatted her legs with the hockey stick, a large gash opened and black blood oozed out and she fell down. Shocked, Kenny skidded to a stop. Instead of crying out, she hissed and crawled after him.

Kenny opened the stairwell door. "Come on, Brownie." The bulldog came into the stairwell with him and Kenny closed the door. Because of the skates Kenny had to go down the stairs sideways, his mother always yelled at him not to go down the stairs in his skates. "Take off your skates or you'll fall and get hurt." Kenny didn't have time to take off his skates. He hurried down the stairs as best he could.

His green Scout flashlight lit the way down the fire stairs. On the first floor short, fat Mr. Serra, the super, was wandering around, his hairy arms and chest stuck out of a dirty white t-shirt. He wore his tool belt over faded white boxers. His pony tailed black hair was dripping with sweat. He held a claw hammer in his hand, black goop dripped from the head of the hammer. He was walking back and forth in front of the front door like he was standing guard.

"What's going on?" he said.

"I don't know," Kenny said.

"I had to kill Mrs. Rothberg," he said holding up the hammer to show him. Mr. Serra shook his head. "She tried to bite me." He showed Kenny the bloody wound on his arm to prove his point. "TV said it has something to do with a meteor."

Kenny looked past him at the empty street. Serra was blocking the front door.

"Excuse me, I have to go."

"Where you going at this hour?"

"To get my mom."

Short, fat Carlos Serra looked him over then turned and looked out the door debating whether it was safe for a kid to be out on a night light this. "Can't let you go."

"You got to. My mom needs me."

"You can stay with me and Mrs. Serra, until your mom gets back." Mr. Serra motioned at his apartment.

Kenny looked down the hall and saw the door to the super's apartment door was open.

"Come on," Mr. Serra said, holding his hands out, the hammer in his right hand, like he was herding a pet down the hall. Kenny skated backwards just out of his reach.

"You have to let me go."

"Too dangerous for a kid on a nightmare like this." He realized what he'd said and grinned as though he was starting to lose it.

Kenny skated backward until he saw Mrs. Serra on the floor inside the superintendent's apartment. Her head was lying in a puddle of green-black blood like it had been bashed in. The smell from the apartment was terrible.

Kenny tried to skate around Mr. Serra, but the super backed him into a corner. Mr. Serra's wound had turned black and black veins spread out from the injury.

Brownie sat by the front door and barked.

"What are you doing with Mrs. Brown's dog?"

"She's, you know, one of them."

"Where is she?" he asked like he was concerned if she had made a mess in the hall he would have to clean up.

Just then they heard something hard thumping down the stairs.

"She's coming down the stairs, right now."

Mr. Serra stepped to the stairwell doorway and opened it. Something was thumping slowly down the stairs. While Serra was distracted Kenny tried to skate around him, but Serra suddenly turned to him and grinned like he was wise to that trick. Then he started to shake like he was shivering. His lips curled back as he moaned. Just as suddenly as he started shaking and moaning, he stopped; now Kenny saw his eyes roll upward so only the white could be seen.

"Oh my God," Mr. Serra cried out.

Before Serra did anything or anything else happened Kenny tried to skate around him. Serra raised his meaty arm with the hammer to stop him and Kenny ducked down and headed for the front door. Serra turned after Kenny and started shuffling toward him. Brownie barked at Serra and Serra stared at the old dog. Kenny opened the front door and went down the steps. Brownie lumbered alongside.

No sooner had he made it down the steps then what was left of Fran Weezer came at him. Brownie barked at her, but she ignored him and shuffled toward Kenny. Brownie grabbed the hem of her dress and pulled, knocking the babysitter down. She hit the ground like a rotten watermelon, stinking, making sounds like she was hollow inside. But as soon as she hit the ground her head came up and she snarled at him.

Just as he'd been taught to hit a puck Kenny smacked

her in the head with the duct tape hardened hockey stick. Like a coconut her head cracked. Black-green goo spattered the sidewalk and splashed on Mr. Serra descending the steps. He reached down and grabbed a handful from his shoe and started eating it.

Kenny skated down the street. There were zombies in the street and Kenny easily skated around them as if they were an obstacle course. Brownie ran at his side, running ahead to bark at and block any zombies that got too close. When a zombie came within range Kenny slashed at it with the blade or smacked it with the bludgeon. As he skated away he left a wake of dead or seriously injured zombies.

"Don't worry, Mommy. I'm coming. I'm coming."

*****

Chapter 27 - Crazy World

Yankee Stadium was quiet. Emergency generators powered the spotlights. A feathery wind blew the pennants and flags on the flagpoles. Scraps of paper littered the green baseball field. Bodies lay in the stands, on the steps and on the field. No cheers, no shouts of protests interrupted the silence. No one was singing, "Take Me Out to the ball game." Everything was quiet. Only zombies were shuffling about the baseball field and in the stands. The smell was atrocious, rotten eggs, ammonia, shit and piss mixed together.

Cathy whispered in Mike's ear. "Wake up. Wake up."
His hand went to his head. "Ow."
"Shssh." Her eyes darted about. It was dark in the aisles now with only the emergency lights on. She could see dark shapes in the dugouts and up on the promenade by the food courts. "They're all around us."
"Give me a minute." Mike rubbed his eyes.

"You've been out for a long time. I have to get home to my little boy."

"My head hurts. Just give me a minute."

"You'll be alright here if you don't move. I can't wait. Kenny's in danger. I can sense it. You stay here until you feel better then catch up."

She turned away from his eyes, unable to look at him. Unable to take the condemnation she felt, certain she was leaving him to his death. It's because of Kenny, she told herself. She had to leave him because of Kenny. She'd stay if it wasn't for her boy.

Each time the zombies had shuffled by, she'd played dead; they'd almost stop until she vomited. The smell of vomit seemed to keep them away. That's when she started shaking Mike. Kenny needs me, she kept telling herself. She'd have to go even if Mike couldn't come.

Like a mouse between cat's paws she got to her feet. She stood up slowly; she had seen that fast, sudden, movements attracted the zombies. If she could move slowly and not attract any attention, she could get out of here and get home to her son. Trembling she glanced about and saw a zombie looking in her direction and ducked down.

"Wait a minute." Mike reached out to her.

She batted his hand away. "My boy needs me. He really does. Been trying to wake you for over an hour. Can't wait no longer."

Keeping low she crawled to end of the row. Heart pounding, she looked around. The emergency lights were dimming as she watched. Damn, she'd waited too long.

Now Yankee Stadium was almost in complete darkness. Only a few pale emergency lights remained lit. Bodies lay in aisles and under the seats. She had seen the zombies eating people; when a person went down the zombies would eat their limbs, their face and rip out their intestines. And sometimes a person became reanimated and even though they were missing parts they tried to attack other people. It was crazy, the whole world was crazy. What caused it? She didn't care. She only wanted to get out of here and get Kenny and hold him.

Mike moaned something.

"Shssh."

Bent over, she scampered up the steep stairs to the concourse. People had dropped drinks, food, making the walkway slippery, treacherous. She was winded from fear before she reached the concourse. Her breath rasped in her dry throat.

Zombies wandered about as if confused. They paid no attention to her. At first she shuffled like she was one of them, trying to not make noise, until she couldn't stop herself and started running. She trotted past empty hot dog stands and dark bathroom doors. Looked at the sign, the icon of a woman. Had to go real bad, but wouldn't step into one of those rooms now, no way.

It was very dark, but she hurried toward where the exit ramp should be. There were signs, but in the darkness and shadows she couldn't read them. Along the concourse she heard hissing sounds. A woman lying on the ground looked like she had been trampled. The woman reached up and she jumped away from her.

The woman reached her hand up as if to get help. No, she shook her head and backed up. As she backed up the woman dragged herself forward, and when she did she saw the woman had no legs. She gasped. Then the woman dragged herself into a ray of moonlight and she saw the woman's eyes were whitish, her lips were black, and ugly wounds exposed what was left of her face.

Cathy backed away, trying not to look like she was running. Her heart pounded in her chest. The darkness got deeper, closed in around her. She trembled so violently, she clutched her stomach and didn't move for several moments.

She told herself to keep moving until she found an exit ramp. Now she could see a little better in the moonlight coming through the structural openings. She picked up speed on the incline and stepped around a human skeleton.

She gasped and paused to look down at it. Yes. It was a child.

She took a few backward steps and tripped and tumbled to the ground, skinning her elbow, banging her chin. Blood oozed from her swollen lip. She tried to get up; a hand grabbed her left foot and yanked. She tried to whirl around, couldn't and kicked. The hand dragged her through a ray of moonlight and she saw the size of him and cried out.

He was huge. A zealous Red Sox fan, dark red sweatshirt with Red Sox printed on the front, and his bald head and face painted white like a baseball. There were even baseball stitches drawn on his head in black. His whitish eyes blended in with the baseball, but his mouth was a huge black maw of yellow teeth.

Now that she knew what she was fighting, she kicked and punched, but he was bigger than any wrestler or football player she'd even seen. She could have been hitting a brick wall for all the good it did as it dragged her into the dark shadows by the vending machines.

She had searched for a weapon while Mike was unconscious, everything was plastic now; plastic bottles, plastic cups. It had been hopeless, until she'd found a tiny baseball bat with a ballpoint pen. It was the biggest, most dangerous, thing she could find. As the zombie dragged her to where he could feast on her alone, her purse almost came off. She caught it at the last moment and found the bat pen. She leaned toward the zombie and whacked him in the head with the small bat and it shattered. He didn't even notice. She kicked him in the groin so hard she hurt her ankle; he didn't notice. She savagely kicked him in the side of his knee and finally he went down and let go.

For a moment she couldn't believe her luck and lay there frozen, afraid to move, then she started to slide away. Slowly at first to avoid his attention, then she turned over to crawl faster. She'd just started to crawl away when he reached out with his long arms and grabbed her foot again

She started kicking the hand, then the face, when he

looked at her. He pulled her to him and she savagely
kicked him in the face. Then he ripped her right shoe
away and went to bite her toes off. She still held the
broken remains of the pen and stabbed him in the head. It
was like stabbing a bowling ball and although chunks of
skin and flesh came away it didn't stop him. Closer and
closer his mouth came to biting her, until she swung
wildly and stabbed him in the eye; the pen sank into his
eye like it was going into a rotten tomato.

The zombie froze. Quivered. Black blood oozed from
his mouth and he fell on top of her. It was like a one ton
bear on her. His weight almost crushed her, shards of pain
shot through her leg. She cried out and quickly put her
hand in her mouth lest she attract other zombies.

She lay still for a moment and now she could see them
in the darkness. Hundreds of whitish eyes. They were all
around her. She lay perfectly still, but they were still
coming toward her so she tried to shove the huge body off
her. She couldn't do it, he was too big. Then she started to
move him and he began to roll on her injured foot and
when he did electric jolts of pain shot through her. She
stifled the scream of pain, but her movement had done
something. She heard sounds. She searched on the
ground until she found her purse; in it was her key ring
light. A small led light. She pressed it, the light blazed.
Dozens of eyes stared at the light. She was surrounded by
dozens of zombies and they were coming to her.

She let the light go off and lay perfectly still, but it was
no good. She could hear them coming from everywhere.
How could she get out of there? They were too close, too
many and she was injured. But she had to, she had to, she
had to get to Kenny.

Then she heard a voice, "Cathy. Cathy."

He's coming to rescue me. Thank God, he's coming to
rescue me. Tears ran down her face. "Mike!" she called.
"Mike! Hurry. Please hurry."

He was running down the ramp. His footsteps loud in
the quiet, echoing in the tunnel. The zombies stopped

coming at her and turned to this new sound.

"CATHY!" he called in the darkness.

She wanted to stay quiet, so they would go to the sound and leave her alone, but she couldn't do that to him. He was coming to rescue her. "They hear you," she shouted.

He didn't answer. In the quiet she heard the sound of someone hitting a coconut or a watermelon, a hollow meaty sound. She turned on the led light. Mike Sato was surrounded by zombies and swinging the bat like a baseball player. With every swing at least one zombie went down. Soon the wall of zombies was no more.

He hurried toward the light.

"Turn off the light," he said.

"We won't be able to see."

"What's to see, they're all around us!"

"Swing the bat," she said and he did and hit zombies to his left and right. He hit and hit and hit and they went down, but never stopped coming. Mike must've had some muscle behind that bulk for he knocked many of them back into others and soon he was next to her.

"You alright?" he asked reaching in the darkness for her hand. She took his hand and held it.

"No," she cried. "This thing tried to bite my foot and fell on me and he's big as a bear."

Mike felt around and grabbed the zombie by the dirty sweatshirt. She could see the other zombies shuffling toward them. They didn't have much time.

"You can't lift him. Try to roll him off me."

"You sure?"

"Just do it."

Mike grabbed the zombie's arm and tried to roll him back into the wall.

"Not enough room," she said. "The other way." She saw the wall of zombies shuffling closer. "Hurry."

Mike grabbed the zombie and pulled and rolled him off her. She cried out when the its weight rolled over her foot, but it was off her.

She reached up and Mike grabbed her hand and lifted

her out from behind the vending machine. She put her arm around his shoulder. "Hurry."

Gripping her with one hand and the baseball bat with the other he moved away from the wall, slugging zombies with every step. They made it to the center of the concourse, but it was evident they couldn't make it far like this.

"Stand ran behind me," he said. "Grab my belt."

Normally she would have argued, now she did as she was told. She moved close behind him. With her against his back he dodged left and right down the concourse, sometimes he smacked a zombie or two with the bat to get out of their way. Soon they were out of the area where the zombies were concentrated.

You played football?" she said.

"Never," he panted. "Too short."

"Stop running," she said. "Just walk fast."

He held her hand and together they walked fast. He found a bat on the ground and handed it to her. "Hit them in the head. Head shots only." She clubbed any that came close.

"We're coming, Kenny," she cried. "We're coming."

They made it down the concourse and around the bend and hurried to the exit. They went out the front entrance of Yankee stadium and stopped. In front of them was a sea of monsters lurching, shuffling toward them.

*****

Chapter 28 - Run Ryan Run

Ryan sat on the floor of the subway car staring at Hector in the ray of his flashlight. He'd found new batteries in the backpack. Hector was dead; he'd made sure of that. He choked back a sob. Hector wanted him to go save Mary Anna and he would, but he didn't want to leave him. It was so quiet. He couldn't hear the other passengers, not a sound. Where'd they go? Could he have been sitting here that long? Seemed like only a few minutes, but it was so quiet. Everyone must have gotten off the train, left him here alone.

He glanced at the back door. The glass was black. The tunnel was dark as a mine shaft. He hated small dark places. When he was a kid he would never hide in a closet. Emergency lights glowed on the walls, but were getting dimmer.

He picked up the flash and shined the beam down the car through the glass in the front door into the next car. Nothing. He didn't like it. It was too quiet. He took a last look at Hector and stood up, his knees creaking like old stairs in a haunted house. He shook his head and swept the flashlight beam over Hector.

He grabbed the backpack and walked to the door and shined the beam into the next car. Empty of people, there was debris on the floor: a newspaper, plastic water bottle, a purse, a blue METS baseball cap.

He pulled the door open, tried to be quiet, but it squealed like a rusty wheel. He stood in the open doorway listening. Not a sound. No, that wasn't correct. In the distance he heard an almost inaudible hissing and he smelled rotten eggs. There was no wind, not even a breeze, only darkness and that odd sound and terrible stench. Not even sounds of traffic or people up above on the streets. He crossed to the next car. So used to catching his balance when the train was swaying down the tracks, he bumped the door. The chain made a loud ghostly sound like a door in hell opening.

He walked across the empty car to the next dark car. With the emergency lighting growing fainter he shined the flashlight around. The beam moved across the car, a shaft of light in a haunted house. A woman's purse on the floor. A green Jets cap. A wooden walking stick with a brass handle of a wolf's head.

He looked back at Hector and didn't like leaving him. With the backpack slung over his shoulder he walked through the car to the next door. Listened and again didn't hear anything. No rumble of other trains, no sounds of traffic up above. Quiet on the streets. The police, maybe the army must have everything under control.

Halfway through the car he breathed that bad odor again. The rotten egg smell was very strong here. Must be a bad gas leak. He didn't like it, but maybe subway tunnels always smelled bad when the trains weren't running.

He shined the flash into the next car and froze, stopped breathing. The hair on the back of his head stood on end. His heart skipped then hammered. His skin grew pebbly with chills.

The people were there. They had made it that far and died. A window was smashed. The front door was open.

The people, what was left of them, lay on the floor. Three other people were feeding on the dead, only they looked horribly wrong. They had gray skin, whitish eyes, green-black blood oozed from superficial wounds, and their black lips were pulled back from their teeth. They had open wounds on their faces exposing muscles and blood vessels. They looked like they were dead or should be. What the hell was going on?

A word, a memory came to mind. "Zombies," Hector's voice said in his mind. He hadn't paid much attention. He didn't think Hector was right. What did he know about zombies? Practically nothing. He couldn't remember seeing a movie with a zombie in it. He was not a horror movie fan like Ron and Hector. Unlike Hector, he'd never read a book with a zombie in it.

He slowly opened the door; it made a loud grating sound. The three things turned to him. "Stop that right now," he said. One of them stood up and came toward him. The guy raised his hands like a sleepwalker.

"Stop," Ryan said.

The guy hissed at him and kept on coming.

Ryan raised the .357. "Stop right now."

The guy kept coming.

Ryan shoved the guy back. The guy stumbled back and stopped for a moment, then came at him again. And now the other two were coming at him.

"Stop where you are."

They kept coming. Ryan batted the first guy's arms out of the way and tapped him on the head with the heavy .357. The guy went down. A blow like that should have put the guy out for a while. A little harder and Ryan would have sent him to the hospital, but he hadn't wanted to seriously injure him. However, no sooner did he go down, than he started to get up.

"Stay down," Ryan warned.

The guy climbed to his feet.

Then Ryan heard the door move behind him and spun around. The squirrel-faced punk he had killed was shuffling toward him with his arms raised and he looked like the weird people in this car: gray face, whitish eyes, and black lips. In his mind, Hector said, "They were dead; the dead come back to life as zombies." Green-black blood oozed from two wounds in his chest.

"Stop!" Ryan warned, the guy was almost to him.

Ryan aimed at his face. The guy tried to bite his hand and Ryan fired. The .357 was like a cannon in the small space. Ryan's ears rang. It knocked the guy back into the other car; he tumbled backward, the back of his head missing. He lay on the floor and didn't move.

Ryan felt something behind him and whirled around,

the guy he slugged was reaching to bite him. Ryan shot him in the head. The slug lifted him off his feet and slammed him into the two monsters behind him.

Ryan's ears hurt. The gunshots had pounded his ears and he couldn't hear. His eyes watered.

The two guys that the shot guy had knocked to the floor were trying to get up. One was seriously injured by the bullet to the other guy, his ear was missing, but he ignored it as he got to his feet.

Ryan backed away from them, his hands and knees trembling. He felt weak, wanted to sit down. A thought slithered through his mind. His head snapped around. Where are the others? He breathed in the rotten egg smell. His heart beating hard and fast. He couldn't stop shaking.

The two guys, things, zombies, got to their feet and shuffled toward him. He backed up, his heart in his throat. He backed into the open door and tried to slide through. The worn backpack caught on a broken piece of metal next to the door. He tried to jerk it free, but it wouldn't come. He started to slip it off and remembered the walkie-talkie inside and yanked again. Something tore and he spun away free. A zombie on the floor next to the door lunged at him and Ryan shoved it into the others.

He closed the door, putting it between them. They beat on the door mindlessly. His heart pounded the walls of his chest. His reflection in the glass was looked scared, very scared. He backed into a pole and almost jumped. Grabbed the pole and held on or he might have fallen down. He was shaking, he'd just killed two people, one person twice, and he felt terribly weak. The zombies were shaking the handle as if they didn't know how to operate it.

Ryan shivered violently. Sooner or later they would open the door. His whole being shifted as if the world had tilted on its axis. Suddenly, the door opened. Ryan glanced down at his gun. How many bullets had he fired?

He ran back through the car. He picked up the walking stick. It was heavier than it looked. It wasn't wood, it was metal. The zombies were coming. He faced them.

"Stop," he said and pointed the gun at them. His ears were still ringing and he couldn't hear his own words. "You saw what I did to your buddies; I'll do this to you."

The zombies did not stop. Ryan holstered the gun and swung the walking stick. He hit the first zombie in the head. The monster went down like a sack of rocks. The second zombie stepped over the fallen zombie and came at him and Ryan poked it so hard in the head and it went down. Ryan stood there for a moment, but neither one moved. His heart was pounding in his chest.

He still couldn't hear that good, but sensed movement and turned around. The other cars were full of people -- the other passengers -- coming toward him. One was missing an arm, another part of a face. They were shuffling toward him. Then Ryan froze; in among the zombies was Hector shuffling toward him. Hector with his eyes frozen open and his lips bared in a snarl. Hector was a zombie.

Ryan shook his head, not believing his eyes. He backed away from them, his eyes locked on Hector. He bumped into a pole and whirled around nearly hitting it with the walking stick. He went to the door. The door between the subway cars had closed. He grabbed the handle and pulled. It would not open. It was jammed.

He looked behind him. The zombies were coming and Hector was still among them. They'd just entered his car.

Ryan tried to break the glass. He hit it with the walking stick. It shattered, but did not break. He was going to hit it again when an idea came to him. He used the walking stick like a pry bar and levered the handle to move. The handle unlocked and the door slid open. Ryan jumped into the car and slammed the door. It banged shut and bounced open. The mechanism was broken.

He scanned the car, saw the body of the fat woman and ran to it. He couldn't see her gun. Then he saw her lying on it and shoved her off the Colt .45. The gun lay on the floor in a puddle of green-black blood. He reached for it, shivered and pulled his hand back.

Now they were in this car. He grabbed her red scarf and picked up the Colt and wiped it off. He raised the .45 and aimed and fired. He missed Hector but two zombies behind him went down. His next shot hit Hector and he went down. He fired again and again killing two more. He decided he would kill those in the doorway to barricade it, but he was out of bullets and they were still coming.

He threw the gun, turned and ran to the door of the conductor's cabin. The conductor was gone. He opened the front door. The tracks strretched into the darkness. No lights in the tunnel. Now the tunnel emergency lights were almost out. No sounds. Just darkness. He hesitated before jumping down to the tracks. He remembered how when he was a kid he'd always slept with a light on, even when he was a teenager he slept with a light on. He didn't need a light, but, dammit, he was still afraid of the dark.

He saw a body lying on the tracks. Felt like he was running from the frying pan into the fire. He stopped. Maybe he could do something. He shined the flash back at the car. A tidal wave of zombies was coming. They were halfway down the car.

Ryan jumped down to the tracks almost tripped and fell down. That would have been a bad move; sprain an ankle and just see what happens next. He took one last look at the train and started running. When he'd gone pretty far down the tracks he shined the flash back at the train. Some zombies had gotten down to the tracks and were coming. Suddenly one lunged out of the dark at the side of the tunnel and came at him. It looked like a homeless man. Ryan swung the walking stick and nearly took its head off. He ran down the tunnel. His hearing returned and now his footsteps seemed very loud in the empty dark tunnel. He tried to run quietly, the light bouncing on the ground, his breathing ragged in his throat. That's when he noticed his flashlight beam was beginning to fade.

*****

Chapter 29 - Nowhere To Go

The metal garage door rumbled up and the black limo drove into the warehouse. The right front headlight was smashed and a severed zombie hand clutched the chrome grill. The metal door clanked down behind the limo. With the engine running the car sat motionless in darkness. The sunroof opened and Alexei stood up and shined powerful flashlights over the walls and the metal shelves and rafters, as Luka shined a flashlight through the windshield.

"Turn on lights," Alexei said.

Luka turned on the car's bright lights and Frankie stood next to Alexei and helped inspect the interior. Dusty steel shelves ran the length of the warehouse and up toward the high ceiling, shelves mostly filled with cardboard boxes. Steel rafters with fluorescent lights hanging down on thin chains. High up, along the cinder block walls, under the roof were dusty windows covered by thick wire.

"It okay," Alexei said.

"Looks okay to me," Frankie said.

"What you know? Check no zombie inside."

Luka drew stainless steel .45 caliber Colt Double Eagles from each of his shoulder holsters and opened the driver's door. He flicked off both safeties and stood up out of the car. He held the guns in front of him like he was holding two cannons. The muscles under his cheek bounced. His hard eyes darted over the floor. He looked up to check the dusty rafters.

"Come on, go," Alexei said and shoved Frankie.

Luka lumbered over to the cinder block wall. For a big man he could move fast. He flicked a switch and a generator puttered to life. He flipped other switches and rows of lights in the high ceiling came on, illuminating aisles and shelves with crates and boxes and a dark green camo Humvee. Single bulb light fixtures hung down from the beams. Metal shelves of cardboard boxes and wooden crates filled the Soho warehouse. The crates were so covered by dust it was impossible to read the lettering stamped on the side. Mouse droppings littered the cement floor. Luka gazed up at the rafters, at the dark places where he thought a zombie might hide. He turned in a slow circle, checking everything, sweat dripping down his square face. He wiped his face with the back of his hand. Nodded once that it looked clear.

Frankie had climbed out. He noticed the large car parked to the side. "A Humvee?"

"Armored," Alexei bragged as he looked around. "Bullet proof. Solid tires. Air filtration."

"How long has this been here?" Frankie said, motioning at the warehouse.

"You should see one I got in Brooklyn," Alexei said.

"Shame we can't get out of city," Luka said.

"Wonder what other bosses got?" Frankie said.

"Nothin'," Alexei said. "They think with crotches. They got nothin'."

"You think they dead?" Luka said.

"Hiding," Frankie said. "Other bosses hiding."

"Nyet, they dead." Alexei chuckled.

Frankie walked over to the wooden crates and rapped on one. "What you got here?"

Alexei grinned. "Guns, food, clothes."

"We could hide here for months." Frankie said, glancing down the long rows.

"Da, I have," Alexei said.

"That time the D.A. said you went to South America and they couldn't subpoena you?"

"Never come close. Let's see what's going on." Alexei headed to the little office against the wall. Inside a light glowed in a lamp on a bookcase giving the office a cozy look. Above the bookcase was a portrait of a dark haired man in a military uniform, his dark eyes staring down.

"What you want me to do?" Luka moved to a folding chair next to a folding table with a deck of cards on top.

"Load Humvee with guns and food." Alexei motioned at the crates. "In case we have to leave."

"Go to cabin upstate? Be nice if we had broads."

"Always thinking of yourself," Alexei said.

Luka said, "Was thinking how nice Frankie's going to start looking after few weeks."

Frankie turned to Luka. "Don't even think that."

Luka laughed meanly.

Alexei shook his head. "See what I can do." He opened the door, turned on the light and looked around inside. Then he hurried to the desk, yanked a drawer open and slammed a bottle on the top. He filled a glass with liquor, raised it toward the painting and drank.

"Who's that?" Frankie quietly asked Luka.

"Stalin. Boss idolizes him."

"All those books at his house?'

"At house, at apartments."

"How long boss have place?" Frankie said as he walked to the table.

"Long time." Luka picked up a deck of cards, blew the dust off them.

Frankie shined a flashlight down the dark rows, at shelves filled with crates and boxes. "Nice setup."

"Lot you not know about." Luka tossed the cards on the table and went to the limo and opened the trunk.

"What we gonna do?" Frankie said.

"Load guns. Shotguns for cops or zombies. Assault rifles to shoot deer. Cases of food. Got army fatigues borrowed from Brooklyn armory."

Luka dragged a wooden crate to the table. It made a loud scraping noise on the gray cement floor. In the quiet that followed the loud sound Luka looked around the shadowy warehouse as if he'd heard something.

"Check," he told Frankie.

Frankie hurried to the metal street door and opened it and looked up and down the street, "Coast is clear," then closed the door.

"I mean in warehouse, you idiot."

***

Frankie's opening the door attracted the attention of a zombie and it shuffled up the street, another one breathed in the scent of man and followed and soon more zombies came up the quiet street.

***

Luka glanced at Frankie, he was already starting to bug him. He picked up a crowbar and pried open the crate. The wooden top came up a little and Luka worked the crowbar under the opening. He pulled on it again and the wood splintered as it opened.

Frankie whistled softly.

Luka lifted an automatic shotgun. "Stole from store in Jersey."

"Ammo?" Frankie said.

Luka ripped open a cardboard box. Brass bullets fell to the floor. He tossed a shotgun to Frankie. "Load it."

Frankie caught the shotgun and picked up shells.

They heard Alexei bang the phone down in the office. "Fucking phone not work." He drew his gun and shot the phone off the desk.

"Not good day to ask for raise," Frankie said.

"Not worry about it," Luka said. "Got police radio, CB and shortwave. Boss find out what happening."

"Shssh." Frankie pointed at the garage door.

Luka looked at the large door. Something was scratching on it. "Zombies search for way in."

Frankie shined a flashlight at the windows near the ceiling, where the office was. Outside the window were zombies. Some were trying to reach through the heavy wire on the glass; others were trying to bite their way through.

"How they get up there?" Luka said.

"Maybe from roof of building next door."

"No matter, got heavy wire over it."

"It'll hold?" Frankie said like he wasn't so sure.

Luka lifted the top off a crate, took out two dark gray tanks with a black hose coming out of each, joined to an odd looking metal tube and placed it on the ground.

"Flamethrower?" Frankie's jaw hung open.

"Doors not hold, you tell me."

Frankie moved out of the big man's way. With a shaking hand he lit a Camel and sat on a crate watching the windows while Luka loaded the Humvee.

*****

Chapter 30 - No Place to Run

The black Mustang idled quiet as a ghost on the side of the road. The lights were off, gray smoke rose from the exhaust. The front windows were open and three pairs of eyes peered out the windshield. Shadows crossed their faces. They sat very still for a long time as if unable to process what they had seen and were seeing.

The roadway was filled with wrecked cars, dead people and zombies, they could see the Hudson River choppy with little white caps and the George Washington Bridge, from Manhattan to Fort Lee, New Jersey. Two hundred feet above the dark river, about a mile and a half from one end to the other, eight lanes of traffic on the upper level and six lanes of traffic on the lower 'Martha' level. The lights usually made the bridge easy to see at night, but there was little light tonight. The emergency lights powered by a backup generator had weakened to dim yellow globes.

In the moonlight they could see the bridge was jammed with vehicles. No cars were moving. Dark shapes shambled about in the shadows. A gun discharged -- a bright flash and loud bark echoed across the water -- and the dark shapes moved, shuffled, toward the sound. As the gunfire continued more and more shapes converged on it, then screams echoed in the dark, then silence. People had climbed onto the suspension cables and steel towers and every now and then a flashlight shined up there or a scream echoed. A rancid, rotten odor floated on the breeze.

A ferry or sightseeing boat drifted out of control down the dark river. Across the Hudson in Jersey, they saw flashes and fires; maybe cars were burning, maybe small buildings, maybe it was the start of a big conflagration. They didn't know. In between the noises, the silence was frightening. Then they'd hear noises, the sounds of a few people running, yells, gunfire, screams. Silence again. A silence darker than night.

"Look at all those zombies," Howie said, his voice sounding small and faraway.

"Millions," Tommy said as though there was nothing left to do, but crawl in a hole and die.

"Now what?" Diane brushed a tear out of her eye in a manner that suggested she would never give up.

"Don't know." Howie watched the boat floating aimlessly in the river. In the moonlight there appeared to be things, probably zombies, on the deck. "Think it's a sightseeing boat."

"Ferry," Tommy said.

"Let's go back to the hotel," Diane said.

"The hotel?" Howie said. "Why?"

"We know where it is. Maybe it's safe there."

"For the price I paid it ought to be safe," Tommy said.

"They won't be charging for it now," Howie said.

"Yeah, they won't," Tommy said and chuckled as if he pulled off another one.

"Maybe we can hole up there until the army or someone comes," Diane said.

"I don't know," Howie said, not sure anything was safe.

"Hey," Tommy said, "if she wants to go back to the hotel, we go."

Howie glanced at Tommy staring at the bridge, playing big man, like anything he said was so. "Don't get mad at me. It isn't my fault your hot weekend is a dud."

"You were pretty anxious to come up here, too." Tommy stared behind Diane at Howie; his eyes saying this whole thing was Howie's fault.

"Shut up! Both of you," she said. "Just go back to the hotel. We'll our clothes. Maybe there's someone there we can talk to. Or they know an emergency place we can go."

"I wonder how Atlanta is. "If it's like this here?"

Tears rolled down her face. She brushed them away with her fingers.

"Stop it, you're scaring her," Tommy said his anger finding an excuse to vent.

Howie glanced at Tommy, Diane still sitting in his lap. Tommy patted her shoulder, "It'll be okay."

Howie shook his head. He'll use anything to get laid.

"Besides I'm hungry," Tommy said.

"The truth at last." Diane wiped her face with a tissue.

Howie drove down the parkway. In the moonlight the tall buildings of Manhattan were ghosts in the night, no lights on anywhere. The dark buildings radiated an eerie despair as though the city had been deserted for decades.

"Maybe we should try the other bridges," Diane said. "The east side of Manhattan might be--"

"No way," Howie said. "We almost got stopped coming here. If we turn down the wrong street, next time we'll need a bulldozer to get through."

"You wouldn't think that creatures that move so slow would be such a problem," Tommy said.

"Out in the country they're probably not this bad, but here with so many of them clustered together...." Howie shook his head.

"I haven't seen many survivors," Diane said.

"They're hiding," Tommy said.

"All of them?" she said.

Howie licked his lips. He didn't want to tell her, afraid it would scare her too much, but he felt he should tell her, so she knew what they were up against. He opened his mouth to speak, but he didn't want to be the one to tell her.

She turned to Howie. All the years she knew him he was the only one who would level with her, tell her the truth no matter what. But he stared straight ahead debating what to say.

"Are there a lot of survivors?" She nudged Howie's arm to get him to speak.

Howie turned to her and saw Tommy shake his head no, don't say anything.

Howie swung his eyes to the road. "I--I don't know."

"Yes, you do. You think the zombies ate them and you're afraid to tell me."

"No," he lied.

She faced forward, her expression drawn. "You're right." Then she started crying. "Mamma and Poppa." She fumbled in her purse for another tissue.

Tommy slapped Howie on the arm. "They're okay, Diane. Back home ain't like New York. People know how to take care of themselves."

"Poppa doesn't own a gun." She wiped her eyes with a tissue. "Momma wouldn't let him."

Tommy motioned Howie to bail him out.

Howie stared at the road, thinking about his folks, his brother. Were they alive? Were the zombies bad in Fayetteville? The car hit a bump and it brought him out of his thoughts.

"Let's go back to the hotel; maybe we can call them."

"Try your cell phone," Diane said to Tommy.

Tommy took out his iphone, noted the look in Howie's eyes, and pretended to turn it on and feigned it wouldn't turn on. "Battery's dead."

Diane dried her eyes. "Hurry, let's go to the hotel."

Manhattan was dark; few skyscrapers had emergency lights on. Cars were abandoned on the sides of the road. Every so often there were corpses on the pavement.

"What a mess," Howie said.

"What if the phones don't work?" she said.

"We'll take our stuff and leave," Tommy said.

"How?" Howie asked. He wanted to hear what 'Mr. Git-her-done' had to say.

Tommy made a face. He didn't care. They'd just leave. And if they didn't follow him, he'd leave without them.

He'd be the one to lead them away. He'd find a great car, not anything like this piece of shit, and he'd drive over zombies, anything, to get them back home.

"We'll take some food, too," Tommy said.

"Why?" She turned to him.

"In case we get hungry." Howie looked past her at the Hudson River, dark with small choppy white caps. Would they find anyone else alive?

"What if we can't get through? What if they've taken over the world? What if we're the only people left alive?" A note of hysteria rang in her voice.

"Then I've dibs on the first date with you," Howie said.

"Silly," Diane playfully slapped him, but a smile appeared in those tears.

Howie peeked past her at Tommy, but T.N.T.'s eyes were miles away. Must be thinking about all the girls he won't be able to screw.

"We can always drive up to New England. Maybe the zombies can't stand the cold."

"Neither can I," she said and shivered.

"I'll keep you warm," Howie said and she smiled at him and he felt like a million dollars.

Then she started crying. She put her head on Tommy's shoulder and sobbed and Tommy patted her back and looked at Howie as if to say look at what you've done.

Howie bent over the steering wheel, trying to see the gas gauge. How much gas was left? With the dash lights not working it was impossible to tell. How far will we get before we run out of gas? Should we even try? Maybe we should just stay here and hole up. Then he looked in the rearview mirror and blinked and felt the air sucked out of him; behind the car were zombies, a lot of zombies, shuffling toward them. The hair rose on the back of his neck. He grabbed the steering wheel with both hands and stepped on the gas.

*****

Chapter 31 - Fort Ron

"Why would beings from another planet do this to us?" Pat asked as they sat in the flickering candlelight in their quiet apartment.

"Disrupt our society, make it easier to take over," Ron told her.

"They must really be terrible creatures."

"Maybe they didn't mean this to happen. Maybe the virus was supposed to evolve a few of us into something like them so they could communicate with us. Or maybe it wasn't supposed to come here at all. You're assuming it was, but maybe it wasn't. Maybe they were throwing it away and something happened and it came here by mistake."

"Throw it away?" she said.

"Hazardous waste they meant to send into their sun, but something happened."

"Why didn't they just destroy it?"

"Maybe it was supposed to be destroyed. This could've happened millions of years ago and the virus has been drifting in space for eons. The aliens might not even be alive anymore."

"So what can we do about it?" Pat said

He looked at her. He'd been wondering that himself for hours. What could they do? How bad was it? Was enough of society left to keep functioning? He heard something in the hall. Steps. Someone knocking on the doors.

"Ron," Pat said, fear quivering her voice.

The wood veneer metal door to the apartment was bolted but in the flickering candlelight they now heard hands tapping, searching, and scratching on the door.

"Where's Ryan and Hector; why aren't they back? They've been gone hours."

"Our power's out. Maybe the subway's not running. They could be stuck on a train or taking the streets."

"You think something happened?"

He turned so she couldn't see his face. His expression always gave him away. When she was finding the candles, he'd tried to raise Ryan on the walkie-talkie. All he got was interference. "They'll come," he said, but he wasn't so sure.

She flinched when there was banging on the walls next door and Ron held up his hand for her to be quiet. "Why worry? We have a metal door."

"The walls aren't made of metal. I don't know what they're made of or if they're reinforced. They can come through the walls."

"Are you sure?" she said and he nodded. "Why don't they go away?"

"They're persistent." He swallowed his mouth so dry he could almost taste lint in it. "And hungry." He tried to blot out the mental picture of the monsters eating people.

"We should see what we have that can kill 'em."

"They seem to be able to sense movement. We move and they'll know we're here. They'll know there's food on the other side of the wall."

"You think they can smell us in here?"

He shook his head. He didn't know.

Something scratched on the door. Something strong and determined. It wasn't the door he was worried about. Suppose there was an army of them in the hall? If there were a lot of them out there then he and Pat couldn't leave and Ryan couldn't return. He breathed out and as his eyes swept over the walls he noticed a poster from when he covered a balloon race in Arizona. Hundreds of pretty balloons high above the city, blue sky above, clouds in the distance. He'd promised her they'd go for a ride in a balloon one day, but something always got in the way. He looked at the balloon poster and wanted to listen to the old Louis Armstrong classic: 'What a Wonderful Day.' He'd put it on his Ipod. She said the music might resonant through the walls even if he wore earplugs.

"We're almost out of Raid." She put what they had on the kitchen counter.

"You're going to kill them with bug spray?"

"What else do we have? We don't own guns." He wanted to remind her that she was the one who made him get rid of the M9 Beretta, but now wasn't the time.

"Knives."

Immediately she shook her head. "I'm not getting that close. No way."

"Do we have a broomstick?"

Pat who could have been a cover-girl her face was so pretty, so photogenic -- small nose, full lips, big brown eyes -- looked at him like he was crazy.

"And duct tape?"

She stared at him as if she wanted to say what the hell was he thinking?

"Do we?"

She went to the closet and took out a sponge mop and unscrewed the top. On a closet shelf was a roll of duct tape she'd bought after she saw an episode of '*Myth Busters*' about duct tape. He hurried into the kitchen and grabbed a long pointed cook's knife from a wooden block. She held the knife and pole and he duct taped them together, winding on layer after layer of the gray tape.

He held it like a spear and practiced thrusting forward a few times. "What do you think?"

"It scares me." She crossed her arms; she didn't want to get that close.

"I don't think they get scared," he said missing her point. "Maybe we should give it a try."

She said, "With just one?"

They both went to the hall closet. Inside was a long thin plastic rug shampooer, great for cleaning the rug, not very good for a weapon. She picked up the old plunger.

"It has a wooden handle." She unscrewed the rubber end.

He looked in the closet, expecting to see a wooden

clothes rod; there was only a metal shelf. He ran into the bedroom, yanked open the closet door. Now he remembered, they'd redone the closets. No rods, only wire shelves. He went into the guest bedroom, his office, same thing. By the time he got back to the kitchen she had duct taped a long pointy boning knife to the wooden plunger handle. Something about what they were doing felt wrong. With the telescope they had seen people fighting zombies, and for some reason he couldn't put his finger on this seemed wrong.

"What?" she said.

He shook his head. "I'm not sure."

She handed him an oven mitt to put over his hand as she lifted an Emeril Lagasse glass pot lid to use like a shield. She looked up at him, "Ready?"

"The Emeril pot lid?" he said remembering how much it had cost.

She shrugged. "Should be zombie proof."

He looked into her brown eyes and in that moment he loved her more than he'd ever loved her before. He got choked up and nodded his head.

Holding the pot lid in one hand and the makeshift short sword in the other, she walked to the front door.

"Too bad we don't have any cast iron pots," he said as he followed.

She put her hand to her mouth for him to be quiet.

He went to the door and shoved the Lay-z-boy aside. She moved the bar out of the way, undid two deadbolts, opened the doorknob lock and looked to him to see if he was ready.

"Do it quietly," he told her fearing the sounds would attract the zombies.

She gave him a look like how was she supposed to do that and swung the door open.

He almost jumped, expecting a zombie to be on the other side of the door, but the hallway was empty. He relaxed and smiled at her and started to step into the hall. All of a sudden a zombie standing at the side shuffled in the doorway.

"Mr. Chen?" she said. Mr. Chen his face gray, black lips pulled back in a snarl, came at her.

Ron lunged forward with the spear, stabbing the him in the chest. Mr. Chen, the zombie was knocked backward and grabbed the spear as Ron continued to shove it in. Then Ron pulled the spear out and the zombie stumbled before attacking again. Ron thrust the spear into him again and this time the zombie grabbed the makeshift spear, and it broke.

Ron looked at the broken mop in handle and stepped back.

Mr. Chen, the zombie with the broken spear still sticking in his chest, came at him. When Ron backed into his apartment, it followed and turned toward Pat standing at the side. Pat froze with fear and shock as the zombie reached for her.

On seeing the zombie reach for his wife, Ron woke from his shock, charged the monster, shoved the broken broomstick into the zombie's side and shoved it back into the hall. The zombie fell in the hall, but even with the broken broomsticks sticking in its chest, it struggled to get up.

Ron stood there, not knowing what to do to stop it. Pat stepped past him, knocked the zombie's grasping hands aside with the pot lid and thrust her short spear, the plunger with the pointy boning knife duct taped to it, into the monster's face. It twitched once and lay still.

Ron backed up into his apartment, pulling Pat with him, and slammed the door and locked the dead bolt. He turned to Pat to see if she was okay. She was shocked, scared and looked at Ron through fearful eyes.

"Did I kill Mr. Chen?"

He shook his head. "He was already dead."

The sound of something beating on the door echoed through the quiet apartment. Ron grabbed the short spear from his wife before he looked through the dirty peephole. He could barely make out other zombies eating Mr. Chen.

"Is it him?" she said.

"Other zombies are eating Mr. Chen."

"What happened to Mrs. Chen?"

He shrugged, he didn't know. As quietly as he could, he locked all the deadbolts.

"Stabbing them in the chest doesn't kill them."

"Maybe you didn't do it in the right place."

"Should've been seriously wounded, unable to continue."

"Then how are we going to stop them?"

Ron shook his head.

"How are we going to get out of here?"

"Maybe we shouldn't leave," he said.

"How are Ryan and Hector going to get back?"

They heard beating on the door and Ron looked through the peephole.

"They are more of them in the hall."

"Will the door hold?"

"I don't know." He put the door bar in place, pushed the La-Z-boy in front of the door and backed into the living room.

"Call Ryan and see if he's alright."

"Maybe I shouldn't. They're attracted to sound."

"You have to find out if he's okay. We can't stay here. What happens when they're done eating Chen? We have to find out if Ryan knows of a place where we can go."

The knocking on the door got louder and more insistent.

"Ron, we have to do something."

He faced her; unable to tell her he'd tried and didn't get through. "I'll call. Maybe Ryan's found out something."

*****

Chapter 32 - Uncle Black Jack Ryan

Ryan ran until he was out of breath then hurried on as best he could. He heard zombies stumbling along behind him. Every time he looked over his shoulder there were more of them. At a bend in the tunnel, when he was out of sight, he squeezed into an alcove in the wall and waited.

The shuffling monsters came closer and closer. The stench of death got stronger. His mouth opened and he felt bile coming up his throat and fearing that he'd make vomiting noises he clamped his hand over his mouth. Holding his breath, Ryan tried to push himself back into the grimy narrow recess. He was afraid they would see him or smell him and come get him. To his relief the monsters kept going down the tunnel.

Ryan thought about fighting them. He might have a chance, they moved so slowly and were not organized and he was quicker and had an idea what he'd do, but if he tripped or misjudged just one of them, he'd be hopelessly outnumbered. He could always use the gun, but sound attracted them and it'd be to his disadvantage. So with the odds against him, he decided to fight another time.

As quietly as he possible he eased out of his hiding place. Suddenly a zombie that had fallen behind the pack lunged at him. Ryan ducked away and the zombie lurched past him. Ryan clubbed it on the head with the cane and the monster went down. Its head hit the rail with a loud bonk and Ryan stomped down on the back of its neck and heard a breaking sound.

He stepped back gasping, trembling. He looked down the tracks where the pack of zombies had gone. He didn't see any of them returning. He looked in the other direction and didn't see any stragglers in the darkness.

He was shaking all over. He had to get away, to keep moving. He proceeded in the direction the pack had gone.

He thought of Sergeant Alvin York in World War One. In the movie Gary Cooper sneaked up behind the enemy and killed and captured a boatload of the enemy. He thought of doing that as he followed in their direction. Take them out one at a time, just like they do in the movies. But in the blackness he tripped and stumbled down onto the middle of the tracks. A zombie, a young kid, shuffled out of the darkness at him. He shoved it back with the tip of the cane. The zombie growled and came at him again. He put his hand up for it to be quiet. The zombie growled, got up and came at him again. He shoved it hard and it fell down in a sitting position. As it sat there it started to growl loudly. Afraid that its growling would attract others, Ryan swung the cane like a golf club and hit it in the head. The zombie recoiled backward and lay there. It was then Ryan recognized the girl in the red leather outfit he'd bumped into earlier.

Ryan limped on holding the stabbing stitch in his side. He breathed in the damp rotten egg smelly air. He was nearly breathing normally when he heard the shuffling feet again. He stopped and turned his head to listen. The zombies were just up ahead. They weren't moving away or coming back, simply hovering in place somewhere just up ahead.

He moved over to the curved wall and sneaked ahead. Staying close to the wall he felt his way forward in the inky darkness. He wasn't sure how far away they were. Were they waiting for him? Could they see in this inky blackness? Were their senses heightened by their affliction?

His foot kicked an empty soda can and it bounced making a racket. He froze and listened. The zombies weren't coming toward him, yet. He eased ahead carefully. The tunnel opened, the track branched from one to two. The single track he was on divided into two leading into two separate tunnels. The monsters had stopped at the branch and were milling about confused which way to go. Unfortunately Ryan couldn't continue down the track he was on without being seen.

Moving silently, he sneaked back the way he'd come. With his foot he felt the space between the track and the wall and found a loose brick. He picked it up, it was half a brick, and went back to where the single track ended.

He took a breath and tried to stop shaking, then eased ahead and threw the brick down the right hand tunnel. The brick sailed over the head of a few zombies and past a few more, then bounced and knocked about as it rolled away. The zombies turned and moved toward the sound.

While they shuffled away, down the right branch, Ryan sneaked down the left track. The monsters were almost down the other tunnel and he was almost clear of the open area and heading down the track when he stepped on an empty pint bottle. The whiskey bottle broke loudly in the darkness. He froze. He couldn't tell if they were coming back. He felt a stabbing pain and looked down at his right foot. A sliver of glass from the bottle had broken off and stabbed his ankle; he was bleeding over his sneakers onto the ground. He moved his foot to the side. It wasn't a serious wound, but he certainly bled easily. Could they smell his blood?

As if in answer he saw several zombies raise their heads and sniff the air. Then they started turning their heads left and right. Turned left breathed in, sniffed the air. Turned right and breathed in, sniffed the air. Turning left and right as if checking which way the human smell was stronger.

Up ahead was a stone pillar and he decided to get out of the open and hide behind it. It was only a few steps away. He hurried to it. His first step was okay. His second step kicked a can full of soda. The red can bounced a few feet, then sprung a leak and sent a noisy squeaking geyser of foaming soda into the air.

Ryan glanced down the branching tracks. The dozen that had been chasing him were coming to the sound and another dozen, visible in the moonlight, were climbing through a grating.

Ryan bent over, grabbed the can, and tossed it over their heads. It landed on the track and continued to spray a little longer. The zombies turned to it.

Ryan hurried down the tunnel. He kept tripping and stumbling, afraid he might fall and hurt himself, be unable to continue, so he switched on the small led flashlight and hurried ahead.

He heard a commotion behind him and paused to see what it was. The two dozen that had been chasing him were joined by another dozen that came from way down the tracks behind him. Now there were at least three dozen after him. Not the time to stop and fight.

He started running again, his breath ragged in his throat, trying to move faster and yet be careful so he didn't fall down. He pointed the flash on the ground, shining it on and off to get his bearings. When he saw something white next to the tracks he shined the light, it was at a station. He ran up the steps to the platform.

Down the tracks lurched the gray faces. They had not closed the distance, but they hadn't given up either.

He raced down the platform. Dodging around a knocked over garbage can he stepped on something, slipped and went down. He tumbled into another garbage can and sent it flying off the platform and crashing down on the tracks where it made enough noise to wake the dead. He'd whacked his left knee on the garbage can. It hurt like hell and he almost cried out. He managed to remain quiet while the garbage can bounced and then rolled clicking and clacking down the tracks. He saw more monsters coming from everywhere, further down the track, other tracks, all heading toward him. He climbed to his feet, his knee hurt, but it wasn't so bad; it would stiffen up before long and slow him down. His right sneaker squished with blood, it was not a serious wound, but these not so serious wounds were adding up. He went to the stairs and used the cane to take some of the weight. When he started up the stairs he saw zombies on the top steps staggering down to him.

Ryan stayed in the middle of the stairs and used the cane as a club. He hit them or knocked them out of his way, down the stairs. Some he hit in the legs so they'd fall and tumble down the stairs. A few he grabbed by their coat sleeves and yanked them down the stairs. He tried not to listen to them falling down the stairs sounding like hollow mannequins breaking on the hard cement.

At the top of the stairs he came to a large red Coca-Cola machine. It must've had a backup battery. On the front in large letters:

THIS IS IT !

He went though a turnstile, smacked a zombie with the cane and shoved the dead zombie in the turnstile so the revolving arms couldn't turn. He hobbled up the stairs. A few steps up he froze. A huge zombie blocked his way.

It was six foot six and thick as a side of beef. In one hand it carried a severed arm. The zombie had been eating it, when it turned and looked at Ryan. It looked back at the arm and then at Ryan, then came down the steps after him.

Ryan backed up. He reached for his gun and halted, his sweaty hand on the walnut grip. A bullet would kill it, but the sound would bring a tidal wave of monsters.

He left the gun in his holster and held the cane like a bat as he backed away. His hands shook, the cane trembled like he was a rookie baseball player.

The monster's big white eyes stared at him, thick pasty white drool oozed over his split black lips down his gray chin. With its long broken jagged teeth it ripped a big hunk of flesh off the severed arm and dropped it and hungrily chewed as it shuffled toward Ryan.

As Ryan backed away, he glanced over his shoulder and saw monsters coming up the stairs from the subway platform and other monsters coming to the stairs from the other end of the station. The big zombie stepped down and its big hands reached out to grab him.

Ryan took a breath and squeezed the cane tighter. The

big monster came closer. Suddenly, Ryan darted to the left and the monster reached to him and Ryan dodged to the right, ducked under the outstretched hands and raced up the stairs, but his knee was bothering him, slowed him, and the monster's thick hand bumped him and he tripped and went down.

He tried to get up quickly, but the big zombie took two steps and was almost on top of him. Lying on his back he backed up the cement steps, poking the monster with the cane, as it reached for him. There wasn't enough room and he wasn't in the right position to swing the cane like a bat. He shoved the tip, like it was a sword at the monster. To his surprise the cane sunk into the monster like it was going into a rotten watermelon. It slid in until only the handle was sticking out. It went in and didn't seem to bother the monster.

The zombie grabbed Ryan and picked him up. Ryan punched and kicked it, but it had no effect. Ryan took his gun from his holster; the .357 was heavy as a hammer. He wanted to shoot it, but he didn't have many bullets left and gunshots attracted monsters, so he clubbed the zombie in the head. The zombie's gray skin and scalp came away like it was shedding sunburned skin. Ryan hit it again and heard a cracking sound and the monster let go and fell down.

Ryan kicked it away. The monster rolled down the stairs colliding into the zombies coming up the steps. The monster was huge. There was no way around him. With other zombies pinned under its massive bulk, it was a logjam.

Ryan saw the cane sticking out of the big monster. He hated to leave it, but zombies were trying to swarm over the logjam. The zombies under the big monster were still trying to reach Ryan, still trying to get to him, rather than trying to get out from under. One of them appeared to be broken in half.

Ryan's stomach churned as he hurried up the stairs. He didn't know what he expected. Whatever it was, it wasn't the nightmare scene that greeted him. The street was quiet. No people hurrying to escape. No cars rushing away. Cars were stopped in the street, on sidewalks, crashed into other cars. A wrecked police car sat only a few feet away, bones on the sidewalk next to it. He went to the body of a policeman. The gun was missing, but there was an ammo clip on his belt. The bullets were for a 9mm. and not for Ryan's Smith and Wesson .357.

In the moonlight he could see far up the street. Bones lay everywhere, gleaming whitely in the moonlight. No streetlights were on. No car headlights. No house lights. It looked as if the city had been abandoned. He turned off the flash and walked to the corner to get his bearings. He didn't think Mary Anna and the kids were okay, but he owed it to Hector. He wasn't far from Hector's apartment. He'd come this way before. Just up the street and around the corner.

He looked around as he limped. Nothing moved in the breeze except a curtain hanging out a broken window. The smell of rotten eggs was bad. A man had hung himself by tying a lamp cord around his neck and jumping out a window. Now he'd come back to life as a zombie and struggled to get free. There were no sounds, no sirens, no noises, unsettling in a city this big. He heard nothing, no radios, no calls for help, only smelled that rotten stench all around him.

He didn't know how much time he had. How long would it be before some zombies came after him and then others followed them?

He hurried up the street trying to move silently as he could. A car had crashed across the sidewalk. He detoured around it. He stepped on broken glass and his feet crunched as he went up the street. For a moment the smell of gasoline overpowered the stink of rotten eggs. The street was wet with gas, one spark and a giant fire would erupt. A dead man lay in the puddle, an Ipad in his hand.

Ryan saw a baseball bat lying on the street as if some

kids had been interrupted playing ball and picked it up. No sooner had he done that then a zombie came at him. It had been a woman, was wearing a faded red housedress, and had curly gray hair. It came right at him. Ryan stepped back, tried to dodge it, but it came right at him. Ryan shoved it back with the baseball bat as he went past it, but it came after him again.

Ryan slowed to go around another wrecked car and it almost grabbed him. He hit it with the baseball bat. It backed up a few steps and came back at him and he had to hit it again. Ryan swallowed his heart, breathing hard. His hand tingled like he'd hit a home run. He didn't want to look at someone's granny, now a dead zombie and he hurried on.

At the corner it looked as though a war had been fought. It was impossible to tell who had won. It looked like everyone had lost. The delicatessen on the corner had been broken into and looted. He heard movement in the deli and stepped closer. It looked abandoned.

"Hello," he called. "Anyone alive?"

"Leave us alone," a young voice said.

"I'll try to bring you to safety."

"There is no safety," a woman said.

"It's better than in there."

"You're one of them."

"No, I'm not. Have you heard any of them talk?"

"Go away." He saw a trap door in the floor behind the counter open and the shadow went down there.

He looked around. The street was empty of movement. He took his gun out and checked the cylinder. Two bullets. He reached in the backpack and touched something long and cylindrical and pulled it out. An emergency flare. His hand fumbled through the sack and grabbed another flare. He shoved them into the pack and stepped through the broken window. His foot crunched on broken glass. He went to the trap door and knocked softly.

"Let me help," he said.

"We have a gun, go away," a woman said.

"It's not safe down there."

The gun fired, probably a rifle. The bullet missed him, but shattered a hole in the wooden trapdoor and sent wooden splinters into his face. Ryan jumped back and backed away.

He tried to touch his face and got splinters in his hand. He searched the shelves and found a mirror. He set the bathroom mirror on the counter. He shined the led flashlight in his face and took out several splinters. Then he walked down the aisle and found a claw hammer and put it in his backpack.

"I'm going," he said. "If you want to come along, I'll be up the street. I don't know how long I'll be there."

"Go away."

He walked to the window and looked around to make sure the coast was clear. As he stood there he realized he'd been shot at and wasn't pissed. Wasn't that upset. If that had happened a few hours ago he'd have been on the warpath, would've done something, but a lot of shit had happened since then. Now he sort of understood, felt sorry for them. He shook his head, now wasn't the time to go soft.

He climbed through the broken window. Now scattered along the street were zombies; they'd heard the shot. With the baseball bat in one hand and the hammer in the other he jogged up the street. When any monster came close to him, he hit it in the head. He dodged left and right killing zombies, no longer dodging away, but veering toward them. Maybe he'd gotten pissed about those people shooting at him and was taking it out on the zombies. He was so carried away, that he ran past Hector's apartment. He hurried back and stopped.

A woman was sitting on the stoop. She was crying.

Oh my God! It's Mary Anna.

"You're okay." He was relieved.

Her jaw moved. Her muscles twitched. It seemed an impossible effort for her to speak but she struggled to have the words make sense.

"Ryan?"

"Yeah, we have to get going."

"Where's Hector?"

He didn't want to tell her. He looked back up the street. The zombies were coming, but they were far enough away he had some time.

She sighed. "I thought so. I felt it."

"We have to go."

She shook her head with such a pitiful look on her face. She had long black hair, was petite, with a movie star figure, but today she looked sickly, so skinny.

"No," she gasped, her voice sounding raw, hurting.

"You'll be okay. I'll get you out of here."

"You-- got-- to-- pro--mise me. . ." She coughed.

"Sure, anything."

She nodded at a dead child lying on the ground. She was holding a child wrapped in a green New York Jets blanket in her lap. She opened the blanket. Inside was Alex her older boy. Ryan didn't know his age, but remembered that he was in elementary school. The kid's skin was gray and his ghoulish white eyes bulged.

"We'll take him, maybe there's something someone can do."

"No." Blood tears were running down her face. "I killed one child, I can't kill another."

"What!"

She showed him her right arm. There were small tooth marks on her arm like she'd been bitten by a child. Black veins radiated out from her arm. Her arm was turning gray. It didn't look like it belonged to her body. She'd put a tourniquet on her upper arm and that had slowed the spread, but not stopped it. The zombie virus was still spreading.

"You have to kill him and me."

"Are you crazy? Why would I do that?"

"Heard about it." Her dark eyes stared at him. "You know what it'll do to us."

He shook his head no, but knew. By God he knew.

"Hector would do it."

"No, he wouldn't."

"Yes," she said and she was right. Tears tumbled out of her eyes.

"I can't."

"You have to. I don't want to eat my neighbors, my friends, you. I want it to end here and now."

She cried harder. She held her right arm as if the pain was unbearable.

He stared at her hand, at the fingernails turning black. Smelled the rotten egg stink coming from it.

"You have a gun?" she said.

"Yeah."

"Give it to me. I will do it then."

He couldn't swallow. His mouth was dry, his lips cracked. He wanted to run away, wanted it to be someone else, anyone but him. His hand fumbled in his holster and pulled out his .357. It was sledgehammer heavy in his hand.

"Give it to me."

He went to hand it to her, but she couldn't get her 'good' hand to grasp the gun. She cried and tried to switch the baby from her left arm to her right arm and couldn't. "Help me," she pleaded.

Ryan lifted the child from her arm and the child tried to bite him. He tried to hand the child back, but now she couldn't make her arm work; the poison was spreading fast.

Her tearful eyes looked to Ryan. "Put him in my lap."

He carefully laid the baby in her lap.

"Hand me the gun."

He gently handed her the heavy gun. She was too weak, she could barely hold it. She didn't have enough strength to lift the gun and pull the trigger.

"I can't," she sobbed, tears running down her face. "I'm too weak." Her eyes begged him. "You'll have to."

He took the gun from her.

"Mary Anna?" he said softly.

She was quivering as the virus worked its way past the tourniquet. Abruptly she stopped and was still. He was about to touch her when he saw her hair was falling out. He backed away. He stared at her face. Black veins radiated across her face, the once red blood vessels crisscrossing in an evil looking blackish web as he face turned gray. Now she was one of the undead. She was beyond pain.

"Kill ussss," she begged, her voice turning into a hiss.

Ryan stood there, chilled to his soul. He didn't feel alive. He felt old and rotten. He shakily staggered to the child. His whole body was numb. Couldn't feel his hands or feet. Like he was a robot telling his body what to do. Stumbled up to the child in her arms like The Pieta; the Virgin Mary holding the dead body of Jesus.

He tried to remember the boy's name and couldn't. Last Christmas he'd given him a present and the boy had called him Uncle Ryan. Uncle Black Jack Ryan, he teased. He kept on calling him that while they ate Christmas dinner. "Pass me the gravy, Uncle Black Jack Ryan." "Pass me the stuffing, Uncle Black Jack Ryan."

The kid struggled to get free so it could bite him. Ryan tried to speak. Couldn't. Wiped his nose with the back of his arm.

Mary Anna started to convulse and the blanket holding the child in place started to come undone. Ryan pointed the gun at the child, the barrel inches from the young boy's face, and pulled the trigger. He turned away as the dead boy tumbled to the ground.

Then what had been Mary Anna stood up and hissed. It started to come down the steps. He shot it in the head, knocking it backward. The explosion was a blast from hell: loud and evil. It echoed up the street. Blood splattered across the steps, the front door.

Ryan sat heavily on the apartment steps, crying so hard he couldn't see. Couldn't think, his head hurt, he wiped his eyes on the back of his hand.

In the moonlight, up and down the street, were many

more monsters, the loud gunshots had attracted them. Ryan leaned forward and threw up. He looked up the street at the bones gleaming in the moonlight. White bones on the black asphalt. Piano keys of the devil.

He put the barrel of the gun against his head. It was hot. Looked at the stars twinkling down at him. "Why?"

No answer. The city was silent except for someone crying. It took him a moment to realize it was him. Then came the sound of shuffling steps.

He pulled the trigger. The gun didn't fire. He pulled it again. After a bit he looked at the pistol and realized he was out of bullets. Then he remembered the new pistol grip and popped it open. There were two inside. In the confusion, fleeing from the zombies in the tunnel; he'd forgotten. He took out the two bullets and fumbled them in, reloading. He put the barrel of the gun against the side of his head and counted down. Three. Two.

When he got to One he heard something, he wasn't sure what. The monsters down the street turned toward the sound and a hockey stick flashed into view and one by one the zombies went down.

Now Ryan knew what the sound was, it was the sound of inline roller skates. A small boy holding a hockey stick skidded to a stop in front of him. "Come on, Mister," Kenny said, "the zombies are coming."

Ryan looked down the street. Many more monsters were coming, filling the night with the sound of their shuffling steps. The gun barrel tapped against his head.

"Mister, don't." The small voice was scared. "I don't want to be alone."

But Ryan wasn't listening. He squeezed the trigger.

With lightning reflexes Kenny swung the hockey stick. The gunshot echoed up and down the stone canyons, far into the night.

Ryan fell to the ground and Kenny cried out.

*****

Chapter 33 - Hotel Death

Howie slowed his old Mustang in front of the Palace Hotel; one of the tires was flat. Several vans were parked along the curb or abandoned on the street. Some of the panel vans displayed the image of a hot air balloon on the side: Bart Simpson's head: a Coca-Cola bottle, a rainbow balloon, a Pterodactyl balloon. Some vans looked like they had been parked, but others had doors open as if the passengers had just run away.

"They're for storing the balloons in," Howie said. "Driving them away."

"Why not fly them away?" Diane said.

"Trump wanted to, but a federal agency wouldn't let him, said the air currents were too dangerous, that the balloons would never rise high enough, fast enough to avoid the skyscrapers around the park."

"They must have been trucked into Central Park," Tommy said.

Howie motioned at the intersection of Central Park South (E. 59th Street) and Fifth Avenue. A van had collided with a Mercedes; the van was on its side, the sedan's hood crumpled. The doors of both vehicles were open and no one was around. Two large cylindrical tanks stuck out the back of the van. On the asphalt next to them were four bright red fire extinguishers. "There were more vans here when we left."

"I guess the others left," Tommy said, "before the world ... ended."

"Look at that!" Diane pointed up the block by the Ritz-Carlton Hotel. People wandered, shuffled about as if unable to get inside. Then one of them turned toward the car and they saw it was a monster. One after another the zombies turned and started coming toward them.

"Get going," Tommy said a hysterical tone in his voice.

Howie raced to the intersection of E. 59th Street and Fifth Avenue and slowed. Up and down every street and sidewalk, every place he looked there were monsters shuffling along on the sidewalks, in the streets. As they stayed there, engine idling -- thank God the lights were off -- more and more monsters turned toward the car.

"Second thought the garage might not be a bad idea."

Howie drove up Fifth Avenue, right on 58th Street. Cars, vans, delivery trucks were stopped, crashed, in the street. He rode up onto the sidewalk; hit one monster coming at them with arms outstretched, knocked him down and rolled over him, then hit a few more. They bounced off his fenders and tried to grab the sides. He zigzagged across the street, careened around a white FedEx van and a brown UPS van crashed in the center of the street and pulled past the broken barrier, 'Please take a ticket', into the parking garage. It was dark, but at least they didn't see any zombies.

The parking garage was unusually empty. A Lexus and a Caddie had backed into each other and been abandoned. Howie pulled into an empty parking place under a dimly lit sign: Pla Ho el.

He shifted into park, turned off the engine and the quiet engulfed them. The hot engine ticked as it cooled. A few emergency lights glowed in the garage. They looked around and saw only a few cars and a lot of empty parking places.

"No zombies," Diane said. "Why?"

"No food," Howie said.

"Shssh." Tommy motioned Howie to be quiet.

"Stop it," Diane said to Tommy. "I'm okay now. I need to know what's going on."

Howie said, "I think the zombies are outside because their food source is out there."

"You mean man?" she said. "Us."

"They don't seem to be afraid of anything," Howie said.

"They're too hungry to be afraid," Tommy said.

"They don't seem to eat dogs or any other creatures,"

Howie said. "That virus in the cloud the radio talked about must've genetically re-engineered them."

"Maybe the dogs and cats sensed it and went into hiding."

"Oh, gross," Diane said.

"Like cannibals," Tommy said.

"The Donner party," Howie said.

"They were starving," Diane said.

"So are the monsters," Tommy said.

"Like Easter Island," Howie said.

"Easter Island?" Tommy said. "Are you sure about that?"

"That's what I heard."

"I never heard that."

"Their population swelled and they didn't have the food to support it, so they started eating each other."

"They have a crop failure or something?".

"You mean like the potato famine?"

"The Irish didn't suddenly start eating each other because they were hungry."

"The Irish were Catholic, Easter Islanders were pagans."

"Must be the zombies aren't Irish."

Tommy turned to Howie, not sure he should smile.

"Guys, guys," Diane said. "Stop it."

Tommy gave Howie like what's the matter with her? We were just fooling with each other.

"Why don't they attack and eat each other?"

"Maybe they do," Tommy said. "We've just been too busy running away to notice."

Howie shook his head. "I'm sure."

"What are we going to do?" Tommy said.

"Get some food," she said. "See if we can contact someone. Maybe the Red Cross has some safe places in the city."

"And some weapons," Howie said.

Tommy grinned and Diane rolled her eyes.

Howie and Diane climbed out of the car and looked

around at the dark parking garage. Tommy climbed out, straightening his dark green blazer, running a hand over his blonde hair.

Howie opened the trunk and handed out flashlights. Under a mat was a Ruger .22 rifle he lifted out. "Keep it for when I get flats on the highway."

"Why didn't you pull it out yesterday?"

"No stranger approached the car."

They shined the weak flashlights around the garage; it was empty. And silent.

"Notice how quiet it is?" Howie said.

"Not even this quiet in the country," she said.

"The city's dead," Tommy said.

"Dead?" she said.

Howie twisted around, checking the area, his neck creaking.

Tommy walked to the wall. He broke the glass and pulled out an axe. He hefted it like he knew what he was doing.

Diane said, "Hand me the fire extinguisher."

Tommy laughed as he handed the red cylinder to her. "Going to give 'em a wash?"

"Maybe we don't have to kill everyone," she said.

"No, we have to," Tommy said. "They're zombies."

Howie shook his head. "You don't know. Maybe we don't. Maybe their DNA is only slightly screwed up and something could set them straight."

"Gimme a break," Tommy said. "We just drove through 'Zombieland' and you want 'Mary Poppins'."

"You got any ideas?" she said.

"One," he said. "Sister Diane or should I call you Nun, I wouldn't risk my life trying to convert the zombies to a vegetarian diet."

"They might lose weight," Howie said.

Diane shook her head and Tommy gave Howie a high-five.

They approached the metal door. Tommy grabbed the handle and Howie aimed the gun. Tommy shoved the door open. The hall was empty; it had beige carpeting and waist high oak veneer wainscoting, was painted light beige from the waist up to the white ceiling. The round dome lights in the ceiling were off as were the decorative seashell sconces. Dim emergency lights glowed along the wall next to the ceiling.

"Come on," Tommy said, wanting to sound like he was in charge, but his voice betrayed the panic in him.

They walked down the hall. The metal door closed behind them. Thunk! They almost jumped.

Diane stood with her hand over her heart.

"Where to first?" Howie said.

"Our room," Diane said.

"The room?" Tommy said.

"Yes."

"Tell me," Tommy said. "If this hadn't happened, who were you going to let sleep in the bed with you tonight?"

"What?" Howie said. "I can't believe you asked that."

"Just a friendly question."

"Both of you." Diane gazed at the shocked expressions on their faces. "I was going to sleep on the floor."

"The floor?" Tommy said.

"So?"

"But I paid for the room," Tommy said.

"That's all you paid for," Howie said.

"That isn't what I mean."

"Let's not get into it now."

"Why bother going to the room?"

"So we get some clothes," Diane said.

"Clothes?" Tommy said.

"You see how I'm dressed," Diane said.

They both looked at her in the black cocktail dress.

"Guys, this isn't a low budget horror movie. I'm not going to go running around in high heel shoes and a skimpy dress. I want jeans and my running sneakers."

"Oh," Tommy said.

"Then we go downstairs," she said. "See if anyone else is alive. Anyone knows anything. Maybe they have a communications center here."

"Since when do you give orders?" Tommy said.

"What're you talking about?"

"Who put you in charge?" Tommy said.

"You're not in charge," Howie said.

"You're not either," Tommy said.

"I vote for Diane," Howie said.

"A girl? You're voting for a girl?"

"What's wrong with that?"

"You're ganging up on me," Tommy said.

"No, we're not," she said.

"Either him or me," Tommy told Diane.

"What's wrong with a girl in charge?"

"Guys are used to action."

"Yeah, I can see that, Paul Bunyan." She regarded Tommy and the way he held the axe.

"Hey, I'm just saying it would be better if you voted for someone who knew what he was doing." He stood taller, lifting his strong chin as if he was running for office.

"T.N.T., you running for school council again?" Howie said.

"Since when did you ever know what you were doing?"

"You didn't seem to mind New Years."

Howie looked from Tommy to Diane. New Years?

Diane was glad they were in shadows; her face felt like it had a sunburn.

"I vote for myself," she said.

"That's two to one," Howie said, still thinking about of last New Years. "Diane wins."

"She can't vote for herself."

"Since when?"

Tommy's eyes darted from Howie to Diane and his mouth became a hard straight line. If that's the way they want it, he'd go along with it, for now.

New Years ... Diane had arrived at Bonnie's house late, Howie remembered. She'd immediately situated herself between him and Bonnie, but now that he thought about it, Bonnie must have been keeping him busy, since he'd asked her where Diane was. Diane said a friend had dropped her off. Tommy arrived a few minutes later looking like he'd dressed in the car. Oh!

He looked at Diane who turned away, and then his eyes went to Tommy who grinned like he was so cool. Tommy knew he'd had it bad for Diane since high school. Tommy had repeatedly said she wasn't so hot, that he could take her or leave her. As a friend she was okay, but as a girlfriend she left a lot to be desired. So Tommy had made it with Diane before the party and that's why he'd acted so full of himself. Of course with T.N.T. it was hard to tell, he was always full of himself. And that's why she didn't want to take Tommy's car to New York.

"Come on." Diane led the way down the hall.

Tommy gave Howie a look to convey that if Howie wanted to be a fool then whatever came his way was his fault. Howie stared at him remembering when Tommy said they should not go after Diane, she was friends with both of them and it'd only split them up. Howie followed Tommy, who followed Diane, up the hall.

"How many times?" Howie whispered.

Tommy grinned at him and held up his fist and opened it, showing five fingers, then closed and opened it, until he reached twenty.

"Twenty times?" Howie whispered, shocked, then remembering Tommy was a liar.

"It's none of your business," Diane said, only hearing part of the conversation.

"I think I have a right to know if my two best friends are playing me for a cuckold."

"We're not married," Diane said and Tommy laughed.

"If the shoe fits," Tommy whispered.

"So you were screwing like rabbits and getting me to cover for you so Tommy's ex-wife didn't find out."

Diane turned to him. "So what if Denise found out, they were divorced and she was seeing other men."

Tommy was shaking his head no to Howie, don't speak.

"He was trying to get back with her." Diane looked at

Howie like he was making it up, so Howie added, "That's why I had to drive you home."

Diane turned to Tommy, her expression one of disbelief, but one look at Tommy and she knew it was true.

Tommy held up his hands like he was innocent. "She was having trouble with a peeping Tom. I knew if I told you, you'd react like that. That's why I didn't tell you."

Howie paused in the hall, a puzzle of history suddenly making sense. "That's why you kept asking me what Tommy was up to?" he said to Diane. Then he turned at Tommy, Tommy shook his head no, "And you didn't want me to tell her about Flo."

"Who's Flo?" Diane demanded.

"He's mixed up," Tommy said.

"And Bonnie."

"You slept with my best friend?" Diane displayed disgust at having been cheated on with her friend.

"What about me?" Howie said. "You said I was your best friend."

Diane turned to Howie to see who else he knew about, but Howie was staring accusingly at her. "What?" she said, but didn't need an answer, she'd seen the look in his eyes. "It was just a one time thing. A mistake."

Howie walked past her, down the hall. "Come on."

"Howie," Diane said, but Howie kept walking away.

Howie wanted to shout at her, tell her off, but it hurt to speak about it and he was afraid what else he might find out.

Diane looked at Tommy like she could kill him. Tommy shrugged his shoulders as if to say it wasn't his fault, but Diane turned away and hurried after Howie.

"I'm sorry," Diane said, not sure what she was sorry for or that she should apologize.

"Shsssh," Howie said, fed up with both of them.

They quietly passed several rooms with the doors open. Diane didn't want to shine her light into the rooms for fear of attracting something that might be in there. Howie was worried about lighting the dark hall and the other open doors in front of them. Tommy, taking up the rear, shined his light into each room, and in two rooms he saw something glittering on the floor or a table. He dashed into one room holding the axe and picked up a woman's watch. It was a Tiffany Gemea watch in white gold with many small diamonds in the watch face and bigger diamonds in the case: hundreds of diamonds. It took his breath away, it was so expensive looking. He looked around, no one was watchin, and quickly pocketed it.

"What're you doing?" Howie stopped when he heard Tommy go into a room.

"Checking it out."

Diane felt the lie, she was certain of it. She'd caught him in fibs several times and this felt like an out and out lie. She noticed the flap on his green blazer pocket was tucked inside and the pocket bulged slightly. Tommy who prided himself on not having anything out of place was the last one to be messy.

"What's in there?" she asked as they stood in the hall.

"Sure is quiet," Tommy said.

"You already said that," Howie said.

"Still is."

"What do you have in there?"

"Come on." Tommy motioned at her to go on.

She gave him a look and walked down the hall.

At the next open room Tommy hurried inside, Howie stopped in the hall and turned to follow him. "Stand guard," Tommy whispered and paused just inside the door to make sure no one followed him.

Diane turned her flash off and stood outside the door in the hall. To her horror she watched Tommy picking jewelry off the floor. The diamonds earrings and rings glittered like ice in the spill of moonlight coming in the window. Tommy unclasped a diamond watch around an arm -- the arm ripped from a body and left on the floor.

Tommy stood up and did not see her in the hall.

"They don't need it."

"Leave it," Diane ordered.

Howie whipped around and saw her in the hall staring at Tommy, a look of disgust on her face.

"We may need it to survive tomorrow. We might have to pay for water or food with it," Tommy said.

She stared hard at Tommy. Now she understood what her instincts had been telling her for years. Now she knew why she couldn't stay with him.

Her eyes swung to Howie. He looked away. She had hoped he would say something to Tommy, finally stand up to him, but he only teased him like an immature man-boy.

"That's robbery," she said.

"They're dead," Tommy said.

"You don't know that."

"He might be right," Howie admitted. "We might need it."

"So we rob from the dead?" she said.

"The rules have changed," Tommy said.

"The rules haven't changed and neither have you."

She stormed down the hall.

"Tomorrow it might buy us food and water," Tommy said.

""You mean buy YOU food and water," she said over her shoulder.

"Shssh," Howie said.

Tommy was about to tell Howie off, tired of his always siding with Diane against him, as if that was going to get him some of what she would never give a schmuck like him. Then he heard it. Hissing. Shuffling from the room next door. The rooms were connected by a double doorway. The door must have been open, but now only one door was closed. Something was in the other room. Diane came back into the room to see what they were up to.

Tommy stepped up to the door and raised the axe. Howie stood where he was aiming the rifle. Diane stepped to the side holding the fire extinguisher.

Tommy nodded at each of them, and then opened the inner door. The other door was almost shut. His hand was shaking as he shoved the other door open.

A gray haired fat woman stood there in the tattered remains of a blue sequined dress, folds of fat hanging down from her like wet gray towels; in her hands was a slender arm she had been chewing on. A young boy lay dead on the floor.

Tommy turned away and threw up.

Howie held the rifle, but didn't shoot. Diana nudged him and Howie raised the rifle, but his hands were shaking too much to aim.

The gray-haired monster hissed at them and Diane sprayed her with the fire extinguisher and she disappeared in a gray fog. Then Diane tried to yank the rifle away from Howie.

Howie shrugged her off and aimed.

"Fire," she told him.

"Can't see her," he said. Then the zombie lunged out of the fog at them and he fired. Hit her in the eye, black blood oozed out of the eye socket, and she fell backward, dead on the floor. The small caliber .22 sounded like a firecracker in the silent hotel.

Diane quickly closed the door. Then she turned to Tommy still throwing up.

"Why didn't you try to get her jewelry?"

"Come on." Howie walked into the hall.

She stared after Howie, angry he wasn't on her side.

"Won't the sound attract more?" she said.

"Then why were you yelling at me to shoot?"

She turned to Tommy still puking on the carpet.

"Next time, Mister Action, either use the axe or give it to me."

Diane stepped into the hall. Howie had already resumed going down the hall. She caught up to him. A moment later Tommy stepped into the hall and hurried after them, the axe shaking in his hands, drops of pale puke on his dark green blazer.

"It was smart using the gun," Tommy said, like he'd purposely not used the ax. "If the gun doesn't work, I'll use the axe."

"T.N.T.," Diane said. "Big man."

Tommy gave her a look like he wanted to hit her.

Diane elbowed Howie aside and took the lead.

"Go ahead, Daisy Crockett," Tommy said.

She shot him a glance over her shoulder. "Just shut up, Tommy-bird. Shut up."

Howie whispered to her, "I froze."

"Happens," she said and wanted to kick herself for coming to New York with these boys. What was she thinking? Diane heard something and she and Howie exchanged looks and stopped and turned to Tommy.

"What?"

"The thirteen pieces of silver in your pocket are making noise."

"We might need it tomorrow for food," he insisted.

"We?" she said. He would only look after himself.

"Whoever's alive," he said.

She looked at Howie, Howie shrugged he might be right. She wanted to slap some sense into him. Didn't he realize that Tommy would only take care of himself? That Tommy had lied to Howie, said hands off, so he could get her for himself and would lie to Howie about everything and anything he wanted for himself.

"What?" Howie asked.

"What is this, a soap opera?" Tommy yanked the fire extinguisher away from her. "I'll take that."

"Hey, gimme that back."

Tommy shoved Howie aside. "And I'm tired of your crap, too. I'm gonna get out of this alive and that means you two assholes are not leading me anywhere or telling me what to do or giving me orders. And we're not voting on it. I'm in charge and you and him either come along or get the hell outta my way. Taking his car to New York almost got us killed; I'm not rolling the dice on that again. I'm not gonna take orders from you or him. Get that through you heads."

Howie started to come forward and Tommy threatened

him with the axe. "Stay where you are until you promise undying loyalty to me."

Howie stared at him. "W--what?"

"T.N.T.," Diane said.

"You two can get in that P.O.S. car and go back to Podunk, before you get me killed." Tommy turned and went down the dark hall.

"Come on." Howie said to Diane and they continued down the hall, not really following Tommy, but going in the same direction. Tommy glanced back at them and hurried ahead.

Tommy went into the fire stairwell and they reached it a few moments later. They opened it and heard Tommy clumping, running up the stairs, then a door opened and closed. On each landing a pale emergency light glowed.

They climbed up the stairs.

"He's just scared," she said.

"Well thank God our lives are not at stake or anything."

She smiled as they went through the fire door. The hall to their room looked almost exactly like the other hall, except the carpet wasn't as worn and there were fewer emergency lights. Sections of the hall between the fixtures were very dark.

"Ut oh," Howie said.

"Come on," she said.

They hurried through the pools of light and paused at the edge of the blackened areas and tried to peer ahead. In a few minutes they were outside their room. The door was closed. They stopped and looked at it.

She raised her hand to knock and Howie grabbed it and shook his head. "It's our room too."

"Open it," she told him.

"Now you're giving me orders?"

She gave Howie an angry look and reached forward and opened the door. The room was dark and the light coming in the windows only made shadows where the beds were and where the dresser was. They shined their flashlights around and saw Tommy's legs on the floor between the bed and the window. His legs were not moving. Howie and Diane were stunned.

"Tommy?" she said and ran into the room to see if he was okay. Howie stepped in cautiously behind her, swinging his rifle left and right looking for zombies.

Diane ran to Tommy. When she got to him he suddenly sat up and said, "Boo."

Diane yelled and jumped back, her hand on her heart.

Tommy was laughing. "Just wanted to scout ahead and make sure the coast was clear."

Howie knew Tommy was making that up to save face and show her he wasn't such a bad guy. Maybe being on his own for a few minutes in such a nightmare world made him realize he needed all the friends he could get. By the look in Diane's eyes she thought the same.

Tommy tried to hand her the fire extinguisher.

"I want the axe," she said.

"An axe is a man's weapon," he said. "You need someone with meat on his shoulders to use it."

She looked at Tommy. What did she ever see in him? For several moments there was silence. Then she reluctantly took the fire extinguisher from him.

"Now what?" Howie said.

"Pack what you really need," Diane said.

"Let's run for it," Howie said. "Go back to the car."

"Not that wreck," Tommy said. "We need to find something better. Something that can get us somewhere."

Diana agreed.

"We'll search the parking lot," Tommy said, thinking he saw some neat cars in the shadows.

"Too slow and dangerous," Diane said. "Let's go to the front desk, check the register or something, and see what people have. We're sure to find something faster, safer."

"Unless they left already," Howie said.

"He's got a point," Tommy said.

"Let's just pack," Diane said.

"We didn't really unpack," Howie said.

"Then just take everything, it'll be quicker."

They gathered their suitcases on the beds and started throwing in the few things they'd taken out back in them. Tommy had taken over the credenza. Had placed his expensive suitcase on it and taken things out and spread them around. Now he couldn't fit every back in his luggage.

Tommy laughed. "With the lights off we should call 'Marco' when he get separated. You know, 'Marco'," Tommy said in a high voice, "Polo," in a deeper voice.

Diane stared at him and sighed. What had she ever seen in him?

Then they heard a sound at the door and turned. Marco, the bellmen, now one of the undead, shuffled into the room.

"I'll take care of this," Tommy said. He grabbed the fire extinguisher near Diane and handed her the axe and headed for the little undead bellman.

"Take the axe," Howie said, but Tommy waved him aside like he was making a big deal out of nothing.

Using the red fire extinguisher like a battering ram Tommy shoved the little zombie bellman into the hall. Then he shoved it down the hall and sprayed it with the CO2 foam and lifted the fire extinguisher like a club and disappeared from view.

They heard the sound of the fire extinguisher hitting something and returned to their packing. Diane stepped out of her heels, quickly got into jeans, took off the dress, pulled on a red University of Georgia sweatshirt, a black 'G' on the front, and slipped on her old Nikes.

"Why isn't Tommy back?" Diane said.

Howie gave her a look, then grabbed his rifle and ran into the hall. At first they didn't see Tommy, there were so many monsters, and then he saw T.N.T. on the bottom of the pile. Diane ran back into the room for the axe.

Howie went up to the first zombie and shot it in the back of the head at point blank range. Then he put the barrel against the head of another zombie's head and fired, and then another. He fired a total of five times and handed

Diane the rifle, "Out of bullets," grabbed the axe from her and hit the last two in the head.

They pulled and shoved the monsters off Tommy. He was at the bottom of the pile. His dark green blazer was smeared with black zombie blood and fresh red blood. His face had been clawed, his neck gouged, his hands had been bitten.

"Oh Tommy." Diane sat on the floor and cradled his head in her lap.

Howie took the rifle from her and ran into the room. He found his multi-tool in a side pocket of his duffel bag and extended the screwdriver. He unscrewed the plastic butt plate on the rifle stock, two long deep screws. Took off the butt plate. Inside the stock was a thin metal rod with extra rounds. He heard Diane struggling in the hall.

"Tommy, stop it," she said loudly.

Howie shoved a round in the small magazine. Shoved the magazine back in place as he ran to the door. He pulled the bolt back to load the round into the chamber and jumped into the hall.

Diane was against the wall and Tommy was trying to bite her neck. Howie ran forward, aimed at the side of Tommy's head and -- Tommy turned to him -- as he fired. "NO," Diane shouted. The blast put an ugly red hole in Tommy's head and he fell to the floor.

Diane stared at him not believing what he'd done. Her face paled. She looked down at Tommy and back at Howie.

"What the hell did you do?" She glared at him, then turned to Tommy and sobbed. Her knees buckled and he had to hold her up before she fell down.

"What?"

"He was kidding," she cried.

"But he was bitten and ... and ... everything."

"You know him. It was a joke." She looked down at Tommy lying on the floor and sobbed and ran into the room and stopped near the window and grabbed tissues from her purse and kept on crying.

In the distance behind her was Central Park and in the blackness a balloon was lit up by a solar powered spotlight.

"But ...."

"It was a joke," she cried. "He had fake teeth. He was going to wake you in the middle of the night and pretend he was a vampire."

"The blood, bites marks on his face and hands?"

"Fake. He must've put them in his coat pocket when he came in the room.

He looked from her standing at the window crying, to the large balloon in the distance behind her moving in the breeze, to Tommy on the hall floor. He was not moving, blood was seeping from the hole in his head. He saw he hadn't really shot Tommy in the brain, he'd shot him more in the face, in the side of his mouth. Then suddenly Tommy's whitish eyes opened, his lips had turned black and curled back from his teeth.

"Diane," he called.

"Leave me alone."

He ran into the room and grabbed her arm. She shook his hand off her.

"Come with me," he said.

"No, I've seen enough."

"Come with me."

She stared angrily at him.

"Please."

She went back to packing and he grabbed her arm and dragged her into the hall. He stared at her and pointed down the hall. "Look."

"Oh my God," she said. "Where's Tommy?"

Howie's head snapped around. He saw the dead zombies, but didn't see Tommy. He looked up and down the dark hall. Tommy was nowhere to be seen.

"He was one of the undead," he said.

She looked at him. "Not Tommy."

"Then how do you explain what happened?"

"You shot him in the head. He's wounded, confused."

"I shot him in the mouth. Must've knocked him out."

"Don't shout at me."

"The dead simply do not get up and walk away."

She glowered at him and shook her head.

"Unless they're zombies."

"Tommy," she called.

"Shut up," Howie said.

"Don't tell me to shut up."

She glared at him like she was going to slap him. Then a noise came from down the dark hall.

"Tommy?" she called.

Howie ran into the room.

"Tommy?" she called again then almost cried out when she saw an undead man walking, shuffling toward her.

Howie was back in the hall. He aimed the rifle and fired. The bullet hit the zombie in the forehead and he fell to the floor.

"Keep your voice down," Howie told her.

She gave him a look. "You've never gotten over my sleeping with him." She walked into the room.

"I just found out about it," he said and followed her into the room.

"I'm not going to talk about it."

"I don't want to talk about it, but you might want to explain why you played the virgin princess with me."

"Because you're a boy."

"A boy?" He looked at the rifle in his hands and the blood on his hands. "Who just save your life. Twice."

"Hurry," she said. "We have to find him. God knows where he's wandering about."

"He's a zombie."

"Maybe he's not completely turned."

"How could you?" he said to her back as she was carrying her suitcase out of the room.

She paused and looked at him; tears running down her face. "He could be quite charming at times."

"Tommy? You know why we call him T.N.T.?"

"His initials?"

"Every relationship he's ever had explodes or he does."

"Why didn't you tell me?"

"I thought you knew. Everyone knew. Bonnie, Flo, everyone."

"Come on." She marched down the hall.

He yanked the magazine out and loaded six bullets into it, shoved it back in place; put the metal rod on the stock. Screwed one screw in to hold the butt plate in place, grabbed his suitcase and the axe and hurried into the hall.

Diane was nowhere in sight. "Oh God, now what?"

The hall was empty except for the dead zombies. He looked up and down the dark hall, not sure which way to go.

Just then the fire door opened and he saw Diane in the dim light. "You coming or not?"

Lugging the fire axe, his heavy suitcase, and the rifle, he hurried after her. "For years you've been saying a girl would have to be a slut or brain-dead to sleep with him."

"Let it go," she said and let the door close.

He lumbered to the door, had a difficult time opening it, and saw her going down the stairs. "Why were you keeping this secret from me?"

She groaned as she continued walking down the stairs.

"This explains some of his strange behavior."

"Shut up," she said as if she was trying to hurry away from him.

"And your equally bizarre behavior."

Howie rushed down the stairs letting the door close behind him. Zombie Tommy came out of the room next to theirs chewing on a foot and went to the fire stair door and struggled to open it.

*****

Chapter 34 – Out of the Fire

They hurried along the street. The little hand gripping his hand pulled him away from the grisly scene. When his thoughts cleared a little he looked back. He couldn't see the porch, too many zombies in the way. And more were coming after them.

The little boy skated faster and he had to jog to keep up. Zombies were everywhere and he would zigzag around them and pass them by. Ryan jogged faster and faster to keep up with the boy. The Inline skates were loud in the quiet night and even if the zombies didn't turn fast enough to grab the boy, they did turn fast enough to hassle Ryan. At times he couldn't dodge them and had to slug and punch his way through.

Most of the zombies shuffled, but a few had long legged stiff knee strides. Some seemed confused and when they looked up and saw a pack of zombies they followed them, but sometimes they veered off in a strange direction, their faces blank as ever. And it was not unusual for other zombies to follow the zombie detour. Thus a pack could go from a focused hunt to a confused mass and back to a focused mob in a few minutes.

Zombies to the left, zombies to the right, and they ran through the middle like bait in a trap.

The boy was fast on the skates. And he was young and in shape. Ryan was not young, was not in shape, and he'd never been what you would call fast. But he'd always been persistent, not one to give up.

The boy would get ahead of Ryan and the zombies would close in on him. The gun was out of bullets so he used it like a 20 ounce hammer. He hit a zombie in the face feeling the bone crack and cave in. The zombie was knocked back, but not dead, the side of the face caved in, the chin hanging by tendons. And, after a bit of struggling to regain its balance, it came after him again. Another zombie lurched at him and he hammered it in the head and the skull cracked and blood splatter flew in the air as half of the creature's head was gone and now it was dead, really dead, before it hit the ground.

Mostly the zombies reached for him and he shoved them aside or dodged out of the way. One of the times the boy got far ahead of him, the zombies closed in and blocked his path. He shoved them and clubbed them and knocked them down; the more time he took, the more zombies closed in. One zombie he knocked down grabbed his leg and tried to bite him and he had to immediately crack its head with the Smith and Wesson. Then the boy was attacking the zombie hoard with the hockey stick. Three, four zombies went down and he could get through and they ran up the street together.

"Thanks, kid."

"Kenny," the kid said as he skated up the street and Ryan jogged alongside.

"Ryan," Ryan panted.

"You need something longer."

"Or bullets."

"The noise will attract more."

"How'd you get so smart?"

"My teacher doesn't think I'll ever amount to anything."

Ryan struggled to keep up with Kenny's skating.

"How far did she make it out of this?"

"Good point."

Suddenly Kenny made a left turn in the middle of the block. "Be right back."

Ryan stopped and whirled about. At that moment there weren't many monsters directly behind them. Ryan looked around. They had made so many turns, he wasn't sure what street they were on, if they were headed east or west or what. The street sort of looked familiar, but in New York that didn't help him. As he was trying to sort it out, looking down the long straight block he saw zombies coming out of the side streets behind him joining in with the pack chasing them. And zombies were coming out of the buildings joining the pack. The pack has swelled to the size of a small army and it was still growing.

"Hurry, kid," Ryan said and killed two zombies that came at him.

"Stop calling me kid," Kenny said as he skated over and handed him a wooden mop.

"What's this?" Ryan asked as they continued running up the street.

"Your new weapon."

Ryan looked at the white mop head covered with gooey black blood. He hammered a zombie with the gun then leaned the mop handle against a car and stomped down on it, breaking the end.

"You didn't have to do that," Kenny said as he hacked a zombie in the face with his hockey stick. "It unscrews."

"Now you tell me," Ryan said as they hurried up the block.

"You can use it like a spear," Kenny said.

"I know. You spot a knife, you let me know."

Kenny took a kitchen carving knife with a nine inch blade from his back pack.

"You come prepared."

"We gotta rescue my mom," Kenny said.

"Where is she?" Ryan said as they ran and he took a roll of gray duct tape from his pack. He used the duct tape to attach the knife to the end of the wooded mop stick.

"She went to Yankee Stadium."

Ryan turned to the boy. "What did you say?"

"Yankee Stadium, the Bronx."

Ryan stopped running and stared at the boy.

Kenny froze and turned to him.

"Did you hear something about Yankee stadium?"

Ryan didn't have to say anything. Kenny saw the look on his face and tears ran down his face.

"I know she's probably dead." Now he started crying, his shoulders shaking, tears falling down his face. "But we have to at least try."

Ryan spoke at gently as he could. "We'll never get across the river."

"We have to try."

"The bridges are blocked."

"How can you say that?" Kenny shouted at him as he wailed. "How do you know?"

"See all these cars?" There were cars and buses abandoned in the streets, on the sidewalks, some crashed into each other, most just left where they were.

"That doesn't mean anything."

Ryan whirled around and speared a zombie in the face that came close. He shoved it back, trying to create a little barrier that would slow other zombies.

The zombies didn't stop. They stumbled over the bodies and continued to come.

"If one bridge was open all the cars and zombies would be headed to it."

"No. No. You don't know."

"None of the bridges are open, or the tunnels, or the subways. They're all blocked with zombies, people trying to escape and more zombies."

"You don't know," Kenny wailed as he turned about hacking zombies with his hockey stick; dark blood and gore went flying. The business end, the blade, was cover with bits and pieces of flesh, with ripped clothing, so that every few swings he had to wipe it off on a dead zombie.

"If she's all right, she probably got to a place of safety and will wait it out, until the army or whoever is in control."

"She's all right," Kenny insisted.

"She probably is," Ryan said as he turned around using the makeshift spear to stab zombies in the head and kill them.

"You're just saying that."

"It's us that I'm really worried about."

"Then what are we doing here?"

They hurried up the street. A zombie got in Kenny's way and he took its legs out from under it with the hockey stick. But it stilled struggled to get up and get him, so he kicked it in the head with the skate. The zombie's head cracked like a rotten melon and he skated away. Only he couldn't. He tried to and tripped and almost went down. The front wheel of his Inline skate was gone. He looked back. It was embedded in the zombie's head.

He couldn't skate anymore. He had to limp. Skate with his left foot, step with his right.

"You need to take them off," Ryan said.

"When?" Kenny said angry that his skate had broken. "How?"

"Soon." Ryan assumed the lead.

At the corner they stopped. None of the other streets offered clear passage. Walls of zombies were coming down each of the streets. There was no way out. Ahead of them zombies came at them. Left and right the streets were packed with zombies. They looked behind and saw more zombies chasing them.

A few zombies were close and Ryan speared two and Kenny hacked one in the head and the blade of his hockey stick broke.

"What?" Kenny shouted angrily. "If I'd known this dumb thing was only rated at a hundred zombies I wouldn't have gotten it." Then he started crying.

Ryan grabbed him by the shoulder and pulled him.

"Come on, kid, snap out of it."

"Get your hands off me."

"Don't give me any lip, kid."

"Help, help," Kenny shouted. "The man won't leave me alone."

Ryan turned to the boy and Kenny tried to smile, but mumbled, "Mommy," and cried.

Ryan pulled him to the corner.

"Where we going?" Kenny said blinded by tears.

"An empty delicatessen."

"I'm not hungry."

"Shut up."

Kenny wiped his eyes and saw the windows were

covered by a wire grill that was lowered at night. So was the door. There was a big Yale lock on the door.

"How we going to get in?" Kenny said.

Ryan took the gun and started beating on the lock.

"You're attracting them," Kenny said.

"Must be my aftershave," Ryan said as he continued to hammer the lock.

Kenny stepped forward and stabbed zombies with his broken hockey stick. Then he was grabbed from behind and yanked backward. He twisted around to stick the zombie and saw it was Ryan.

"Why'd you do that?"

"You didn't hear me."

"Hear what?"

Ryan shoved him into the open doorway, then closed the gate and used duct tape to keep it closed as zombie fingers reached through to grab him and then the zombie hoard came and pressed against the grate.

Ryan broke the glass door to open it. He and Kenny went inside, then he closed the door. The zombies were pressing on the wire grate. Ryan pulled the shade down, so they couldn't see them.

Zombies crowded at the door. Other zombies crowded the windows, but the framework of metal held them back.

Ryan and Kenny moved back into the dark store. They crawled back into the dark shadows. The sound of the wall of zombies pressing on the grate was loud.

Ryan pulled Kenny down and they crawled into the darkness. They crawled behind some displays where they couldn't be seen from the windows. After a few minutes the sound of the zombies lessened.

"Maybe we can sneak out in a while," Kenny whispered.

The sound of his voice brought new attacks on the grate. Then he heard the sound of the grate bending, the metal straining to hold the monsters back.

Ryan put his finger over his mouth.

Kenny nodded.

They sat on the floor in the darkness, behind a display of pickles; a shaft of moonlight barely lit them.

"My mom," Kenny breathed and put his hand over his mouth to silence his own sob.

"I know, kid," Ryan whispered softly.

"Mommy," Kenny said and started crying quietly, his shoulders shaking and heaving.

Ryan put his arm around the kid's shoulder and hugged him as Kenny buried his face against his chest and cried and cried.

Ryan sat stoically still, his eyes darting left and right examining the shadows of the zombies on the ceiling, listening to the grating, making sure it didn't break, as tears ran down his face.

*****

Chapter 35 – Sounds Like a Plan

Alexei stomped out of the warehouse office, his hard eyes angry, his mouth a thin red line. He walked to the steamer trunks on the floor of the warehouse and stopped when he heard gunfire outside. His eyes scanned the wall following the sound of gunfire up the street. The machinery that opened the warehouse door started making noises. He turned toward the door and his long fingered hand reached under his expensive pinstriped jacket and from a black vinyl shoulder holster that fit like a vest, pulled out a Glock nine-millimeter sixteen rounds pistol with laser grip sights. He took his shooter's stance, right arm rose holding the pistol. When his right hand squeezed the pistol grip, it activated the laser sight and a red dot shined on the middle of the door as it rose.

Alexei made ready to shoot in case zombies followed the idiots in or if either of the idiots had been infected. Briefly, he considered just shooting them to get it over with, but relented; he might need them. As the gray metal door rolled upward he breathed out and moved the red dot left and right prepared to shoot to kill.

The noisy warehouse door opened and Luka and Frankie rode in on police motorcycles. Alexei deftly holstered the pistol and stood there inspecting them for cuts and scratches as if nothing was wrong. His expensive pinstriped dark gray suit coat hung on him perfectly concealing the shoulder holster.

Luka and Frankie wore large black backpacks and gun straps over their shoulders; Luka had a Tech-9 machine pistol and Frankie an Uzi. Luka pressed the automatic door control and the big door started closing. In the street Alexei could see the bodies of several zombies and further up the block other monsters hurrying after them. Frankie jumped off his stylized Orange County police motorcycle and hurried to the door and shot down any zombie that came close. Then the door slammed shut and after a moment the undead started beating on it.

Luka and Frankie rolled the motorcycles to the three steamer trucks.

Aware that the a few zombies could draw an army of zombies, and an army of them could interfere with his plans, Alexei hurried to the Humvee. From a backpack in the rear he took two small canisters that looked like gray soda cans. He walked back to the door; next to it was a small mail slot. He opened the slot and immediately a gray hand reached inside. He pulled the Glock and fired two shots to get the hand out of the slot. Then he pulled the pin on one can and tossed it out the slot. He did the same with the second can. The eye-burning smell of tear gas started filling the street when he closed the mail slot. With the sound of zombies trying to get away from the burning gas Alexei strolled to the steamer trunks.

"No other bosses alive," Alexei said. "I last of bosses. I last boss. I boss of bosses."

"Congrats," Luka said.

Alexei stood tall, proud; it was an honor for him to

outlive his contemporaries. War, zombies, plague, it didn't matter. He survived, they didn't.

Frankie said, "We saw some people, maybe cops taking apart First National, so we left it. Some vigilantes tried to stop us so I lit box of firecrackers as we left. They didn't follow." Frankie grinned. "Too busy fighting zombies."

"No crime families left," Alexei went on. "No organization. On shortwave they say country devastated."

"What about Russia?" Luka asked.

"Worse," Alexei turned away. "People no own guns. People strong, but monsters too many."

"Where can we go?" Frankie said.

"Why we have to go?"

"I mean we can't stay in the city, it's getting worse out there.

"Right now we worry about stayin' alive. We will have to get out of city. Too many monsters here."

"How we do that?" Frankie said. "Bridges are crap. We can't drive over them. We can't walk and carry enough bullets to fight our way across."

Alexei nodded and rubbed his chin as if he had been considering the same thing. "How to leave."

"We did like you said," Luka told him, "went to harbor. No boat available. Whatever float is gone. We see big yacht in river, people on it fighting. People shooting at monsters, then fire start. People jumping overboard. Shooting and fire attract monsters to dock. We leave."

"I worry about them starting a fire in city," Frankie said.

"Yeah, who will fight it?" Alexei said.

"How about other countries? Maybe we go there."

"How we get there?" Luka said.

"Many places destroyed," Alexei said. "Cuba burning. Ukraine, Georgia not good."

"All my family and friends," Frankie said. "Gone."

A tear rolled down Luka's cheek. "Always thought I would visit home one more time."

"Worse than Hitler," Alexei said.

"Zombies running outta food," Luka said. "They eat people till only bones left."

"We shoot a lot of them." Frankie held up two empty ammo clips.

"When they really run outta food, that when things get bad," Alexei said.

"How we survive in here with thousands of zombies beating on the doors?" Frankie said.

"If stink not get us, bugs and disease will," Luka said.

"I can shoot zombies, but how I stop disease?"

"And rats." Luka shook his big head. "Saw some as big as small dogs, weren't they, Frankie?"

Frankie nodded. "Mean as Cujo."

"So how we going to do it, Boss?" Luka said.

Alexei looked from one to the other, judging their loyalty to him.

"Thought we going take over country?" Frankie's brown eyes jumping around at every noise. The zombies were beating on the walls searching for a weak spot or there were so many of them that's what it seemed like.

"We might have to stay here," Alexei said. "In few days zombies be dead. Then come rats. Then bugs. We can't poison all of them. Too much poison. We could force people to burn parts of city down."

"Slaves?" Frankie said.

"Forced labor, like in old Russia."

"Hate to be here when fire starts," Luka said. "Fire easy to spread."

"I come to same conclusion," Alexei said.

"So what we do?" Frankie said.

"I working on it."

"How we survive until then?" Frankie blurted out. "Need to get away. How we going to...."

Glass broke, a tinkling sound. It fell from a high window and landed on the cement floor.

They all ran to the side and shined their flashlights up in the darkness. Somehow the monsters had made it to the roof of the building next door. The thick iron mesh welded to the window prevented them from getting inside.

"Not last forever," Frankie said.

The zombies shoved their fingers through the thick mesh trying to reach through to them.

"Only hold for time being," Luka said.

Alexei walked back to the motorcycles, the weight of the world on his shoulders.

"You had success?" Alexei said.

"Like taking money from dead," Luka said.

"Jewelry stores, banks," Frankie said. "Everything waiting to be taken."

The first steamer trunk was overflowing with diamond rings, diamond earrings, diamond watches, gold rings, and money. As were the second and third trunks. The fourth trunk had a little room left.

Next to the fourth trunk was a mound of paper money. Some of the money had bank wrappers around it.

Frankie grabbed the pack from the back of his chopper and dumped the contents on a card table forming a pile of money, diamonds, and jewelry. "How much?"

Luka looked at the trunks and shrugged. "Millions." He emptied his backpack on top of the pile and more money and jewelry spilled onto the floor.

"Over twenty million," Alexei told them.

"Hear anything?" Frankie said.

Alexei glanced through the windows of the warehouse office at the CB and police band radios lining the shelves below the portrait of Stalin.

"Disorganized crap. Everyone ask for help. No one do anything. Go to this hospital for medical help. Then hear hospital overrun, everyone not infected fleeing. Go to police station, same thing. City coming apart." Alexei turned to Luka. "You see anything?"

Luka shrugged his shoulders. "People running around. A few fighting. Most hiding in apartments, waiting for zombies to attack. Zombies everywhere. Getting worse. By tomorrow city gone."

"City not last twenty-four hours," Alexei said.

"I figure eighty percent dead," Frankie said. "Less in country, but city real bad. No place to run, nowhere to hide. Defenses overrun." Luka nodded in agreement. "Pretty soon won't be able to get out there be so many zombies in street."

"What we do?" Luka said.

"Stow trunks away."

"Then what?" Frankie asked.

Alexei's gray eyes looked at him hard, not happy that he should be questioned. He was about to answer with his pistol when one of the radios in the office, squawked.

"What that?" Frankie said and Alexei held up his hand for him to be quiet.

"Ryan, Ryan," a voice on the radio said. "I know a place to go, where are you? Over."

"Hurry, stow trunks," Alexei said as he ran to the office and closed the door.

"What's up?" Frankie asked Luka.

"We find out when Alexei find out."

Luka took handfuls of diamonds and money and put them in the fourth trunk. He pulled out any loose bills in the pile and dropped them on the floor. Frankie scooped handfuls of loot and transferred it to the trunks, pausing to pocket a particularly big diamond ring or two.

"Robbing hotel good idea," Frankie said.

"All right already, everyone know it your idea," Luka said. "Now shut up. Be sure to tell boss when we stop for coffee and donuts."

Frankie looked at Luka, angered, but if he didn't speak up Luka would take the credit for it.

When the loot was stuffed into the trunks Luka closed the tops and pressed the clasps closed.

"You gonna lock 'em?" Frankie said.

"What for?"

"So no one rips us off."

Luka almost laughed, as if that would stop someone. He shook his head. "Lot you not know." He grabbed two hand trucks. He gave one to Frankie, put his under a trunk and lifted another trunk on top, straining with his massive shoulders.

"Must weigh a ton," Frankie said.

"Ton and half," Luka said then he helped Frankie load the last two trunks onto his hand truck.

Luka grabbed the red handles of his hand truck and pulled back lifting the trunks and pushed it across the warehouse. Frankie struggled to pull his handle back, and then he followed, wondering where Luka was going.

Luka walked down an aisle to the wall. They could hear the hissing and growling from the zombies pressed against the heavy wire high up on the warehouse windows.

On the wall was a triple light switch. Luka walked over to them.

"They not work," Frankie said.

Luka made sure all three switches were pointed down. Then he pushed the third one up and pressed in the second one. Machinery in the cinderblock wall made noises and the wall started moving. Frankie's mouth flopped open as the cinderblock door swung open revealing a large room.

Luka and Frankie stepped inside. Luka turned on a lamp on a table. A portrait of Stalin looked down at them in the small apartment. The room was ten feet deep and ran from one end of the warehouse to the other. One end contained a bathroom and a small kitchenette and a dining area and a couch with a large flat screen TV. At the other end were two freezers, a refrigerator, filing cabinets and storage crates and boxes. The cement floor was painted gray with a grassy green outdoor carpet in the living area.

"How the boss hide out so feds not serve warrant few years back?" Frankie said.

"Lot you not know."

Frankie saw a trapdoor in the floor.

"To sewer system for escape."

"Why we not stay here?" Frankie said then heard the metal roof creaking from the weight of the zombies on it.

"That why." Luka looked up at the ceiling. "When they completely out of food they smell us. You see how they hunt. They smell us here and thousands can break in. Not now they can't, but a day, maybe two, so many even walls not stop them."

Luka wheeled two trunks inside, dropping them next to three other trunks.

"What's in there?" Frankie said.

"Money or guns, not know."

Frankie, with Luka's help, dropped his trunk next to the others. They went out of the secret room and Luka pushed the door closed. They rolled the hand trucks back to the other end of the warehouse.

Alexei was coming out of the office with a cool grin on his face. They could hear the zombies pushing on the wire mesh over the windows, the wire starting to bend, the windows creaking. A zombie in front had been crushed to death; his black blood leaking down inside, the metal was making a sound like it was starting to give.

"Won't be long before they inside," Luka said.

Frankie's eyes were wide open as he stared up at the windows. "What we do? Where we go?"

Alexei walked to the card table and gave Luka and Frankie each a quart size baggy filled with diamond rings. "For each of you." Then he tossed each of them three bank wrapped stacks of hundred dollars bills.

"You know how to get out?" Frankie asked.

Alexei glanced at the office, on the wall a few feet away from Stalin's portrait was a poster for Donald Trump's New York Balloon Fair.

He said, "Load Humvee."

A squawking sound was heard in the office.

"The scanner's picked up something." Alexei hurried to the office. "Hurry it up."

Luka climbed into the Humvee and turned the key. Nothing. The battery was dead.

"Hurry," Alexei shouted as he ran from the office, "We have to go."

*****

Chapter 36 - Unexpected Events

Ron Parker carried an orange backpack to the kitchen counter. When he put it down, it thumped, it weighed so much.

"Did you get a hold of Ryan?" Pat said when she returned from nailing more boards over the bedroom doorway. Three zombies had broken through the bedroom window from the fire escape. So many were on the fire escape it had made a metal wrenching sound and they'd run into the bedroom. The zombies saw them and busted through the thin glass after them.

Ron took his brand new Nike driver and hit a five hundred yard drive with the zombie's head. The zombie was dead before it touched the carpet. The next zombie Ron swung at put his hand up to block the shot and the club broke. The zombie paused in its attack to notice its arm was broken and wasn't doing what he wanted it to do. Then after the pause it resumed its attack and Pat handed Ron his Nike putter. "Not the Tiger Woods," he cried, but she smiled and handed it to him. "C'est la vie."

He grabbed the expensive putter. "Showing off you went to French immersion school again?"

"Tres bien." She smiled and he clobbered the zombie in the head with the putter.

When that zombie, the former Charles Larry Bundy, insurance salesman, fell down Ron charged the third zombie coming in the window. He pushed it, the previous Mrs. Smith who had such nice long legs and showed them off in short skirts, back out the window, blocking the other zombies from coming in. Ron smacked it in the side of the head with the titanium putter and it was dead sitting on the fire escape, a barrier to other zombies entering; at least for the time being.

He glanced out the window and saw zombies coming

up from two floors below, Mrs. Goldstein's place. Apparently the idea was catching on, for zombies were busting through other windows, getting on the fire escape and climbing up, looking for food. There were well over a dozen climbing up.

Just then the dresser whacked him in the side.

"Ouch," he said pulling back.

"Get out of the way," Pat said, pushing the side drawer dresser in the way.

He limped back holding his knee. "It isn't high enough."

"Why do you always have to find fault with everything I do?"

"I'm just saying ...."

"Then you do it and she stepped away and folded her hands over her chest.

"Hey, now's not the time to get all pissed."

She gave him a look. "You would say something like that."

"Here." He handed her the club. "Keep 'em out."

"I know what to do." She walked up to the window and with her first swing missed the zombie outside the window and smashed the framed picture of his mother on the dresser. "Oh, I'm sorry."

He glanced over as he struggled with the bed. "Yeah, I bet."

"I am," she said and swung the club angrily killing monsters outside the window left and right, until a wall of dead zombie bodies was piled outside the window.

"Help me," he said.

"Now what?"

He half carried, half dragged their queen size mattress to the window. She helped him put it over the window. Then he lifted up the dresser, all the pictures, keepsakes and junk on top slid to the floor as they put it on end lying against the mattress.

"Will that stop them?" she said.

He looked at her deciding between the truth or a good

lie.

"Well?"

"Not for long." She looked at him, like she couldn't believe him. "They've got our smell. The animal part of their brain that's still functioning will focus on it.

"Now what?"

He turned to the door. The hollow door opened into the bedroom so he couldn't nail it closed.

"Take what you need," he told her.

She ran to the closet and grabbed some blouses, slacks, a jacket and threw them in the hall while he pushed and shoved the taller five drawer bureau to the door. Pat hurried back in and took underwear and socks for him and her out the door. He stopped the dresser a few feet from the door. He lifted off the box spring and wedged it against the dresser leaning against the window. He grabbed the slacks from under the bed and handed them out the door to her. Then he had her hold the door open enough for him to get through and leaned the bureau against it. When he went through into the hall and closed the bedroom door he heard the bureau fall against the door, jamming it closed.

"That should hold them," he said.

"Tsk, tsk," she said. "You forgot your golf clubs. What will Tiger say?"

"Damn, they were good weapons."

"Right," she said. "Weapons."

"I gotta make a phone call," he said and rushed to the living room.

"Don't order any more golf clubs," she said when she came into the kitchen.

He looked at her. "Very funny."

Using a small hammer with a handle that came apart and turned into a screwdriver she started nailing bed boards over the doorway with some picture hanging nails she'd found in a kitchen drawer. As she finished she heard crashing in the bedroom and shivered and knew beyond a doubt that more zombies had come in the window.

"Terrible connection," Ron said. "He sounded ... I don't know, different."

"He's probably been through a lot."

The sound of a board breaking down the hall grabbed their attention; the hollow bedroom door was starting to break. They dragged the dining table down the hall, turned it sideways and wedged it between the open bathroom door and the open hall closest door. They stacked a wall of chairs in front of it and upended the coffee table to hold everything in place.

"He sounded funny."

Breathing hard, she said, "He's probably been though a lot. He's lucky to be alive."

"The connection was. . ." He shook his head.

"How's Mary Anna?" Pat said. "And the kids?"

"Didn't say. When I asked, he said he couldn't hear me, but I could hear him."

"Something must be wrong with his walkie-talkie."

"How come sometimes I could hear him fine like he was talking on a telephone?"

"Newer batteries," she said like she really knew instead of making it up as she went.

Ron touched old Mrs. Moon's pistol under his jacket.

Ron looked back at Pat, what was she talking about? Pat put her hand over her mouth, as if she was surprised and even more scared.

He looked at her, glanced at the big gun. He wasn't sure. Should he just put it down or put it somewhere out of sight? Maybe if he put it in his pocket.

"I'm pregnant," she said.

"So I can keep the gun?" He thought she'd misspoke.

"Didn't you hear me?" Her voice rose as if she was going to start screaming. "I'm going to have a baby."

"So we'll keep the gun?"

She looked at him with tears running down her face.

"The hell with the gun, do what you want with it."

He shoved the gun behind his belt.

"I meant to tell you about the baby. But I was nervous.

Worried how it would change our lives."

"Thought that's why you wanted Ryan, Hector and Mary Anna to come over tonight."

"You knew?"

"Us news hounds are trained to sniff out fast breaking stories." He felt the heavy gun pulling his pants down.

She stared at him. "So you're not upset or anything?"

"Bought you a present." He started down the hall toward the bedroom and stopped. "You would have like it."

She hurried to him and put her head on his shoulder and hugged him.

"You're not upset I didn't tell you?"

"You were going to, weren't you? Why should I be?"

She wrapped her arms around him and held on.

"You don't mind about the gun?"

"We need one. It's not just you and me now." She leaned back and looked at him. "What?"

"Ryan?"

"Haven't heard from Ryan."

That's when he started using the walkie-talkie to get hold of Ryan.

"Now what?" Pat said coming down the hall, the hammer in her hand.

An automatic weapon started firing, the bullets slamming through the walls. He grabbed Pat and they both flattened on the floor. Plaster dust floated down on them.

"Mrs. Moon?" she said.

"Or Johnson," he said.

"We have to leave."

Ron twisted to his side and looked at the window. The sky was starting to lighten in the patch visible above the buildings across the street. Dawn was on the way.

"Might as well leave now."

"Dressed like this?" She looked down at her Saturday night outfit.

"You want to go to the bedroom and change?" Ron

said.

Now Pat made a face. "Very funny."

Suddenly, a cracking sound came from the bedroom. The hollow door was finally breaking. The zombies hadn't tried to move the bureau aside, something any human or even a monkey would have done. They climbed on the bureau and clawed at the door until there were so many of them on the bureau their weight cracked the door. Ron and Pat listened to the wood break, then the surge of monsters crashing into the dining room table. Their weight kept the table in place. Their hands, gray fingers with black fingernails, came over the top of the table reaching for them, searching for them.

"God, what a smell." She put her hand over her nose.

"Come on." Ron lifted a red backpack. "I'll help you into it."

"We still have this from when we used to go hiking?" Pat said. "What's in it?"

He adjusted the shoulder straps.

"Gorp, water bottles, Gatorade, whatever candy we had," Ron said. "Some canned food."

"You have the walkie-talkie?"

Showed her a holster on his belt as he put on the orange backpack.

"How we going to get there?"

"That black Volkswagen Gabe Kelly's rebuilding."

"It's a valuable antique. We can't take that."

"The world's an antique."

"But he's been. . ."

"I'll do anything to save you and Little Ron."

"You don't know it's a boy."

"Grandma said, 'conceived before the full moon, a little boy be coming soon.'"

"That old wives' tale."

Ron carried a baseball bat autographed by Derek Jeter and Pat held the Tiger Woods putter. They went to the door and looked through the peephole, couldn't see anything.

"Ready?"

She held up the hammer. "Open it."

He undid all the bolts and lock and a zombie came into the room trying to bite him. He jumped back and she smacked it in the head with the putter. The blow hardly did anything, so she pulled and swung like she was still playing tennis and trying to hit an ace. The monster's head cracked like a coconut, a jagged line when down the side. The zombie toppled to the floor.

It was like the top taken off a bottle of perfume. The stench that came from the dead monster was terrible. Almost instantly the air was air was unbreathable. Waves of terrible horrible smell seemed to rise upward, each one worse smelling than the last one.

Ron put his hand on his pounding heart.

"It was like you were playing tennis, right?"

Her frightened eyes rose off the dead monster on the floor to him.

"Who were you playing against?"

"Don't ask."

"You were playing me, weren't you?"

"It was just a swing, just a swing."

"You were imagining beating me again."

"Ron, let's go."

Ron led the way into the hall.

Pat followed and made an invisible mark in the air.

He stopped and looked at her.

"One point for me and none for you."

She was doing that just to get him fired up to swing the bat with more force. "Did I tell you I love you?"

"Go," she said. "Let's get our son to safety."

*****

Chapter 37 - A Way Out

Alexei rushed from his office. "Hurry up. Get in Humvee. Got us way out." Then he stopped. He saw the hood on the Humvee open and Luka and Frankie looking at the engine. "What fuck's the matter?"

"Engine not start," Luka said.

Alexei saw the hood of the limo open and a black cable running from the caddie to the Humvee. "You jump it?"

"Try," Luka said.

"You need limo engine running."

"See, I told you," Frank said.

"What about this being closed space, garage?" Luka said.

Alexei took the nine-millimeter from his vest holster and shot at a window high on the walls. The glass broke and partly fell out. Almost immediately there was pounding on the metal garage door.

"See what you did?" Frankie said.

Alexei looked at him, a strange look on his face. He did not like a punk like Frankie speaking to him like that. If this is where this new world was going, there were going to be a lot of dead Frankies around.

"Sound like a lot of them," Luka said.

"Way more than before," Frankie said.

Alexei turned back to the door, the pounding by a dozen dead fists unnerving him. "Hurry, get car started."

Frankie rushed to the limo, jumped inside and started the engine. The engine roared to life, gray plumes of smoke billowing up to the rafters. More monsters beat on the metal garage door. Frankie rushed to the front of the Humvee, had Luka get behind the wheel as he attached the jumper cables to the battery.

Luka turned the key and the Humvee rumbled to life. Frankie took off the jumper cables and closed the hood.

There was just enough room for the Humvee to pass the limo.

"Wait." Frankie ran to the limo and disconnected the jumper cables. Then he took pliers and unhooked the limo's battery. He lifted out the battery. Alexei was looking at him as if he'd gone nuts. "In case we have to jump Humvee again." He put the battery and cables in the back of the Humvee.

Alexei picked up the garage door opener from the limo as he marched to the Humvee.

"How we get out of the city?" Frankie asked as Alexei climbed in the front seat of the Humvee.

"Never mind. Go."

Frankie looked at Alexei. Mika had been right. He was certifiable. He always thought Alexei was a little mad to do some of the things he'd done. This proved it. The world had gone insane and Alexei was a mad man. Frankie picked up the Uzi and climbed into the back seat.

Luka drove to the door and Alexei pressed the button that opened the garage door. Slowly the metal door rolled up. Outside in the street was an army of zombies. The moment the door started to rise, the zombies surged inside.

"Jesus."

Frankie looked at Alexei; the sight of all those zombies scared the boss. He smiled; glad something scared him.

"Go."

Frankie leaned out the backseat window and started shooting with the Uzi. He mowed down those in front so the Humvee had some room.

Luka shifted into four wheel drive and the green camo Humvee rolled forward. The zombies crashed into the sides and he kept going. When they were outside Alexei pressed the automatic door switch and the heavy metal door came down crushing a few and trapping some inside.

"Reminds me of Halloween," Alexei said as he opened the front passenger window a crack and tossed out a grenade. "Trick or treat." Immediately smoke stated pouring from the grenade.

"Tear gas?" Frankie said.

The zombies moved more erratically as if in pain and unable to do anything about it.

"Trick," Alexei said and laughed.

"Turns my stomach," Frankie said.

"Is that all it takes?"

"Which way?" Luka asked.

"Central Park."

Frankie said, "We should go to river."

Luka didn't reply as he headed toward Central Park. He stepped on the gas and the big car plowed through the zombies crowding the street. They bounced off the front bumpers, off the sides of the car. Then the big tires rolled over their bodies, bones crunching and cracking against the undercarriage. There were so many of them the vehicle slowed and Big Luka had to gun it.

At the corner Luka turned left and accelerated.

One zombie grabbed onto the side mirror and held on. Alexei opened his window and took a Bic propane cigarette lighter from his pocket and lit a flame. He increased the flame till it was a mini blow torch and aimed the flame directly onto the hand of the zombie.

The zombie kept holding on as his hand caught fire. Alexei closed his window and stared at it, amazed. The flame quickly spread over the whole body. The zombie let go and dropped to the road and his skin continued to burn.

Alexei turned and watched the zombie burning on the road. "If these zombie things start a fire, they'll burn like hell and turn the whole city into a tinderbox."

"It's like they are dipped in kerosene. Must be part of their changes, the smell, the sweat is flammable."

They went on for a bit in silence.

"See," Luka said, "Told you boss would get us out."

Frankie said, "Boss, you were born lucky."

Alexei shook his head. "Nyet, you make own fucking luck. And fuck 'em that get in way."

*****

Chapter 38- - Nuke 'em

Paul Dachtera felt a hand on his shoulder and opened his tired eyes. Lying in the dark he felt the rolling motion of the sailboat on the sea, breathed in the fresh salt air and wanted to go back to sleep. He was very tired, but the crisp sea air made him feel alive, like he should get up and do something. Gina was standing over him holding a small flashlight.

"My turn to stand watch?"

She shook her head. "No, Dad. We didn't work that out yet." Her brown eyes looked away like she was troubled.

"What's a matter? Helen okay?"

Gina motioned to the bunk across from him and he heard his wife's heavy breathing as she slept, listened to how rhythmic it was and wanted to crawl in next to her. In the bow the kids were sound asleep in sleeping bags, rocked by the gentle motion of the waves.

"Jack wants to talk to you."

He unzippered the sleeping bag, pulled his legs over the side and rolled to a sitting position. It was chilly outside the zippered bag. Behind Gina through the open door and porthole it was still night. A lantern swung from the ceiling.

"At this hour?"

"It's important."

He rubbed his eyes. God, it's cold out on the water.

"You want a cup of hot coffee?"

"Yeah."

Gina left the little cabin. Helen snored lightly on the bunk above him. He stood up and gazed at her peaceful face. Boy, could she sleep. Through a hurricane.

He picked up his tan canvas pants and sitting on the bunk pulled them on, slipped on tennis shoes and pulled on an old blue sweatshirt, the shoulders still baggy on him until Helen had washed and dried it a few dozen times. He grabbed his jacket off the back of the door, better suited to windy Florida golf courses than the Atlantic Ocean, and putting it on, made his way down the narrow passage, a few uncertain steps holding onto the walls, before moving with the rolling sea. Must be what they mean by getting your sea legs. More and more he liked sailing.

Gina waited in the compact galley holding a steaming cup of coffee. Her face was so serious it brought him up short. "What's going on?"

She pointed topside. "He'll tell you."

She never used to be like that. Daddy, I have a cut, will you make it better? Daddy, this boy pushed me in school. Daddy, I want to talk to you about something. Now it was Jack this. Jack that. What happened? Was it growing up or was it all the times he was working and wasn't there for her?

He climbed the short ladder, spilling only a little coffee on his fingers.

Jack sat at the wheel, staring off into the distance. Captain Ahab, he wasn't. Jack looked soft on shore like he'd eaten too many donuts, but out here his jaw line was set and hardened and the Navy peacoat gave him a brawny appearance. Jack had been there when he went to bed. Did that mean he'd been there all night? He didn't look tired. He seemed ... scared.

"How's it handling?"

"She."

"Huh?"

"You call a boat she."

He thought about it a moment. "How's she handling?"

Jack's expression was like he'd seen the shark in Jaws following the boat.

"You don't want to speak to me about the boat?"

"Have a seat."

Paul sat on a cushion and sipped his coffee. It was terrible. Gina never did learn how to make decent coffee.

Even her instant coffee was awful. Jack seemed to enjoy it. At first he'd thought Jack was just humoring her, but after so many years, Jack must like it.

The night sky was all around them, a big upside down bowl full of stars. He'd never seen so many stars in his life. A million stars shining, twinkling in the black dome of velvet sky. He'd missed something not sailing until now. Pretty awesome, now that he got a look.

"See that?" Jack pointed at a notebook computer open on the seat.

"Yeah." His son-in-law loved anything to do with computers. Had a web page, whatever that was. Built his own computer. Thinking of opening an online computer store.

"The Victory has a shortwave and phone."

He shook his head.

"The boat."

"Ah huh." Why didn't he just say he had one on the boat, why does he talk as though the boat owns it?

"Talked to a guy last night, in Bangor."

"Where that writer lives?"

"What writer?"

"Never mind, go on."

"He's been monitoring Navy transmissions. Most of it in code. Wanted to know if we were close to New York. He. . ."

He looked back behind them. Didn't expect to see the city, but thought he should at least see the glow from all those billions of lights. It was dark in the west.

"Why is that?"

"I'm getting to it. He says he decoded some Navy communications. The fleet isn't far from where we are."

He scanned the horizon.

"We can't see them, but they can probably see us on their radar screens."

Paul didn't like the sound of that. Breathed the salt air. How can anything be wrong when the air smells so good? And the coffee didn't taste too bad either, once you got used to it.

"So?"

"According to this guy, the Navy is going to nuke New York at sunrise."

"What?!"

"They're going to send a plane over to see if anyone's alive and if they see just monsters, they're going to bomb New York and a bunch of other cities."

"You're kidding?"

"I've been talking to the guy for hours. They want to wipe out the monsters before the infection or virus, whatever it is, spreads anymore."

"Who is 'they'?"

"The military, army or navy, whoever's in control. They're going to nuke San Francisco and Seattle, too."

"Who the hell gave them permission?"

"They say some admiral is now in charge of the country."

Paul thought about what he remembered of the chain of command in the constitution. With all that had happened, it might just be possible. It was always that way. Once the safeguards were removed, some asshole got carried away. Business, government, you name it, always some asshole looking out for himself.

"I thought you'd want to know."

He stared out to sea. Couldn't see much. In the moonlight he'd catch the white cap on a small wave.

"What're you planning to do about it?"

"Me?" Jack turned to him. His grimace said he shouldn't have said anything.

"Yeah, you. What are you gonna do about those fools nuking YOUR country?"

"I'm heading as far out to sea as we can go." Jack looked ahead as if that ended that. He was fulfilling his responsibilities, thank you very much. "Depending on the blast yield and the fallout we might not be far enough away."

Paul stared hard at his son-in-law, the soft face, young

for his years. They all seemed to be young for their years nowadays. Whatever happened to real men like Chesty Puller, Patton, and John Wayne? "That's what you plan to do about it?"

"What can I do? He's an admiral, for chrissake."

Paul sipped the coffee. As it cooled, it got worse, now tasted like warm grease. He took a big sip and his stomach rumbled. Didn't need much, maybe this would do.

"Can we contact this A.H.?"

Jack faced him and smiled.

What the hell's he grinning about? Then he realized, that's what he wanted, someone else to do the dirty work. Someone else to put their balls on the line while he sailed his boat.

Jack pointed at the computer screen. It had numbers on it. He handed him the microphone. "Everything's set. I press the enter key and in a moment you'll be connected." He looked at his father-in-law. "Then you just press the button and talk, the frequency's set."

He nodded. The kid didn't have balls, but he was smart, he'd give him that. He pressed the button. "Hello?"

"Now release the button and listen."

He couldn't hear anything. Jack reached under the seat and turned something. Static came louder over the speaker. "Try again."

"Hello, I want to speak to the Admiral."

"Get off the air," a voice boomed. Jack quickly turned the volume down. "This is a secure military channel."

Paul held the mike up and took a breath. "Listen Sonny, go find the Admiral and you tell him his boss is on the line."

"Excuse me?"

"You heard me. Get off your ass and get your Admiral. By the way, what's his name?"

"Admiral Frank Rogers."

"What's your name?"

"Petty officer Don Boyer."

"Okay, Boyer, move it."

Released the button. "Yes sir."

Jack was smiling. The pride was unusual on his face.

"Who the hell is this?" came a loud rusty reply.

"Sounds like his vocal cords have been aged in bourbon."

"What's your name?"

Pressed the button and spoke, "This ain't the President."

"Who is this?" the voice growled.

"Paul Dachtera, registered voter from Orlando, Florida. Since everyone else is dead I am the senior Senator from Florida and my son-in-law, Jack McKenna, is a Senator from New York."

"I know of no elected Senator from either state by that name."

"I was just elected, you must a missed it, you must of been too busy sailing off somewhere. I'm also Chairman on the Armed Services Committee, the Ways and Means Committee and any other committee or branch of government it takes to get your attention."

"I hear you. What do you want?"

"You're planning to nuke New York City and a bunch of other cities."

The Admiral cleared his throat. "That is classified information. You have violated national security."

"Like hell I did."

"I'm sorry to have to tell you this, everyone is dead, all the members of the cabinet and the congress are dead --"

"Good riddance, you ask me."

"-- only myself and a few other senior officers are alive."

"I want to know who gave you permission for such an asinine plan?"

"Asinine!" Admiral Rogers boomed. "Our best military minds working all day and night came up with the most feasible solution."

"That's the best you can do?"

"At five P.M. last night the Speaker of the House. . ."

"That drunk. Who sobered him up?"

"According to the Constitution, he's now the President of the United States."

"He's been sworn in?"

He released the button. No response.

"Has he or not?"

"Well, no. They couldn't find a judge alive and by the time we did he was infected and had to be ... shot."

"According to the Constitution, I'm a voter and you work for me. And if he's dead, I've got just as much say as you do. Probably more."

Silence when he released the button.

"Didn't think he'd like that," he said to his son-in-law. "These career soldiers always like to think they're above us."

Jack said, "Strictly speaking, Pop, (He called me pop.) you don't have any authority. If the President is. . ."

"Don't hand me that. I haven't heard any report that the President is dead."

"It was on the radio while you were sleeping. His bones were found. . . ."

"His bones! How do they know they're his? They don't know. Been too soon. Maybe it's some aide. They're just trying to take over."

He pressed the button and continued, "I don't want you or another other branch of the military to bomb any city until you've fully explored other alternatives for getting rid of the zombies."

"Sir, we've discussed our options at great length. There aren't any alternatives."

"Came to that decision real quick in my opinion. Too damn quick, you ask me. "

"Sir, Mr. Dachtera, you have no authority. I'm talking to you out of courtesy. I don't have to listen to you."

"Is this what we fought wars for?"

He released the button and heard the admiral talking to someone, asking them to pinpoint his position. He took a breath and continued.

"Do you want to go down in history as the man who

destroyed America?"

"What I'm doing is for the good of the country."

"You can't come up with a better plan than that? History will not talk kindly of you and the other geniuses who came up with this plan, no matter how many times you rewrite it."

"I'm sorry you don't understand. We're all agreed, the other Admirals and Generals who are still alive have agreed that the best course of action is to annihilate the monsters."

"And any cities the monsters are in?"

"Yes, there will some losses."

"LOSSES? That's not acceptable."

"Dad."

"If you're all that's left then you have to lead. Not destroy. Leading is not destroying. Leading is not wiping the slate clean."

"You don't understand, the zombie virus is very contagious. If we don't wipe it out, it will resurface again and again."

"There are seven of us on this boat who didn't catch it. If there are seven of us here there are lots of people all over the place. People you haven't heard from and can't see. People hiding in cellars, in the woods, in their homes. It might be months before all of them come out."

"You don't understand, we'll all be in danger if one zombie is left alive."

"I know you have to make tough choices, but perhaps staying the hand that presses the button and using the minds at your disposal to come up with a better plan is the tougher and better way to lead."

"I'm sorry. It's out of my hands."

"And what about the culture, the works of art, books, paintings, those people who haven't turned into monsters."

"I don't have to listen to this."

"You're not just destroying cities; you're destroying history, our heritage, the future, your own children's future."

He released the button. Silence.

"That got him," Jack said.

"We have to get rid of the monsters," the Admiral said, his voice was losing its arrogance. "They're spreading the virus out of the cities."

"What's the rush? The cities are probably already overrun. You have all day tomorrow to explore new options."

"But every time a zombie bites someone they infect another person and so on, their numbers are increasing."

"Have you seen any baby zombies?"

"What?"

"Then their numbers are probably going to decline and rapidly if what I heard on the radio last night was true."

A jet plane flew over them low enough for them to hold their ears.

"Now you know where I am. And you know I'm not some spy." Crying echoed from below. "And you've woke the grandchildren."

"I'm sorry. I had children and grandchildren, too."

"Had?"

"Jacksonville. Tampa. Houston. We are in communication with other ships and bases. Many land bases, Army and Marine Corps bases, have been destroyed. Most of the country has been flown over. Except for some rural areas, most of the United States is destroyed. Denver, Chicago, San Diego, NASA, all gone."

Paul sat back. That was quite a shock. He won't miss Rat World, but the grandkids will. He suddenly felt very old and very tired.

"It's like that all over the world. We, the U.S., have the only two functioning fleets so we're not in any danger of attack, but that doesn't make it any easier."

"There must be another way to take care of them. You don't want to go down in history as the man who bombed America back to the Stone Age. If some of the reports I heard on the radio late last night are correct, much of rural America is still left. True, we've lost a lot people, but we still have libraries and museums and enough canned goods to last us till we get up and running again."

"I've agonized over this all night long."

So that's why you've been drinking. You're tormented over the decision.

"Other countries might not have lost so much and if you bomb what little we have left you'll be leaving us open to invasion. Maybe not today, but tomorrow or the day after."

A short pause.

"We discussed that. The chance of that is very remote. It's taken us hours just to re-establish a chain of command."

"If you bomb the cities with no one to fight the fires, there'll be fire storms. Whole cities will be gone."

"It's a chance we'll have to take."

Paul looked over at his son-in-law and shook his head. "You notice he said 'we'll have to take'. Jack looked at him and shrugged as if the discussion was a lost cause.

"Don't forget about the canned goods and dry goods in all those warehouses and supermarkets in and around those big cities. The zombies ain't gonna eat 'em. The bigger the city the more depots and bigger warehouses. Those of us who are left will need those supplies to make it through the next few years."

"You have a point which our experts have considered."

"Surely not experts who live in those ... infected areas. Surely not citizens, middle men, truck drivers, who know about things like that."

"As a matter of fact, no."

"If you bomb those cities you'll be condemning the surviving population to starvation."

"The country has food supplies stockpiled at various locations around the continent."

"I've read about that. You have maybe a month's worth, probably more like a week's worth and you won't have the rail system or the highway system to deliver it."

"We have soldiers who drive trucks."

"And can they also handle the distribution and find ways around the central hubs, the cities that are burning and will burn for quite some time?"

"We'll replant. We've already discussed having the troops do that."

"With all those bombs there will be a nuclear winter."

Doggedly Admiral Rogers said, "It's a chance we will have to take."

"While all you good Admirals and Generals have all your troops in the field helping and rebuilding, who's going to be watching the one or two officers who are loose cannons and decide they want to be Caesar?"

There was silence on the line. He had finally hit a nerve the Admiral was worried about; his own loss of command. He continued while the iron was hot,

"Surely you can wait twenty-four hours."

"It's not just me. There are other Admirals and Generals involved."

"Admiral, do you mind if I call you Frank?"

"No. Go right ahead."

"Frank, your biggest enemy is fear. If you do all that bombing, you won't have ports to go back to. And you won't have food to feed your men with. You won't have fuel for your ships."

"We're atomic powered. We have enough fuel for two years."

"How many hammers and nails and screwdrivers do you have? It takes a lot to rebuild a city. More to rebuild a country."

"We have enough."

"Your crews have wives and family in those cities. Bombing them after all that has happened will be bad for morale. There will be a much greater chance for mutiny."

Jack gave him thumbs up.

He swallowed a dry bitterness. The pause was so long he pressed the button on the microphone to make sure he had released it.

"I don't know if I can get the others to go along. They

wanted to start bombing last night."

"Frank, by nature you're a fighting man. It's easy to kill. It's tremendously difficult to grow and preserve life. You'll have to talk those others into waiting. Try a few things. God, there must be something that can save our heritage. Something. Don't let our heritage be that when the going got tough, we bombed ourselves. You don't really want to do this."

"No, I don't, but Goddamn it, they eat people."

"And their supply must be running low. Try something. Anything is worth a try. Anything."

"I'll see what I can do," he said, sounding exhausted.

"God bless you."

"We'll have a plane keep watch over you. High up so as not to wake your grandchildren. And if you need any supplies or you want to come aboard, just let me know."

"Thank you, Admiral."

"It's Frank."

In the east they could see the sky lightening. A band of gold across the arc of the sea. High up, thin feathery clouds were tinged with red like the wings of a great angel.

"Good going, Dad," Jack said.

Paul breathed out. Pops and pop sounded so impersonal, but dad sounded real. That was the first time Jack had ever called him Dad. It sounded funny coming from him, but not bad. He put the mike on the seat and started to get up. That's when he felt a constricting pain, high across the left side of his chest and down his left arm. The pain increased and he winced and stumbled for the hatch.

"You okay?"

He nodded once, couldn't speak.

Gina helped him down. "You did great, Dad." She looked at his face. "Are you all right?"

"My cabin."

She helped him down the hall and he staggered to his bunk. From the night table he took a small plastic bottle of pills and put one under his tongue. "I'll be all right now."

She put her hand to her mouth and stared at the pills. "I didn't know. Are you all right?"

"Don't you worry. I'm okay."

"Are you sure?"

"Jack's been up all night. He needs a break."

"Okay." Obediently, she made her way to the stern.

Held up the bottle. Only six pills left. Of all the things to forget. But he'd thought he could go to a drug store on Long Island and get a refill. Course, that was before the end of the world.

Maybe the Admiral has some pills he can lend me. Sounds like the kind of man who's been around.

He put the plastic bottle on the night table and lay down. He coughed and the pill flew out of his mouth. He struggled to get up and grab the bottle off the night table, but the boat rolled sharply. Gina must have taken the wheel. The bottle rolled onto the floor and he fell back into the bunk as a new wave of searing pain rippled through him.

*****

Chapter 39 – Only Way Out

Ryan woke suddenly; he'd been having this terrible dream and … he looked around. He was sitting on the floor of a store in the dark. It wasn't a dream. The nightmare was real.

Kenny was sleeping against him. The little guy had been through a lot. Ryan wasn't sure if he was Kenny if he could handle it.

Dark shadowy items sat on the shelves. The small store smelled musty and old and … and picklely. He felt a draft and remembered the window on the door was broken. Why didn't the place stink of zombies?

He eased Kenny off him. The kid slept like a brick. Carefully, quietly, he got to his feet; his knees popped and cracked like chicken bones breaking. He paused afraid he'd awakened the kid. Kenny continued to sleep.

Hunched over he made his way down the aisle. When he could see out the big plate glass window, he stopped. Outside a sea of zombies wandered aimlessly around.

He went to the narrow door and peeked past the curtain to get a better look. The delicatessen was on a corner and he wanted to see down the other streets.

The zombies were everywhere. Thousands of them. They could never slug or shoot their way through that many. None were blocking the store entrance, so they could get outside, but once outside, then what? They could never make it to the bridges. No one could.

His eyes fell on the metal grate. He had broken the lock and duct taped it closed. Now as he looked, his heart stopped. Most of the duct tape had been clawed away. Only a thin strand held the grate closed.

He looked at the walking dead wandering past and backed away. He didn't want to attract them. Any sound, any noise might cause them to lurch against the grate and once they did that, it would open and they'd flood inside.

He heard Kenny stirring and turned back to the aisle. He had to stop him from making any noise.

"Ryan," Kenny called softly.

Ryan froze. The shuffling noises outside ceased. He glanced out the plate glass window. The zombies on the sidewalk had stopped shuffling. They were looking around. He had to get to Kenny before he made anymore noise.

"Ryan," Kenny called a little louder, his voice a little higher, sounded frightened.

Ryan rushed down the aisle, motioning Kenny to stay quiet.

Kenny saw the shadowy apparition coming at him and swung his hockey stick.

Ryan started to duck and then realized if the hockey

stick missed him it would hit the glass counter, probably break it and make a lot of noise. Knowing it was going to hurt, he blocked it with his forearms and stopped it. Pain exploded in his forearms. Kenny tried to pull it back, but he wouldn't let go. He put his hand up and Kenny saw who it was and nodded.

"I thought you were …."

Ryan covered Kenny's mouth with his hand. He looked over the top of the display row and saw zombies outside looking for where the noise came from. As long as the zombies didn't know they were in here, they were safe.

Ryan turned to Kenny. The boy nodded that he understood.

Ryan let go of the hockey stick.

Kenny moved it back, away from Ryan. The end of the stick hit the display shelf of pickle jars. One jar smacked into another and within moments the whole shelf was raining glass pickle jars on the floor and the pickles and the smelly liquid.

The jars broke loudly and continued to break and break. And while they were breaking the pungent smell of pickles drifted up with the sound of breaking glass.

"Sorry," Kenny whispered.

Ryan didn't wait for the last jar to break or the zombies to start hammering on the door. He took Kenny's hand and pulled him to the back of the store while the waterfall of breaking pickle jars continued. No sooner did they go into the small storeroom than the front of the store exploded inward with zombies.

Rya hurried through the small storage room. The back outside door was locked.

Ryan hit the door with shoulder. It was metal. It didn't budge. He bounced off the door, his shoulder hurting. He heard zombies flooding into the front of the store, knocking more things down..

He turned to the door to kick it, but Kenny was in his way.

"I have locks like this at home," Kenny said and in a

moment he had the door open and they were out the door into the alley behind the store. They closed and locked the door.

"We're safe," Kenny said.

Before Ryan could reply he heard noise behind them and turned. Two men, two zombies, in black raincoats came at them. Ryan realized he had left his spear in the store and took out his gun and clubbed both of them to death.

Kenny stood over them his broken hockey stick in his hands, he was shaking.

Panting, they leaned against the metal door, feeling the zombies in the store pounding on it.

"What were they doing out here?" Kenny said.

Ryan pointed at the gates in the alley. "They couldn't open them. They were trapped."

"So are we," Kenny said.

Ryan stared at the dead zombies as a disgusting thought came to mind.

"What?" Kenny said. "What's the matter?"

Ryan turned to Kenny and the boy shook his head.

"Just by the look on your face, I don't like it."

***

A few minutes later Ryan and Kenny wearing black overcoats emerged from the alley at the end of the street. Keeping their heads down, they shuffled slowly down the street filled with zombies. As the sea of zombies shuffled aimlessly, the two were soon gone from view.

*****

Chapter 40 - How's Your Trip

Howie heard Diane cry out and raced down the stairs. She was cornered by two monsters, a skinny woman in a slip and a chubby man in baggy white boxer shorts, but he couldn't get a shot with her dodging left and right. He'd aim at one of the zombie's head and be about to pull the trigger and she'd suddenly be in his sights.

"This way," he shouted, hoping one of the zombies would come to him so he could get close and kill it. Instead, they both turned and Diane shoved them aside and came up the stairs. Both zombies came after her.

He aimed, but she kept moving in the way. He stepped to the side, next to the railing and she swerved toward him. "No, the other side," he said and she gave him a look like shoot already.

He aimed when something fell down next to him. It was a piece of clothing. He looked up and saw many monsters were coming down the stairs; more than he had bullets for. Now Diane was next to him.

"Well, shoot already."

He aimed but the zombies were bobbing their heads in that shuffling, stiff kneed walk they had.

"Hurry," she said and he pulled the trigger.

The .22 rifle shot echoed in the stairwell and soon he heard monsters pounding on doors above him. He'd hit the zombie, but only taken off part of its ear. It didn't even seem to notice.

He aimed again, but there was just too much movement and he wasn't firing a cannon.

"Hurry," Diane said and he squeezed the trigger. The shot echoed up the stairwell, the zombie's head snapped back, then came back up. He'd hit the monster in the chin, its chin was bleeding black blood, but it didn't seem to notice. The zombies on the stairs noticed; the sound agitated them and sped them up.

"What's the matter? Can't you hit anything?" Diane shouted. "Where did you learn to shoot?"

He turned to her and yelled in her face. "Shut up." Then he took his suitcase and flung it down the stairs knocking the closest zombie into the one behind it and they both tumbled down the stairs. He rushed down the stairs to them, put the rifle almost against the face of the first zombie and fired. The head snapped back and the monster was still. He pulled the bolt back and seated another round and put the barrel against the forehead of the second zombie and fired. The head recoiled and the zombie was still.

He breathed, relieved they were dead. He turned to shout to Diane, but she was not there. Then the emergency light on the wall started to dim. The white led dimmed and then went out, not just on this flight of stairs, but on all the stairs. One by one the emergency light blinked off. Now the stairwell was in complete blackness.

***

Diane listened for movement, but she didn't hear anything. When Howie ran down the stairs, she backed up into the stairwell wall afraid he going to do something stupid and die. She didn't see him aim the rifle point-blank at a zombie. When the rifle fired, the sound hurt her ears and she jammed her fingers in her ears and took a few steps further along the wall and squeezed her eyes tightly closed so she didn't see anything. But when she opened her eyes, she was standing in blackness.

If she called Howie, the monsters would hear and would come to her. She had entered the stairwell on floor eight and had gone downward, but she hadn't counted how many flights she gone. And it wasn't as if one flight of stairs equaled one floor. She thought two flights of stairs equaled one floor, but maybe not. She didn't know where she was.

She heard a sound and looked into the blackness. Was that sound from above or below her? She couldn't tell.

Sounds echoed in the stairwell. Had Howie sneaked past her in the dark searching for her?

"Howie," she whispered, now it was absolutely quiet. Before there had been this strange noise in the background, now it was gone and there was quiet.

"Marco," a familiar voice said.

She knew that voice. "Polo." Then she remembered that voice wasn't Howie's, it was Tommy's. Was Tommy okay? Was this another joke?

She heard steps now, coming closer and closer.

"Marco," came a voice very close now

"Polo," she said and backed into the wall.

Then she remembered. She was still carrying her purse slung over her shoulder. She had quit smoking; everyone had made such a big deal about it, and reached inside and rummaged around trying to find it.

"Marco," said a voice that sounded a lot like Tommy's.

She wasn't going to answer now, until she found it. She grabbed it, no, that was a small box of tic tacs; she moved it aside and felt around.

"Marco."

She could almost feel that breath on her.

She found it, her old Bic butane lighter, hoped there was still fluid left, and took it out, held it up and pressed the switch and a flame rose in front her and between her and the wall of zombies, Tommy stood at the front of the pack.

She backed into the wall and the zombies came at her. Tommy was reaching for her, when a metal barrel hit him knocking Tommy back into the other zombies and she dropped her Bic.

Howie caught the lighter and pulled her away. He had her hold the lighter over her head and pulled her down the stairs, the zombies momentarily blocked by Tommy on the floor.

Howie grabbed his suitcase, he might have to try that maneuver again, knock them down with the suitcase so he could get a good shot.

He saw her lugging her suitcase. "You don't need that." She gave him a look. "Why not, you're taking yours." He wanted to tell her he had his reasons, but didn't have the time to get into it with monsters only a few steps behind them.

They came to a door; she flicked her Bic and the sign on the door said: Lobby. He motioned her to be quiet. She pointed upward at the monsters pursuing them, meaning they didn't have time to stop. He shook his head; he knew about them, just don't rush him. He carefully pushed opened the door into the lobby. What they could see of the lobby was empty of monsters.

"Come on." He hurried out of the stairwell. She rushed into the hall after him and he pushed the hydraulic door closed. It made a loud metallic clicking sound and he looked around, no monsters were coming.

"We have to bar the door," he whispered.

"What?" she said.

He thought she hadn't understood him and enunciated, "We have to block the door."

"Okay."

He put his suitcase in front of the door.

"That won't stop them," she said.

"Put yours on top."

"That's not enough."

"For once, just do it."

She dropped her suitcase which was at least twice as heavy as his on top of his suitcase and gave him an I-told-so look and now he was pretty sure why some men beat their wives. She was right, but she didn't have to rub it in.

He looked around for something to use. In a nearby alcove was a large ornate imitation Grecian urn. He ran to it and carried it back. He put it on top of the two suitcases and stepped to admire his work and wondered if red roses were heavier than daffodils or orchids or whatever.

"Hey, Liberace," she called. "Gimme a hand."

He saw her trying to lug the small table stand the vase had been on over to the door. He reconsidered his suitcase-flower vase pyramid and saw how flimsy it was and ran over and helped haul the small but heavy table to the door.

He stood the table next to the door. "No," she said.

"Well, why don't you show me," he said pissed that according to Diane he couldn't anything right. He'd save her life, but apparently he hadn't even done that right and now he couldn't build a barricade without her expert advice.

She quickly handed him the vase and shoved the two suitcases to the side. She pushed them aside so easily. What the hell he was thinking trying to use them as a barricade? Then she laid the table down on the floor so that it was lengthwise against the door. She put his suitcase on top of it, and placed hers against the bottom of the table.

He was impressed; it was quite a good barricade. She must have a lot of tomboy in her. He was still holding the vase. "What about this?"

She considered him for a moment, then took the bouquet of red roses out and held them and smiled. "Thank you."

He looked at her as if didn't know what to expect.

"You can put that down." She motioned to put it down by the door.

She walked to the lobby carrying the roses and he followed. Had he underestimated her? He hurried up next to her so it wouldn't feel like she was leading and he was following.

"Slow down," he whispered.

Then she turned to him. "You want to carry the flowers and I'll carry the gun?"

He was about to tell her a thing or two, when he saw the lobby and his mouth fell open.

She saw his face and whirled around.

It reminded him of the railroad track scene in *'Gone With The Wind'*. Everywhere he looked were dead bodies. There were no injured. No one crying, pleading for a doctor. There were dead bodies and parts of dead bodies and torn clothes and wrecked furniture. The smell of death was atrocious.

"You remember that rotten egg smell," he said and she nodded. "It's gone."

"Does that mean the infection or virus is gone?"

"No, it's hiding behind the stink of death."

Rana, the front desk clerk who had greeted them was munching on someone's forearm, suddenly dropped it and came at them.

Howie took a stance like he'd seen Clint Eastward do in the movies and aimed.

"Don't." Diane gently pulled the gun down.

"Why the hell not?"

"They'll hear you." She pointed across the foyer at the front glass door. The street was littered with bodies and zombies shuffled about as if they didn't know where to go or what to do.

He looked at Diane. She gave him an I-told-you so smile that angered him. By now Rana was almost to them. He took the rifle and swung it like a club and smacked what had been Rana in the head and felled it in one blow.

"That's more like it." Diane carefully explored the lobby. Howie didn't know if he wanted to kiss her or hit her. He could envision twenty years of being married to her with her advising him on everything from how to dress, to hammering a nail. On the other hand she wouldn't hang all over him waiting for him to come home and kill a spider.

They walked across the lobby stepping over the bodies. He found a dead policeman and took the Glock automatic off him. He put the pistol behind his belt and quickly turned away before Diane wanted it.

They went to the front desk.

"What did we come here for?" she said.

"We were going to ask if they had a safe place nearby and maybe take a car."

"No place is safe, or they would have gone there. And

we're not going to drive away from this."

He motioned to the front doors. Two revolving glass doors flanked each side of the foyer. They crept up along the wall to the doors on the west side. The six lane street, Central Park South, was filled with bodies and wrecked and abandoned cars. Zombies shuffled along the street. In Central Park they could see a few inflated balloons.

"Now what?" she said.

He was about to answer when all of a sudden the lobby went dark.

They turned to the dark lobby.

"The emergency generators must have stopped."

"Do you have a flashlight?" she said, knowing he always carried stuff for emergencies with him.

"In the car. What about the lighter?"

"Out of fuel."

"You have any matches?"

"In my suitcase."

"Now what?"

"I'm not stumbling in the dark over dead bodies."

"Dawn's only a few hours away. We'll wait."

She slid down the wall and sat on the floor with her back against the wall.

Howie slid down the wall next to her. He looked out the glass doors at zombies shuffling up and down the street, at the dark lobby with dead people lying on the floor. "Well, how's your trip to New York so far?"

Diane looked at him and her lower lip began to tremble and then she started crying. She wrapped her arms around him and held on while she sobbed.

He shook his head; he'd done it again and held her while she cried.

*****

Chapter 41 - VW

Ron and Pat went down the stairs and out the back alley. The narrow alley was empty of zombies and bodies, but the smell of death from the streets was almost overpowering. Pat started to gag and Ron put his hand over her mouth so she wouldn't make any noise.

He took the gun he was holding and shoved in behind his belt in his back and took her hand. He'd heard that pregnant women are subject to mood swings from the sudden urge to eat weird foods, to crying, to feelings he could not begin to fathom. So he held her hand to comfort her and lead her quickly without seeming like he was bossing her around.

They went down the narrow alley, tall apartment buildings on either side, and into another alley and into the back entrance of the parking garage. He stopped at the gray metal door. She was right at his shoulder. He leaned forward, putting his ear against the door, and listened.

"Come on," she whispered.

He pointed down the alley with his chin at zombies shuffling past in the street. Then he grabbed the doorknob and suddenly got a bad feeling about this. Aw, it was just nerves and he pulled open the door.

Light from the open door flooded inside and he saw she had stopped to look down the alley. He pulled her inside and tried to quiet the door closing.

"Don't do that," she said.

He put his hand up to his lips and she gave him a look. She didn't like being shushed. He scanned the dark garage. It was ground level. He didn't know how many levels there were.

To his left he could see light coming in from the exit. No cars were parked between them and the exit. The black and yellow exit barricade was broken. A car was in the street.

He looked down at the ramp going underground.

"I'm not going down there," she said.

They turned to the right and went up the incline.

"I don't like it," she said.

"Neither do I."

They walked up the ramp and around support columns where the darkness was very thick.

Suddenly a match flared in front of them. Ron jumped back, pulling Pat behind him. The match moved to the side and lit some candles.

The match was blown out. A man smiled at them. He was very dark, not African-American, but Middle Eastern, average height with short curly hair. Ron remembered him from the building, his name was Kadar. He was wearing a green hat, a black leather topcoat, black face-paint; black fingerless gloves and his eyes glowed as though he was insane. He motioned to a hunting rifle next to the candles on the hood of a yellow Corvette.

"You want it?" Kadar grinned, cradling a hunting rifle in his arms.

"Out of my price range," Ron said.

Kadar nodded as if they were playing cards and he had the winning hand no matter what.

"You can have any car in this garage," Kadar said.

"Thanks," Ron said, waiting for the rest.

"But it'll cost."

"Yeah?"

"Yeah."

Kadar motioned along the wall behind him and a match flared and someone lit candles on the trunks of two cars, throwing more light on the nearby parking places. Three dark sedans lined up along the wall. At the rear of each sedan was a man with a rifle or rather the shadowy silhouette of a man.

"What do you want?" Pat said and Ron glared at her, angry she had spoken.

Kadar smiled like it was nice they could all be friends.

"We don't have much," Pat said and put her backpack on the ground in front of her.

"Not what I want," Kadar said and coughed, his faced glistened with sweat.

Pat took off Ron's backpack and as she lifted it, she took the Colt .45 from behind his belt. She struggled to put the backpack in front of Ron and slipped Ron the heavy Colt. As she did, she gave him a look that she was ready for whatever he did.

"Not that either," Kadar said and Pat and Ron exchanged a look. They could sense it in the air; they were in Crazyville, Arizona. Ron tensed, he didn't' know if the safety was on or if it was loaded, if a round was chambered, how many rounds it had.

"What?" Ron asked, not faking how nervous he was. His hands were shaking. He glanced toward the guy that had lit the other candles and could barely see him in the dimness. He stood like he was holding a gun in his hand, but the barrel was the same width as a broomstick.

"You," Kadar said to Pat and laughed. His round face glistened with sweat. Sweat dripped off thin goatee.

Ron pretended to gently push her away as though if this nut wanted her she would do it for their survival.

Pat took a step and stopped like she was scared. It wasn't an act, she was very scared.

"I want her too," a voice said from the back.

In the candle light Ron could make out two men with guns at the rear of every car, they had not moved or said anything. Behind Kadar on the right was the man who had lit the other candles. He also wore a black leather topcoat, but he had painted his face black and dyed his hair blonde. He placed his 'gun' down on the car; it tapped the hood, not sounding like metal, maybe wood, maybe it was a broomstick. Ron remembered seeing a squirrelly guy hanging around with Kadar. The name Fitz came to mind, but he wasn't sure.

"What'll you give me in return," Ron said.

Fitz laughed meanly. "Your life."

"What about my wife," Ron said, stalling for time, he felt a button on the side of the gun and pushed and it went in, but he didn't know if the safety was off or on. He pushed it back the other way from the other side; it was much harder to push: did that mean anything?

"The needs of the many outweigh the needs of the one," Kadar said and smiled.

"I want my wife back when you're done with her," Ron said.

"She ain't gonna want to come back to you when we get done with her," Fitz said.

"Please," Pat said, standing there, trembling. To the others it probably sounded like something else, but he knew she wanted him to do it already.

"We?" Ron said. "How many of you are there?"

"What's it to you?" Kadar said.

"The more of you there are, the more I want to be paid."

"We're paying you with you life," Fitz said.

"I want cars or gold," Ron said.

"Shit," Fitz said angrily and stepped forward. "You'll take what I give you." He lifted his rifle like he was going to shoot and Ron saw that indeed it was a rifle, but what type he did not know.

Pat stepped back into Ron. "Shoot and you'll have two zombies. You boys anxious to make it with a zombie?"

Kadar quickly glanced over his shoulder at Fitz.

Pat twisted her head and whispered to Ron. "Shoot already."

"What did you say?" Fitz demanded.

"We're discussing payment," Ron said angrily.

"Who are you to tell us," Kadar said. He angrily took a step closer, leaving the rifle on the hood of the vette.

"Now," Pat whispered.

Ron pointed the pistol to the side and pulled the trigger to see if it would fire. Nothing happened. . He pushed the button and jerked the trigger as hard as he could. The gun would not fire.

"What are you doing?" Kadar demanded.

Ron remembered when he covered the war, how the soldiers would cock their weapons; they would grab the barrel of their pistol and pull it back. He quickly turned to the side, behind Pat, and holding the pistol in his right hand pulled the barrel back. He heard the sound of a round seating in the chamber. So did Fitz and Kadar, they were turning to him.

Ron pointed the gun around Pat and squeezed the trigger. And squeezed. He felt like he was squeezing the trigger so hard he was bending it, but nothing was happening. He didn't know what he was doing wrong. The round must have seated wrong or was a dud.

He grabbed the grooves on the side of the slide and pulled, jerked the slide back. A thick brass cartridge jumped out of the chamber. The shiny brass bullet flew up in the air, spinning, catching the light in the dark garage, a shuttle falling through candlelight.

Kadar turned toward the gleaming cartridge and fired the shotgun he was holding. The blast was loud and deadly in the garage. He missed Ron and Pat by over twenty feet, but he did hit a Lexus and the car's orange parking lights started flashing as its horn beeped.

The loud shotgun scared Ron and he pushed Pat out of the way and fired at Kadar.

Kadar was still looking at the damage his shotgun blast had done to the silver gray sedan when Ron fired and the bullet whizzed past him. He swung his shotgun around to Ron, hoping to hit him and leave the woman unhurt for future desires.

Ron fired again. His shot was wide, missed Kadar, almost hit Fitz and went through the windshield of a Ford Escape, put a hole in the windshield, shattered the rear window and knocked down two of the 'men' standing behind it.

Almost immediately Ron fired again, first moving his aim more toward Kadar and pointed his hand at him he fired. Kadar was knocked back as the heavy .45 caliber slug hit in the chest. He fell onto the hood of Mercedes.

Kadar's hand flew back and the automatic shotgun discharged again. Pellets hit the cement ceiling of the parking garage and ricocheted knocking down several of the cardboard 'men'.

Fitz had dived to the ground and hurriedly crawled behind the Mercedes, knocking down the last two cardboard 'men'.

Ron saw Kadar was wounded and hurried to Fitz. He stepped between the Mercedes and the Ford Escape and in the flickering candlelight saw tall lanky Fitz cowering against the wall, his hands in the air. He had on a black t-shirt and a dark green army type jacket. "Don't shoot," Fitz said. "It was an accident. We thought you were someone else."

He reminded Ron of Alan Rickman in 'Die Hard' when Bruce Willis cornered him on the roof and Rickman says, "Don't shoot." Ron heard Pat crying and started to turn and step away when he heard movement behind and swung around, Fitz was picking up a spear off the ground. He dropped it when he saw Ron point the gun at him. Ron fired twice, both bullets hitting Fitz, knocking him into the cement wall. Fitz slid to the ground leaving a bloody smear on the wall.

Ron hurried back to Pat.

She had gotten to her feet and was approaching Kadar. "You okay?" Ron asked her.

"I'll live."

"Did you just cry?"

Pat gave him a look like he was cracking up. "No."

Ron looked around the dark garage but saw no one else.

Pat picked up a candle off the Mercedes and held it over Kadar. His chest was covered with blood; his face was pale like he was dying.

"Who are you?" Pat asked.

"I'm Kadar," he said.

Ron pulled Pat back. "Don't get too close."

She gave him a look like she knew that.

Kadar had a letter in his inside vest pocket that he wanted them to give or send to his parents in D.C. He reached inside his vest to get it.

Ron saw Kadar's hand coming close to what looked like a gun in a shoulder holster and shot Kadar in the chest again. Kadar's head fell on his chest.

"Why'd you do that?" Pat said.

"I thought he was reaching for a gun."

Pat pulled open Kadar's coat. In a shoulder holster was a metal cigarette case.

Ron said, "Cigarette smoking will - -"

"Don't," she said.

He shrugged.

"The other men were cardboard cutouts," he said.

"I know," she said. "I saw."

She saw the edge of the white envelope sticking out from behind his vest. She pulled it out. Held it next to the candle and saw it was addressed to Washington, D.C.

"We haven't got time for that," Ron said.

"It would be the right thing to do."

"If they're alive how will you get it to them?"

"I don't know." She shoved it in her pocket.

Ron heard movement from the where the garage opened into the street. He turned toward the sound and took a few steps in that direct. A zombie was walking in the garage attracted by the sounds. It took Ron a moment to realize it had been Gabe Kelly, the super.

He lifted the Colt 1911 .45 and aimed and fired. He missed. The zombie was to far away.

"Shoot again," Pat said from behind him.

"He's too far away."

He aimed at the head and waited.

"Shoot," Pat shouted.

He motioned her to be quiet. When the zombie was only ten feet away, he tried to shoot, the trigger wouldn't move. Nothing happened. He thought he'd accidentally put the safety on and pressed buttons on the side until the magazine fell on the ground. He quickly picked it up. it. He was out of bullets.

The zombie was just about to grab him, when Ron stepped back. He went to step back again and tripped and sat down hard. The zombie was standing over him, reaching for him. He pulled the heavy Colt back to throw at him, when a shotgun fired. Now the zombie flew backward.

Ron's ears hurt. He looked around at Pat. She had picked up Kadar's automatic shotgun. She stood there shaking, holding the shotgun.

"You okay?" she said.

He pointed to his ears. He couldn't hear her.

She quickly handed the gun to Ron. She hated guns. That was the first time she'd ever fired one.

"That's was Kelly," he said too loudly.

"I know," she said, mouthing the words so he could read her lips.

"I'm out of bullets." He motioned at the Colt.

"The 1911 Colt only held seven bullets." She held up seven fingers.

"Oh," he said loudly.

They hurried along down into the parking garage.

"Why not take one of these?" she said.

He couldn't hear her. She pointed at the cars they passed. He pointed at the flat tires, the broken windows. "If these cars were in any good Kadar and Fitz would have taken them."

She didn't agree with him, she thought Kadar and Fitz were more likely to hole up, but he couldn't hear her arguments.

She grabbed the candle off the Corvette.

They hurried down the ramp, below street level and around the turn found only a Volkswagen Beetle in sight. It was not what he'd expected. He'd heard Kelly was restoring it; this car was not in any step of restoration. It was, had been, an old VW and there the similarity died. It wasn't black, had no fenders, the tires were large off-road monsters. On the top was a rack with four large spotlights on it. The car had been painted camouflage, swirls of greens and brown, it probably blended into the woods okay, but on the streets of New York, it would stand out. There was no engine cover and the engine looked like it had been souped up.

They climbed in and saw the tiny backseat had been packed for going into the country. There were backpacks and crossbows and quivers full of arrows and targets. Before Ron could ask what's in the backpacks, Pat was going through them. When she continued to search without saying anything, he had to ask, "What's in the backpacks?"

"Jerky."

"Jerky? Just Jerky?

"There's beef jerky and turkey jerky and salmon jerky and pork jerky. There's teriyaki jerky, plain jerky, spicy jerky, honey jerky and jerky jerky."

"That's it?"

"His wife put him on a fat-free, salt-free diet. So I guess he spent his weekends in the woods eating. His wife was telling me the more she cut back his diet, the more weight he gained.

Ron shook his head. "You ready?"

"Is this thing going to make a lot of noise?"

"Probably."

"You know if we lived by my parents we wouldn't be in this position."

"Not now. Please, not now."

She rolled up her window. "Go ahead."

Ron turned the key and the gauges came to life.

"What?" she said.

"Isn't a lot of gas."

"What does it say?"

"It's on E for empty."

"Maybe we should take another car."

"We're here."

"But if it's on empty."

"In these cars I think it means it has a gallon or two left, which should be enough for where we're going."

"And if it isn't? Maybe we should siphon gas from one of the other cars."

"No time." He held up a green garden hose from the floor. "If we have to, we'll improvise."

"Momma said I should have married Richie."

"He's in jail for insider trading."

"But I'd be home, in the country, surrounded by woods and the farm and six very loyal dogs."

"Six vicious dogs."

"Whatever."

"I knew you wouldn't leave out the dogs."

"Are you going to start the car or not?"

He turned the key more and the engine putt-putted to life rather quietly. He looked at her. "Not bad."

"What's that?" She pointed at a toggle switch on the dash.

"Don't know."

She pressed it as he said, "No, don't."

The bypasses on the exhaust system opened up and the engine roared so loud they couldn't hear each other speak. He quickly flipped the toggle switch and it broke off, part falling to the floor.

The car became quieter, but not as quiet as it had been.

"A work in progress," she said.

He looked at her.

"Don't start," she warned. "Just don't start."

Ron shifted into first, only grinding the gears a little.

"You want me to drive?"

"No."

"I grew up driving a stick on the farm."

"No."

He eased off the clutch and the car jumped ahead. He headed down the ramp. A zombie was still coming up the ramp after them, Ron swerved around him and watched him turn and went a short distance and stopped.

"What?" she said and he looked at her.

"I just can't," he said. "If I don't kill him, he'll hurt someone."

"We haven't got time."

Ron shifted into first and drove away.

"This thing has some power," he said as he raced into the street, the little VW skidding sideways out of the parking garage.

He drove down the street; it was easy to control with a lot of pep.

"Take it easy, Rambo," she said.

He drove over the curb, down the sidewalk, driving around any monsters he could. When he couldn't he hit them and didn't stop. After the third collision the windshield cracked and he was more careful. Some streets were impassable and he had to detour around them. A few blocks from their destination the engine started to cough and he eased off the gas.

"You never listen," she said.

He babied the gas and coasted to a stop next to the Pulitzer Fountain.

"Come on," he said and climbed out.

"What about this stuff?" she said.

He glanced at the backpacks in the back seat. They had attracted the attention of a small pack of zombies and they were coming toward them.

"You know, I'm allergic to jerky."

"Not that." She pointed at the bows and arrows.

"Okay, okay." He grabbed a small crossbow and a quiver of arrows.

"Crossbows don't take those arrows."

He saw more and more zombies coming at them.

"Come on." He went around the car and grabbed her hand to make her come with him.

She grabbed a quiver of bolts and stumbled along at his side until she got her footing.

They ran to the corner and turned west, running along the sidewalk. They went up the short drive and into the entrance. They had just gotten inside when a young guy near the wall pointed a gun at them.

Ron pointed the Colt .45 at him.

"We're alive," Ron said.

"We're trying to get away," Pat said.

"So are we," Diane said.

"Everyone calm down and put the guns down."

Howie and Ron lowered their guns.

"Pat and Ron," Pat said.

"Diane and Howie."

"How are you going to get out of the city?"

Ron turned to look out the front door when he heard the rumble of a car. "That's our friend."

"He's meeting us here," Pat said.

"He drive a Humvee?" Howie said. "Cause that's what it sounds like."

"You can tell what a car is by its sound?" Ron said.

"He knows cars," Diane said.

A smile appeared on Howie's dirty face.

"Did you hear our car?" Ron said.

"You mean the modified VW?"

"Ryan must have found one," Pat said.

"He's just gonna attract more of those monsters to us," Howie said.

Pat and Ron exchanged looks.

"He's bringing our friend's wife and children."

"And a hundred monsters," Howie said.

"He's probably had a rough night," Ron said.

"Haven't we all," Pat said and they peeked out the door to see if they could spot the Humvee coming.

*****

Chapter 42 - It's All Happening

They watched the camouflage Humvee drive down
59th Avenue from the west, bullets fired from the vehicle
killing a few nearby zombies, but the gunfire attracted
many more from the surrounding blocks. Zombies
swarmed down 59th Avenue, shuffling down Central Park
South, shambling out of Central Park toward the noise.

Peering out the doors of the Plaza they watched the
Humvee weave around stopped vehicles, continuing down
5th Avenue, it was lost from sight for a moment, perhaps it
was backing up or swinging a turn, then it headed west on
Central Park South.

Suddenly Diane remembered Fred Astaire singing
about Fifth Avenue in a movie; it seemed like a lifetime
ago in another world. How had the world come to this?

"It's coming here?" Ron said.

"That Ryan?" Pat said and Ron shook his head.

Thick glass doors flanked either side of the foyer. With
the electricity out, they didn't open automatically. The
doors on the far left had chairs and tables barricading
them. To the right someone had put a mop handle through
the door handles effectively barring the door. The head of
the mop was black as if someone had started to mop up
zombie blood then decided it was better to use it to bar the
door. Black flies buzzed around the mop head.

"Need more'n a mop handle to block it," Ron said.

"Once the zombies see us inside, they'll be coming."

In the foyer between the doors was a lounging area
with heavy armchairs and two brown leather sofas.

Ron said, "We move the couch over; after Ryan comes
in we shove it back in front of the door. Ron and Howie
tried to lift the leather couch, soon discovering how heavy
it was, and then decided to shove it over. Then they
helped Pat and Diane with the other couch.

The Humvee pulled up outside the hotel and a big guy jumped down. Holding an AK-47 in each hand he mowed down zombies coming up and down the street as he walked to the front door.

Diane and Pat backed away from the door and Luka pointed his weapons showing he meant to shoot through the glass and kill them if they didn't open a door. At the sides of each door Ron and Howie stepped forward, Ron aimed the Colt .45 and Howie his old Ruger .22 rifle, but the big guy only smiled.

Laughter echoed in the foyer behind them and they whirled to face a thin, rat-faced thug holding an automatic pistol in each hand. "Now boys and girls," Frankie said, "we not want to hurt people who not zombies?" He motioned them to get rid of their guns. "Safer you put guns down."

Ron looked to Howie and Howie shrugged. Ron wasn't sure it would be safer, but before he could say anything Howie was already tossing down his gun and when he looked up Frankie and Luka were pointing at him, so he tossed his gun on the floor too. Diane stepped to the door and pulled the mop out of the door handle. Luka turned and shot some zombies in the street, then pushed the door open and walked in, not pointing the AK-47 at anyone.

Luka nodded at Frankie and then his heavy eyes went over Ron and Howie and settled on Pat and Diane and a smile lit up his mean face.

"You my prisoners now," Luka said.

"What?" Ron said and saw that the big man was serious. He glanced at his gun on the floor and Luka saw him and grinned.

"I'm sure we can all work something out," Pat said.

"We have," Frankie said. "You my prisoners."

"No, my prisoners," Luka protested.

Howie stepped back figuring the two thugs might open fire on each other.

Frankie and Luka stared and pointed their weapons at

each other. Ron, Pat, Howie, and Diane backed against the wall out of the way. Luka and Frankie approached each other like it was a TV western and there was going to be a shootout.

"We split them up," Luka said as if it was a threat. "You take boys, I take girls."

"No," Frankie said. "We shoot guys and split girls."

"What fun in that?" Luka said and they turned and saw the others looking at them and laughed.

"We not shoot you," Frankie said. "We need you all."

Howie sighed with relief and Frankie added, "Girls sex slaves; men just plan slaves."

"Yeah," Luka said.

Just then there came a strange sound from inside the hotel, from way back in another room behind the lobby.

Everyone turned as a kid blades raced out of a back room. Frankie turned quickly, pointed the Beretta and saw it was a kid and grinned, after all it was only some kid. The boy smiled as he ran toward him as if he was having trouble staying on his feet.

"You play hockey?" Kenny said.

"Damn kid, "Frankie said. "You come over here."

The boy wobbly ran toward Frankie as if he was obeying him. But when he got close the boy swung the broken wooden hockey stick and clobbered Frankie in the head. As Frankie tumbled to the carpet, Kenny whirled around and tried to hit Luka, but Luka had played hockey and easily blocked the stick with one of the AK-47s, sending the boy flying across the room. Luka aimed one AK-47 at the boy and the other AK-47 at the rest. He gazed down at Frankie. Frankie lay on the carpet dazed, a red welt on the side of his face.

As Frankie went down a baggy fell out of his coat and split open, diamond earrings, pins and rings spilled across the floor, some of the diamond rings had blood on them. One ring still had a finger attached.

Ron, Pat, Howie and Diane looked at the bloody jewelry with disgust.

"That isn't a zombie finger," Howie said and Ron silently agreed. Their eyes met, both realizing terrible things could happen to them and the women. Ron gestured at their guns on the floor and Howie gave a barely perceptible nod. Ron held three fingers out at his side. Howie did likewise. The communication unmistakable, on three they would dive for their weapons. Ron held two fingers out at the same time Howie did. They looked at each other and nodded.

Ron and Howie had just held one finger out when Luka turned from the kid and aimed his AK-47's at them. Ron and Howie froze. Luka stared at them like he knew what they were up to.

Luka nudged Frankie with his foot. "Get up idy-ot."

Frankie groaned, but didn't try to move.

Luka stepped over Frankie and stared at his captives. Luka smiled at the kid. Little Kenny smiled back until Luka scowled and pointed the AK-47 at him. "Not funny." He motioned with the AK-47 for him to move next to the others. Kenny carefully stepped across the carpet in his roller-blades to Diane and Pat.

"Nice liddle family."

Diane gazed at the boy. "We're not related."

"No matter," Luka said and nudged Frankie again with his foot. "Get up."

Luka stood gawking at the woman and glancing down at Frankie, when from around the corner a man hurried into the lobby behind him. Pat and Diane looked behind Luka and almost started to give it away when Kenny fell on the floor to distract them.

Luka shook his head at how clumsy the kid was and then the next time he looked uup from Frankie, a man was pointing a Smith and Wesson .357 at his face. Luka didn't know the make or model just that it was like looking down the barrel of a cannon.

"No shoot," Luka said and raised his hands.

"Drop the guns," the man said and Luka obeyed.

Luka noticed something strange about the .357. He

stared at the barrel. There were no bullets in the cylinder. The gun was empty. Before he could react, the man bent over and picked up one of Frankie's M9 Berettas and pointed it at Luka and dropped the empty .357. Then he picked up Frankie's other Beretta and pointed it at the gangster on the floor.

Luka shook his head at being tricked, but was not angry. He still knew something and would teach this American dog a lesson. One swing and he would take his head off. He would show this dog why they not let him become a professional wrestling star. He slowly moved his fist back to swing.

"I wouldn't do that." Ryan flicked off the safety.

Luka paused. The guy knew. He did not like that. "Who you?"

"The man with the guns," Ryan told him.

Ron and Howie relaxed, putting their hands down.

Kenny tried to step forward and pick up Ron's Colt .45, but Diane held him back. "Let the grownups handle this," she whispered. Kenny gave her an angry look, who was she talking to, didn't she realize all that he had done, been through today?

Ryan motioned Luka to get against the wall and take Frankie with him. Ron and Howie hurried to bar the door. They closed the door and put the mop through the handles as Luka bent over to lift Frankie to his feet, by his jacket and stepped to the wall. Frankie struggled to stay on his feet.

"Hey, be careful, I injured." Frankie glanced around. "Where kid with hockey stick?"

"Shut up," Ryan said. Over his shoulder to Kenny, "I told you not to."

"It worked, didn't it?"

"You shouldn't point guns at ladies." Ryan turned to his friends and noticed the expression on Pat's face.

"Where's Hector?" Pat said and Ryan shook his head.

"Where are Mary Anna and the kids?"

Ryan opened his mouth, but he couldn't speak. How

could he tell her? She didn't need that nightmare.

"They're dead," Kenny said.

Ryan nodded in agreement.

"You need us." Luka motioned at the street outside.

Ryan's glanced outside at the zombies shuffling down 59th Avenue. The zombies had already forgotten about the commotion with the Humvee. When he looked at Pat, he realized thinking about Hector and his wife had distracted him and he'd missed something. Before he could spin around a gun rapped him on the head and he fell to the floor.

*****

Chapter 43 - Escape is Easy

When Ryan came to, Diane was holding a cool washcloth against his head. He was lying on the floor, his head in her lap. He looked up and she smiled at him. He stared at that pretty smile for what seemed a long time and she stared back. He studied every detail of her face; the intelligent blue eyes, the soft lips that looked like they wanted to be kissed, the face of an angel, right there. Then he realized he was in a hotel lobby and struggled to sit up. A wave of dizziness hit him and he rested against her for a moment. Some time must have passed since he was knocked out; more furniture was piled against the glass doors. The sun hadn't risen, but it was lighter outside.

The notorious gangster Alexei 'The Butcher' Antonov was at the left side of the front doors looking up and down the street. Frankie pointed the nine-millimeter Berettas at Ryan, Diane, Ron, Pat, Howie and Kenny, all sitting on the foyer floor, their backs against the wall.

"That was close," Alexei said. He grinned at Ryan. "You have thick head."

Ryan took the washcloth from Diane and held it against

his head. "Not thick enough."

Alexei frowned. "Wonder how long before we can go?"

"I've seen your face on TV," Kenny said.

"That me, TV star." Alexei smirked.

"On *'America's Most Wanted'*."

"You too young to watch that."

"What type of parents you have?-" Frankie said to Kenny.

"Dead, that's what," Luka said.

"You take that back," Kenny said and jumped to his feet. Pat grabbed him and pulled him back to the wall.

"Like spunk in kid," Alexei said, "but be careful, little one, I have no patience for fools."

"My mom's not dead," Kenny said as Pat tried to soothe him and calm him down. Kenny put his face against her and started sobbing.

Alexei shook his head.

"What do you plan to do with us?" Diane said to get his attention off Kenny.

Alexei looked at her, undressing her with his gray eyes. "Well?" she said.

"Nothing. Too much killing already."

"Then you'll let us go?" Pat said.

Alexei shook his head. "Kid already call me gangster."

Kenny wiped the tears from his eyes and pointed at the baggy of bloody diamonds rings still on the carpet. Then he pointed at Frankie, "This guy dropped that, that makes you a gangster."

Alexei looked at Frankie and sighed. "Look at idy-ots I got work for me."

Frankie scrambled over to the baggy and hurriedly crammed everything in his coat pocket.

"So, for now, we keep guns and you stay there. We not want to harm you so you not do anything foolish. When we leave, you go on your way."

Ryan stared at Alexei, not believing him. "What are you planning?"

"We wait till afternoon, then heat and lack of food, monsters not so many. Then we take balloon and fly to upstate New York." Alexei smiled at them like he was such a nice guy for not killing them.

"The wind's not blowing in the right direction," Kenny said.

"What you know."

"You're going to let us live?" Diane said.

"Why not?" Alexei said. "I not monster. Monsters outside eating people."

"Boss," Frankie said and Alexei glared at him like he wanted to shoot him.

"What? What?"

Frankie motioned at the women. "You know those lonely nights."

Alexei stared at him; his dark eyes ordering the fool to keep his mouth shut and stop putting foot in it.

"What about the bomb?" Ron said.

"What bomb?" Diane said.

"An atomic bomb," Ron said.

"Military change plan, not until sunset." Alexei made a grand gesture. "Give you plenty time to get away after we do."

"You didn't hear?" Ron said to Alexei.

"Hear what? What you talk about?"

"They're no longer going to Nuke New York,"

"What you mean?" Alexei said.

Howie said, "They're going to set off an atomic bomb above New York, set off a gigantic electromagnetic pulse; an EMP. They figure the zombies will look up and the blast will blind and disorganize them. It will be a lot easier for the military to come in and take over."

"Are they out of their minds?" Ryan said.

"They figure it will mess up the zombies, but won't damage the infrastructure."

Alexei stared at him, not sure what all this meant.

"Hey, I see you on TV," Luka said to Ron. "You reporter."

"Yeah."

Alexei stepped closer to Ron waving a Beretta at him. "This EMP, what it like?"

"It might start a few fires, but they plan to send in troops to put the fires out."

"What fires it start?"

"Cell phones, computers, TVs, GPS devices."

"Cell phones will be like fire crackers," Kenny said.

"Shit, there zombies walking around with cell phones still in pockets," Frankie said.

"More than a few," Diane said. "They're all wearing the clothes they had on when they became zombies."

"So?" Pat said.

"You don't understand," Kenny said.

"Of course we understand," Frankie said angrily.

""Shut up," Alexei said. Then whispered, "We just leave earlier."

"What don't we understand?" Pat said.

"Zombies are like human torches," Kenny said. "Somehow their sweat is very – very. . . ."

"Flammable," Ryan said

"When we were coming here we tried to keep them away with a torch and one of them went up like he was soaked in gas. He just touched another zombie and then both were on fire. Ryan had to shoot them before them ran into other zombies and the fire spread."

Pat stared at Alexei. "You knew that, didn't you? You're not surprised. You're going to let the city burn."

"I not know what you talk about," Alexei lied.

Frankie whispered to Alexei. "Maybe we leave one with big mouth behind."

"What did you say?" Pat said.

"We have to warn the military not to set off the bombs," Ron said.

"Warn them?" Alexei laughed. "Why should I warn them?"

"So many cell phones," Howie said. "Thousands of human torches. There aren't enough people to fight the fires."

Ryan said. "They're going to spark a few million cell phones; thousands of zombies will become walking torches. All the major cities of the world will go up like bonfires."

Alexei said. "You sure of this?"

"At noon," Ron said, "they've sent out a warning to everyone, not to look up at noon. It could blind you."

Alexei looked from Ron to Luka and Frankie as he figured out what this meant to him.

Ron went on, "They're going to do it above all the major cities of the world at the same time. The armies are coordinating this worldwide. Every major city in the world will be hit at the same time. "

Alexei looked at his watch.

"Less than two hours," Howie said looking at his Timex.

Ryan said, "We've got to warn them."

"Radio in Humvee not work," Alexei said. "We try to get helicopter to pick us up."

"We've got walkie-talkies," Kenny said.

"Give to me," Alexei said.

Ryan started to reach for it and Alexei waved his gun at him. He motioned the kid, Kenny, to get it.

Kenny ran to the backpack at the side of the lobby and took out the walkie-talkie.

"Give it me," Alexei shouted.

Frankie yanked it from Kenny and handed it to Alexei. Alexei motioned Frankie to point his gun at the hostages, to make sure they didn't try anything. Then he turned the radio on. Every channel he tried was a recording:

BE ADVISED. AT NOON AN ATOMIC BOMB WILL BE DETONATED HIGH ABOVE THE CITY. THE BOMB WILL NOT DAMAGE THE BUILDINGS. BUT DO NOT LOOK UP AT THE SKY. THE BLAST COULD CAUSE BLINDNESS.

"What's going on?"

"I think I know," Ron said. "They're sending the signal out on thousands of radio and TV channels to make sure everyone gets the message. Because of that no one can contact them and warn them."

Howie said "Or jam the drones carrying the bombs."

Alexei said, "No way to get word to them."

"We got to get up in the balloons and warn them," Ryan said.

"Why not just get on roof?" Luka said.

"In Manhattan?" Kenny said. "Almost every building is a skyscraper and lots have antennas on them."

Alexei said, "We came here to get balloon, but there so many zombies we never get to park to launch balloon."

"Unless someone led them away," Frankie said.

Alexei smiled at Ryan.

"That's suicidal," Diane said.

"It is noble," Luka said and they all pointed their guns at Ryan. "You be hero, the motherland honor you."

"We can figure out another way to do it," Ron said.

"We like this way," Frankie said.

"Not enough time," Alexei said.

"He's right," Ryan said and everyone turned to him.

"You brave man," Alexei said.

"Ryan, no," Ron said. "I've seen what those monsters can do."

Ryan climbed to his feet. He was a little shaky and had to stand still for a moment.

"No, Ryan, don't," Pat said.

"Please," Diane said trying to hold him back.

"Someone's got to," Ryan said. "That way all of you can make a break for it."

"I don't trust them," Kenny said. "He's not going to let us leave, we could tell people about the bloody fingers in their bags."

"Who care about diamonds in this?" Alexei said.

"No one believe you," Luka said.

"Who care if we take ring off zombie?" Frankie said.

"Zombie blood is almost black," Kenny said. "Your

rings are covered with red blood."

"People were dead," Frankie protested. "They not need it anymore. We need it to trade for food and water."

"Now," Alexei said to Ryan, "you have to leave now."

Ryan tousled Kenny's light brown hair and said, "It'll be okay." He turned to Alexei. "I need a gun."

Alexei shook his head. "So you change mind and shoot me?"

"I need to protect myself to keep the zombies chasing me."

"Give him .22," Alexei told Frankie.

"How are my friends going to get to the balloons?" Ryan asked.

"We escort them."

"Don't believe him," Kenny said.

"He believe me," Alexei said.

"No he doesn't."

"Want to see?"

Alexei pointed his gun at Ryan, then aimed it at Kenny. "And I no trust your father." To Ryan he said, "I shoot your son, if you don't."

"I'm not his son."

Alexei grinned like a wolf. "You two lie good, I no trust either one of you."

Ryan started to object and Alexei fired into the carpeted floor next to Kenny. Kenny jumped back into Pat. She grabbed him and held him tightly.

"Okay, leave him alone," Ryan said.

"My kind of man." Alexei grinned. "We have deal?"

*****

Chapter 44 - Gunfire

Ryan walked to the glass door. His first steps were a little shaky, but once he got to walking he felt a little better. Sunlight shined into Central Park across the street; several colorful balloons could be seen above the treetops. The trees were still, there wasn't much wind today. He wondered how it was once the balloons rose above the protective wall of the skyscrapers. He watched the zombies wandering about and motioned for Luka to help move the sofa away from the door on the right, so it would open.

"You go east down Fifth Avenue," Alexei told him, standing next to him, pointing a Beretta at him. "Yell to make zombies follow you."

Ryan looked at the balloons in the park.

"Well?" Alexei said. "Stop stalling."

Ryan nodded, but continued to look at the zombies to see if he could discern any pattern in their behavior. He noticed as the sun went up they moved into the shade, in alleys, indoors, inside buildings.

"We not got time to wait, he leave now." Frankie tapped his watch as he became more nervous.

Alexei said, "Need hero to lead zombies away."

Ryan stared at Alexei. He glanced at Luka and Frankie, his glance saying what he couldn't say.

"Don't," Diane said.

"And you promise you're going to let the others get to a balloon?"

"Of course," Alexei said. "You have my word."

Ryan went to the door and looked outside.

"Don't go," Diane said.

"Don't, Ryan," Pat said.

"I'll try to catch up with you in the park," Ryan said and went to the door.

Luka opened the door and shoved him outside.

When Ryan was outside Frankie tossed him Howie's .22 rifle, and then Frankie helped Luka push the couch back in front of the door.

After Ryan headed right, toward Fifth Avenue, Frankie opened his hand. The gleaming brass cartridges fell from his hand to the floor. Luka and Frankie laughed.

"You bastard," Pat said.

"He got two bullets, that enough to lead zombies away," Alexei said.

"But not enough to fight for his life," Pat said.

"He brave man," Frankie said.

Then Alexei saw the look on Ron's face. "What you find so interesting?"

Ron turned to him. "He's an ex-marine. With two bullets he can win a war."

Frankie laughed and Alexei whacked him. "No make fun of brave man."

Then they heard a gunshot and a car horn blaring on Fifth Avenue.

"He use rifle to push car horn to attract zombies," Luka said.

The zombies passed by the front of the hotel heading for Fifth Avenue. Soon there was a break in the parade of shuffling monsters.

"Come on," Alexei said.

"We have to hurry," Ron said.

Alexei gave Luka a nod. Luka shot Ron in the leg. Frankie clubbed Howie and blood ran down the side of Howie's face, as Kenny raced around the corner of the lobby.

Alexei turned to Diane and Pat. "You two come with us."

Pat was kneeling next to Ron. "I'm not going anywhere." When Frankie approached her she brandished a knife at him.

Luka grabbed Diane by her arm and lifted her up.

"Take her," Alexei said.

"What about the other one?" Frankie said.

"She remind me of mother wolf. No trust to be close to at night."

Frankie backed away from Pat.

"We share this one," Alexei said.

Frankie shrugged.

Luka smiled; the boss wouldn't share. They would find more women or Frankie would do.

When they opened the door the stench of death was so bad, it was like getting breathed on by the devil.

Alexei hurried out of the lobby to the Humvee. He opened the back door and Luka threw Diane inside. Alexei grabbed Diane by the wrist to stop her from jumping out the other side and she spun around and slapped his face so hard, he rocked backward. Alexei blinked and pointed the gun at her. Diane stared at him expecting to be shot.

"Shoot me, but you still won't get me," she said.

Alexei swung the gun toward the lobby and aimed through the glass doors at Pat tying a tourniquet around Ron's leg.

"Okay, just don't shoot anyone else." she said and he lowered his gun.

He smiled as he climbed in the backseat. Luka got behind the wheel. The Humvee roared to life. Luka drove across the street up East Drive into Central Park.

Some zombies turned toward the loud car, others turned toward the door and the smell of humans.

*****

Chapter 45 - Run for it

A fire door in the back of the lobby opened and Ryan stepped into the lobby. He fired a small pistol crossbow down the hall behind him and closed the door. He jammed a table in front of the door and ran into lobby.

Pat had stopped the bleeding in Ron's leg and Kenny was helping Howie, holding a cloth on the side of his bloody head. "How'd you get away?"

"Jammed the horn in the VW and ran."

"They took Diane," Pat said. "She went with them so they wouldn't shoot us."

"Come on, let's get out of here." Ryan pulled Howie to his feet. Pat helped Ron limp to the front door.

Suddenly the back door of the lobby burst open and Tommy came in followed by a horde of zombies.

"Tommy," Howie said and the zombie growled at him.

Ryan took the backpack off his shoulder and tried to load another arrow in the pistol crossbow, but it took too long. He lifted the hunting knife he found in the VW, from his belt and threw it at the lead zombie. It hit the zombie in the chest. The zombie fell back into the pack in the doorway blocking it for a moment.

"We have to go," Pat said.

Ryan carried Howie to the door. Pat helped Ron out the door, Ron's thigh was bleeding badly; Pat was afraid an artery had been nicked and hoped the belt tourniquet would keep him alive until they found a doctor or someone who could help him. With Kenny holding Howie's left hand and Ryan helping him on the right, and Pat supporting Ron; they went out the front door of the Plaza, as the zombies crossed the lobby after them and other zombies in the street were coming toward them.

After he was outside Howie tried to walk on his own.

"Wait a minute," Pat said and ran back inside for the

backpack Ron had carried into the hotel. She grabbed it and hurried away, a step ahead of the zombies. Ryan picked up a rock off the ground and threw it at the swarm and the lead zombie went down.

Howie spotted a hotel limo at the end of the drive.

"Check it for keys," Howie said.

Kenny ran to the driver's door of the black Mercedes, opened it and looked inside. The keys were dangling from the ignition. "They're here," he yelled and immediately regretted it.

The others hurried to the car. Ryan deposited Ron in the backseat. Pat crawled in the back to be with Ron. Howie feeling better, went to the driver's door.

"I can drive," Ryan said to him.

Howie wanted to tell him to move over, but he kept his mouth shut and slid over the hood, leaving a trail of blood from his head wound and climbed in the passenger door. The dash looked like the control of a plane and the car was filled with amenities; wet bar, stereo, refrigerator, flat screen TV and black leather seats.

Ron sat in the backseat as Pat worked on his leg.

Suddenly there was knocking on the window and Ryan jumped. It was Kenny knocking with his hockey stick; he'd gone back for his hockey stick. He was locked outside the car. Ryan looked at the buttons, not knowing which one to press.

"That one." Howie pointed and Ryan pressed it and the windows opened.

"Try that one," Howie said and Ryan pressed it and the sunroof opened.

"Try them all," Howie shouted.

Ryan did but the doors did not want to unlock. Meanwhile, Kenny climbed on the hood, over the windshield and came down through the sunroof. Ron cried out when Kenny landed on his leg.

""Sorry," Kenny said noticing how white Ron's face was turning.

"Let me drive," Howie said.

"Okay, you drive." Ryan climbed out of the front seat and stood in the open sunroof and loaded an arrow in the pistol crossbow and aimed at a zombie and squeezed the trigger. He aimed at the lead zombie's head, but missed and the arrow went through the two zombies behind it.

Howie slid behind the wheel and looked at the snazzy controls and instruments.

Pat opened the backpack and spilled the contents onto the floor. Inside was a roll of duct tape, a small roadside emergency medical kit. Pat grabbed the medical kit and the duct tape. Pat applied a small dressing to Ron's leg, then wrapped duct tape around it. Finally the bleeding stopped.

Kenny climbed into the front seat and poked Howie in the arm.

"What?"

"Well, start it already.

Howie turned the key and the limo's engine coughed to life.

Kenny pointed at the shift lever.

"I know. I know." Howie shifted into drive and the limo rolled heavy like a tank.

"Don't follow them," Ryan said from the sunroof seat and Howie looked at him in the mirror.

They heard shooting from where the Humvee had entered Central Park.

"Turn around," Ryan said.

Howie stepped on the gas and made a turn on Central Park South and hit a Yellow cab abandoned in the street. The crossbow arrows that Ryan had placed on the roof next to him to make it easier to reload went flying off the roof. He grabbed for them and managed to seize three arrows.

Howie turned trying to avoid zombies. The zombies reached for the car, clawing at the windows, one even crawled onto the hood. Ryan standing in the open sunroof aimed the pistol crossbow and shot the zombie on the hood.

Kenny inadvertently pressed the button which closed the sunroof.

"Hey," Ryan cried as he ducked into the back seat, but lost the arrows to the closing sun roof.

"Don't touch anything," Howie yelled nervously.

"Sorry," Kenny said.

"Just hit them." Ryan pointed at the zombies.

"They were people once," Pat said.

"There isn't enough time to go around them," Howie explained. "Just driving is attracting more of them." He pointed at the horde of monsters coming toward them down 59th Street.

Howie headed west weaving around stopped cars and delivery vans.

"Watch out," Kenny said. Coming out of the shadows on West 59th Street were hundreds of zombies.

Central Park Drive was up ahead on the right; Howie had driven it last night. Only a short distance to go. Then he saw all the zombies pouring out of 6th Avenue and he stepped on the gas before they cut him off blocking the entrance to Central Park.

The heavy limo plowed into the zombies, they hit the hood and bounced off, and some bounced and rolled off the sides. They pounded the windows, grabbing and clawing the windows and the sides of the cars. A few made it onto the hood and clawed the windshield trying to get to them. Others grabbed onto those zombies on the car and pulled themselves onto the car. Zombies were lying on other zombies on the hood. They grabbed onto the windshield wipers until they broke off. The car slowed to a crawl.

"What are you doing?" Ryan shouted

"I can't see where I'm going," Howie said.

"Just step on the gas."

"Go right," Kenny said.

"Why?"

"Think the park entrance is on the right."

"You think it is?"

"Just do it," Ryan said.

Howie turned the steering wheel right and the car almost came to a stop.

"FLOOR IT!" Ryan shouted.

Howie stomped the gas and the big limo surged ahead. He started to break free of the zombies, almost hit a post on the corner of 59th and Central Park Drive, swerved in time to avoid it and headed into Central Park. Zombies chased after it.

*****

Chapter 46 - Central Park

The sun shined brightly in Central Park. What would have been a gorgeous day for a picnic was a nightmare of zombies. There weren't as many in hte Park as there were behind them, but they were there, in the shadows of the trees, and were attracted to the big limo. They came from the streets surrounding the park attracted by the sound of car engines and shooting and especially the smell of humans. A wall of zombies chased the limo. On both sides zombies were closing in.

There were deflated balloons to the right and left, the car bounced, lumbering, as if the right front tire had gone flat and there was something wrong with the suspension on that side. Now the engine started coughing and smoke was coming from under the hood.

Ryan leaned forward to the back of the front seat.

"Can you go faster?"

Howie spoke with a British accent, "Well sir, the picnic grounds seem to be a little crowded today, but I trust we'll find a spot that your lordship finds suitable." As Howie was speaking he was zigzagging left and right, trying to avoid abandoned vehicles and not hit too many zombies.

Ryan replied in a cockney accent, "Make sure there's a

nice balloon handy."

"Yes sir."

Kenny looked from one to the other. "You guys cracking up?"

"They were born cracked up," Ron said.

"Just, please hurry," Pat said.

Then they heard shooting from their right and through a break in the trees saw the Humvee stop in a field and Alexei, Luka, and Frankie shooting their way to a balloon. Alexei was just about dragging Diane to the balloon.

Howie veered to the right and Ryan shouted, "NO!"

Howie put his hand over his ear, Ryan said, "Sorry," and pointed to the left. "That one over there."

"How are we going to rescue Diane if we go over there?"

"We can't rescue her if we're dead."

Howie swung a left and bounced over the curb and across the grass.

The front bumper hit a rock and stopped. Howie shifted into reverse and tried to backup, but the limo wouldn't budge. The undercarriage was hung up on the rock. He shifted from reverse to drive and stepped on the gas. The tires spun, the car would not move.

"Now what?" Howie shouted.

"WHAT!"

"The car is stuck."

"CHILDREN," Pat shouted and they quieted.

"Let's make a run for it," Ryan said.

"Where?" Ron shouted, sending jolts of pain up his leg.

"Over there." Ryan pointed at a balloon across the field. The balloon was not completely inflated. It was made up of colored panel squares that when inflated and up in the sky would look like a rainbow.

Howie grabbed his door handle and opened it and jumped out, almost into the arms of a zombie. He shoved the zombie back, but it came at him again. "Here," Kenny said, handing him his hockey stick. Howie whacked the zombie in the chest and knocked it backward.

"In the head." Kenny pressed the button to open the sunroof and climbed out the sunroof. "In the head."

Howie swung again, a vicious slicing blow, and hit the zombie in the neck and a waterfall of black blood came out of the wound and down the chest.

"The head," Kenny shouted. "The head."

Howie swung again and hit the zombie in the head and it went down and lay still. Howie stared at it a moment, looked at the hockey stick and shrugged.

Ryan opened the back door and climbed out and helped Kenny off the roof. Pat helped Ron out of the car.

A mob of zombies lurched down Central Park Drive and more were coming across the fields on both sides of them. They heard shooting to the northeast.

"The Russians," Ron said.

"Come on." Howie hurried across the field toward the rainbow balloon. Kenny was at his side ready to help him.

Pat helped Ron limp after them. The pants on Ron's right leg was soaked with blood, the makeshift tourniquet had slowed the flow of blood, but not stopped it. Ryan held Ron's right arm, Pat the other. Ron tried to pay attention and do his own walking, but the loss of blood had taken its toll. It was a struggle just to remain conscious.

Kenny ran to the left and right smacking any zombies that came close and knocking them down.

They hadn't gone far when Pat remembered, "The backpack." She looked back at the limo.

"Leave it," Howie said.

"It's got survival stuff in it," Ron said.

"I'll get it," Kenny said.

"No," Howie said. The zombies were closing in on the limo. "You help Ron, I'll get it."

Ryan held Ron up while Pat took off her own belt and tied it above Ron's wound. Kenny raced, after Howie, back to the limo. Ron almost fell down and Pat staggered under the weight.

Howie ran to the limo. A zombie shuffled by the rear door and Howie shoved him so hard he flew over the trunk. He turned to see if Diane was watching. He could see the other balloon rising across the park; it looked like a rainbow ball, all yellow and reds, and he hoped that was her at the side of the basket. He waved at her.

Then he ducked in the open rear door and grabbed a shoulder strap on the bright orange backpack. He pulled, but it wouldn't come. He yanked again, and then as his eyes adjusted to the dark interior inside the car he saw the other shoulder strap was caught on the bottom corner of the small refrigerator door. He yanked again harder and the strap came free. The refrigerator door popped open and bottles spilled out.

He turned to go and stopped and looked at the tiny bottles on the floor. Inside the refrigerator was a bottle of Cold River vodka and more mini-bottles of other liquors. He nodded, they could come in handy and started shoving the booze in the backpack. He was just about finished when he felt something grab his foot. He whirled about and saw it was a zombie. He kicked it in the face, sending it back into the zombies behind it. There was a wall of zombies trying to get at him, he closed the door.

He looked left and right at all the windows. The limo was surrounded by zombies. "You done it this time," he said to himself. Then he noticed the sunroof was open and thrust the backpack up through it and climbed up on the roof. Zombies surrounded the limo. How could he get down? Immediately the zombies started climbing on the car to get to him.

Then he saw a zombie wearing a dark green blazer climb up on the hood of the limo and come at him with its thick arms outstretched. There was several black holes in the zombie's chest as if it had been shot, but the clincher was the knife stick stuck in what he used to call the Mouth of the South, Tommy.

"So you did Diane." Howie kicked it in the groin.

The zombie backed up a few steps, then shuffled toward him again, as if it wasn't even bothered.

"Oh, shit."

Howie had fallen down on the car from the force of his kick and scrambled backward. He was almost to the sunroof. If he fell through or climbed back into the car he would be trapped; a dead man. Suddenly an arrow hit the zombie in the head. Zombie Tommy's head recoiled, and he fell off the car into the zombies around the car.

Howie stood up and yelled, "Thanks."

"Come on." Ryan turned to run back to Pat.

"Stop fooling around," Kenny called.

Howie was angry that a kid should say that, think he was fooling around.

Filled with anger he ran across the hood of the car and leaped over the wall of zombies and fell to the ground, knocking a few down. He clambered to his feet and ran after the others carrying the weighed down backpack. . He ran fast leaving most of the zombies far behind.

Ryan stayed in front of the group firing a policeman's Glock he'd found on the ground by a body. They caught up to Pat still supporting Ron and Howie went to Ron's other side to help her.

"What do you got in there?" Kenny said.

Howie opened the backpack to show off the booze. Many of the bottles had broken.

"Great going," Kenny said. "Now we've gotten broken glass to use on them."

Pat shook her head.

Howie was crestfallen and looked at the soaked backpack and at the wet trail of booze he'd left on the ground; his eyes followed it back to the wall of zombies chasing them. Then his face lit up as an idea came to him.

"Anyone got a lighter?"

Pat struggled with Ron'. "I gave up smoking."

"It's not for me," he objected.

Pat shook head no.

"Here." Kenny reached in his jeans' pocket and took out a Bic butane lighter.

"Thanks," Howie said and stopped and kneeling down started to put the flame to the wet trail of liquor. Kenny kicked the lighter out of his hand.

"Ow! Why'd you do that?"

"They burn," Kenny shouted. "Remember?"

Howie stood up, pale, deflated and looked at Pat for a word of encouragement.

"Give us a hand," Pat said.

Howie handed her the backpack and put Ron's arm over his shoulder and just about lifted Ron himself to show he could do his share.

He hurried, trying to catch up to Ryan, Pat struggling to help and keep up with him, when Howie noticed Ryan had stopped and was looking back behind them.

"Oh no," Kenny said.

Howie looked over his shoulder. A zombie had picked up the still flaming Bic butane lighter. The zombie tried to grab the flame and the flame spread to its hand and ran up its arm. The zombie turned and continued after them as flames quickly covered its body like it had been soaked in kerosene. It took a few steps and fell into the backpack.

There was a momentary flare from the liquor soaked backpack and then a small explosion.

Glad the flames had not spread; Howie turned to the front and saw Pat sitting on the ground. "What are you doing down there?"

A piece of wreckage from the explosion had knocked her down. She picked up a small red Coca-Cola can the explosion had sent at her like a missile. She was so angry, she couldn't speak. She hurried over to Ron's other side.

Howie glanced at her to see how pissed she was and she gave him a look not to say a word. He turned front and helped her with Ron.

They heard gunshots and saw Alexei's red and yellow rainbow balloon rising, zombies holding onto a tether line being lifted off the ground, Alexei shooting at them and the zombies falling.

*****

353

Chapter 47 - Up, Up and Away

The balloon that looked like a red and yellow rainbow was rising up into the air. They could see three men and a woman in the small baske, the men leaning over the side shooting zombies. Then they were aiming over the tops of the trees, trying to shoot them. The bullets kicked up dirt near Ron. They took turns using the hunting rifle. When Diane tried to stop them, someone hit her.

"Why are they shooting at us?" Kenny said.

"Remember the bag of bloody rings and jewelry?" Pat said.

"War crimes," Howie said.

Ryan reached the blue, red, and white balloon and signaled them to hurry as now bullets kicked up the dirt around the balloon. Ryan climbed inside the balloon and reached up and pulled the handle. Only a little propane flame rose up into the balloon. Then they heard an automatic weapon firing. "An AK-47," Ryan said and ducked. They heard the heavy 7.62 millimeter bullets smacking through the balloon fabric above them and saw the colorful balloon begin to sag.

"We better find another balloon," Ryan said.

"Over there." Kenny pointed at a balloon on the other side of a wall of trees.

Ryan hurried out of the basket before the balloon collapsed on him. They had just started out toward the trees when a shot rang out.

Howie felt something hot hit him and stopped. He looked down; blood was coming from his belly. He'd been shot. It didn't hurt yet, but he felt trembly weak. He took a few more steps then saw the grass come up and smack him.

Ryan hurried back, shooting at zombies coming toward the fallen Howie. The zombies went down in a splatter of

Zombies

blood. Most stayed down, some struggled to their feet to attack again.

"Can you walk?"

"Leave me."

"Come on." Ryan helped him to his feet.

Howie was about to insist on being left when Kenny grabbed his arm and growled in his face. "You better come."

Howie found himself walking with Ryan's help.

Ryan fired the nine-millimeter Glock at zombies that were nearby. Every zombie he hit went down, only a few got back up.

"Does it hurt?"

"No. Will it?"

"It might."

"That's the best you got? It might?"

"It might not," Ryan said.

"Oh, now I'm relieved."

"Probably will."

They went through a wall of trees to a balloon that looked like a giant blue-and red-ball. The bottom was dark blue, the middle dark red, the very top blue. When they emerged from the trees they checked and the other balloon was too far away to bother them.

The basket was large enough for all of them, bigger than the previous one.

"Heard about this," Kenny said, "it was on TV. They were giving kids rides."

Around the balloon were two large propane tanks and black hoses to fill the propane tank in the basket. Two security guards lay dead on the ground; around them were the bodies of several zombies. It looked like the men had killed the zombies then one of them turned and the other guard shot him in the head, then committed suicide.

Ryan lifted Howie into the basket and then deposited Kenny alongside him. Pat climbed into the five person basket and he handed Ron up to her. Ron looked a little better. There wasn't much room inside the basket with propane tanks and a little instrument panels and lines.

Ryan went to the two guards. Both had Glocks, but their guns were empty, on the ground near each of the bodies was one empty magazine. In the hand of the body of the older guard he found a full magazine. He took it and the security guard's gun and tossed them to Kenny in the basket.

Ryan directed Pat to the propane burner mounted on a metal frame above the center of the basket. A small propane flame, on a whisper burner, had been on an automatic computer setting and the balloon was filled, not really straining at the tether lines, but ready. Ryan had Pat grab a red cord that opened a blast valve. Once Pat pulled the spring loaded valve, a hot blue flame shot up into the balloon and it tried to rise pulling the tether lines.

Ryan ran around cutting the tether lines away from ground stakes. Zombies were closing in and he shot a few, cut a line, ran to the next line and shot zombies, cut it.

When the tether lines were cut he ran to the rising basket and jumped in, but Pat hadn't been inflating the balloon at the maximum rate. The hot flame so close overhead frightened her. Ryan grabbed both cords and pulled sending two hot blue flames upward as he turned around and around shooting zombies. Very soon the balloon rose about seven feet and stopped. Zombies held onto a tether line that hadn't been cut while others tried to grab the bottom of the basket. Some were trying to climb up the line. Ryan looked for his knife but couldn't find it. He had run out of bullets and zombies had climbed on fallen zombies and were trying to reach up and grab the basket to get at them.

Kenny handed Ryan a magazine he'd found on the ground and then went around with his hockey stick clobbering zombies that had grabbed the bottom of the basket. Ryan gave Pat the cords and told her to pull as he took bullets out of the Beretta magazine and put them in the Glock magazine. When he reloaded the Glock, he put the muzzle of the gun against the tether line and fired. The line split and the balloon sprang up into the air.

Ryan looked around and the balloon still wasn't rising fast enough. Once above the trees, the wind coming down the cement canyons from the west would blow the balloon east toward the skyscraper cliffs. One zombie was holding them down. The zombie in the dark green blazer, a hunting knife in his chest and a crossbow arrow sticking out on one eye was trying to climb up the basket. Ryan aimed at the face and squeezed the trigger. The hammer fell on an empty cylinder. The gun was empty.

Howie looked over the side, saw who the zombie was, climbed over the side and kicked the zombie in the head knocking it off. Howie watched the zombie fall and splash down in Central Park Pond. Ryan, Kenny and Pat had to help Howie back inside the basket. When he was inside, Howie looked at all the blood on his shirt and plopped down in the basket. He felt cold and started shivering.

Pat had stopped pulling on the blast cord and Ryan shoved her aside and yanked on it.

"What's your problem?"

Ryan pointed at the wall of buildings along Fifth Avenue.

"But the other basket easily made it over them."

"More lift, less weight," he said and she didn't seem to catch on. "Less people."

Her mouth formed a big silent, Oh.

"Where is the other balloon?" Kenny said.

They looked around, but couldn't see it.

Ron was standing at the side. Howie struggled to his feet and stood over the side and stared at the wall of skyscrapers coming at them. He looked down at his ankle, at the claw marks zombie Tommy had left there. Would he change one? Not everyone changed into a zombie when a zombie clawed them.

Pat had to stop the flow of blood and wrapped a gauze bandage around Howie's waist, but it was soaked through and blood was dripping down his pants. Kenny took one look at him and shook his head. Howie held onto the railing as he shivered and felt his life draining away.

"Does it hurt?"

"Now that you mention it." His face was pale and he looked sick.

"Hang in there."

"Why?"

"I care." Pat grabbed his hand and held on.

"There they are," Kenny shouted and pointed.

Howie looked across the city's skyline at the rainbow balloon, at Diane in the other basket. "A dollar short and a day late, story of my life."

"What?" Pat said and he shook his head.

"Are we going to make it over them?" Kenny said and motioned ahead.

Ryan looked at the buildings and how slowly they were rising. And behind the buildings on Fifth Avenue were taller buildings. For a moment he felt he was back in the helicopter looking down at the black hole, the explosion, the helicopter shifted and he was falling. He blinked. He was in a balloon. He wiped the sweat from his face. Abruptly, the wind changed slightly and blew them down E. 61st Street, like wind funneled down a canyon. Skyscrapers towered on both sides of them. The balloon bounced on the wind coming precariously close to the sides of the buildings. Their blue and red balloon was not rising, the tops of the buildings were higher than the balloon.

"Need more altitude," Kenny said.

"Too much weight." Ron started to climb over the edge. Pat grabbed him and pulled him back.

Pat said, "We need to throw things out."

"What?" Kenny said.

She ran to the tall cylindrical propane tanks; they were stainless steel, mounted vertically with red insulating covers. Each had a fuel gauge on top and a round chrome handle. There was one in each corner.

"Only the empty ones," Ryan said. "We have to keep the balloon inflated."

"They're both full." She looked at the fuel gauges.

Ryan motioned Kenny to grab the cord and went to the tanks. He studied the gauge, tapped them to make sure they were working. When he tapped the left tank the red needle moved to the red 'E'. Empty. He freed the empty tank from its harness and lifted it over the side. It reminded of the tank on Ron's grill. He watched it crash on the empty street below.

Now they were rising, but still not fast enough. The balloon barely made it across Madison Avenue when a cross wind hit it. The basket swung like a pendulum. The wind hit the balloon and it rocked and descended. The balloon might make it over the roofs, but the basket would not. The towers would snag it.

"It's okay," Howie said and they turned.

Howie was sitting on the side of the basket.

"Oh no, don't," Pat said.

Howie showed her his scratched ankle. The nearby veins were turning black "It's either now or later."

"Please don't."

"Story of my life."

"We can figure out something," Ryan said.

"Not enough time." The wind blew them over Park Avenue and the balloon was buffeted in the cross currents toward the buildings.

"Please," Pat begged, tears in her eyes.

He waved goodbye and jumped over the side.

They rushed to the side and watched him fall down as the balloon rose higher.

He splashed into a pool in a Park Avenue penthouse, blue water rose up and covered him. Before they could see if he was okay, the balloon moved and the pool was blocked from view.

The balloon rose, the wind rocked it and sent it on its way as Pat cried. Kenny started crying and Ryan held him.

*****

Chapter 48 - Blue Dome of Sky

The tall fortresses of steel and cement rose up, but they watched the tops of the buildings go by beneath them, the gray ribbon of streets, wrecked vehicles like little toys; zombies wandering and dead bodies everywhere. At times the breeze brought the smell up to them. The stench was so terrible it made them gag. Broken windows gaped like black holes, sheets hung out some buildings. In building after building someone came to a window and waved. Some shouted. Many cried for helped. On a few streets battles still raged; other streets were empty like in an abandoned city.

They flew over the East River, the United Nations to the south, traffic permanently jammed on the famous Queensborough Bridge. Way to the side and below was Queens Boulevard. Over the Brooklyn-Queens Expressway, they saw the parking lot that was the Long Island Expressway. Here and there survivors waved to them. Some held up signs. HELP US. They left Queens behind for Long Island, the wind more southeasterly now.

The other balloon with the larger basket was behind them. A trailing tether line had been grabbed by survivors clinging to the top of the Queensborough Bridge and tied to the top of a tower crown. Alexei and Frankie had shot the survivors as they tried to pull the balloon down until Luka cut the line. A few people clinging to the bridge shot back when they were fired upon and Alexei shouted for everyone to stop shooting. Everyone stopped. "Take us," some people shouted. "We have no room," Alexei shouted. "Then we'll shoot," someone warned. Then Luka cut the line and as the red and yellow rainbow balloon floated away, Alexei, Frankie and Luka opened fire on anyone on the bridge before they shot at them.

They had only been delayed a few minutes, but it was enough for the wind to blow the lighter balloon further away.

Now the rainbow balloon was to their northeast.

"Why are we going this way?" Kenny said.

"I don't know," Ryan said. "A lighter basket, the wind pushes us a little differently." He shook his head.

"You're making it up," Kenny said.

"He always does," Pat said.

Ryan looked down at her sitting next to Ron, the basket beneath Ron covered with blood.

"How's he doing?"

Pat shook her head; she couldn't speak as fear filled her eyes.

Ron searched the backpack. His hand came out with binoculars and he extended them to Ryan.

Ryan lifted them to his eyes and sighted in on the other balloon. He saw Alexei looking through binoculars back at him. Alexei said something and Luka grabbed Diane by the arm, raised her up and licked her face as she struggled to get away from him.

Meanwhile Frankie was aiming a rifle at him. Ryan didn't know how far away they were, but he doubted with the wind and balloons moving he would hit anything. Then Ryan saw a puff of smoke and then heard the shot. He hoped the bullet didn't come anywhere near them or the balloon.

"What was that?" Kenny said.

"Nothing. Keep your head down."

"What do you see?"

"Nothing." Ryan looked at Pat and her eyes said she understood.

"This is as bad as home," Kenny said. "Don't do this. Don't do that."

"Really?" Ryan motioned at the sky.

The sky was a beautiful blue vault above them, few clouds, and the stench of the city fell behind them. No cars moved on any of the roads below. Occasionally they saw people and zombies moving about. As the sun shined down, the zombies retreated to the shadowy places and they saw people out in the sunlight scavenging for food, a few waved at them. Some held up signs. One person flashed a mirror as if the knew Morse code.

Ryan tried Ron's walkie-talkie, but got only interference.

They floated over part of Long Beach, the tip of Jones Beach, no bathers, the beaches empty – a few bodies on thewhite sand -- the roads empty, the fresh salty wind shoving them eastward over the deep blue Atlantic Ocean.

They watched the other balloon behind them. It had changed altitude and seemed to be closing the distance between them. The other balloon floated closer and closer and soon it just behind them almost level with them. Now they were over the ocean and saw small boats of people heading away from shore.

Ryan looked at his watch; it had stopped at 11:45.

Ryan tried the walkie-talkie. Nothing. No interference, no sound, nothing. It was like it was dead. He checked the batteries, licked the ends and put them back in. Still nothing.

"Try again," Ron said.

"Hello, this is a balloon leaving New York, can you hear me? Over." He released the button and listened. Silence.

They heard shouting. The gangsters in the other balloon were waving at them.

"What do they want?" Pat asked.

"Maybe they want to apologize for how they treated us," Kenny said, "so we won't get them in trouble."

"Not Alexei the butcher," Ron said and coughed up blood. He looked at the blood on his hand and wiped in on his side, hiding it from Pat.

Ryan didn't trust Alexei. Kenny tapped him on the shoulder and made a face and Ryan agreed with him.

Then they heard shooting. Alexei was shooting at them.

"What's he doing?" Pat said her voice high and frightened.

"Russian mafia," Ron said. "Leave no witnesses."

"You can't be serious," Pat said and stood up to see for herself. "Even he wouldn't stoop so low after what happened." The next shot nicked Pat's shoulder and she fell down.

Ron reached out to her. "Are you alright?"

She looked at her shoulder. "It's only a flesh wound."

"That bastard," Ron said and tried to stand up to curse at Alexei, but Pat pulled him down.

"They don't want us to tell anyone about the bloody jewelry," Kenny said.

As if Alexei had heard, the next shot hit the basket and they all ducked down.

"Can that gun shoot through the basket?" Kenny asked. He looked to Ron, Ron turned to Ryan. He pointed at a bullet hole in the woven wicker basket.

"This has got to stop right now," Pat said and stood up and waved her hands for them to stop.

The next shot almost hit her again and she ducked down.

"How many bullets they have?" Kenny said.

"Too many," Ryan said.

"Where's the small crossbow," Ron said.

"I threw it out when were trying to lessen the weight.

"Don't we have anything?" Kenny said.

"No," Ron said.

A few more shots were fired and one hit the basket. Ryan saw Ron jerk and knew he was hit, but when he went to say something Ron shook his head. He didn't want him to say anything. What good would it do?

Suddenly Kenny jumped up and grabbed both burner cords. The blue flame shot out of the blast valve and the whisper burner.

"What are you doing?" Pat said.

"Something," Kenny said. "Anything is better than doing nothing."

Ryan peeked over the edge. They were rising. The other bigger balloon had been caught flatfooted or was in a different air current.

"We'll run out of fuel," Pat said.

A smile crossed Kenny's face. "We're rising out of range."

Ryan didn't think so, but he peeked over the side.

***

The three Russian gangsters were paying so much attention to the other balloon's rising they ignored Diane.

They argued back and forth to shoot and don't shoot. They started shouting at each other. Luka wanted to shoot. Frankie said it was too far away; afraid he would get blamed it he missed. Alexei shouted that in his younger days he could make a shot like that.

Their arguing became more violent. Diane had no illusions about being trapped any place with these thugs. They would rape her. Alexei would keep her for his own only as long as it suited him. Then would give her to others to help themselves or kill her.

She saw only one way out. She pulled on the parachute valve cord to let the air out of the top of the balloon. The balloon would fall and she would probably die, but that was better than being Alexei's sex slave. But the cord was stuck. She yanked and yanked, nothing happened. She thought she wasn't putting enough pressure on it, not enough force. She reached way out of the side and pulled just when the wind shifted. The basket rocked and she tumbled out, and held onto the cord for dear life.

She almost screamed, but she saw them in the basket and something came over her and she held it in. She would not ask them to help her. She would rather fall in the sea and die than ask those animals to help her.

Diane had been the best rope climber in her gym class. She could climb up a rope hand over hand. Mrs. Smith had complimented her, told her if they had a rope climbing event in the Olympics she'd win the gold medal. Diane used to make bets with the boys, even give some of the jocks a head start, and still beat them. She didn't know why: Emily said it was working on her uncle's farm in the summer. She was so small and skinny, yet she had powerful muscles. And her fingers were tough. From all those weeks of hard work. She had a grip like a weight-lifter. Diane had dated a rock climber, but he became discouraged at how easily she could scale a rock face and stopped seeing her. He had said she was like that girl that went around world climbing everything with just her hands like she was a spider while experienced climbers had a difficult time even with the help of ropes. Diane didn't like rock climbing. On the farm she felt she was accomplishing something, doing something important, not just going up a rock.

Now as she hung over the side of the balloon hundreds of feet in the air, those experiences came back to her. She held onto the cord, and arranged it through her legs just like she'd seen Bear Gryls do and like an inchworm, she started ascending. She had no real plan. She just figured she was safer getting away from the gangsters where they couldn't lay their hands on her.

After she had climbed some distance, they noticed she was gone and ran to the side of the basket and looked down. For a long time they didn't see her, then Frankie looked up and the others did too. She was above them against the side of the balloon. They shouted at her, warned her if she didn't come down they would shoot.

She looked down at them. She had seen them shoot. Even at this close range they were more liable to hit the balloon than her. "You'll hit the balloon," she shouted.

When she wouldn't come down, Alexei grabbed the rifle from Frankie and aimed at her.

"Boss?" Luka motioned at the basket. "Too close to balloon."

"We need women," Frankie said.

"Where she go?" Luka said,

Alexei angrily lowered the gun, but he told Frankie and Luka to grab the cord that dangled a few feet away from the basket. They tried and tried and couldn't grab it. Finally Luka held Frankie's belt as he leaned out of the basket and the wiry gangster managed to snag the end of the cord. He pulled Frankie and the cord back into the basket.

"We pull this," Alexei shouted. "No come, we pull."

Diane looked down at them. She was glad they were holding the end. It made climbing a little easier, but she had no plans to go back down into the basket. She'd stay out here till they floated to England if she had to. She looked up; the webbing holding the balloon in place had become slightly unraveled. Maybe I'm not climbing up a cord connected to the parachute valve. Maybe the cord is part of the webbing. If she could make it up another few feet she could let go of the parachute cord and grab onto the webbing. If it was the parachute cord? She was beginning to hope it wasn't. The webbing was like a net over the balloon, and she would use it to climb higher.

"Come in or we pull," Alexei shouted.

"You know what this cord is?" Diane said as she struggled to climb upwards. She only had to go another few feet.

The three gangsters looked at the cord.

"Stop stalling," Alexei warned.

"Look at the label," she shouted, almost to the webbing. At the end of the cord was a small white plastic label with black printing.

"Parachute valve," Alexei said. "What that mean?"

"It lets the air out of the balloon," she told them. "You pull that and you'll let the air out of the balloon and it will fall."

Alexei stared angrily at her.

Luka dropped the cord and stepped back from it.

Frankie said. "It not open when you climb."

"I don't weigh that much," she shouted angrily.

Diane transferred from the cord to the balloon. Now she was holding onto the webbing and had no weight on the cord. Her hands were blistered and cut up from climbing up the rope. On the webbing she tried to find a way to hold on just using the uninjured parts of her hands. Her hands hurt so much she wanted to cry.

"I pull it now we see what happens," Frankie said.

Diane pointed at the sea far below them. "Go ahead."

Frankie was about to yank on the cord, when Luka grabbed his arm.

"What?"

"Where she go?" Luka said. "Nowhere. Let her stay up there out of way."

"Go get her," Alexei ordered.

Frankie paled. "Boss, I can't."

Alexei shoved Frankie, but he refused to climb up after her.

"Let her go," Luka said.

Alexei didn't like anyone telling him what to do. If it was their girl they would not let her go. Who are they to tell him to let go of his woman?

While they argued Diane climbed as high as she could. The blisters on her hands burned, the blood made her fingers slippery, but she continued up the side like a bug on a rounded window pane. She reached a point on the side of the balloon where she couldn't push her sore fingers between the webbing and balloon fabric. She had run out of steam, it required every ounce of energy she had just to hold on. She wedged her bleeding fingers into the webbing. She glanced down and couldn't see the basket, but she could still hear them shouting at each other. She liked that, hoped they got so mad they killed each other.

The three gangsters continued to argue, and while they did they didn't notice the other balloon maneuvering.

***

Ryan looked around, trying to think of a way to help Diane. He shivered as the image of his falling out of the helicopter flashed across his mind. He had nothing. He was in a balloon he didn't know how to steer. Then he got an idea. He cut the tether lines that were in the basket and tied them together into one long rope.

He heard shouting and used the binoculars to look at the other balloon. Alexei was shouting at Frankie, but the little gangster cowered in the corner. Alexei took out a pistol and Frankie said something, Ryan could see his red face, as Alexei fired. Frankie slumped down.

"What was that?" Pat asked.

"Alexei shot Frankie."

"Why?"

"I think because he wouldn't climb up after Diane."

"What?"

Pat, Kenny and Ron looked over the side. Their smaller balloon had risen, while Alexei's bigger balloon had not or maybe it had gone down a little. Maybe Diane had done something to the parachute valve. Now they could see into the large basket of the other balloon.

Diane had gotten up on the side of the balloon, but it didn't look like she could climb anymore. She waved at them.

As the other balloon descended, it floated toward them, under them.

Ryan saw the gangsters looking at Frankie and examining a tank behind him. Ryan figured when Alexei shot Frankie he hit the tank and it was leaking. Frankie didn't seem to be dead, his hands moved and he tried to stand and Alexei shoved him back down.

Alexei looked up and saw that the other balloon had risen and started shouting instructions to Luka. Then Alexei picked up the AK-47 and aimed.

Ryan moved, almost stumbled and when he did Alexei fired. The bullet missed Ryan, but hit one of the aluminum support posts. The bullet took a hunk out of it, but didn't break it.

Ryan stood there, ready to dive down next time, but Alexei shook the rifle. He handed it to Luka, but Luka was unable to fix it. Alexei yanked the rifle from him and threw it over the side. Now he took out his automatic pistol and waited, watching as his balloon came closer and closer to Ryan's balloon.

Ryan kept on pulling on the cord and his balloon was rising; not as fast as he wanted. Rising as the other balloon slowly sank or so it seemed.

Alexei's red balloon was coming closer fast.

Everyone was peeking over the side.

"They're coming too close," Ron said.

"Stay down," Ryan said.

Ryan watched the Russians bending down, doing something. What were they up to? Now the Russian gangster stood up holding an M9 Beretta and grinned at them.

The balloon was coming into range of the M9.

Ryan quickly drew the pistol from his holster and aimed it at them and they ducked. Ryan scrambled to the tank. He unscrewed the fuel line from one tank and connected it to the other. He turned it on and went to the burner and ignited the flame and pulled the blast valve cord. The hot blue flame shot upward and the balloon started to rise again.

"I'll throw out the old tank." Ron said struggled to his feet.

"No." Ryan saw the back of Ron's shirt was bloody from being shot. The basket must have slowed the bullet and prevented it from killing him.

"Why not?" Ron asked and saw Ryan staring at him. Ron shook his head and glanced at Pat; she hadn't noticed.

"Just don't."

Ron's expression said he thought he was losing it and was going to do it anyway, and started to lift it when Ryan shouted, "Duck."

Alexei peeked over the edge and pointed the M9 up at them, looking up into the sun.

Ryan aimed his pistol and Alexei and Luka ducked. Ryan was out of bullets. He could only keep this up so long. He kept pulling the cord and the balloon kept rising.

When he didn't fire Alexei looked over the edge of his balloon, the sun bright in his face, and aimed the Beretta. But this time they didn't duck. When Ryan didn't fire the

Glock, Alexei fired the M9.

Alexei's aim was off or the wind took the nine millimeter bullets for the first few shots were way wide of their mark. Eventually Alexei hit Ryan's basket, but it was not the result he wanted. Alexei and Luka argued among themselves.

Ryan kept pulling on the cord, making his balloon rise higher and higher. He glanced down at his side watching the blood coming from where he'd been hit.

Alexei stood up and aimed at the balloon itself. He fired a few rounds then the M9 jammed.

Ryan said, "Must be an old one or one he bought on the black market." He noticed Kenny looking at him. "The new ones don't jam."

Ryan saw Diane waving at him. What did she expect him to do? He had lowered the tether line, but the wind took it and it kept dancing around.

Alexei grabbed another M9 from Luka and aimed and fired a few rounds. Ryan could hear the rounds whistling past. None hit the balloon.

***

Luka pulled the M9 down and pointed at the balloon.

"Get your hand off me," Alexei warned.

"Boss, our balloon will go under the other balloon."

"So?"

"Once on other side we pull burner cord and rise up and then you can shoot them."

"And if we not rise fast enough?"

"We throw Frankie out to help us." Luka grinned at Frankie.

"No," Frankie cried and Alexei shot him again and killed him.

***

Diane was hanging on the side of the balloon in her blue jeans and red Georgia sweatshirt, shouting, "Help. Help."

Ryan tied the empty tank to the end of several tied together tether cords and lowered it over the side. But they were not floating directly over Alexei's balloon. He started moving the cord, swinging the tank back and forth like a pendulum.

As the Russian balloon started to pass underneath Ryan's balloon, Ryan swung the tank more and more, the pendulum arced higher and higher.

"Suppose they grab it?" Kenny said.

"It's not that long," Ryan said.

He had managed to get the tank close to the other balloon as it went under them, but he didn't think it went close to Diane and was about to give up. Suddenly the tank didn't swing back. Ryan was sure Diane hadn't grabbed it, so he wondered if it had snagged on the other balloon. What would happen if it had snagged the other balloon? Would they both be pulled along or would they be pulled down?

Ryan tried to jerk the tank free, when suddenly the tank swung out with Diane holding onto the end. The added weight started pulling their balloon down.

"Help me," Ryan said.

Ryan sat on the floor and they all grabbed the line and pulled it in hand over hand. They heard shooting and Kenny looked over the side.

"I'm shot," Diane said. "Hurry."

Hand over hand they pulled the line up and in a minute Ryan helped Diane into the basket. She had been shot in the thigh and only just managed to hold on. Ryan hugged her tightly and she hugged him as though she would never let go.

"We're too heavy," Kenny said. "We're falling."

Ryan looked over the side. They were descending, but the other balloon was not rising as fast.

Ryan grabbed the empty tank and looked around. "We have anymore medical tape?"

"I'll bandage your wound," Pat said.

"It's not for me."

Pat glanced at Diane and handed Ryan the tape. Diane moved to the side so Ryan could wrap the tape around her, but Ryan grabbed the hockey stick. She looked at him thinking he was going to put a tourniquet on her leg.

"I'm not bleeding that bad," she said.

"It's not for you," he said and she gave him a look.

"Hey, that was my dad's," Kenny said.

"Sorry," Ryan said, "I'll get you another."

Ryan taped the empty propane tank to the hockey stick; he hurried to the side and looked over the edge.

The other balloon, a red and yellow rainbow ball, was moving away from beneath them. Ryan leaned over the side holding the makeshift bomb by the hockey stick and swung it back and forth.

The balloons were moving apart. Ryan could almost see down into the Russian basket. Luka picked up Frankie and moved the body to the side like he was going to throw him out. Alexei was leaning out over the side of the basket trying to get a shot at Ryan's balloon when Ryan released the hockey stick taped to the tank and watched it sail, tumble toward the Russian balloon. Alexei must have figured out what it was, for he fired at it and hit it.

At first Ryan thought his grappling concoction was going to tumble into the side of the Russian balloon, but then the bullet from Alexei's gun hit it, and knocked it away from his balloon. The empty tank with the hockey stick taped to the side fell into the sea.

Alexei shouted and Luka let go of Frankie's body. The body fell and the wind shifted and Russian balloon moved closer, almost under their balloon.

"Where's the knife you found?" Ryan said.

Kenny took the knife out of his pocket and Ryan grabbed it.

"Only one thing left to do." Ryan started to climb up on the edge of the basket.

Ron lunged to his feet, grabbed Ryan's belt and yanked him back. Ryan crashed into the basket, into Diane, Pat and Kenny. Ron, picked up the knife and, blood seeping from his wounds, climbed on the edge.

"Ron!" Pat cried out.

"I'm dying, honey." He motioned at his wounds. "Won't be long anyway."

"Ron," she cried.

"I love you, baby," he said and dived over the side. Once he was away from the basket, he folded his arms at his side and kept his legs spread. He fell like a missile.

Kenny leaned over the edge watching him. "He's falling sideways, like he's flying."

Alexei fired, but missed him.

Ron crashed into the side of the balloon and with his last bit of strength slashed a hole in the side as he slid down. Then he was unconscious and fell and the balloon plummeted to the sea.

Ryan went back to pulling on the cord. Their bullet-ridden balloon would not stay aloft much longer, but he tried to ease their descent. He glanced at Pat and Diane, both wounded, and saw the scared look on Kenny's face.

Everyone watched the other balloon crash into the Atlantic when this loud noise came from behind them. They turned. A helicopter was coming toward them. Soon it was beside them. Marines stood in the open door pointing weapons at them.

A voice over a loudspeaker said, "You are under arrest for causing the death of the people in that other balloon."

Everyone starting shouting at once, but they could not be heard above the sound of the helicopter's rotors.

High in the air overhead Ryan saw a small white drone making its way to New York City. He held up his cell phone and pointed at the guys in the helicopter. One of the Marines in the helicopter wrote some numbers on a white board.

Ryan dialed the numbers and was soon speaking to the Marine in the door of the helicopter.

"This is the guy in the balloon."

"This is Captain Greene. You all are under arrest for killing those people in the other balloon."

"There's something I got to tell you."

"We'll talk on the ship."

"This is about the drone."

"It will be at its target in a few minutes."

"You can't let it go off. The zombies are like they've been soaked in kerosene. The EMP will explode their cell phones and MP3 players, and the zombies will be like torches, they will spread the fire to each other and the city will become a fire storm."

"You sure about that?"

"Take you only a few minutes to find out."

"Stay right where you are; don't try anything." Then he saw the captain signaling the radio operator and talking rapidly on his headset.

"What could we do? Where could we go?"

"I don't know. Bleed to death."

"That really wasn't my father's hockey stick."

Ryan turned to him.

"My mom said it was, but I knew it wasn't. He never even married my mom."

"Well, I'll buy you one, first chance I have."

Kenny looked at him and wiped the tears from his eyes. Diane limped over to them.

"What are you two talking about?"

"Guy stuff," Kenny said.

Diane turned to Ryan, who nodded. "Guy stuff."

*****

Chapter 49 - The God of Tomorrow

The Victory sailed to where the balloon came down. Jack pressed a button to lower the sails and the boat slowed and he threw lifesavers into the water and pulled each of the survivors aboard.

**

Hours later, after being patched up by Navy doctors, Ryan sat on the hatch with Diane. Sitting on the bow fishing was Kenny. Pat had stayed on the Navy ship.

"How you people feeling?" Jack said from the wheel.

"You doing this all by yourself?" Ryan said.

"Well, the Navy's kind of busy," Jack said.

"We were lucky you were right there," Diane said.

"It wasn't luck, my father-in-law told me I had to help you," Jack said. "He heard about it from the Navy and said we should do our share, the Navy had enough to worry about."

"I'll have to thank him."

"He passed away. My mother-in-law, wife and kids were aboard, but dad had a heart attack and they all took a helicopter to the aircraft carrier where he died."

Ryan looked at the ocean. Little white caps on the rolling waves.

"How 'bout some coffee?" Jack said.

"Want a hand?" Diane said.

"No, got it all taken care of." Jack smiled. "Guy I rescued when you were on the carrier getting patched up will bring it on deck."

Up the stairs from down below appeared a tray with six steaming mugs on it and a bottle of Jack Daniel bourbon. The man came on deck and turned around and smiled at them.

Alexei grinned, his dark eyes almost glowing.

"This is Alec," Jack said.

"You Alexei," Kenny said.

From under the tray Alexei took a Beretta and pointed it at Jack.

"What's going on?" Jack said.

"Go over there next to others." He motioned with the gun.

Jack fastened a rope to the wheel and backed up.

Alexei handed him the tray.

"Condemned should have ... how you say, last meal."

"I want K.F.C. and fries," Kenny said.

"Shut up."

Jack walked around the side of the boat and put the tray down on the hatch.

Ryan eased away from the others.

"Stop. You tire me. You first to go."

Alexei motioned with his gun and Ryan slowly took the .357 from his pocket.

"I know that empty," Alexei said.

Jack not knowing who Alexei was going to shoot first and his nerves frayed after the night he'd just had, starting laughing.

Alexei glanced at him like he was crazy.

Kenny still on the tip of the bow had reeled in and now cast at Alexei.

The lure hit Alexei. He turned from Jack to Kenny as Ryan, in a smooth motion, threw the pistol at Alexei as hard as he could. Alexei shielded himself with his arms, but the heavy .357 smashed into his chest and knocked him back. The back of Alexei's legs hit the safety line. His arms windmilled. He fired hitting the mainsail and the mast as he went over the side into the water.

Jack rushed to the wheel, turned the ship about and sailed back to where Alexei fell in. He had splashed around for a bit, but when they got to where he'd fallen in, the water was smooth and still. They sailed around the area for several minutes, but never saw him again.

*****

Chapter 50 – Harbor

That evening Victory and other small boats sailed with the fleet into New York harbor. Smoke from fires clouded the view. A few skyscrapers had been damaged in the small wars that that been fought, but most of the city had been spared. Dead zombies lay everywhere. People came out of hiding and stood on the waterfront cheering.

Torches had been lit around Lady Liberty and she glowed proudly in the firelight.

Ryan sat on the bow with Diane. They had both been treated and bandaged by the Navy doctors. Diane's hands were covered in white bandages. A gauze bandage was wrapped around her thigh.

"What are you going to do now?" Diane said.

"Probably settle down and help rebuild."

"Yeah," she said. "I'm from Atlanta, but I can't see myself living in a big empty city."

"Out in the country will probably be safer."

"That sounds nice," she said.

"Lots of room," he said.

"Kenny really likes you."

"He's a nice kid."

"I like you too."

He kissed her and she smiled and he put his arm around her as the Victory sailed into harbor.

\#\#\#

About the Author

Ted Stetson is the author of several books, including the science fiction/horror thriller 'Night Beasts' and the western 'The Legend of Sweetwater'.

He was born in Brooklyn and grew up on Long Island. He went to Seton Hall and Hofstra. After being honorably discharged from the Marine Corps he graduated from the University of St. Thomas in Houston, Texas. He lives in Oregon with his wife and son.

His other work can be found on Amazon and Smashwords.com.

*****

www.ingramcontent.com/pod-product-compliance
Lightning Source LLC
Chambersburg PA
CBHW060152260626
47160CB00001B/239